C000054475

BY THE SAME AUTHOR
(WRITING AS JASON FOSS)

Darkness Rises
Byron's Shadow
Shadesmoor
Lady in the Lake
When the Dust Settles

NON-FICTION

The Story of Guernsey

GLINT of LIGHT on BROKEN GLASS

JASON MONAGHAN

Copyright © 2016 Jason Monaghan
The moral right of the author has been asserted.

Apart from any fair dealing for the purposes of research or private study,
or criticism or review, as permitted under the Copyright, Designs and Patents
Act 1988, this publication may only be reproduced, stored or transmitted, in
any form or by any means, with the prior permission in writing of the
publishers, or in the case of reprographic reproduction in accordance with
the terms of licences issued by the Copyright Licensing Agency. Enquiries
concerning reproduction outside those terms should be sent to the publishers.

Matador
9 Priory Business Park,
Wistow Road, Kibworth Beauchamp,
Leicestershire. LE8 0RX
Tel: 0116 279 2299
Email: books@troubador.co.uk
Web: www.troubador.co.uk/matador
Twitter: @matadorbooks

ISBN 978 1785891 946

British Library Cataloguing in Publication Data.
A catalogue record for this book is available from the British Library.

Printed and bound by CPI Group (UK) Ltd, Croydon, CR0 4YY
Typeset in 11pt Aldine by Troubador Publishing Ltd, Leicester, UK

Matador is an imprint of Troubador Publishing Ltd

MIX
Paper from
responsible sources
FSC
www.fsc.org   FSC® C013604

For Emily

Holiday 2016

Don't tell me the moon is shining;
show me the glint of light on broken glass.

Attributed to Anton Chekhov

THE LAST BOY

No one in Guernsey is now called Bazin. The name has died along with everyone who carried it. Some say the family was cursed, but life is strange and so is death. Georges Bazin was the last boy born to the family, baptised in July 1897 at Ste Marie du Castel. As holy water marked the forehead of the baby, saints stared down from fading mediaeval frescoes, and the congregation said their prayers on a spot where prayers had been chanted for four thousand years. Outside the church door stands *la Gràn'mère*. Carved in stone, she watches over the cemetery as she has watched over the north of the island for two hundred generations. Now her shape is almost gone, her face is weathered away and just the hint of one breast remains.

Marie Bazin carried her baby from the church. Holy baptism over, she paused by the *Gràn'mère* and gave a slight nod of her head. From within the folds of her coat she found a copper double and placed it on the head of the statue-menhir. The coin was for luck – her boy would need luck. Her husband frowned, but young Artie asked a question.

'What's that funny stone, Pépaen?'

'Never you mind. Don't worry about the old ways.'

Henri Bazin looked down at baby Georges. A second son may never rise to the heights expected of a first son, but young Georges would face a tougher struggle than most. He had almost died at birth, saved by a mix of love, care, luck and every folk remedy any female member of the family could find. One leg was growing wrong and the child seemed to stare straight through any adult who dandled him. It was hard to catch his eye and raise a baby smile.

Guernsey has superstitions to explain everything from squint eyes to lame legs. The Valpied sisters stood by as the family emerged from church. Unmarried and likely to stay that way, they muttered in the ancient language of the island, that version of Norman called Guernesiais but never properly written down. *Cor là!* Here was another crippled child for the Bazin family, surely being punished for its sins or omissions. Baby Georges would be fortunate to live longer than his poor dead sister. He was not right, that boy. If he survived, his life would be hard.

In the same month, a baby girl was baptised at Our Lady Star of the Sea, newly built by the Catholics up on the rock at Delancey. Her red-haired father held her up proudly, and handed the child back to her mother. Ruth Mullane was a beauty, and her daughter would be too. Service over, the family walked back to the tiny cottage on La Route Militaire, which quickly filled with quarrymen and Le Page relatives from Ruth's side of the family. Edith Mullane was shown to the world, and then the drink was opened.

PART 1:

LES JAUNNES

CHAPTER 1

Her hair was storm-black, her eyes as blue as the sea at dusk. The woman held both beauty and terror, and if she appeared in the flesh George Bazin would love her forever. He would be her slave.

'A woman? Was she old, young?' the stranger's voice broke into the story he was telling.

'Both. It's hard to tell,' he said.

He resumed by describing how he had been watching a kestrel hovering, looking for rabbits in the furze above the little bay at Albecq. Behind him there had hovered another figure.

'I was used to her by then,' he explained, 'I'd seen her since I was seven – and I was turned thirteen by that day at Albecq. I wasn't scared any more.' For all his words, cold fingers still crawled down George's back each time he saw the woman.

He had kept his focus on the kestrel and the woman drew closer – closer than she had ever come before. She lifted her face, but it was veiled to conceal her expression. In her hands was a black cushion and on the cushion sat a glittering crown. His heart thudded as she stood, silent and sombre.

At last he could take no more. The thrill of the supernatural turned to fear and he scrambled to his feet, limping his way home and constantly looking around for the phantom.

'And did she pursue you?'

'No, no, she's never there if I turn. She's only behind me.'

By chance George had heard of this Mrs Lake who lived up in the north of the island at St Sampson's. She had a reputation for being far-sighted and for knowing remedies for ills the doctors could not treat. In Guernsey's ancient language she was a *désorcheul'raesse*, a white witch. Of course few believed in such things any more, or at least would not admit it if they did, but if anyone could explain this beautiful terror, it was Mrs Lake.

It was a fair walk from the Castel to St Sampson's and George had needed to ask a few people before he found La Robergerie, after walking straight past it the first time. Mrs Lake lived in an ordinary cottage on an ordinary lane and her looks were unremarkable. He expected strangeness, so did not glance too deeply into the alcoves when welcomed inside. The curtains were drawn, even though it was still light, and the white witch had lit a single candle.

Mrs Lake narrowed her eyes. 'But you told me you see the future? How's that? Do you use tea leaves? Cards?'

She sat in an armchair, while George sat on the little sofa, glancing nervously at the antimacassar that trailed over his shoulder. Children were playing out the back, somewhere.

'Ah, well, I went home, kept myself busy, me,' George continued his story. 'I went to bed, had bad dreams. Next day was a school day – she never came to school.' George paused. 'My father came home from the quarry and cleaned up. Then Artie – that's my brother – he came in from the Intermediate, him. Then Uncle Jack, bringing the paper. I was in the yard and they called me in. Uncle Jack stood there, all formal, holding his cap like at church. And he said, "The king is dead".'

'King George?'

'No, King Edward.'

'But he must have been dead three years now, eh?'

George nodded and an icy shiver doused his whole body.

'It was the May of 1910, I remember to the day. The girl carried a crown on a cushion and she wore mourning clothes. She'd told me before anyone else on the island knew. I knew before Uncle Jack or even the newspaper!'

Mrs Lake was sceptical. 'Are you saying you knew before King Edward even died?'

'Yes! Well, I don't know.'

She made a humming sound. 'Was that the first time this spirit told you secrets?'

'I… I think so. She might have forewarned me about other things, but I never noticed what she meant. Not until the cushion. And it keeps happening, now and again.'

'And do you tell people about these things you foresee?'

'I told my brother – but he just teased me. He don't believe in *pouques*.'

'Is that what she is, a *pouque*?'

'She's very beautiful. She looks like a girl not much older than I am now. Yet you can see she's not a girl. Her eyes are old – like your eyes.'

'I'm old, am I? The old witch?'

'Are you really a witch?'

'There's folks say I am. And what are you, boy who consorts with *pouques*? Back in the old days they used to hang people like us. Burn them sometimes, like the Cauchés women under Queen Mary. But it's a precious gift, being far-sighted.'

'It's scary.'

'Yes, isn't it just? You're on the edge of two worlds, George. A very special person who can live in this world, yet have a glimpse into that other world we know exists just beyond…' She reached out a hand. 'Out of reach… behind us. Not quite in the sight of ordinary folks.'

'Yes, that's right! That's just what it's like.'

She drew back. 'Be careful, that's my guidance. People come to see me, women mostly, and I help with their pains and their fears.'

'Do they pay money?' he asked.

'You pays the doctor money?' She snapped out of the guise of sage in an instant. 'You pays money to the advocate and you pays money to the church who pays the preacher. Some people brings me presents from time to time.'

'Ah.'

'But don't you go charging money, George Bazin, it's not seemly in a boy.' There was a warning in her voice. 'And have a care for who you tell about your gift. Adults smile at children's stories, but you're what – sixteen now? So beware. They'll rate you mad and have you down the Country Hospital quicker than you can say knife.'

He nodded. A fear of hospitals ran through the rural community. People went in and did not come out. It was a place to die, or go insane.

A carriage clock chimed.

'I am expecting a visitor,' she said. 'But I would be glad to speak to you again.'

Now he had told Mrs Lake, he felt better. One person at least did not think him mad, or stupid, or slow. Mrs Lake at least understood how his world had changed forever the day that King Edward VII died. This foresight was a gift, but not even Artie believed in the spirit woman, and George would tell nobody else. Spreading stories of fairies with morbid black cushions would do him no good at all.

CHAPTER 2

Before Edith Mullane's father had run off with that French maid, the family lived in a cramped cottage off La Route Militaire, within sight of the Vale church. Tourists would stay in the guest house nearby, and from time to time stop to ask Edith for directions as to where to catch the bus into Town, or where the famous prehistoric dolmens were. Tumbled old stones and smelly tunnels seemed to be of interest to these well-spoken English gentlefolk. Edith would embellish her directions with an old legend or two to add spice to the tourists' day. Her mother knew a great store of these tales, which were by turn incredible, bizarre or macabre.

'You must know everyone on an island this small,' a tourist once said.

'Do you know forty thousand people?' Edith replied tartly.

'Ah,' said the tourist, embarrassed, and gave her an English halfpenny for her trouble.

The tourist had a point. Days came when it felt like Edith knew everyone and everyone knew her. When her father abandoned his wife and two daughters, leaving only debts behind him, the Vale felt very small. People would point at her back and whisper. Thank God she was no longer in school, and did not yet have a respectable job where she would have to hide her shame daily. Instead she learned to be useful around the house and trudged around the parish and into St Sampson's, picking up odd pieces of work to help her mother.

Her older sister Leila did the opposite – keeping out of the house and out of the way as often as possible.

'I blame myself,' said her mother, a bottle of gin already empty above the label. 'I blame myself.'

Edith watched her from the other chair, the one that should have been her father's. *Yes,* she thought, *I blame you too.*

'He'll come back,' her mother insisted, as if it were only a matter of time.

Of course he did not come back, because the French girl he had run away with was only twenty-two years old and Patrick Mullane carried too much devil-may-care about him to stay chained to a rock barely five miles by seven for the rest of his life. Edith's overriding memory of childhood was of her parents drinking heavily and then arguing afterwards. Losing her father brought a peace to the house, but respectability left with him. The Vale had once been a separate island and was too intimate a place to keep your business to yourself, so it was time to leave.

'Uncle Nico' said they could live with him in St Sampson's…

…after the briefest stay, the three women moved in with Aunt Marguerite in Town…

…then moved to a shared house in the Canichers with 'Uncle Clive'…

…then moved to the Castel to be close by 'Uncle Tom'.

'It's like coming home!' Ruth Mullane declared to her daughters. 'I was born not five minutes' walk from here. That little white cottage down by Le Préel.'

Home would be the dower wing of a granite farmhouse part way between the Castel church and the Bailiff's Cross. It was at the dead centre of Guernsey and Leila echoed that word 'dead'. She soon moved back to live with Aunt Marguerite in St Peter Port.

It was only two miles, but coming down to the Castel from the Vale was like crossing continents. Even the accent was different here, and a good many of Edith's new neighbours spoke no English at all. All the young men and women around Edith had known each other since childhood, and half of them were related to the other half, but somehow she was to pretend that this was like coming home.

Baptised Catholic, she'd found her father cared little for the faith and her Aunt Marguerite was constantly chiding her mother for marrying a 'papist'. Now safely back in the Castel, her mother pushed young Edith to attend the parish church. It was her last swipe against her Catholic husband and the latest swipe against her Methodist sister. God would be on Edith's side, even if nobody else was.

Ruth Mullane was 'far too busy' to attend church on a regular basis, so told Edith to go with Adèle Le Page – a distant cousin via this aunt and that brother and all kinds of family complexities which Edith forgot immediately after it was explained.

Adèle topped Edith by a good four inches and was altogether bigger and darker. When they met outside the church, she had begun the conversation in patois, and then quickly switched to English and started the introductions again.

'How old are you?' Adèle asked, as the parishioners started to file past them into the porch.

'Sixteen, just,' Edith said.

'Me too! You don't speak patois?'

'No.'

'You might want to learn it – a lot of the boys round here hardly speak English, even them that aren't Frenchies in the first place. How's your Good French?'

Edith shrugged.

'Me neither. Never had time for it in school. What's the need? The cows don't speak French, eh?'

Within the church, high on the wall of the nave, ran an old fresco of The Last Supper. Edith Mullane glanced at it before taking her seat. During the prayers, beneath the saints, she cursed her father – then realised that his blood ran in her veins. Patrick Mullane had not bothered to learn patois, did not pretend this rock was his home, had not let marriage vows or family duty stand in the way of what he wanted. He had simply followed his heart off into the world. Wickedness and selfishness and fecklessness had been rewarded with freedom. How did that square with the message the preachers hammered out Sunday after Sunday? How did virtue have its reward? A hymn began and she stood to her feet. *Lord lift me up now*, she thought. *Take me away with the angels.* She fitted new words to the tune, writing her own hymn of salvation. Even getting out of that half a cottage and away from her mother would do.

CHAPTER 3

Private Arthur Bazin, 2nd Battalion, Royal Guernsey Militia, had dressed for the occasion in his scarlet uniform with its royal blue facings and blue-black helmet. His younger brother George had been called to the Militia headquarters at Les Beaucamps a few months after his sixteenth birthday, and the two would march there, side by side. Leading them from the gate of La Vallée went their father, wearing his own Militia scarlet with a pride not normally seen on ordinary parade days, when he muttered about wasting his time and listed all the jobs he had to do on the land. Today he puffed out his chest and led his boys up the lane.

Two girls approaching womanhood leaned over a field gate, but Artie was determined not to give either more than a glance. One was Adèle Le Page, who lived down by the school and whom he had known since childhood, but the other was new to the parish. Copper-red hair was rarely seen out on the west coast, so Artie did in fact spare her a second glance, then a wink.

'Who's the cheeky one?' the redhead asked, too loudly to be discreet.

'Artie Bazin,' Adèle said.

'He's got a glint in his eye, that one.'

Artie could just hear their voices, and imagined the admiring stares at his back. He felt ten feet tall in his dress uniform, and with his love of history knew what a special honour it was to be a Militiaman. Ancient charters decreed that Guernseymen were not to be conscripted or pressed by the British. Instead all fit and able men served in the Royal Guernsey Militia, and it had been so for six or seven hundred years. Artie and his fellows accepted it as part of life, offering a whiff of adventure to the farmers and office clerks who formed its ranks.

It was only a short walk from La Vallée to the training camp at Les Beaucamps. Just down the hill there had once been a mighty battle between the Militia and the French. Artie had told the story to his little brother one dark winter night. It had been back in the days of knights and bows and arrows, and the Militia had lost with terrible numbers slain. Since then, they had defended the island against all comers, while seldom doing any actual fighting. Even the wives and sisters had taken turns on guard duty when the men were out fishing or gathering the harvest. Artie clapped George on the shoulder, grinning to know they were part of this long and noble tradition.

Artie's grin was a false grin. He knew the Militia took *fit and able* men. He knew his brother fell into neither category. His left leg had grown wrong and, until he was given spectacles, it was an effort to gain his attention and more so to pull him into games. George had been a disappointing playmate and would never make a soldier.

Les Beaucamps sits at the edge of the plateau on the western side of Guernsey, just before the land starts to fall towards the sea. Here was a camp, a chequerboard of grey huts spreading out from the original granite Militia hall, with a parade ground and fields for training. Around the camp, men were drilling in small groups. Artie's romantic side wished soldiers still wore scarlet uniforms with brass buttons all the time. The parade uniforms looked so much smarter than the modern khaki the men were wearing, which was neither green nor brown. Soldiers lying prone, pretending to shoot their rifles, looked like so many *bousaettes* dotted around the field in the wake of Guernsey cows.

Artie had been supporting his brother as long as he could remember, and now he led George into the Militia hut while their father waited outside. Seated along one wall, boys of George's age who had tormented him at school passed him leery glances but looked at their feet when Artie glared at them. Boys of the parish knew better than to make Artie Bazin angry. He caught the bare end of a snigger but did not react, as officers were present and he was ambitious to gain a stripe.

The Bazin brothers sat down, and waited as two officers in full uniform checked other boys one by one. Next it was George's turn. Artie bit his lip, waiting.

The captain was a grocer they sometimes visited. 'Can you see without those glasses?' he asked.

'Course I can,' George said.

'Whip them off, then.'

George removed his glasses.

'How many lads are sitting on the chairs across there?' Just a twitch of the captain's finger indicated the chairs on George's left.

George looked the wrong way, back towards Artie. 'Four,' he guessed.

The captain looked at him. 'They are on your left.'

'Ah, those lads. Er, four.'

The captain held up his hand and raised his index finger. 'What colour is this pencil?'

'Brown, woody colour.'

'I'm not holding a pencil.'

The captain looked down at the special shoe George wore on his left foot, the one with an extra-thick sole. 'March around the room.' To Artie he added, 'March with him, mark time.'

'Come on, George!' Artie marched around a neat square, with George following with his awkward limping gait.

Two of the boys on the chairs laughed.

'Quiet!' the captain barked. 'That's enough, Bazin. You'll get a letter saying you are not required to serve in the Militia.'

'But, sir!' George protested.

'You're not fit, Bazin. You'll never be fit.'

'But the Militia don't do no fighting. It's just parades and practice.'

'You can't even march, boy. If we give you a rifle you'd as likely shoot your brother in mistake for a target. Now run along.'

'Can't run,' he said.

The officer scowled, and glanced away. 'Next one. Yes, you!'

Artie clapped his arm around his brother's shoulder and led him out into the spring air. Now the inevitable had happened, he felt relief. Their father stood some way off, smoking his pipe, watching rifle drill. He looked back at Artie, and Artie merely shrugged.

'Hard luck, George,' said their father, with not the slightest surprise or disappointment in his voice.

'It's not fair!' George protested.

'Never mind,' said Artie. 'Your Sundays are your own now. You don't have to worry about parades and drill and calling Mr Bessant the grocer "sir".'

'But I wanted to be a soldier like you and Père.'

'We're not real soldiers, George, just play-soldiers.

Quarrymen and growers and office boys, that's all we are. And the officers, well, just shopkeepers and advocates and men with too much money and not enough work to fill their week. We're friends with the Frenchies now, so there's going to be no war round here. You're not missing nothing.'

CHAPTER 4

For all the confident words of his brother, George knew that yet again he was set apart from the other young men. Artie had just been trying to be kind. The day was warm, so George left his father and brother soon after leaving Les Beaucamps and walked on inland, alone.

Of course he was not alone, he was never alone.

She was with him now, hair dark as a crow, eyes blue as the evening sky. Her face was young yet sometimes looked older than the earth. The girl was off to his right, over his shoulder somewhere. She only came close when he thought no one was there – and so it had been since he was seven years old. Novelty had long since worn off; George had first tried to ignore her, but later welcomed her company. Whenever he was at his lowest, she came to comfort him.

George knew that if he turned to see her full in the face, she would nip out of sight – ever just out of his direct view. So he kept his eyes on the spire of the church, willing her to leave. He was sixteen, he was a man whatever the Militia thought; he should leave childhood behind.

For some reason lost in stories about fairies and curses that George only half believed, Ste Marie du Castel was built on the eastern edge of the parish, close to the border with St Andrew's. Quite where the 'Castel' came from always puzzled him, as there was no castle up here, although legend says there was once. Behind the church, where the ground fell away steeply to the north, was where Gràn'père Bazin lay.

At the end of the last century, the steamship *Stella* had struck a rock off Alderney in fog, taking a hundred people to the bottom of the English Channel. It was a well-known story, often revisited around the kitchen table at home.

'Gràn'père Georges was a hero,' Artie had told the younger George many times. 'A great hero. He saved lots of tourists, helping them to the lifeboats. But the ship sank all of a sudden, before he got himself a lifebelt, so he was drowned.'

In a drawer at La Vallée lay an old newspaper that told all about it.

Some days passed before Gràn'père's body had washed up, then more before it could be brought back from Alderney. George had been named Georges in the French manner after his grandfather, but he had no memory of him. Young Georges had been barely three years old by the time the funeral was held on this spot here at Ste Marie du Castel, and he had been left at home with the women.

He'd have seen nothing even if allowed to go. For the seven years before his parents bought the spectacles, he could see no further than the end of his arms. Everything beyond had been a blur. He could dance his fingers around like birds, imagining how they flew, but he had been seven before he had seen a wild bird in full focus.

Those glasses had changed his life in so many ways.

Today the air was clear enough for him to see Alderney from the churchyard; a distant wedge of brown on the northern horizon. Just to the left, a white blob was the Casquets lighthouse, warning of the reef where the *Stella* went down. George removed his glasses so he could forget who was behind him, and touched Gràn'père's headstone.

'Wharro, Gràn'père.'

A little way on from Gràn'père was the unmarked spot

where Drusille lay. The sister George had never known must have been too small to rate a headstone. Instead, a clutch of dandelions had planted themselves above her tiny grave. He would have liked to have met her, but there was not even a photograph. The family never spoke about her, but plenty of unlucky children fell sick, suffered accidents or simply failed to thrive. It was the way of things.

Still alone, George moved back up to the *Gràn'mère*. Someone, perhaps a newly wed bride, had left a coin, a copper 8 double piece, on her head for luck. He put his hand against the stone, feeling the rough texture of the granite, sensing every grain but knowing nothing of the people who had shaped this rock thousands of years in the past. He sat down in her shadow, where cold stone blocked out the brisk wind blowing in from the west.

Without his glasses, George could not see the Casquets, or Alderney, or even the sea. He slipped them on again, just making out the distant lighthouse marking where Gràn'père had drowned. They would never let him be a hero like Gràn'père had been.

George sat by the *Gràn'mère* until the sun fell, playing with his glasses in his hand, watching the light catch in that little chip on the right lens. He had not told Mrs Lake about the day he chipped his glasses, the day it had all begun. He had told no one of how his familiar had suddenly appeared, nor asked anyone for an explanation.

Of course there were certain people on the island he might have asked. A pair of figures entered the churchyard by the lower gate: the Valpied sisters. Always in black even in the height of summer, they carried an aura of knowing all those things that men were meant not to know. Every sniff of gossip came their way, although quite where they obtained it was a mystery as they kept no company but each other and their cats. The old spinsters lived just along the lane and he had been afraid of them since childhood. The Valpieds may be able to explain the crow-haired woman, but George dared not ask them. Perhaps they would know no more than Mrs Lake. One of the Valpieds saw him, scowled, and pointed his way. He hurried to his feet, turning his back on the pair. As quickly as his lame leg would allow, he made for the top gate and worked his way home, not caring if he was followed or not.

Gràn'mère Bazin had always insisted the family go to the parish church, even though St Matthew's Cobo was a shorter walk. Chapels aplenty were scattered across the parish, but she told the family repeatedly these were not proper churches. Even after she died and was laid above her husband in the graveyard, the family Bazin kept up the practice.

Church was, of course, the place for boys to meet girls. George had once thought straw-blonde Perotine Guille to be the most beautiful girl in the world, but this title he now awarded to another. She was new to the parish, landing like a thunderbolt amid the girls who had ignored or taunted him as a child. Was her hair red or gold? When she turned her head, it was like the glitter of the sun rippling across a glasshouse at sunset. Her skin was paler than that of many of the parish girls and her face more angular and proud. She did not carry the puppy fat which made Perotine so round, nor the big bones which meant that Adèle would never be elegant. Delicate, almost elf-like, she did not look like a woman born to work the land and raise a brood of quarrymen.

In the bustle outside the church door she never even looked towards George. One after another, parish boys edged up, wanting to catch her eye and learn her name.

Edith Mullane retreated to the clutch of girls she was building into friends.

'*Là*, it's market day!' she breathed behind her hand.

Adèle seemed sullen, jealous perhaps of the attention the new girl was getting from the boys. 'George Bazin's eyeing you up,' she said.

'Nonsense.' Edith ignored whatever George Bazin was doing, whoever George Bazin was.

Adèle nudged her, so she glanced towards the boy with the glasses and ill-fitting Sunday suit. She recognised him from a few weeks before when he had limped along to the Militia camp beside the winking hero.

'He's an idiot,' Adèle said. 'You wouldn't think he was Artie's brother.'

She had to admit, George looked the part. He wore glasses that were too small for him and pinched his face giving him an odd piggy look. Artie must be the tall one with the cheeky smile and easy way with the youths around him.

'Is that his brother?'

'Yes, that's Artie. We saw him up by the Beaucamps, all dressed up like a proper soldier.'

Edith sauntered across to where George Bazin stood, and as she drew near he seemed about to melt with fright. She held out her hand.

'I'm Edith Mullane,' she said.

'M-Miss Mullane… I'm George, George Bazin.' He gave her hand the most uncertain of shakes.

'Pleased to make your acquaintance.'

From the corner of her eye she noticed Artie Bazin moving

towards his brother. Blue eyed but dark haired in that Norman way, he carried a swagger across the churchyard.

'Wharro, George!' he said, clamping a large hand on his brother's shoulder.

Edith felt his cheer touch her, smiled and said, 'Good day.'

As she walked away she could feel their awestruck gaze, as if she were a fairy-tale princess of rare beauty such as mortals had never seen before. For the first time in a long while, Edith felt a glow of happiness.

CHAPTER 5

L ife is full of fleeting moments that are forgotten equally quickly, but some have a significance that is felt instantly. A sailor can sense a shift in the wind; a bird's instincts signal the day it should head back south in the autumn; a condemned man knows when his time has come.

Her eyes were paler than that stark blue of the family Bazin, and threads of hazel edged her wide pupils. A few freckles dotted her face around a sweet little nose that turned up cheekily, adding to her pixie appeal. When the red-haired girl turned to leave, both brothers felt the pull of a lever in the machinery of their souls. Nothing now could be the same.

'Edith Mullane,' said George as they came down the lane towards La Vallée. 'That's not a Guernsey name.'

'She don't look like no Guernsey girl either.'

'Do you think we'll see her again?' George asked.

'Well, you tell me,' said Artie. 'You're the one who sees the future.'

George had often regretted sharing his secret with Artie. He once thought his brother would be thrilled – even impressed – by the hidden knowledge. Of course Artie did not believe him, teased him about it, said it was a fantasy, and so the spirit girl was seldom mentioned any more.

La Vallée was an old whitewashed cottage nestling in a shallow valley on the western slopes of the Castel parish. A second, larger house had been built on to its gable by Gràn'père Bazin and his two sons, so that both could have a home in which to raise their families. Both the Big House and the cottage had two rooms on each floor with *la p'tite maisaon* out in the yard. A small rough granite pigsty had stood empty since the last pig was eaten at Christmas 1911. Behind the cottage lay fifty foot of glass, and a small field ran uphill and served as a kitchen garden. Measuring more than a vergie yet less than an acre, the whole could not be called a farm.

The brothers went round the Big House and into the yard. Behind the cottage ran a scullery and dairy, although the Bazins had never kept a cow. George made for the dairy and picked up his fishing gear. 'You coming?' he shouted back from the door. 'I'm off to the rocks, me.'

No Guernseyman would say 'I'm going fishing' in case the fish heard him and stayed away.

'Tide should be good.'

Artie grinned and came in for his own rod and bag. Their father had taught Artie to fish, and in turn Artie taught George. He didn't need to run to catch fish, nor even to see them. As boys they would pick their way to what Artie called 'a good place' beyond Albecq where the rocks fell sheer away and the water was deep. They cast their lines then waited. George could hear when his hook did not make the water and would try again. He could feel when he had a fish. The first one he caught had been a splendid, wriggling shimmering thing and he would not let Artie kill it.

George was pleased his brother would still come down to their usual rock, as he feared that Artie would outgrow him one day. Perched as comfortably as they could upon granite of unimaginable age, the two watched their lines and looked out at the sea. The wind was chill and rain was not far off.

'You know, I could marry me that Edith Mullane, once I've

made a lot of money in the bank.' Artie said this with no more care than if deciding whether to use one worm or two.

George was alarmed, jealous even. 'I thought you weren't staying at that bank? I thought you still wanted to be a schoolteacher?'

'They won't let me be a teacher,' said Artie. 'Not yet. I've got to be older, or wiser, or something. Makes me think I should go off and see the world first.'

'You going to be a sailor like Gràn'père Georges, then?'

'No – the sea's good for fishin', but I like having me feet on the land. I like being in the Militia – it's good training. I could join the Regulars and travel to India or Timbuktu, travel the Empire.'

'That would be good so long as there's no wars going on.'

'There's always little wars going on somewhere,' Artie said. 'Like the African war on the memorial in the Avenue, the one Uncle Jack helped build.'

In George's mind, Artie was already a teacher. It was English history that was taught in school, but Artie had got friendly with that Mr Torode at the Intermediate School who told all kinds of tales about Guernsey to liven up the lessons. George had not moved up to the Intermediate and left school at twelve.

'Guernseymen make famous soldiers,' Artie added. 'Like General Le Marchant, who beat the French. He was fearless and brave and won a big battle in Spain.'

George had ever been the willing audience for Artie's stories. 'What happened?'

'He got killed right at the end leading this big cavalry charge. Then there was General Brock, he beat the Americans in the very same year and saved Canada, even. He got killed too, shot through the heart.'

George turned up his nose. 'Being a soldier's not a very good job if it means getting killed.'

'That was a hundred years ago, almost to the day. Things have changed; the army only fights fuzzy-wuzzies these days. We've got guns and they've just got spears and sticks. The army's more about having adventures than fighting real battles.'

'See, but you should be a teacher, you, knowing all that history. You don't want to be a soldier and go away. You can do that job in Town for now, until you're old enough to teach. Father's proud of you – and Uncle Jack.'

'Yes, that's my plan, give or take,' said Artie. 'The bank will do for now, as you say, but it's scribbling on paper and running errands around Town, and it's pretty boring being in an office all day. Still, once I've made lots of money I can find that nice girl to marry.'

'But what do you want a girl for?' George said with disgust.

'Oh you know,' Artie said. 'To keep me company. You've got that girl who follows you around. She keeps you company when there's no one about.'

George looked away. 'But she's not real,' he said bitterly.

'You get upset when I say that.'

'No, I mean that she's really there, but she's not a real person.'

With a look of mischief, Artie peered to left, then right. 'Is she here now?' he whispered.

'Course not.'

'Course not,' echoed Artie. He jiggled his line and fell silent.

George had been thinking about Mrs Lake, thinking how much better he felt for having unburdened himself. All at once he told Artie the story, the full story of the girl by the sea.

'You know, it was right here I first saw her.'

Artie turned and became attentive, and for once it was George telling the story.

'I was seven – just after I got my glasses. I thought I'd come down here, on my own, now I could see proper. You, Father and Uncle Jack were in the greenhouse, working. I sneaked out without you seeing.'

Quite deliberately he had collected his rod and bag of gear without his brother and the men seeing him leave. So much was good. He was seven years old and he had glasses now. Nothing could stop him.

'Mind you don't lose them glasses, George,' his father had warned when the glass and metal was first pressed into his palm. 'You'll not get no others.'

Lose them! George was freed by those glasses. He would sooner lose an arm or that crippled left leg! He discovered that the sea had white-capped waves and made a curved line where it met the sky. Up above, the clouds had wispy edges and twirled as if they were alive. The island stretched away from him, with cottages and hedgerows and more glasshouses than he had ever imagined. Guernsey seemed enormous.

He could see better than all the other children. He could see more than anyone in the whole world!

So George enjoyed finding his own way to the usual rock by Albecq, and soon caught two bream. The tide was closing in and the sun falling when he decided to make for home. Despite his glasses he was still lame and clumsy, and the rocks from which he fished could be wet and slimed with weed. Worse, the glasses gave him confidence – too much confidence.

The old watch house of the Guet caught his eye. Up on the ridge, stark on the skyline. To see it so clear, from so far away; this was magical!

Distracted for a moment, his left foot betrayed him. Slipping on greasy seaweed, George overbalanced. He made to grab at his rod, then at the fish, and then fell hard on to the rocks, the fish protecting his hand from the impact, leaving him on his knees. His glasses shot from his face and rattled into a shallow pool.

Fish forgotten, he scrabbled for the glasses, the sudden shift of events leaving him almost blind. Desperately he groped in wrist-deep water between a triangle of rocks. In moments he had recovered his treasure and dried them with the tail of his shirt. He slipped them on and could see once more.

The world was wrong. He removed the glasses, wiped them again, then brought them close and examined them with screwed-up eyes. In the bottom of the right lens there was a moon-shaped chip. It almost looked as if a bubble of water were trapped in the glass.

His only pair! There would be no other. He began to tremble, then to cry. No, seven-year-old boys must not cry! Desperate, he looked skywards. The glasses had been so expensive, his father would kill him! George sat glumly on the rock until the tide lapped at his feet and he was forced inland. He crossed the dunes and sat staring across the pools and reeds of La Grande Mare, his back to the setting sun. He did not dare return home, so sat on the rough grass trying to hatch a plan or an excuse while the sun fell in the sky behind him. Glittering glasshouses were everywhere on the rising ground, a thousand panes reflecting the sunlight back at him.

The world was still wrong. He could see that chip, spoiling his vision if he looked down and right, yet there was something else there too. It was off to the far right, further than he could strain his eyes to turn. A flash of sunlight – some sort of reflection in the glass danced and played in the light. Without being aware of it, he became entranced by that ethereal figure, for figure it was – skipping into and out of the periphery of his vision. Mesmerised he watched, playing with fanciful thoughts until those thoughts brought a shiver to his soul.

What was he seeing? Who was it dancing behind him, where he could hardly see? He spun round, but the figure spun faster. Only the rocks and the sea were behind him, both sparkling red-gold in the sunset. He turned back to face east, and there again was the figure. He looked hard and it vanished. Only when he glanced away did it reappear.

He concentrated on *not looking* and there she was again. The sea breeze died with the sunset, but his back grew cold.

Already frightened, his fear grew as the figure stopped her dance and drew closer. He could sense her creeping up from the marram grass behind; he could see her reflection in the glass, yet understood that if he turned about there would be nothing. Trembling, he sat with his eyes fixed on the Guet watch house on its clifftop, but the ghostly figure grew and became solid. It was a woman – ancient, yet young. A girl his own age, yet not his own age.

He had braved this too long – this wraith was more frightening than his father! He struggled to his feet, grabbed at his rod and his basket and ran inland as fast as his crippled leg would manage. George took off his glasses as soon as he came into the cottage at La Vallée and secreted them in his hand. He hid them in his room, intending to only put them on the next day after he left the house. He kept his guilt well hidden too.

After school the next day, he came into the kitchen ravenous and was so looking forward to the evening meal he clean forgot his fright of the evening before, so was wearing his glasses with no attempt to conceal them.

'Georges!' His mother scolded. 'Your glasses, they're broken!'

Then he remembered. It had all seemed like a feverish nightmare. Broken glasses, ethereal girl, blind panic.

'Oh, they're just scratched a bit.'

'Let me see!' She demanded the glasses and he handed them over.

'See, it's just a little bit down here,' he explained. 'I was on my rock and I slipped.'

She slapped his leg. 'Georges! Do you know how much money these cost! Do you know? Wait until your father gets home, he'll tan your hide for this. Breaking your glasses and them not a month old.' She slapped him again. 'And don't you dodge!'

'But I was fishing.'

'You take care of your things! There won't be no more, you hear? We can't afford new spectacles every week. Not with your special shoes and all!'

He was sent to the bedroom hungry, and waited for his father to come back. Fright numbed the pain of the beating. He had already been thrashed a hundred times in his mind, so when it finally came it was no more than part of the same nightmare. Friendless and hopeless George was sent to bed without the supper was craving. Tears misted his broken lenses, and he left them lying on the windowsill and sobbed himself to sleep.

Gràn'mère Bazin died suddenly that night. She died in her sleep and was only discovered when George's mother finally ventured into her room in the Big House. No one had expected this – she had not complained of being ill and not been particularly old. Amid the shock and upheaval, George's mishap was swiftly forgotten. The family grieved and rushed around making funeral arrangements. George, as usual, was ignored.

Out on the pink-brown rocks, Artie frowned as if listening carefully to the story, told in full for the first time. Only at the very end did he ask a question.

'You sure it was the day Gràn'mère died?'

'I am now,' said George.

CHAPTER 6

As Artie trudged back up the hill at George-pace, he worked over the story of George and the ghost-angel in his mind. He'd lived with George's invisible friend for as long as he could remember, but wished it would fade like other childish things. He would fight to the death to defend his brother, and a couple of times he almost had. Once he had looked forward to a new playmate, but the baby christened Georges did not grow up as he should.

'Why can't he walk?' young Artie had asked many times.

Doctors had done what they could, which was little compared to the price they charged. Georges started his early years with his left leg strapped into contraptions of iron and leather. He could barely move, let alone run. When Artie wanted to be helping his father in the glasshouse, his job was more often 'Watch Georges'. He took the mission seriously and would draw immobile Georges into his games. Georges would be the injured soldier who needed to be saved, the trapped quarryman who had to be rescued by Artie in the nick of time. Georges could not be off adventuring, so Artie would bring back souvenirs – a seagull's skull, a perfectly round white pebble, a giant pine cone. His little brother would hold them very close to his face, sniff them and run his fingers over the texture. Once Georges could talk, the brothers made up stories about these little treasures, especially in the winter when the rain swept up the valley from the sea. Artie won a book at school called *Brave Sons of the Empire* and they read it over and again.

Then King George V came to the throne and 'Georges' became 'George' to all but his mother and a few elderly relatives. The French ways were fading and Artie did not miss them. For all his curiosity about the past, he did not want to live there.

It was a time of bright possibilities, and Artie toyed with all the things the future might hold for him. The bank might send him to England, or that opportunity to learn to teach might finally arise. He could just throw it all in and run off and join the Regulars – there had been a good deal in the papers about the need to build up the army to meet the German threat. He might indeed marry Edith Mullane and carry her back to Ireland, or travel the world with her. But George dragged at his heels; George would be his burden for as long as they both lived.

'Hurry up, George, let's get the fish home to Mémaen.'

Marie Bazin fried the fish her sons had caught. With her husband and unmarried brother-in-law she was cooking for five. Over supper, Artie gave vent to his ideas of travel and adventure. He listed friends and acquaintances who had already left the island, fulfilling those boyish dreams to get away and explore the world.

Uncle Jack sympathised. 'You know there are towns called Guernsey over in America and down in Australia? Canada, New Zealand. All sorts of places.'

'Artie don't want to go to such places!' his mother protested. 'Don't encourage him, Jacques, he's got a good job right here.'

She habitually called the men by their names in French style, and rarely spoke English at all. Artie though had always been Artie – no one in the family ever called him Arthur.

'Guernsey once had a great fleet of sailing ships that

travelled the oceans before the days of steam,' Uncle Jack continued, mistily.

Artie knew this, but Jack was the older brother and liked to be the bedrock of family wisdom.

'That's what took your Gràn'père to sea,' Jack continued his narrative.

'But not you, eh, Jack?' his brother said.

'Nor you, Henry,' Jack observed.

Henry Bazin had never profited from a firm occupation. He grew a few tomatoes in the summer, but mostly worked as a stone-breaker at Mowlem's quarry behind Cobo. Jack on the other hand had risen to be a stone-cutter at Mowlem's, and then set himself up as a mason. He styled himself 'Jack' and made sure his English was good enough to do business with Englishmen from the stone companies and the smart families from Town.

'Born Guernsey, we'll die Guernsey,' said Jack, after another mouthful of fish. 'Granite is in our bones and tomato juice in our veins. After the *Stella,* I reckon our family has done its travelling.'

Uncle Jack might profess to be no traveller, but Artie could see a sparkle in his eyes as he looked towards the window and a life he might have led. Perhaps that glint was a tear. There were always adverts in the *Guernsey Evening Press* encouraging people to take the Trans–Canadian Express, and letters from people who had moved across the globe. His uncle might harbour a secret regret that he never got away, but for Artie, the world still beckoned.

The elder three Bazin men stayed at the table after finishing the fish supper. Marie began clearing around, clattering dishes, while George went off to do whatever George did.

'You're doing a good job encouraging our Artie to vanish off to Africa, eh?' Henry moaned.

'Aw, he'll make up his own mind in his own time,' Jack said, winking at his nephew.

'I will,' Artie stated.

'Remember someone's got to look after your *mémaen*, when I'm gone,' Henry said directly. 'And George – someone's going to have to look out for him. Remember how the property gets split two ways, so you'll only get half of a half, Artie.'

'Aw, Henry, it's not like when we were young and all you did was what your parents did,' Jack said. 'It's a big world. Artie was never going to be a quarryman like us. Too much book-learning, eh? Speaking of which, Artie, will you help me with my books tonight? My suppliers need paying, yet everyone who owes me money finds good reason why it has to be next week, or next month.'

'Of course,' Artie said. This was what family was all about. Little obligations, day in and day out, year in and year out. He was no sooner going to Africa than he was to the moon.

'I tell you, though. Our George is going nowhere.' Henry Bazin mopped grease from his chin. 'They were grand fish George caught, but he is a worry. Near seventeen now and what hope has he got of a trade?'

'He makes a good fisherman,' Jack said.

'Two fish are fine, yes, but could he launch a boat?' Henry replied. 'Could he stand firm on a moving deck? He can't see no horizon, no storm coming, can't follow the leading lights, can't even see the shore if he drops his spectacles like he's done before now. You should see the chips and dints in them; I'm surprised he can see at all.'

'Buy him some new ones,' Artie suggested firmly. That offered a solution to more than one problem.

'Oh yes, have you seen the price? He'd only lose them, or break them like he broke the old ones. Or some boys would steal them, even. You know what they're like, always making his life a misery, bullying him. I've seen you chase them off, but a man's got to fight his own battles.'

'He does,' Jack said, frowning. 'Not let his brother do it for him.'

Artie sensed he was being criticised. His uncle was never one to throw away thoughts lightly.

'You be careful about that, eh?' Jack continued. 'It's handy to be a fighter when you're young, but you have to put it aside now you're at the bank. We don't want you troubling the jurats. It goes down badly with the bosses to have a brawler on the team, 'specially in a bank. You'd get away with it once or twice down the quarry, but a banker would never see things our way.'

Artie flexed his right hand, wondering if wearing a suit and riding the bus to Town somehow made him less of a man than these two who chipped stone for a living. The last unwise youth to crack that line had been sent to the floor with a bleeding nose.

'I'll come round later,' he said to Uncle Jack and got up from the table. He walked across the yard to *la p'tite maisaon,* but the latch was down: George was inside. He told his brother to hurry up, half in jest, and went back to the cottage to wait a decent while. By nifty footwork he slipped inside the back door just in time to allow his father to pass out of it and into the yard, an unlit pipe paused on his lips. From over by the pump his mother challenged her husband.

'What's wrong, Henri?' she asked.

'George,' he said.

Through the thin wooden door of *la p'tite maisaon* George

heard his name and paused as he was about to undo the latch. Years of being half-blind had accentuated his hearing.

'What's he going to do?' his father continued. 'How did it come to this? Do you think we're being punished?'

'Never say that!' she snapped. 'Never say that again.'

'But—'

'No!'

'But, Marie, why George, why us again?'

George caught the word *again,* and wondered at it.

'God's testing us,' she said, her voice hushed now so that it was difficult to catch every word. 'It's another chance, so take it as a sign, Henri Bazin. Don't you ever give up on our Georges,' she said. 'He'll find a way.'

'He'll never find a wife.'

'He couldn't support no wife. And it hasn't harmed Jacques to be without a wife.'

'I reckon Jack's happier for it,' he said.

'*Vere*! Your *mémaen* looked after him all those years, and now he eats at our table. He has it easy. And he has the bigger portion, and why does he need it? Jack's well past marriage and children.'

George strained to hear what they were saying, if they were saying anything at all now.

'…So it will all come to us one day, especially as he's the elder,' his mother said triumphantly. 'Two sons, two houses. So it won't be half of a half, as you're always saying.'

They fell silent. Perhaps George had rattled the latch. He opened it casually, smiling at his parents who both watched him with more than usual interest.

'You eavesdropping?' challenged his father.

'You worry about me,' he stated, by way of counter-challenge.

'We do – especially what happens when we're gone,' said his father defensively.

'Well, that's not so much of a problem, is it?' his mother said with a sudden burst of cheer. 'Artie will be fine in the house with some handsome girl, and Georges can have the cottage, just has Jacques has it now. You'd like that, you?'

George nodded. He liked Uncle Jack. He would like to *be* Uncle Jack.

His mother wagged a finger at her husband. 'Luck evens out, see? So you don't need to worry. We do our part, we raise him well. Our Georges will be fine, in his own way.'

She smiled at him and George made a noise of agreement.

'Just you see. It's like God has a plan for Georges.'

CHAPTER 7

Winter grew dark and work grew scarce for the lame young man widely thought a fool. In the years since leaving school, George could only hope to 'help out'. His parents found tasks for him round the home, in the greenhouse and in the yard which earned his place at the dinner table. He caught fish regularly, and by season brought in his share of gulls' eggs and blackberries or picked tomatoes. He chopped wood, he could cut furze or *vraic* intended for the fire. One neighbour or another would need a hand with the animals, with the harvest, with repairing glass, so George was able to earn a few shillings. It was far from a career, but despite his father's worries, he was content.

Bunched in the sitting room for warmth early in the New Year, the family Bazin was buzzing with the latest unlikely news. Aunt Irene had come round to visit her sister and drew all their attention to the story. George's heart went cold.

'A witch?' he asked, feigning ignorance.

'Such a carry-on in this day and age,' said his mother, gleefully running through the details of the case in the *Guernsey Evening Press*. 'My, these English words are hard!'

'There's no paper written in the patois, *p'tite soeur*,' Aunt Irene said. 'Let George read it.'

George had been half-curled up on the green bed by the fire, and took the paper as if it burned hotter than the log in the grate. The story ran down a whole column. Mrs Lake of St Sampson's had been arrested for witchcraft.

'Aloud, boy!' Aunt Irene urged.

He did his best to recite the story of the arrest, choking on the idea of the police searching that little cottage for clues to her guilt, taking down statements and accusations.

'She foretells the future but didn't see that one coming!' laughed Aunt Irene.

'I bet she did,' George said. 'I bet she knew that someone would come for her one day. I bet she was just waiting for that knock on the door from the policeman.'

'Then she's daft. She should have escaped!' Artie said.

'Or brought some goblins up from hell to chase off the policeman,' their father said.

'Or turned him into a *crapaud*,' Artie added.

They all laughed, as *crapaud* meant not only a toad, but a Jerseyman, which in many ways was worse. George's laugh was a nervous laugh, the laugh of the traitor who does not want to be unmasked. Inside he felt bad, fearful for the woman to whom he'd opened up his darkest secret. He'd not dared visit her since that day last summer, and now he would see her no more. Perhaps there would be a witch-hunt and he would be the next to be arrested.

George looked to Artie for support. 'They won't burn her?' he asked. 'Like in the old days? Like that story you told me of the Bailiff burning those witches and their babies?'

'Course,' said Artie, lowering his brow and fixing George with a stare. 'They burn people who consort with fairies and foretell the future.'

'Don't tease, Artie,' said his mother. 'Georges hasn't got your book-learning. He was out working while you were still studying.'

'No, mousse,' soothed his father. 'They don't burn witches any more. If they did, them Valpieds would be first on the bonfire, for sure.'

George checked the paper anxiously each day until the verdict was published. Mrs Lake was convicted of witchcraft, sorcery and telling fortunes. She was sent to jail for eight days and never practised again. People said she was just a wicked lady who tricked people out of money by pretending to lift curses laid by herself, and by warding off bad luck which only she could detect. George decided not to go and see her after she was released. She might have reformed, turned against the craft entirely, and betray him. Suspicious eyes would be watching her house, taking note of the names of those who called. It was a small island, with little to talk about. He too might have the police at his door. George retreated from the world of the white witch. Everything that happened to him from that day forward would be his secret. Not even Artie deserved to know.

Artie was no longer interested in hearing about George's magical woman, as he had found one of his own. More and more she had floated into the brothers' conversation. Now he seemed to have lost her again.

'Have you seen that Edith Mullane lately?' Artie asked as they took a roundabout 'short cut' back from the church through the fields by Le Préel. Walking had begun as a great effort to George, but his years of struggle had made him strong. He limped home with determination, rhythmically clumping down that extra-thick boot.

'Not since Christmas.'

'It's just that you're still round the parish when I'm working. Thought you might have seen her, that's all.'

'You could ask Adèle.'

'I don't gossip with girls. Adèle gets mad jealous anyway – I kissed her once after some cider and she still rates it as a proposal.'

'Never kissed a girl,' George mooned.

'Nothing to it,' Artie bluffed, making clear there was plenty of mystery he would not share with his brother.

The lame boy who had never been kissed by a girl, who perhaps never would be kissed by a girl, stomped onwards, shaking a clod of mud from his left boot. 'I likes Edith, me,' George said. 'But she wasn't to our school, was she?'

'They lived to the Vale when her father was around.'

'Is he dead, then?'

'Nar – ran off with a maid what worked for her aunt, so Mémaen said. Gone back to Ireland or to England or somewhere. Mémaen was talking about her after she first saw Edith at church. You know how she likes to know everything about everyone.'

'That's not a nice thing to do. Run off.'

'You like everyone to be good, don't you, George? Well they're not and you should learn that, you.'

The slate roof of the Big House was soon in sight over the bend of the lane, then the tiles of the cottage. They walked quietly, George thinking first of the elf-slim Edith, then of another sylvan figure. Girls were a mystery to him and the very word 'girl' brought deeper mysteries to mind. His lame leg and useless eyes were not the first curses to strike the family.

'Did you ever know our sister?' George asked.

'No, I was only little when she was lost.'

Baby Drusille had died just a month before George was born. She would scarcely have been two years old, and Artie only a year or so older.

'There's no picture of her,' George said.

'No.'

'And no headstone. She's all on her own, away from Gràn'mère and Gràn'père Bazin. I sometimes wonder, when I sees that girl out of the corner of my eye…'

'George, stop it! Grow out of it. They'll lock you up if you keep talking like that. There's no ghost following you. One day I'm going to sneak those glasses off your bedside, smash them with a hammer, then throw the pieces down the deepest part of that old quarry above Vazon. Drown your ghosts in all that water.'

'You wouldn't.'

'I'd do it to save you – as I always have.'

At the end of their own lane, Artie stepped in front of him. 'Come here, straighten them up.' He made to straighten the glasses, but instead whipped them off George's face.

'Hey!'

Holding his trophy high, Artie sprinted down to the Big House and behind into the yard, George blundering after him. In the middle of the yard, Artie stopped and dangled the glasses. George lunged at them too late, only to have them jerked out of his way like a fish on a line.

Artie waved them aloft, standing on tiptoe. 'Can't get 'em, can't get 'em.'

He dodged around, circling his brother, holding the glasses up out of reach while George boiled at the centre of the ring, trying to grab them back.

'They're my glasses and they're special, they're mine!'

Their parents came from separate doors at the same moment, one from the house, one from the dairy. The boys were in full argument and both were using English, back and forth.

'What's that shouting?' Marie Bazin used the ancient language.

Artie stopped his teasing immediately.

'Give them back!' George said, and took the glasses into his hands.

'Boys!' their father shouted, also in Guernesiais. 'Artie – fetch the wood in. George – what's that you're fighting for?'

George put the glasses back on his face defiantly. 'Spectacles,' he said in English.

'When you get a job, you need to save up for new ones!' Bluntly his father brought the bilingual argument to its close. 'You look like a child, but you're a man now, so grow up!'

He turned to his wife.

'*Eche qué j'étais au païssaon tànt d'temps?*' he asked. 'Or do they always squabble in English these days?'

'I never noticed,' she said.

'We're raising Englishmen!'

George looked at Artie, who smiled back with confidence.

'It means they'll get on,' their mother said, glancing from one to the other. 'Not have to quarry and scrape in the garden.'

Deliberately their father kept speaking the old language as he responded. 'There's nothing wrong with quarrying – nor scraping in the garden. We don't have to pretend to be English all the time.'

'You changed your name. Henri wasn't good enough, you had to become Henry.'

'Only because Jack did the same. We're brothers. He starts getting all English, so I have to keep up.'

'And you were desolate when King Edward died.'

'That's just being respectful. You know, the king, our duke. Doesn't mean I want to be English, and it doesn't mean my boys have to pretend to be English to move on. Is everyone just going to forget to speak like we do?'

'*Y a fin à toute chaose*, Henri Bazin.'

Times were changing, and everything has an end.

CHAPTER 8

Edith's mother's prime excuse to drag her to the heart of nowhere had been that she had found work on a farm near Le Préel where 'Uncle Tom' lived. Uncle Tom was of course not her uncle, in the same way that Uncle Clive and Uncle Nico had not been uncles either. It promised to be a dismal winter in the dower wing of that cottage not quite on the Bailiff's Cross Road, especially once the inevitable quarrel with Uncle Tom left Ruth Mullane with no means of support. Edith and her mother dressed in their worst rags and went to see the *Procureur des Pauvres* at the Douzaine Room. He asked where their husbands were, and Ruth Mullane recited a long and weary yarn until the *Procureur* was quite worn down and compliant. Just enough money came into their hands so they could eat. Something had to be done.

'So you went into service?' Adèle asked, incredulous. The young women had met at a halfway point at the bottom of Rectory Hill, which meant Edith was now doubling back towards the church.

'Yes,' Edith sighed.

'We wondered when we didn't see you – not even at church. We all thought you'd gone papist again.'

'No, I was gone to St Martin's, to some big house full of English people.'

'Bet it was warmer than your little place though?'

'Only once I'd cleaned the grates and made the fires for them.'

As Easter was past, the women of the parish had switched from their winter clothes to their summer ones and there was more colour and life around. Edith wore a cornflower-print dress that was her favourite, and Adèle wore a skirt in green cotton handed down from her mother. Both girls wore bonnets with brims so deep that their faces were hidden except from directly in front.

'Did you get a uniform?' Adèle asked, almost in awe.

'Yes, but it was horrible. Like I'd stopped being a person. And this posh cow who ran the house insisted on calling me Daisy, because she had an aunt called Edith and Daisy was a "more suitable name for a servant".' She mocked the English accent.

'*Là*, sounds snobby that one!'

'*Vere!*' Edith rarely lapsed into patois, but at that moment she had never wanted to be more Guernsey. 'I stuck it until New Year, when they got this new gardener in from Wales. I mean, what's wrong with our men? Even George Bazin could dig up flowers and plant new ones, eh? Why bring that grubby little man in from Wales? Anyway he started going on about "planting Daisy in a bed".'

'The dirty devil.' Adèle seemed more jealous than shocked.

'I was having none of that, I can tell you! I stuck it until last week, then walked out. No notice, no reference.' Edith smiled at her own red rage. She was not born to serve.

'So what you going to do now, you?'

Edith shrugged. 'Smile at the *Procureur* again. Marry a rich, handsome man.'

'You won't find none out here.'

'No.'

Edith returned easily to the Sunday ritual of boy meets girl, girl pretends to ignore boy, boy pretends he's not really interested and is only talking to her for a dare. She was penniless but carried currency in her face.

'The richest folk in the world can't buy good looks,' her mother had told her more than once. 'What you're born with is better than money, my girl. Makes up for having none. But beauty don't last; you can't save it up for a rainy day. You spend it while you've got it.'

Yes, this was currency that must be spent fast. Edith's mother had once been a great beauty, said her mother. Admired by all around her, said her mother. Ruth Mullane still thought that way and still acted that way, though that particular omnibus had departed long since.

Sunshine warmed the churchyard as Edith came out of the porch with Adèle at her side. Dark-haired, dark-eyed and oval-faced, Adèle had an earthy plainness that made her the kind of friend who could never become a rival. She was the perfect companion.

A fair gang of young men and women loitered around the top gate on Rectory Hill. *Les jaunnes* fenced with words; teasing, boasting, chatting. George Bazin, however, was alone among the headstones closest to the porch, studying one with great care. He was a stoutly built young man, with broad shoulders developed by years of compensating for a weak leg when working his odd jobs. He glanced up and met the women's gaze for just a moment before looking away.

'Ooh, the Owl's watching you again,' Adèle teased.

'Do you mean George Bazin? Why do you call him Owl?'

'It's the glasses.' Adèle mimicked owl-eyes with thumbs and forefingers. 'We used to tease him horribly at school. Couldn't read the blackboard, couldn't catch us when we played *djablle*. When he first got them, we all ran away shouting, "*Gerdé cahan!*"'

Beware of the owl, thought Edith.

'And he's strange, him. He keeps to himself when he's not with his brother. Hangs about this 'yer churchyard until past dark.'

Owl-boy stood beside the tombstone. The owl was a creature of night, the familiar of witches, an omen of death. No one would befriend an owl.

'Poor boy,' said Edith beneath her breath, watching George half watching her.

Owl-George smiled that wet-eyed puppy smile of his.

Artie Bazin, on the other hand, was a different prospect. The brown-eyed Guernseymen tend to be short, as it is said they are descended from fairy folk, while their blue-eyed neighbours trace their roots to tall Norsemen. Folklore alone explained why Artie was taller than most. A grin was always lurking at the corner of his lips, even when he brought that heavy brow down to frown. As usual, Artie was at the centre of his group of friends.

'Hard to think that's his brother,' Edith said.

'For sure Artie's got the charm for both of them,' said Adèle.

'For sure.'

Adèle dived in to quash Edith's interest as they approached the group. 'But he'd be impossible to walk out with,' she said quickly. 'He's gone all posh since he went to the Intermediate School. He works in a bank now, in Town. Wears a suit. And his dad and his uncle changed their names so they sounded more English. It's like they're too good for the likes of us.'

Edith gave a smile as Adèle said this, but it was not directed at her friend. Artie caught the smile and moved her way, so she quickly made to ignore him as she had been ignoring his brother.

'It's Edith, eh?'

She pretended to have forgotten his name. 'And you are?'

'Arthur Bazin, at your service,' he half bowed.

Adèle scowled, and Edith sniffed the scent of envy.

'Can I walk you home, Miss Mullane?' Artie asked.

'You? Intermediate boy? Smart boy who works in Town? Why do you want to walk out with a country girl?'

'Nar, I'm as country as you are. Town's just where the job is. Walk with me.'

'Walk alone? People will talk. It will be all round the parish before we get home.' Edith raised her eyebrow at Adèle, but her friend's face had turned dark under her bonnet brim.

George was hovering by Artie's elbow.

'My brother George will chaperone us, then people won't talk.'

'George?' She gave him a glance. 'Your pet Owl?'

'Don't call him that!'

Artie's rebuke was a little too sharp for her liking.

'Fine, I won't. George, you're not an owl. Be our escort. Protect us from gossip and scandal.'

It was plain to Edith that the brothers Bazin came as a set; you did not get one without the other. She would have said something to allay Adèle's hurt feelings, but her friend walked away without a word. The other young people were dispersing, so Edith assented to being escorted home with just enough reluctance as to not seem eager. She lived only five minutes' brisk walk south of the church, but George's walk was a slow walk and the trio was in no hurry. The Owl followed a few steps behind the couple, but not completely outside their talk, as he would throw comments forward to join the conversation. A narrow track with a rutted surface of earth and stones led to a green lane carpeted by grass and fringed by earth banks where primroses, pennywort, campion, bluebells and ivy all fought for space.

Amid the pollen and the scent of the flowers, Edith picked up something else – musty, salt, something she could not describe. She was close to him momentarily; the back of their hands brushed. When she glanced up at him he gave a little laugh and looked away, telling some anecdote about some distant relation who had fallen off a cart round about here when drunk. His eyes were a bright, surprising blue, and he looked upwards and outwards, not down at the earth content with his lot. Edith said goodbye some distance short of her home, as was only decent, and determined to say nothing of this to her mother.

Since Edith's swift failure to get on in service, Ruth Mullane equally swiftly decided that her daughter needed a husband. Artie Bazin was not mentioned on their Thursday walk to Town, although half a dozen other names were raised. The women walked by the lanes leading through the edge of St Andrew's and down past the Foulon cemetery. On their return journey they would take the horse bus part of the way back, but the route was hardly convenient for their home and money couldn't be squandered.

An arcade fronts the Markets, and this is where they headed first. Her mother sold eight eggs to a stallholder for a few coppers, and they went through into the long fish market with its high vaulted roof. Mrs Mullane fought a hard bargain over a piece of conger. Ruth Mullane had far more of a classic Guernsey look than her daughter – the unusual blue eyes paired with hair that was almost black, a wide and eager face designed to smile. Her hair was spoiled now by attempts to make it a shade of ruddy brown it was never meant to be, and on careless days such as today it rose in a wild bundle and fell about her shoulders. A woman with so much natural colour barely needed make-up, but Ruth applied it liberally and cheaply. That *Beauty of the Parish* rosette was a hard one to put away.

Her mother gave a coquette's smile at a man five years too young for her, but Edith pulled her arm to steer her away from misadventure.

Across Market Square, beside the Guille-Allès library, a workman was pasting an advert for a dance at St George's Hall. Two young men studied the poster. Both were smartly dressed in what must be the latest fashion for gentlemen: light jackets and straw boaters.

'That's young Master Carey,' Ruth Mullane hissed. 'Reckon he needs a wife.'

'Oh, Mother!'

'You'd do no better than snagging a Carey. His family are all Bailiffs and advocates. Must own half the Town. Oldest family in the island, they say.'

'I'm not out to snag anyone.' Edith looked down at her dress and its faded green print. 'And men like that don't marry the likes of us, Mother.'

'You can try, my girl.' She pinched her daughter's cheek. 'You're my beauty. You've got more spirit than some posh Town girl. Just look at them sorry boys. Their mothers will find one of them girls from the Ladies' College who only knows Latin and piano. Don't know how to sew, or knit, or cook…'

'No, Mother, they have servants to do all that.'

Master Carey and his even more handsome friend must be back from university for the holidays. Guernsey's rich men were all old men. Their sons for the most part were sent away to school in England or packed off into the army to keep them out of mischief. If they came back at all, chances are it would be with an English rose on their arm, importing stock to improve the breed. Edith turned away.

On her next expedition to Town, Edith formed a trio with Adèle and Perotine Guille: one redhead, a dark Guernsey girl and a pink-faced straw blonde. At seventeen and eighteen years old, they were the finest the Castel would offer that year. One of Adèle's brothers took the young ladies most of the way in his cart. Brushing away the farm dust from their dresses, they headed for Candie Grounds, a regular venue for band concerts of all descriptions. At the top was a statue of old Queen Victoria, then lawns and gardens stretched down towards the harbour. A bandstand was the focal point of a bank of chairs, which enjoyed a view directly over the smaller islands of Herm, Jethou and Sark to distant France. No artist could paint a prettier view of blue sea, sparkling waves and brown islands, all framed by exotic trees and fronted by the steep lawn.

Off to one side, a white-painted kiosk sold ices. Dark-haired Master Carey was there, again in company with his handsome and fairer friend. The pair wore the same sharp jackets as when last seen in the Markets and were queuing for ices from the stall.

Perotine suppressed a giggle, but it was a stage giggle and the men noticed.

'Good afternoon, ladies.' The fair one tipped his straw boater. Master Carey leaned close and said something under his breath.

'Would you care for ices?' he asked aloud.

'That would be so kind,' Edith said.

Three into two does not go, but the men must have reckoned they had the right to pick and choose. Ices were handed out, with introductions.

'Thomas Carey.'

'Peter Le Marchant.'

'Carey, my,' Edith said. 'I was told that's the oldest family in the island.'

'Indeed – they came over with Noah,' Peter Le Marchant was quick with his quip.

'Actually, old boy, we had our own boat.' Carey grinned at Edith and took the first lick of his ice. 'So, Miss Mullane, that's Irish. Is your father with the garrison?'

'Do I sound Irish?'

'No, I admit you do not.'

'The Irish name goes way back,' she said. 'I'm not really Irish at all.'

'She's just a Castel girl, her,' Adèle butted in. 'Like the rest of us.'

'And what does your father do, Miss Guille?' Master Le Marchant asked.

'Farms,' Perotine answered, and then blushed. 'By Kings Mills.'

'Are you related to the Guille who built the library?'

'I dunno. Must be.'

'He made so much money, that man. Made it big in America, brought it home, founded a library.'

'And a museum,' sighed Tom Carey. 'Don't forget the museum. It's not what I would do with several thousand pounds.'

'Old Wilfred Carey's doing much the same; he must be a relative of yours…'

Edith felt her heart sink. She had no family to speak of, and the family she had did not come over with Noah, let alone found libraries or museums.

'Are you going to the dance on Friday, Miss Mullane?' Tom Carey asked. 'At St George's Hall?'

It was a question, not an invitation.

'We might go – is there still tickets?' blurted Adèle.

'There very well might be.'

'We'll see,' Edith said.

As the five strolled downhill, two young women walked up towards them, sheltered by parasols. Both wore light white summer dresses, one with a brocade bow in pink, the other with an embroidered bodice.

'Why Tom, Peter,' one said. Her accent was clipped and educated.

Five women were now gathered around the two men. Edith held her ground, glaring at the closest of the finely groomed pair.

'Ices, my, what a splendid idea,' said one, nudging her friend.

The men tipped their hats and the pair swept past up the path, all eyes following.

'Are they going to the dance?' Edith asked.

'Probably – they usually do,' answered Master Carey.

'Ah, Tom,' said his friend.

'Yes, we really must.' Tom Carey looked Edith in the eyes. 'It has been a pleasure, Miss Mullane. I hope to see you again. Miss Guille, Miss…'

'Le Page.'

The men tipped their boaters, and then walked away to examine a great rock that had been fixed in the gardens as the base for a new statue.

'They were nice,' said Perotine.

'Nice for you two,' huffed Adèle. 'Didn't even remember my name. And see the way he looked you up and down, Edith, when you were leading him on.'

'I was not leading him on! And soon as you opened your mouth we stood no chance.'

'What did I say?'

'"She's to the Castel, 'er",' Edith mocked. 'That's going to go down really well in the drawing room when the Governor and his wife come to tea.'

'Don't go all airs and graces, Edith Mullane!'

'Why not? Look at those houses up there.' A row of villas stretched along the north rim of the valley, looking down on the gardens. 'Don't you want to live up there one day? You happy on that farm?'

'Farming is what I knows. I don't want no big house with snooty ladies coming to tea. You're getting above yourself, and for no reason.'

'Men like them don't marry girls like us,' Perotine added. 'We're just a bit of fun to them. Don't go chasing after them, Edith, or it will turn out bad. They want one of them parasol girls what reads poetry.'

'I read poetry,' she retorted. 'My aunt lends me books. And, she's joined the library for me.'

'Books is not going to get you nowhere,' Adèle scoffed.

'Least we got an ice cream out of it,' Perotine said.

'Yes,' sighed Edith. 'There is that, eh?'

The parish rubbed noses very closely with the Vale to the north, so it was hardly surprising that Vale boys and Castel girls met and married. At the end of June, Edith's cousin Jim Le Page was betrothed to Artie's cousin Molly Brehaut. She came from his mother's side, as there were no Bazin cousins. His grandfather's family tree withered away; populated by genealogical dead ends of premature deaths, childless marriages and maiden aunts.

As was custom there was a flouncing, held in the barn of a mutual relation down in the Marais which formed the border of the two parishes. Last season's hay gave the barn a comforting, musty smell. Tapers and lanterns threw a yellow light into its rafters. An accordion played now and again, punctuated by a fiddler.

Edith had abandoned plans to join the smart set at St George's Hall. She had nothing fit to wear, and feared being humiliated if she played a strong hand with one of the younger men of society. Worse, she could be badly used by one of the wealthy bachelors. In those romances she read, poor girls or boys miraculously turned out to be the heirs to fortunes or married way above their station. Money, land, position and titles fell easily into the hands of fictional heroines. If only real life were like that.

No, this was her society and she must be content with it. She drank not champagne but Guernsey cider. Cakes came in hearty chunks to be eaten in the hand, not served in delicate portions on equally delicate china, and the boisterous dances were hardly the genteel waltzes seen in Town.

Both sets of Bazin brothers were in one corner, amid a clutch of relations. George Bazin had taken off his glasses and was cleaning them with a red kerchief. He screwed up his eyes to concentrate on the job. At least he was in a shirt and tie, she observed, and not his tatty Guernsey. Artie Bazin stood with his arms folded, cider resting in the crook of his elbow. He gave her a wink. Around him stood a group of Castel boys forming his own fief-court, wanting his approval for their jokes, seeking sanction for their admiration of this girl or that.

Castel relatives sat or stood by the far wall of the barn, while the Vale crowd clustered where the drink was. They met in the middle to dance, and met in the yard to fight.

Two quarrymen started it, over a girl from Town whom one or the other or both were sweet on. Squaring up, name-calling, threatening, they edged around each other. Suddenly the blows came and the girl squealed. Cousin Jim dashed out with his friends, and Edith ran after him. Men grappled in the half-dark. Another rushed into the fight, pushing the Castel man off his opponent. Then Castel was reinforced by a friend or brother who knocked down the new man with his fist.

For a moment Edith was amused, and then disappointed, then ashamed. Cousin Jim had always been a ruffian, and so were his friends.

'Oh Jim, oh Jim!' cried the new bride-to-be. 'Stop them. Stop them spoiling it.'

When six men were in the fray, Cousin Jim waded in with his arms stretched wide.

'Hold it! For God's sake, stop.'

But drink and petty rivalries fuelled the brawl, and a man took a swing at Jim. He ducked his head back just in time to avoid the shiner.

'Jim!' Edith shrieked.

The attacker came forward again, a big Irish quarry worker, both knuckles ready. Jim had drunk far too much cider to offer a proper defence.

Just then a shadow stepped from the dark, and the big Irishman went down with one blow. Artie Bazin shook his knuckles, and pulled Jim away by the arm.

'Artie!' Edith said.

'Thanks,' slurred Cousin Jim. 'But I had him.'

'Back to your dance, back to your missis!' Artie said, and squared up to the other brawlers.

Molly Brehaut took Jim by the other arm and pulled him inside. Edith instinctively did the same to Artie.

'Come on, Artie – let them fight.'

In truth the fight was over. The Irishman picked himself

out of the dirt shaking his head, and went off with two others into the night, swearing and shouting insults. The survivors jeered at their retreating backs. A musician started up his accordion and a dance was called.

'Does that hurt?' Edith touched his hand.

'Yes, it do! I always forget how much until afterwards.' He shook away the pain.

'That was very brave.'

'Can't have drunkards like that spoiling your Jim's big night, eh?'

'I hardly know him,' Edith said. 'Not since we were children, and I never liked him then, even.'

'Would you dance with me, Miss Mullane?' He held out the hand which had so recently inflicted pain and humiliation.

'It would be a pleasure, Mr Bazin.'

So they danced *La Bebée, La Gobbie* and the odd-man-out *Après Six Heures*. If the rules of the dance allowed, and the rules of life allowed, nobody else would be their partners.

CHAPTER 9

Drop a cat and it falls on its feet. George was no cat but found his summer employment by accident. A Frenchman normally did the carting around the parish for those without a cart of their own. He had a falling-out with Perotine Guille's father, whose land ran down from Kings Mills to La Grande Mare, and who then found himself short of a carter while they were clearing out *douits*. George had often played at driving Uncle Jack's cart, but down by the Mare he had real call to work. The men were digging out the *douits*, clearing them of mud and weed to keep the streams flowing. Some women were cutting reeds and it made sense to have a cart handy, but little sense in paying a carter to sit around idle most of the day or diverting one of the men from the digging. George's labour came cheap and he stood by the horse, leading it from place to place when needed, and driving it back to the farm at night.

Daydreaming, as he did, George stood by the horse and half watched the others working. He was on the very lip of the newly cleared *douit* when the horse nudged him. Jolted from his daydream, he let go the reins, tried to find his balance – but that leg betrayed him once more. George slid down the bank into two feet of water.

After the splash came a woman's laugh, then a few more.

'Ho, George!' called one of the workmen.

'I'm fine!' he shouted. 'Just clumsy, me!' With boots full of water, and trousers dripping slime, he clawed his way up the newly sharpened sides, his lame leg no help at all. At least he had not lost his glasses.

'You be careful round here,' said the nearest woman, one of the Guille family. 'You with better reason than most. Don't go drownin' yourself.' She gave a snigger, as though drowning was funny, and another woman by her side smiled too. The second woman touched the first on the shoulder and said something under her breath. Then both grinned at him.

Muddy from the hips down, but mostly dried out, George drove the cart back to Uncle Jack's barn at the end of the day. This could be the life for him, he thought. No need to run when you're a carter. No great need to see, either, as the horse usually knew the way to go. He rode high, with his head above the field banks, on the eyeline of the sparrows and finches. Yes, he had a sensation that someone was sitting behind him, but she did no harm. She had slipped away by the time he'd unhitched the horse and cleaned her down.

He related the story of his mudslide to Uncle Jack.

'I didn't see it was so funny,' George said.

'Aw, people laugh at other people's misfortune.'

'But it's the way that old woman said it. Like I was 'specially likely to drown in a *douit* only so deep.' George brushed at his thighs where the muddy watermark remained.

'Oh,' Jack nodded. 'That's just folk talking. Don't put more meaning into it than that.' He patted George on the shoulder, as if he were still a child needing reassurance.

Once Jack had gone, the silent friend returned. She was frowning. She didn't laugh when he fell into the *douit*.

On the days when the other men were away doing paid work but nobody needed George, he found things to do in the backyard. Along the whitewashed wall that supported the glasshouse lay a line of pebbles he had brought back from the beach over the years. Artie used to throw stones into the surf, but George would only collect them. There was no fun in throwing stones when you could barely see the splash where they landed. Holding them close to his face he examined the matrix of the stone, the veins, the black inclusions. The stones were alive with fine lines, cracks, pits and subtle grains that would glint in the sun. Pink *galaots* from Albecq, grey ones from the beaches at Cobo or Vazon. Among the granite he would pick out the alien rocks, the white globular ones, the black and white flint and flat red pieces of sea-worn brick. He had other souvenirs – a *pépie* from a cuttlefish, a green glass net float which could have been a crystal ball – but it was stone that entranced him.

On Sundays after the service at the parish church he usually went into the graveyard, choosing a different section to study each week while his mother talked with her friends and Artie joked with the fit boys and girls beside the gate. He could touch the stones, feel the texture and read the writing letter by letter, admiring the curves and straight-cut lines. If he did not understand all the words, they seemed to carry a kind of magic. Long-dead people lived on here. Their names were carved and they continued to live. Here was old Admiral Saumarez who had beaten the French a hundred years back and done something noble in Sweden. George ran his fingers along the letters. The Admiral was here, right here, just around the corner from Gràn'père, another hero of the sea.

'*Baonjour* Gràn'père,' he said, standing close to the headstone, eyes less than two feet away from the carving. 'And Gràn'mère, even.'

Two souls in a grave – that was a kind of company, he

figured. But his sister was alone. He wandered a few yards further to the little spot where the dandelions had wilted.

'*Baonjour* Drusille,' he whispered. 'I wish we had been friends.'

'Georges, what are you doing?' his mother called.

'Talking to Drusille.'

His mother set her lips in a firm line as she came across to draw him away.

'Grow out of that, George. You're not seven now, come on!'

Yet she talked to him as if he were seven. Everyone did. On the way out he passed the *Gràn'mère*, trailing his fingers against her stony skin. Untold centuries rippled by as fingertips ran over the imperfections in the granite. His own years had rippled by and the world around him was changing.

George was in awe of his Uncle Jack. He could not visit his own father at work in the big quarry, but he could stop by the yard where Jack worked magic with stone and watch for a while. Jack Bazin had been angling to do some work on the big granite block that was being used for the base of a new statue in Candie Grounds, but the work had gone to Mr Martel. All Jack managed, in the end, was a few hours of careful chipping with a gang of other masons when the statue arrived at the end of June and its own base was too big to fit on the rock prepared for it. Jack now had a stake in that statue, so he loaded up the family in his cart and encouraged George to drive them to Town for the grand unveiling. Artie was going to march there with the Militia to form a guard of honour for some French dignitaries.

George left the horse in the usual field behind the Grange and the family Bazin walked over the crest to the top of St Peter Port. From the high ground near the Victoria Tower he could see France on the horizon. The islands of Herm and Jethou sat as if at anchor in the Little Russell channel, and in the middle distance was the brown wall of Sark. Two battleships were moored out in the Russell, huge and grey compared to the little yachts and fishing boats that darted around them.

Bands played and bunting was strung everywhere that could hold it. All week the *Guernsey Evening Press* had been advertising special events for the Victor Hugo Fête. The family stood well back in the crowd which filled Candie Grounds, and they did not see Artie.

'He wrote some books,' Marie Bazin explained. 'Hugo was a French writer what lived here, very famous.'

'Have you read them, Mémaen?' George asked.

'Don't be silly. With you lot to look after? I don't have time to be reading books. And I never see you with a book, for all your years at school.'

Letters he loved and could trace their shapes, spending time forming the perfect script as he wrote, but George was not a great reader because his teachers had used the distant blackboard to explain how words were spelled. Lessons had of course been in English and he had been thrashed more than once for speaking the patois in class, which added more discouragement to learning. In all, the chance of George reading a thick French classic novel was remote.

Still, here was this great writer, in Guernsey! The new statue was of a bearded man striding towards France, plucking at his beard as if in thought. More than the statue itself George admired the carved inscription, inlaid with gold leaf. George found it odd that someone famous would come to live in Guernsey, but there must have been a good reason for it. Hugo had been in trouble with the law back in France, or something. George was reminded of another day eight or ten years earlier when he was very young and some duke came to unveil the Boer War Memorial further down the hill in St Julian's Avenue, but the hats of the ladies seemed not so large now as he remembered back then. These memorials would stand forever, and carried a magic all of their own. Lying a hand on the fresh-carved script, George prayed to the Great Writer that he too would become a mason, just like Uncle Jack. It was time George Bazin had some luck.

CHAPTER 10

O n the first truly hot Sunday afternoon that summer, the youth bathed in the sea at Cobo. All except George, of course, who had never been trusted to swim. He sat on the yellow-white sand watching the boys and the girls splash and shout. In truth, half of them could not swim either. The tide was falling and gradually lapped away from him. With the sun high above the Guet, the sea took on a deep blue hue, capped by a thousand sparkles.

More genteel society would have frowned at this frolicking between the sexes. The young men wore cut-down old trousers, at least two being cast-off Militia uniform. The ones who worked outdoors had heavily tanned hands, necks and faces, but to a man their bodies, knees and shins were nearly as white as the Militia trousers.

Girls always struggled to remain modest on the beach, with only Perotine wearing a bathing suit of modern style. For Edith and the rest it was a case of making do with shortened skirts, chemises, knickers and old dresses in the most decent combination possible.

Edith was the first to tire of the games, and she was one who'd never learned to swim anyway. As she came back, a solitary figure was waiting patiently on that portion of the sand now dried by the sun. Not many country folk wore glasses. A farmer had no need to see further than the lead animal pulling the *grànd tchérue,* and a quarryman no further than the rock he was about to strike. The spectacles made

George stand out from the crowd, on the rare occasions he was in a crowd.

For a moment, the sun flashed off both lenses like the bulbs of a photographer. Those little circles of glass connected him to the rest of the world and without them he would be lost.

She flopped beside him. 'Why don't you get some new glasses, George? You won't win the girls with your baby glasses on.'

He flinched as she said this. Perhaps without knowing it, he touched his glasses. Of course he needed to replace them, but had resisted it stubbornly. He was not ready for this. He had owned the glasses for nearly ten years. They pinched, and he had stretched the wire frames as best he could to make them fit his broad face. Edith was not the first to tell him to change them, but he was not ready to let go of his security, not just yet. Without them he would be blind, truly blind. There was no guarantee that new spectacles would allow him to see in the same way. Maybe it was the glasses that owned him.

She had laughed a little at his reaction, but George did not find it unkind. A real woman had actually sat beside him, and then talked to him alone for ten or fifteen minutes, as if he were important and as if she cared what he said in response. George drifted home as if carried on sea fret. Edith filled his soul, so that he hardly noticed another figure trying to draw his attention.

The spirit always loved the summer, and in years past, George would often glimpse her; off in the trees to the right, back down the shore, skipping down a lane in his wake. High summer that year seemed different, and her vigour was subdued. She had stopped dancing and she had stopped her playful hide-and-seek, preferring to walk closer to him.

He was irritated when she did that, he saw too much of her. Beautiful women made him think of Edith, while all Edith seemed to think of was Artie. Even when they had sat talking together on the beach, half her talk had been questions about his brother.

Part way home from the beach, she came close. He looked down at his feet, marking where they fell on the hard stony road. Against the bright sky she vanished, but when he brought his head up again there she was. Close enough to touch, a frown on her face, a doom about her which sent him cold.

'Go away! Go away!' he shouted at nothing and batted the air as if attacked by bees.

He closed his eyes, made ten paces, opened them again to maintain his bearings, and then closed them again. A neighbour rode by on a dark bay.

'Wharro, George!'

He waved to the man and hurried on, knowing he had bought some time. He left the spirit woman behind, glimpsing her one last time, far away and weeping. What was the problem, what was the threat? What was she warning him about?

Artie noticed a change in his brother. Yes, he had played alone as a child and worked alone when driving his cart, but for weeks since Jim and Molly's betrothal dance he had shunned company. Several times of late he had seen George standing on his own, in an open field, down by the Mare or on the beach. His brother would twitch his head this way and that as if sniffing the wind, or dodging a wasp, but Artie knew what he was really doing. If life took him away from George it would be like a soldier deserting his post.

As Private Bazin, he had enjoyed the Victor Hugo parade, marching to the band with a rifle on his shoulder. He'd kept his face forward but his eyes would glance at the crowd each time a young woman of the right height and age flickered into view. Yes, in the army he would be a man among men, but that was not a life he wanted. He yearned to be with Edith. More, he yearned to be alone with Edith. Better, he was sure Edith wanted to be alone with him just as much – if he read her signals right. So far she only appeared with Adèle or Perotine glued to her arm, and he invariably had George perched on his shoulder like a pirate's parrot. If life had been different, he and his brother could have hunted as a pair. I'll take the one, and you take the other. That's the way it worked. He'd even tried that manoeuvre with his friends once or twice, nobly taking the less favoured girl aside while his comrade made play for the object of his affection. But George was not that kind of *boti*. This was one mission Private Artie Bazin must conduct on his own.

He'd seen her for just for a moment, flanked by ranks of islanders at the bottom of the gardens, waving a paper flag. Looking straight ahead, he felt prouder than ever. From the corner of his eye he fancied that she waved more furiously as he passed.

On the beach at Cobo she'd been the ragged princess, dressed up in cut up hand-me-downs. He'd see her wear silk and a broad hat one day! When his dreams came true, she'd pick no more tomatoes and mend no man's shirts.

Dreams and worries were put aside, as it promised to be a glorious summer to be young. Summer nights brought out *les jaunnes*, with the moon serving as the parish lantern, full and hanging low in the east. In its light, the boys and girls of the Castel came out to adventure. Artie was determined that George would come and join the fun, break him out of the dark mood that gripped him, but his brother hung back.

'So,' Artie said, 'you coming?'

'Yes, yes! Uncle Jack has lent me his *cro*.'

In a moment, George took up the curved metal implement and brandished it, ready to do battle on the shore.

A banging came from the front door.

'Come on then,' Artie said. 'You can carry the basket, you, and I'll carry the cider!'

The night sky was clear, so the air was cold, even though it was July and the day had been warm and still. Not much of a wind was blowing, there not being the same land-breeze in the islands as happens at night on wider coasts. Three of Artie's friends stood in the lane.

'Wharro, George!' The greeting came from Pierre Du Port, a broad, squat Guernseyman of the old stock.

'Wharro, Dippo.'

Pierre clanked George's *cro* with his own. A greenhouse worker who struggled with English, he was another of Artie's devoted followers. He made a couple of paces forward to become Artie's right-hand man, leaving George following at the back.

Soon the five became seven when they met a pair of girls. Beside the lane was a hollow tree, where a barn owl was known to roost. As children they had avoided it, as owls carried such an evil reputation.

'*Gerdé cahan!*' one teased. 'You brought the Owl. He'll see good in the dark, him.'

'Stop it,' chided Artie. 'He sees things the rest of us can't see, eh, George?'

George bowed his head, almost ashamed, but it was an old joke he barely noticed any more.

Vazon Bay was broad and dark, with the moonlight coming from behind and casting long, weak shadows towards the sea.

As they descended to the coast, other groups came into sight, until there were more than a dozen young men and young women in the troop. Edith appeared last, so that George barely noticed her before she became just another shifting shadow.

With their *cros* gripped hard and baskets in hand, the youths advanced to where the sea had retreated. At the lowest tides, the sand eels came out to play. The *cro* would hook them from their burrows, and the eels shimmered on the sand in the moonlight until plucked up into the baskets. George set his basket down on the wet, faintly yielding sand. He had once tried catching ormers in the winter, but his balance was too unsteady to work out on the weed-infested rocks looking for the tasty shellfish. Sand-eeling was a different game. He was no cripple here; he was quite the master of the little creatures as they fell prey to his *cro* one by one. He looked for the burrows and he struck! Elsewhere there was splashing and shouting and laughing, but George concentrated on the hunt.

The moon caught inside his glasses and he knew he had company. Off behind him, somewhere to the right stood a figure in a white gown. He might have seen her many times before, but he still felt a shiver. Pale, motionless, almost formless, she watched him.

George moved along the beach, away from the others, and she followed him. Somewhere near here, at certain tides, the stumps of great trees could be seen. An ancient forest once grew at Vazon, thousands of years before, when the sea was elsewhere. Animals had scampered beneath its canopy and the moonlight would have slanted down where it could between the branches. Men would have walked here, George's great-great-ancestors. They would have hunted deer instead of sand eels. Now this ghostly woman walked through the ghostly forest.

Was she a ghost? An unquiet spirit, maybe shipwrecked on this very coast, her body never found and buried, her soul doomed to wander the earth until someone gave her a Christian burial? Maybe her bones lay here, under this very sand.

Ice trickled along George's nerves. He turned full circle, but she was not behind him – she never was. The lanterns and the cries of the other youths seemed distant and he felt alone, becoming afraid. Was she here to warn him again? What about? Out to sea he could hear the surf, gentle against the shallow shelving beach. The sea was no danger, even pulled taut by the full moon. Although the tide came in fast here, George could outpace it. Cautiously he moved back towards the shore, basket heavy in his hand.

A fire flared up beneath the sea wall. He moved towards it, looking for the danger he sensed was near. Where was Artie? The boys had gathered driftwood and dry *vraic* earlier in the day, and were now piling it together for a bonfire on the dry sand. George reached the fire, where two boys and two girls were already contriving to cook the eels they had found. One had a *djougue* of cider.

'Owl, Owl, have some cider!' urged Matthieu Ogier.

'He's wobbly enough already,' laughed Adèle Le Page. 'He'll fall over.'

'Yes please,' said George, taking a swig straight from the *djougue*, signifying that he had joined the men and looking sharply at the girl who tried to put him down.

'Have you seen Artie?' he asked.

'Find Edith Mullane and you'll find your Artie,' said Adèle. The other girl giggled.

Yes. Catching sand eels fell a poor second to catching Edith Mullane.

Edith had arrived with Adèle and Perotine, but Artie slipped in as expertly as a sheepdog cutting out a ewe, separating Edith from her escorts. She offered no resistance, and her friends proved good friends and faded into the night. Artie said he knew a good place to catch the little creatures, further along the shore, and Edith willingly played the game. Of course it was not the best place – that's where George had gone. The half-blind boy had a reputation as a champion hunter of sand eels; he must truly be able to see in the dark.

Edith had never caught eels, so squeaked with delight at the first trio they caught, but soon grew bored. Artie made it clear this was not why they were here. Making for the top of the beach, but away from the fire, they scrambled up to where dunes still remained. Here Artie led into a hollow, bathed in bright moonlight. She sat down as best she could on the sloping dune, feeling the cold dry sand against her wrists, ducking her head away from blades of sharp marram grass intent on impaling her scalp.

Artie slumped further down the slope, looking up at her.

'Your skin is so white in the moonlight,' he said, as if his nose had come fresh from a poetry book. 'You are a match for any fairy princess.'

'Flatterer!'

'Queen of the *pouques*,' he said.

'I don't believe in *pouques*,' she said. 'My mum used to tell me so many daft fairy tales – about this dolmen, or that rock. Every corner of the island seems to come with a silly story that no one could ever believe.'

'Well, if *pouques* existed, you'd be their queen,' he said. 'You like some cider?'

She held out her hand and he shuffled up the dune, uncorked the wicker-bound jug and passed it up. Edith took a most un-queenlike swig, laughed, and took another. She wiped her chin on the back of her hand and passed the jug to Artie. It was cold now they had stopped pretending to hunt eels. Guernsey's summer nights hold little warmth and she could feel the sand drawing heat from her body.

'Brr,' she said, hugging herself.

'Cold?' Artie took a very long gulp from the cider and passed it back to Edith, using the manoeuvre to bring himself right up beside her. She drank the cider with two hands, but did not dry her lips.

He carried that manly scent, one she could not possibly describe. Added to that was the smell of apples. She edged towards him and closed the final gap between their hips.

'That's warmer,' she said.

Here was the risk that all couples must take at such a moment: a risk of rejection and the end of a friendship, embarrassment, hostility, a life-long grudge. But oh the reward if lips meet! He put his left arm around her shoulder and she fell into the nest his body made.

'Even warmer now?' he said.

His right arm moved to rest on her left, but she took his hand and gripped it, palm to palm. Completely untrained, both knew exactly what to do.

His lips tasted of sweet apples.

In twos and threes, the young people came back to sit in a ring around the fire. Arm in arm, Artie and Edith finally joined George on the edge of the group. Artie carried his empty *djougue*, Edith a basket with a pitiful number of eels compared to George's crop.

'Wharro, *mon frère!*' Artie cheered as they slumped down close by his brother.

'Hello, George,' said Edith, slightly slurred by drink. She poked his belly with a finger. 'Eaten all the eels yet?'

'Did you get much?' George asked. Edith burst out laughing. 'Look how many I got.'

'Oh, very good, George. You're a fearless eel killer,' said Edith.

'Let's cook them up, them!'

Artie released Edith and another round of cooking and eating began. The eels were eaten on bread as soon as they were cooked. Boys swapped loaves and compared the merits of their mothers' breads to those from the baker. Portions of *gâche* were shared around, supposedly for 'afters' but eaten out of order, and what cider was left quickly ran out. Songs were sung, old jokes were repeated. Artie and Edith were gently teased over their absence, but Edith laughed all thought of scandal away and Artie merely stirred the pot of mystery by saying less than he might, and denying less than he ought.

Without the moon, it would have been ink-black, there not being a single streetlight this side of Town until you reached Newfoundland. The party broke up when the food and drink were exhausted and no one wanted to find more wood to feed the fire. Artie and George walked with Edith as far as the turning for La Vallée. After only a moment's protest, George was sent home alone and Edith and Artie walked on towards the parish church.

Edith had read a good many romances to fill her quiet hours in the dower wing. The very idea of love and courtship was entrancing, but none of the writers truly explained this strange sensation running through her veins. It was not the cider, but something else. For all her mother's enthusiasm to see her wed, there had always been caution too. Snare a man, but beware of him. Hold back, keep your secrets and release your gifts only slowly. Yet here was this new drug urging her to forget this schooling; to misbehave, to yield to the animal side of man, to fall as Eve had fallen.

'First kiss,' Edith said, twirling around in the lane.

'Surely not.'

He kissed as if he had kissed a good many girls already, and she had strained to kiss as though it had not been her first time. She wanted to be sophisticated and worldly, not backwards and naive. He caught her again, this shade of night barely visible where the trees cast solid shadows. He embraced her firmly and kissed her with gusto.

'Second kiss,' he said.

'Nineteen,' she responded.

'You counted?'

'Perhaps.'

'You're going to be awfully late with all this dilly-dallying.'

'I'm hoping the cider will wear off,' she said. 'My mother was raised strict Chapel, you know. No cider. No French wine. No demon gin. My Aunt Marguerite is still Chapel and scolds my mother mercilessly.'

'We're in the better church. A little bit of each does you no harm.'

'Does my mother harm,' she said, pace quickening. 'No Chapel for her in a long, long time. She'll be dead drunk tonight. Snoring away when I sneak in. She'll hardly notice me getting into bed.'

'You still share a bed?'

'We've only got the one. Not like your family that has two whole houses to choose from. It wouldn't surprise me if you have your own wing, one room each...'

'...and servants. And French maids...' he added.

'Don't!' she snapped. 'Don't ever make jokes about French maids. You've heard the gossip, I'm sure?'

'Yes, suppose so.' The mood had been broken.

'Come on, it's late and I'm going to have a bloney big row with Mum if she's still awake.'

CHAPTER 11

George had been told to go home alone. Told. Sent away like a child. Moments after Artie had walked away into the dark, with his arm around Edith, George turned for home. Almost immediately he noticed a companion trudging along behind him, keeping pace like a mourner behind a cortège. Moonlight made her bright white and more ghostly than ever. He could not tell if there was a smugness on her face, an 'I told you so'. It hardly explained the weeping, it did not explain her frantic scurrying to and fro, but surely this was her warning: George was going to lose his brother to a girl.

After the sand-eeling party, the youth of the parish stopped comparing George to an owl. Men ordered him around, women scolded him for being late or getting in the way, but the other young men chiefly winked at him or shrugged their shoulders. He was one of them now, poor and working hard.

He did more carting for a gang of builders working the great estate at St George, the place with the fief hall and the allegedly magical well. A wall was being rebuilt and George was under strict orders from Jack to look out for the first opportunity for some proper masonry work. That day he brought up a load of partly dressed granite and some rubble.

'Hey, George,' said one of the workmen, another cousin on his mother's side.

He left the cart and came over, hands in his pockets.

'See this what we found,' said Cousin John. He went to

the barrow the men were using about the site. He picked up a smooth grey-black stone as long as his palm. It was something like a long narrow axe head, but made from the hardest polished stone.

'I found it built into the old wall. You collect stones, eh, George?'

He nodded, taking the stone into his palm. It felt cold and he felt something else, something he could not quite explain. A tingle maybe, an echo of things past and far away.

'Fell from the sky that did, I reckon,' said his cousin. 'It's a thunderbolt. There's a man in town I hears collects them.'

'Naw, he's dead now,' said one of the other workmen. 'That Mr Lukis? Died long back, him.'

'Aw, thought he might give me a couple of pounds.'

'Not if he's dead he won't.'

George weighed it in his hand.

'Would you like it, George, for your collection? They bring good luck. Let you have it for five shillings.'

'I don't have that much, I'm saving for some new glasses, me.'

'Is it?'

George checked his pockets. 'I've got an English sixpence and some doubles.'

The cousin glanced at the money and mentally converted it to beer.

'Well, seeing as you're family. Some of us needs more luck than others.'

As soon as he reached home, George washed the sky-stone under the pump in the yard and watched it glisten. He placed it in the cottage, beside the chimney, where it would ward off lightning and other evil. To keep the witches away there was already a jar of nails wedged behind a loose stone which

Gràn'mère once showed him, plus a horseshoe over the door, so the house was well protected. Superstition, like religion, makes no sense if analysed by a rational man but is bound into the human condition as surely as the need to eat and breathe.

Perhaps the sky-stone would bring much-needed luck to deflect whatever doom was looming. Mrs Lake had warned him of the dangers of foresight. George tried to read the omens, fretting first about his father. Henry Bazin did have a worrying cough, especially when he smoked his pipe. George was determined never to smoke a pipe, because the smell made him want to cough too. Working the quarries was hard and dangerous. It wore out a man before his time; beaten by the sun, soaked by the rain, smothered by dust and showered by the constant chip-chip of granite fragments. He'd watch his father closely.

But what of Artie, shooting his rifle at Militia practice? Accidents happened from time to time, and Artie had become so much more serious about the Militia in past months. Even Father and Uncle Jack were paying more attention to their Militia kit, as if the French would land at any minute.

Or was it Uncle Jack who was in danger? Wonderful Uncle Jack who seemed to know every important man on the island. He was growing too old to be still expected to march and shoot with the younger Militiamen. Perhaps an accident was lurking for him at the dock where he picked up his stone, in the lane when one of those motor-lorries came by, or in his yard when he was working alone? Nobody had spotted that Gràn'mère had been ill, so George must watch them all from now on.

A deck of cards lay on the kitchen sideboard, abandoned after the men finished playing euchre the night before. He touched the top card. If this was the jack of spades it would be really bad news. If it was a red card; good news. He flicked the card: ten of clubs.

That was just practice. He flipped the next card over: queen of hearts.

Stupid, stupid game! He could make the cards say anything he wanted. That was how Mrs Lake had operated her craft with the gullible ladies of the north.

Oh, but the queen of hearts! Yes, he saw it. Yes, yes, he would lose Artie to Edith. Worse, even, he would lose Edith to Artie. Jealousy burned strong for a few moments as he imagined them kissing, but then foresaw the three of them, walking side by side. If Artie and Edith married, they would come to live at La Vallée. He could secretly share Edith with his brother. She would smile at him – yes, it often meant that she wanted him to go away and leave her alone with Artie, but a smile was a smile after all. Perhaps he should see her as a sister, making up for the sister he had never known.

He flipped a few more cards, made up a forecast brimming with good news, and then picked up the *Press* as a distraction. There was trouble in Ireland, as ever; an Austrian Duke had been murdered in Serbia; and a bloke was on trial for killing another man outside a pub in the high parishes. Plenty of ill luck had struck elsewhere that week. Impotent to stop the impending tragedy, the young man lay awake for another night wishing for the dawn and light enough to see into the future.

George was not as slow as people imagined him to be. He read the *Press* every day, after the other three men were done with it, even a day late if the paper had taken its time passing from hand to hand. It was published in English, so showed the point of all that hard learning at school. The story about the murdered Duke turned into a little war out in the Balkans (he found where Serbia was in the world atlas Artie had won as a prize). Day after day there was increasingly alarming speculation about what the Russians and French and British would do about it. Surely, he began to sense, this must be the dark cloud, the flock of crows, the ill portent, the jack of spades, the reason his spirit girl wept.

In the closing days of July, Henry and Jack were bound for work, but George came across them arguing with Artie in the yard.

'It won't come to war,' said Jack.

'Bet it will,' growled Henry. 'It's just the sort of thing the English would do. And the French, they're all the same. It'll be the Boer War all over again and you'll be carving another memorial in the Avenue with fifty boys' names.'

'No, the king and the Kaiser are cousins…'

'And what do you think of your cousins?' Henry said.

Jack spread his hands.

'Exactly!' Henry noticed George was with them for the first time.

'I had this feeling something bad was going to happen,' George filled the pause with just a hint of his dark fears.

The other three stared at him. Artie frowned, possibly understanding.

Hands in pockets, George shrugged. 'It was just a feeling.'

CHAPTER 12

Artie was working in the back office of the bank when Mr Jepson came in, frowning. He was English, always correctly dressed and always let his staff know exactly where they stood in the ranks of the bank. Of the men, Artie was at the very bottom.

'Bazin? Would I be correct in saying you're in this Guernsey Militia?'

'Yes, Mr Jepson.'

'Well there's a notice going up. You have to report somewhere.'

'What?'

'Don't just say "what", Bazin. There's a notice beside the post office. They want all your Militia to assemble. God knows why they need you all today.'

'Are you in the Town battalion, Mr Jepson?'

'Don't be ridiculous. I can't run a bank and pretend to be a soldier as well. I don't know how we're going to cope if I lose all the men to the Militia. Don't the comedians in your States realise we have a bank to run?'

'I'd better get off to the camp, me.'

'No you won't!' Mr Jepson checked his pocket watch with practised consideration. 'Take another hour to finish up, and then you'd better go and find out what this nonsense is all about. Every minute lost will come from your wages, though.'

Artie's heart began to pound. He could not concentrate on the ledger. Once Jepson was out of earshot he joined the whispering among the clerks who had been out at lunchtime. The word was that the English garrison was being recalled and the Militia were to be embodied to take their place. His pulse rose, his mind began to race. All of a sudden this soldier thing was no longer a game.

Once he was released from the bank Artie rushed up to the post office. A fair group of townsfolk were reading and re-reading a notice, discussing it, jabbing and pointing. Spotting another youth he remembered from Intermediate School, he set off uphill in company and marched home as quickly as he could. He hoped he'd spot Edith on the way but was disappointed.

His mother was surprised to see him back early, hot and dusty.

'Arthur, your suit!'

'Might not be needing this no more,' he said with a grin, pulling off his tie. 'The Militia is called up.'

'Your father's already gone.' Her expression betrayed her worry. 'My, what an affair!'

Artie had to report to the Militia camp at Les Beaucamps, which was just around the corner. He toyed with putting on his dress uniform, but reasoned this was no day for parades. On went the khaki kit and he presented himself for inspection by his mother. She bit her bottom lip as she brushed a little lint off his shoulder and confirmed his flat cap was straight.

'Come back and tell us what's happening, eh?' she called at his retreating back.

'If they let me,' he said with a grin.

He was at the camp before five o'clock. His father was already there, amid a gang of quarrymen of his own generation, some dressed in scarlet, some in khaki and some still in their working clothes. Artie spotted Pierre Du Port and went to join the short, barrel-chested Guernseyman he'd known since childhood. Other men he had trained and grew up with stood around the Militia huts in groups. Nobody really knew what they were supposed to do. Officers should show leadership and initiative, but the Militia officers were just as clueless as the men. Hastily pulled from their offices, shops and studies they exchanged what little information they had.

Was it war, or just an alarm? Were sabres just being rattled or had they been drawn?

The Militiamen were assigned to huts and shared what food they had thought to bring along. Men grumbled that they were losing pay and vowed to demand the States made it up. Crisis turned to anticipation, then to anti-climax. The weekend was spent on camp beds or sleeping on the floor. Kit was checked and parades held but questions went unanswered. On Sunday, the Militia were mustered for church parade and marched off in groups to different churches.

Artie glimpsed Edith across the far side of the Castel parish church and she gave him an anxious wave. His mother tried to talk to her menfolk after the service, but the Militiamen were quickly herded together on Rectory Hill for the march back to camp. In response to her worried frown, all Artie could do was shrug.

With the cream of its men loitering at the Militia camps, the island was almost at a standstill as the week began. If it hadn't been a bank holiday that Monday, the paralysis would have been even more stark. After a couple of days of command, officers worried more about their businesses than some distant war. Complaints poured in from all sides – to the States, to Government House, to deputies and douzainiers. Artie and his comrades were told that when they were not on duty, they could go home to their families and resume their jobs.

The weekend paper said there was 'little hope for peace' and the future looked increasingly black. All kinds of stories were flying round and the islanders spent the weekend fretting about war and invasion and all kinds of perils, which escalated with every new rumour. By Tuesday, the truth was known and Artie was allowed to slip home and see his mother.

As he came out on to Les Beaucamps, he spotted his brother loitering with hands dug deep into his pockets, pretending he was strolling that way almost on a whim. It was likely he'd been there half the bank holiday.

'Wharro, Artie, what's happening?' George called.

'War, George,' Artie said, turning up his chin. 'Them Germans have gone and done it. They've attacked Belgium and the English are going to war to save them.'

The Great European War burst upon a world that had been holding its breath. Edith was in a glasshouse picking tomatoes when she heard the news. She did not always read the *Press*, and when she did, it was usually a week old and she skipped the boring stories. The Balkan crisis had wholly passed her by, so the church full of Militiamen had been more a novelty than alarming. Her mother had come back from some pub with a clutch of scare stories, but like most of Mother's tittle-tattle, Edith half ignored it. By the time news reached her it was either old news or distorted beyond believing.

Two Frenchmen, who were over for the work and knew not a single word of English, came back into the glasshouse after handing in their notice. They saluted 'mademoiselle', one bowed, the other kissed her hand and they were off into the lane and away to defend their homeland.

Confused, only half understanding what they had said in their own dialect of Breton, she followed them outside, watching them go, one with an arm around the other's shoulder. It was hot and damp beneath the glass, but the air was fresh outside. She stood in the sunshine in a daze, knowing that *guerre* meant war, especially when accompanied by hand gestures of shooting, and the saluting. Mr Robins the grower came round the glasshouse, mopping his forehead with a polka-dotted kerchief.

'Gone,' he said, suddenly at a loss. 'My labour. Just like that.'

'Did they say there was a war?'

'Yes, and a big 'un too. Sounds like the French are off to fight the Germans – with us on the Frenchies' side, even. I bumped into a bunch of lads from the Militia this morning, and it's all they were talking about. Who was joining up, and when.'

Faces flashed before her face – the church full of khaki – all the eager young men she knew. It was easy to see why the prospect of adventure would stir them up. Both the French workers had carried a fire in their eyes she'd never seen while they were picking tomatoes.

'So if my Frenchies are gone and all the local lads troop off to join the army, what do I do? The love apples won't pick themselves.'

'So you're not going with them, Mr Robins?'

'Me? Soldiering? I'm too old, my dear, else I might. Young men have all the fun, eh? Leaving us old 'uns and the girls to do the work.'

'You'll be needing me next week then?'

'*Ouai* – if you don't run off and be a nurse. Got any sisters?'

'One, but she's a skivvy in Town. If you're short-handed, there's always George Bazin. He's not in the Militia and don't do much most days. He'd work hard if someone let him.'

'Ah, George, yes. Will you be seeing him?'

'Might.'

'Ask him to drop by, would you?'

Little more work could be done that day. Mr Robins said he was going down to the pub 'to find out the latest news' and that Edith was free to leave. She washed her hands under the pump, collected a basket of tomatoes that made up part of her pay and began the short walk home. Wars were things you heard about in school, in the dullest lessons about why this king killed that king, or how the British managed to paint a particular square of the map pink. In the paper they were always in faraway places like China or Mexico and the stories were brief and incomprehensible. But a war so close? She could actually see France at that moment from the high ground in the centre of the Castel. The glint of glass caught in the sunlight must be from houses atop a cliff as it seemed to float in the air above an invisible shore. Perhaps this new war would be no more than the history stories Artie liked, where various men of the Saumarez family sailed away for a year or two then came back heroes and rich.

Yet, must it be just the men sailing away? One word rattled around her head – nurse. It would be rather like being a nun without having to forswear men, wine and so forth. She couldn't be a soldier, but she'd get a uniform, she'd get away from Guernsey and actually do something useful with her life.

'Edith?' her mother called as she opened the door.

'Who else?'

'Have you heard about this war?'

'Yes, and I'm going to be a nurse.'

Her mother's jaw dropped. 'Since when?'

'Tomorrow.'

'You're too young. And what do you know about nursing?'

'I can learn.'

CHAPTER 13

Often in mid August, Guernsey's weather starts to change, as if making up its mind whether to turn into autumn while at the same time plotting how bad winter will be. There is a feeling that the days of sunshine are almost over and that long nights are approaching.

George had never met a German. He figured he knew where Belgium was, and soon found it in the map book. This is why his secret friend had been weeping; she had known what was coming. Oddly this comforted him.

Of all people, it was Edith who found him work picking tomatoes up at the edge of St Andrew's. It gave him a little beer money, so he seized every opportunity to stand with Artie and the other men as they talked and boasted outside the Cobo Hotel, all mesmerised by glory. At last, men who toiled with no hope of improvement suddenly had an aim, a goal, a challenge to their prowess.

War had come and he was offered work, just like that. War would change things. George read the excited headlines in the papers and could not help thinking, *damn the omens – this is Good News.*

Back from a couple of hours of solid drinking and profound argument at the Cobo, all four of the Bazin men came into the kitchen of the Big House. Marie had fallen asleep in her sitting room chair, but woke to their voices and a slamming door caught by the wind. She called in to bid them all goodnight and then went up the stairs, leaving the men talking.

'You'll not be volunteering.' Henry jabbed his finger at Artie.

'But, Père, all the boys are talking about it.'

'It's talk, son. Your place is here. You've got a good job at the bank. I can't see them holding that open for you while you're chasing off to Berlin.'

'It will only be for a few months.'

'Says who?' Jack said, a tiredness in his voice. 'You, who wanted to be a schoolteacher? Think of your history books. When did a war only last a few months?'

'Anyways,' Henry said, 'we've got no cousins in Belgium. And you'll not go off and get yourself killed for the English.'

'And what you got against the English?'

'My father, your grandfather, drowned on an English ship. Sailing too fast so that one English railway company could beat the other English railway company. English captain too. Not enough life jackets, eh?'

'They had enough life jackets,' Jack said wearily. 'Père just didn't put one on.'

Henry was not one to be deterred by facts. 'All the money they make carrying tourists and they can't even buy enough life jackets. It's a scandal!'

The family had heard this complaint many times before, but for George the sinking of the *Stella* was only a vague tale from childhood memory in which Gràn'père had died a hero.

'Gràn'père won that medal,' Artie said.

'Oh, fat lot of good that did him. And fat lot of comfort for your poor widowed Gran. I'd rather have my son than a whole dresser full of medals.'

George said nothing. It was as if he did not exist. It was as if he were no more real than the face he saw reflected in his glasses. His father had only one son to worry about, only one who had a career that could be dashed by the war.

'I'm tired, me,' he said, and made his way to bed.

George, Jack and Artie went along to a meeting at the parish hall where one speaker after another explained why the war was important and why Guernsey should 'do its bit'. Even the rector put in his eight doubles' worth, hinting that God was 'on our side'. Men of the Channel Islands had for centuries been exempt from conscription into the king's army, yet singly and in groups men began to volunteer. In the pub and in the streets of Town, George saw their smiles – they were getting away at last. The *Press* carried stories about those who had enlisted, sometimes with photographs. The letters column contained calculations and tight arguments about how Guernsey should really send more men – a whole company, even. His father sneered that no doubt they were written by men who were conveniently too old to volunteer themselves, or who had no sons to lose.

When the war was two weeks old, George found his brother in the scullery, cleaning his Militia kit with great care.

'Artie, are you joining the army?' George asked cautiously.

'No.'

'You once said you wanted to be a soldier, to get away.'

'Well, I'm thinking the war's a long way off and it will be over before I get there anyhow.'

'Oh. Père will be pleased.'

Artie snorted. 'Père hates the English, without good reason. I reckon Uncle Jack would volunteer if he wasn't too old. They won't have the over forty-fives. He sometimes says things after a few beers, like life's passed him by, or he's still waiting for his big chance.'

'He must miss not being married,' George said.

'He doesn't like children,' Artie responded. 'And you can't have one without the other.' He spat on his boot, and continued to rub. 'Anyhow, no army for me. The Militia's been called up. We're going to do our bit here.'

'The Germans won't attack Guernsey?' George asked, alarmed. The *Press* was full of stories of atrocities being committed in Belgium, people being murdered or roasted alive as their houses burned down. 'They won't come here?'

'Not until hens have teeth, but the garrison is shipped over to join the fighting so we're taking their place guarding the island. Some of the boys talk about transferring to the Regulars, but not me. I'm happy in Guernsey, me.'

'And me,' George beamed.

As he said it, George doubted his own words and it made him feel queasy. He went out into the sun, up to the top of the little field and looked steadily about himself at these familiar hedges, trees, rooftops and the glinting of glass. Must he stay here? Was this his entire world? Was the war the one chance stupid young George Bazin would ever have of joining the other men in a great enterprise?

Looking around for her meant she would not be there. Good, for perhaps here was the real reason the spirit cried. She feared to lose him to a higher cause. She had always been his friend, yet suddenly George saw her as something different. The spirit was a hawser securing him to this rock. She was the ball and chain that slowed him down as surely as his leg. Her love for him was an obsessive love, a smothering love. He was her spoiled child, her attentive dog, her happy slave. But she was anchored in Guernsey, doomed never to leave the island – surely she would not follow him to war.

Putting on his Sunday best, George travelled to Town the

next day he was free of tomato-picking. As he went out of the house and into the lane, the spirit came up behind him, an angry look on her face. He ignored her. The horse bus came up from Cobo and he caught it, choosing to sit facing forwards. He took off his spectacles and slipped them into his pocket, feeling strangely free as the fuzzy world slipped by. Once in Town, he put on his glasses once more. She never came to Town, with its crowds and noise. She was a spirit of the country and the coast.

He stopped at the post office and asked for the place where the navy was recruiting. He did not need to march if he was to join the navy. He could find a job on a dreadnought where his glasses would not matter, pulling levers to make the great engines go, down in the dark depths of the ship. He would be an engineer, like Gràn'père Georges Bazin. The bearded petty officer did not share his conviction.

'You don't meet our standards and you're only seventeen,' said the man. 'Have you tried the army? They might take you.'

'I tried the Militia.'

'If the Militia won't have you, son, the Royal Navy certainly won't. Be on your way – ask the next man to come in, as you go.'

George could not walk straight. He could not run. He could not clamber up a ladder in a companionway. He would be a hindrance when the men were rushing to action stations. If he took off his glasses he could be like Lord Nelson and say 'I see no ships' and it would be true, all of the time. Worst of all, the petty officer had seen the way he squinted when trying to read a notice on the wall. He thought that George was stupid. Everyone thought George was stupid. He was the one who had been warned the war was coming, yet everyone thought him stupid.

In a grey mood he walked all the way along the seafront, around the harbour, and then out along the breakwater to Castle Cornet where the army had set up its stall. Perhaps now, with a real war to fight, they would want him for a soldier. The papers said the British needed a hundred thousand more soldiers – and that was a lot – more than every person in the Channel Islands as far as George knew, women and babies included.

He had never been inside the castle before. It was bigger than it looked from the shore – a huge, sprawling place that grew from a rock at the harbour mouth that must once have been a separate island. It had no fairy-tale turrets or towers, but simply rose in tier upon tier of grey-brown granite stonework until it reached the pole where the Union flag flew. Crenellations and gun ports threatened any who dared approach.

'Hello, George,' said the man behind the desk. It was Mr Torode, once a schoolteacher in the Castel, but wearing his Militia khaki and sitting alongside a Regular lieutenant.

Now he was in with a chance! At least the man knew him.

'What are you doing here, George?'

'I've come to fight.'

'You've come to get killed,' he said, quite kindly. 'I remember how easily the girls used to be able to catch you at hide-and-seek. I remember the day the boys threw pine cones at you, and you just curled up because you couldn't run and you couldn't dodge. What are you going to do when a six-foot Prussian grenadier comes after you with a bayonet?'

'I want to fight. I want to serve the king.'

'Serve the king in a different way. Someone's got to keep the island running when the rest of the young men are away. You're what? Sixteen?'

'Seventeen.'

'Well, no one under nineteen is allowed to serve overseas, so I'm not sure what use you would be even if you were the fittest youth on the island. Have you got a job, George?'

'I help out, round the parish. Been picking tomatoes in St Andrew's this week, me.'

'Well, now you can get a real job, George. All the business men I know are crying out that the army is taking their best lads away. Bide your time. There's more to a war than just soldiering.'

'Yes but I want to go, before it's all over.'

'Ah, you're listening to those people who say it will be over by Christmas? The curse of being a teacher is you actually learn those lessons that history tries to teach us. I wish to God politicians did. It took us fifteen years of fighting to beat Napoleon. It took three years to beat the Boers, and they were just farmers, for goodness' sake. No, George. The army needs food, the navy needs our harbour. All the lads who march away need to know they'll have an island to come back to one day, not fields full of weeds and vineries falling down. It's no disgrace, George. You learned a long time ago that there's more to being a man than fighting.'

He nodded, wiping away a tear that was unbidden. His glasses misted and just for a moment he imagined a smiling face just behind him. She had him trapped; no escape.

'Thank you.'

'Good luck, George.' Mr Torode gave a firm, yet rather wan smile. He did not want to go to war either.

'Good luck to you too, sir.'

It was a dispiriting walk back from the castle along the breakwater to the shore. Yes, he could have taken the quick way home up Fountain Street, but he had all the time in the world now – he was going not going anywhere anytime soon.

He walked all the way along the Esplanade in a dark gloom, and then had a slow pint of beer in The Swan. No happier, he trudged up the Avenue, pausing in front of the Boer War memorial. One fine Saturday when George had been eight years old and still routinely called Georges, Uncle Jack had organised one of his cart rides to town for the whole family. His friend Mr Newbury had allowed him to help out on the memorial to the South African War, so the Bazins had mixed with the crowd that filled the Avenue below Candie Grounds to see it unveiled. Bunting was out in red, white and blue and the Militia band played. Father lifted his little son as high as he could manage so that he at least got a glimpse of Prince Arthur, the Duke of Connaught in his scarlet uniform and feathered hat. All the great and good men of Guernsey were there: the Bailiff, the jurats, the deputies and the Militia officers. All were in their finery, their uniforms, their formal robes, and to one side were their wives and daughters in enormous hats. Young George had only just got his new glasses so the wide world was still a very special place.

'What's it for, Pépaen?' George had asked.

'It's like a gravestone for the Guernsey soldiers who were killed in Africa.'

'Why were they in Africa?'

Henry Bazin put him down. George was heavy to hoist for so long.

'I don't know. It was where the English sent them to fight the Boers, round about when the old Queen died. Don't ask me who the Boers are, because I'm not sure anyone round here rightly knows. It were a waste of life, sending boys off like that.'

'Have you been to Africa?'

'No.'

'Has Uncle Jack?'

'No, but I reckon your *gràn'père* might have, when he was a sailor boy travelling the world.'

'I want to travel all over the world.'

Uncle Jack had been in his Sunday suit, talking to Mr Newbury who had designed the monument. When they got chance, the boys went close enough to examine the statues of two British soldiers. One was wounded and the other was helping him.

'That's like me and you,' Artie had said. 'When them Ogier boys tripped you up and I had to stand and fight them all off!'

George wanted to be the man standing, not the one on the ground. He brought himself close enough to read the names of the men who had been killed. There was something magical about inscribing names in this manner, as if it made them live forever. Robins and Guille and Tupper were all gone somewhere in Africa, but their names lived on.

That afternoon long ago, the boys of the parish had played Boer War on the slopes of the Guet. George had to be a Boer, so Artie volunteered to be a Boer too. The Guet became Spion Kop and they defended it to the last drop of their blood, but in the end, the British Empire had to be victorious.

In August 1914, the Boer War was fading into memory. Rejected by both army and navy, George read the names on the memorial again. A lot of Guernseymen seemed to have died fighting those farmers. Perhaps the spirit knew what was best for him and could have put Mr Torode's words of comfort into his mouth. Perhaps she cared for him and George had been wrong to try to abandon her. He brushed these thoughts away, did not care to wait for the horse bus and began the hour's walk back home. It had never seemed so far. Only one person was happy. She danced along the lane behind him. Escape had been foiled and he was back in her hands again.

CHAPTER 14

The war was going well, according to the headlines about crushing German defeats, their sunk cruisers and heroic Belgian resistance. Artie read the paper carefully, and found that the smaller stories told a different story – it was going badly. Despite the headline victories, the Allied armies were advancing backwards. The British Army was forced to retreat from Belgium to France and had only been saved after the Battle of Mons, it was said, by the intervention of a host of angels. He was immediately reminded of George and his guardian-angel woman, which no longer seemed such a mad idea. The *Guernsey Evening Press* carried the names of a few local men who had been wounded, as well as some Frenchmen who once worked here but had gone back and died for their country.

With the front page filled by advertisements as usual, the second page of the paper had been taken over by war news. Jack finished that day's paper quickly and passed it to Henry with a deep sigh.

'Good God,' he said, the moment he had turned to page two.

Artie came over to stand behind the chair, reading over his father's shoulder. Unprompted, Henry Bazin started to read the names of British officers listed killed. It must have been the sixth day of these lists and they seemed endless.

'That's your war for you,' Henry muttered. 'If we're winning, that's a lot of dead officers, so thank God we're not losing. It's every day this week – what in God's name is going on?'

'Don't they even list the privates?' Artie asked glumly.

'No, they don't bother; it would fill the whole paper. If you was killed, the English wouldn't even waste one line of ink on you.'

'I don't like to say,' Jack added soberly, 'but there's going to be a good trade in headstones.'

Artie no longer had any illusions about the war, unlike many of his friends. In the Cobo Hotel, he talked a couple of the Ogier brothers out of enlisting with the Royal Irish by a deluge of arguments. In 1914 Guernsey offered no Isaac Brock or James Saumarez who could change the course of history. This was much too big a fight for little Guernsey to make an ha'peth of difference.

On a Saturday afternoon in November, the young people went to see the electric theatre at St Julian's in Town. Artie was with Edith, who brought Adèle Le Page as chaperone. George made up the fourth member of the party, but Adèle took pains to see she was not paired off with him. They chose to sit well forward and in the centre block, square to the screen, so that George could see easily. Adèle led the way into the seats, followed by Edith, with Artie and George last of all.

Magic sparkled at the electric theatre. Moving pictures told stories from a flickering black and white world. First came a story about a little dog, then a comedy where a woman was being chased by an ugly rich suitor and a handsome but poor one. At the end was an adventure set in the Wild West of America. A group of bad men tried to steal cattle from some cowboys and it ended with them all shooting at each other round a farm. It was not like a real play or music hall, in that there was no sound, but a woman played along on the piano to set the mood.

'I'd like to go to America,' said Edith, as they walked back up St Julian's Avenue.

'That's a long way,' said Artie. 'Straight out from Cobo and steam for a week. And what would you do in America?'

'Act in the moving pictures.' She halted and struck a pose of terror, in the style of the blonde woman in the second feature.

'I reckon you'd be good,' Artie said, truly believing what he said.

'Would you move to the Wild West?' asked George.

'I already live in the Wild West,' she said, with a hint of cynicism in her voice. 'The Wild West of Guernsey.'

'But we don't get men in black hats stealing our cows,' said George.

'They can have them, and welcome,' she said. 'When I've saved enough money, I'm moving to America. Will you take me to America, Artie Bazin?'

'Gladly.' Artie offered his arm and she took it.

George offered his arm to Adèle but she just scowled.

'My brother saw you at the navy recruiting station,' Adèle said to George.

Artie paused in his step when he heard this. 'George?'

He shrugged.

'You joining up, George?' Edith was genuinely impressed, although she hugged Artie's arm tight.

'I tried,' George said. He removed his glasses and held them at arm's length. 'Can't see a thing, me. So, they won't have me; Militia, army or navy.'

Edith released Artie and laid a hand on George's arm. 'But that was a truly brave thing to do, George.'

'My brother signed up with the navy,' Adèle added.

'Old Mr Torode says I have to stay here and look after the island.'

'While all the brave men are away?' Edith looked slyly at Artie.

'What?' said Artie.

'Nothing.'

'You're saying I should join up?' His pulse began to rise, and an acid taste came into his throat.

'My brother has,' Adèle said again.

'Even George volunteered,' said Edith.

Artie was affronted. 'No,' he said.

'Cowardy custard!'

'Don't be stupid, Edith. You've read the papers, we're getting a right licking over there. Thousands have been killed already; it's not a lark like they all said it would be. I'm not joining up for a dare, or for a pretty smile.' He glared at Adèle. 'Or because someone's brother has got no sense.'

Adèle glared back for a moment, and then looking as if she would burst, let out a squeal and ran up the hill away from them in tears.

'You're a bloney coward, Arthur Bazin!' Edith said, and turned to follow her friend.

He grabbed her arm.

'And don't grab me!' She shook him away. 'Remember, I'm stupid. You said so yourself.'

It was as if she had slapped him. Artie stepped back, restrained his brother by the arm and let the women go. He made a gesture towards The Swan. Leaning on the bar for an hour would allow the women a good head start back to the parish, so there was no danger of catching them up.

'Women!' Artie cursed. 'Happy to see us all killed.'

George nodded agreement, both his elbows on the bar and glass of beer gripped in both hands.

'You never told me you tried to enlist.'

'Was no point,' George said. 'Père would be angry.'

'He'd be proud.'

'But he doesn't want us to fight for the English.'

'No, and we've got to respect that, but he'd be proud that we were men enough to want to.'

'Thought about asking if I could fight for the Frenchies, then Père might not object,' George said. 'But my Good French isn't that... good.' He laughed at his own joke.

'Just stay out of it,' Artie said. 'Let the others go. The loudmouths, the boasters, the ones who used to bully you at school when they thought I wasn't looking. Let them go and bully the Germans.'

'So you're not going? Whatever Edith says?'

'Not if the king himself comes to ask me,' Artie said. 'I'm in the Militia and we might be needed yet. The Germans nearly captured Paris, they say. Might be a blessing if they had done, then the bloney war would be over.'

'The French wouldn't just give up!'

'No, I guess not, and they say the Kaiser won't stop at Paris. Could be we'll still see them Prussians over on the coast by Granville, sailing their dreadnoughts up and down the Russell. I reckon the army would even take you on that day, George. It's not over yet, *mon viaer*, and if we have to go fight it won't be because of some stupid girl.'

CHAPTER 15

Fate also seemed to be against Edith Mullane. She made an enquiry by letter about becoming a nurse and was discouraged by the tardy reply. She had rarely written anything since leaving school, and her grammar was being ruined by the mixture of languages and dialects she met out in the fields and vineries. Her second attempt was more careful and she went into Town and asked Aunt Marguerite to read through the second and third drafts. Her aunt took a stern delight in editing the letter and correcting the spelling, and offered her opinion that being a nurse would 'improve' Edith.

It was October before she was summoned to Victoria Cottage Hospital in Amherst on the edge of Town, where she met a severe lady from the Red Cross, who had a posh English accent and little regard for country girls. Edith's fingernails were chipped and her once dainty hands had acquired grime from a summer picking tomatoes and an autumn picking potatoes that a single scrub simply could not remove. The sun had caught her at odd angles beneath the bonnet, giving her a flushed and blotchy complexion with girlish freckles. That, or her naturally pale skin suggested she was anaemic. Her slight build made her look simply thin, undernourished and incapable of taking care of herself, let alone wounded heroes. All this was plain to the severe lady, and she said so.

Edith persisted in the interview.

'I know I left school at twelve, but I've learned a lot. I can cook and sew, darn and repair. And I read – I read lots of books.'

'Such as?'

'Well, the one I've just finished was about farming in a place a bit like Guernsey, and it was called *Far from the Madding Crowd.*'

'Thomas Hardy?' asked the woman with surprise, making a mark on the piece of paper before her.

Hardy at least seemed to be on Edith's side, but the message was coming through that a nurse should be *an educated young lady from a good home.*

'Well, I suppose you could learn,' the woman admitted reluctantly. 'If you start at the very bottom, and were instructed over a number of years you would have a chance to prove yourself.'

A number of years? 'In France?'

'No, in Guernsey – here, or at the Town Hospital, or the Country Hospital. As you improve I would hope you might one day free up a trained nurse to go to France. Thereby, doing your bit for king and country right here.' The woman actually beamed. 'Without ever having to leave home.'

Edith nodded mechanically and thanked the severe lady for her time. There would be little point in enduring long nights tending the sick, lame, infirm and insane if it kept her on the island and living with her mother.

She needed another way to escape.

Winter turned cold and very wet. To English people, Guernsey winters feel more like a long autumn with blustery days, lashing rain and gales that come worst at night. A crisp, frosty morning is rare. Edith retreated to the little dower wing by the Bailiff's Cross and filled dark evenings knitting balaclava helmets for the troops. She had heard they were stuck in trenches with a wet and cheerless Christmas ahead. The wool was provided by an emergency committee set up by women with rich husbands.

Ruth Mullane was constantly fussing about men she knew, or their sons, who had joined up or might join up. She started bringing yesterday's paper back from Uncle Tom's each day – they were, it appeared, friends again. Every name in the paper had to be studied and cross-examined over the dinner table, and his pedigree worked through. 'He's the son of that man who ran the little shop, you know, that one where we used to buy the groceries when we lived to the Vale,' and so on. It was as if she wanted to take a piece of every triumph or tragedy for her own.

The pair spent La Laongue Veille at Aunt Marguerite's, eating a perfectly presented, if rather sparse dinner in a stretched atmosphere. Leila had met a commercial traveller from Birmingham who had come to stay at the guest house and she was full of all the things they planned to do in a year or so's time once his business came together. Edith half believed her older sister's tale and was half-jealous of the better parts. Her mother wanted to know all the details, again and again from different angles. Marguerite chipped in from time to time with words of caution to downplay the whole scenario. Mother and younger daughter came home when Marguerite went to chapel, pulling Leila with her, which meant Ruth Mullane could have 'just the one' to celebrate Christmas.

Caught in a compromise between Catholic father and Chapel mother, Edith had been sent to the Anglican churches since she was young. It gave her mother an excuse to go to neither chapel nor church where there were plenty with stiff necks willing to pass judgement, cast the first stone and many other things good Christians ought not to do. On Christmas Day, Edith saw Artie across the parish church and he caught her eye just for a moment. She buried her face in her hymn book. Many times since the autumn she had kicked herself for starting the argument about the war. Of course she didn't want Artie stuck in those trenches with shells falling all about him, but were not the best of the men already signed up? He was built like a hero, talked like one, even acted like one among the youth of the parish. She remembered vividly how he had taken that brawler down with a single blow, and his hug was strong and manly. And yet he held back when lesser men were trooping off to fight for the king. And he had called her stupid. She might be many things, but Edith was not stupid.

CHAPTER 16

M r Torode was proved right and the war was not over by Christmas. Flanders seemed very far away as the Bazin family settled in front of the Yule log, and it seldom snowed in Guernsey. With half the globe in turmoil, George Bazin's own little world began to improve.

School had been difficult as he lost his early years to squinting and thereafter was treated as a fool by the teachers and widely ignored. He could count, but was no mathematician. He could read the prayer book on Sunday without too much trouble and pick through the *Guernsey Press* after Uncle Jack, Father and Artie were done with it. Beyond this, George saw no great point in reading books. The family only owned three; *La Grande Bible,* a book about the Empire Artie had won as a prize and his other prize that had maps in. Many times as boys, Artie and George had gone through the maps in the world atlas, imagining far-off places they might visit, but Bechuanaland and Kashmir might as well be mythical for the chance that two Guernsey boys would end up there.

What George brought away from school was his letters. He copied the teacher's letters with great care. He copied lines from poetry books, without troubling to consider what the lines themselves actually said. He copied the headlines from the newspaper, trying to get every kern and serif right. In Uncle Jack's yard he had sometimes taken up a slate and copied the letters carved on the gravestones by the mason.

À la Mémoire Chérie
En Mémoire Affecteuse

Sacred to the Memory
Peace

Soon into the New Year, Uncle Jack and his father were talking in the parlour of the Big House when George came in from the yard. They must have heard him making his way down the passageway.

'George, a word with you,' his father called.

George sat down on the green bed in the nook beside the fire. Both older men looked serious.

'You know young Len Batiste? My apprentice?' Uncle Jack asked. 'He's gone and volunteered, him. He's joining the Royal Irish Regiment. Irish, I asks you.'

'Only the Irish will take Guernseymen,' his father added. 'We don't speak good enough English for the Coldstream Guards, or the Household Cavalry. It's a travesty. Our blood's as good as anyone's.'

'Still, I'm losing Len,' said Jack. 'Thanks to my age, the Militia don't want me no more, but I'm still short an apprentice. Would you come and work with me, until the war's over and Len comes back?'

Henry nodded his assent and approval.

'Carting?' asked George.

'Now and again, when it's needed. You know that Frenchman? Him what used to drive the cart round most of the parish? Well, he was one of the first to go back home to join up, him. I heard he got killed just about straight away.' Jack bowed his head and gave a little shake. 'Anyway, I need help.'

'I'm not much good at lugging things,' George said. 'I can lift stuff, but not carry a long way. I'm sorry, Uncle Jack, I'd really like to work with you in your yard.'

'Helier Le Poidevin can do the carrying for both of you. He's only got one good eye, and the army will never want him before the Kaiser is marching up High Street. I've seen your little drawings, I see you like stone. Come and learn to cut. If you've strong arms and a steady hand, you'll do.'

'There'll be no tomatoes to pick for a few months,' Henry said. 'And it's good money.'

Uncle Jack used the palm of his hand to suppress expectations. 'I'll start you on what Len got when he started. Not what he gets now, mind. We'll see how you get on.'

'It's a proper wage, son,' Henry said. 'And you can still help round here.'

'And while we're at it,' said Uncle Jack, 'you may as well move in with me, have your own room.'

Leave Artie? The brothers had always shared a room, indeed in the early days had even shared a bed. This was the way life went, he knew, people moved forward, moved away, changed and took over the space left behind by others.

'*Monifique!*' he said. 'Thank you, Uncle Jack!'

'Just call me Jack from now on.'

Regular money was good, as prices had started to climb since the war started. His job gave George pride; it gave meaning to his life when the world was boiling all around. It seemed that Guernsey was a tiny place amid this great war of Kaisers and kings, and the Castel even tinier. When empires clashed, the concerns of one young man seemed terribly insignificant.

He started work the following week at Uncle Jack's yard. At first he watched, and then he held the spring jumper while

Uncle Jack heaved the mallet to split the stone. Soon he was the one heaving the mallet and roughing out the granite for Jack to work. Each kind of stone had its own name, like species of trees or birds. Each had its uses and its own temperament. Cut it this way, polish it that way. This was close work, for which he could take off his glasses, throw away the name of Owl and be just George.

He put his chisel to the stone. The war was going well.

CHAPTER 17

M arch was the yellow time of year when daffodils, primroses and celandines burst into life along the lanes. Later in spring would come the pinks, the whites and the blues. One Sunday afternoon, when the air carried the warmth of spring, Artie and George walked down past Kings Mills towards the back of La Grande Mare. From a distance, two girls could be seen picking flowers from the bank of the lane. The plumper one with straw-blonde hair falling over her face as she bent looked like Perotine Guille. A flash of red-blonde escaping from beneath a white bonnet meant that the other could only be Edith Mullane. Artie's pace quickened, but George fell back.

'Come on, let's say hello!' Artie urged.

George had trod this path once before. In his last summer of school he had thought Perotine Guille the most beautiful girl in the world, indeed the only girl in the world (apart from his secret companion). Spotting Perotine standing alone in the playground, he had moved towards her. Behind his back was a bunch of dandelions.

'Here,' he said. 'You're so pretty, I brought you these flowers.'

Perotine looked startled, and blushed. She put out her hand to take the flowers, and then drew back. 'You mustn't pick dandelions,' she said. 'You'll wet your bed.'

'What?'

'Everyone knows.'

'They just looked pretty and…'

'I don't want them, George!'

Two other children had by now seen what was passing. George looked ruefully at his flowers, and retreated as the girls closed in to share the gossip.

'What's that, George Bazin?' one called.

'Nothin'.'

'Let us see!' She dodged around, and her friend moved the other way.

'Flowers! Flowers for Perotine Guille!'

'I wouldn't have them,' Perotine called.

'Dandelions. Wet-your-bed dandelions from little Owl.'

'Bet he does, too. Wet-your-bed, Wet-your-bed!'

'Stop it!' George hurled the flowers down and ran from them, ran from the school yard into the lane and away as fast as he could manage.

Someone followed. One of the girls? He kept hobbling down the lane, but she swiftly caught up with him. A teacher? He was in for a whipping!

A friend came from behind and from the right. He slowed, panting. He stopped. She drew close, bearing a flower in her hand, a dandelion clock. She smiled and his panic eased. She puckered her lips and blew the dandelion seedlings towards him. A shower of fairies surrounded him, glowing as the sunlight struck them, scattering on the breeze. He closed his eyes, felt it was night and he could still see the fairies glowing around him. On opening his eyes again he found himself alone in a summer lane, with a thrush singing and a cow lowing somewhere close by. He was not an owl – and he would not wet his bed.

Five years had passed but he had not forgotten the humiliation and had scarcely glanced at Perotine since that day.

'What you frightened of?' Artie asked. 'Girls don't bite.'

Even in their drab working clothes, the young women looked gay and bright. Perotine's star had long faded in George's eye as Edith's beauty burned so much stronger. She was the spirited one who stood out from the crowd of local girls. The plain ones, the fat-faced ones, the ones who took too little care with their hair, or who shouted too much with voices that would carry halfway to St Saviour's. None could rival her for the crown of parish beauty. Where other girls made vain attempt to flatter the handsome Artie, Edith would tease and set herself just out of reach. When she rose to greet Artie, George watched with both love and jealousy in his heart.

Not for you.

Just for a moment George glimpsed an angry face, a figure with her arms folded and her visage rippled with frowns. George turned away as Artie and Edith met. She was right. A cripple was no match for the parish beauty. He had no wit to equal hers, no strength to carry her across a threshold as Artie would surely do.

'Afternoon, ladies,' Artie said, doffing his cap.

'Why, it's the brothers Bazin.' Edith put one hand on her hip.

A company for an Irish regiment had been formed of volunteers from the Militia and had taken ship that month. The island had given those men a splendid send-off and Edith had cried when she spotted Cousin Jim among the two or three hundred young men marching past on their route from Beaucamps to Town. Everyone was talking about the 'shirkers' – in the shops, in the papers and Edith's mother made it a point of daily discussion. Just now, in the sunshine, there was something wrong about a fit young man casually strolling around the lanes sweet-talking girls when so many more were risking their lives to save the Empire.

'Not seen you around much these days,' she said. 'Began to think you'd gone off and joined up after all. Didn't see you in the parade though.'

'I've been working, and doing my bit with the Militia.'

'*Cor, là*. Toy soldiers,' Edith said.

Artie started to lose his famously short temper. 'You're not getting me on that army thing again.'

'No? My cousin Jim's gone away to the Royal Irish.'

'More fool him. 'S not a question of bravery, you know, it's principle. See, if someone were to offend my mum, or set about George here, then I'm up for a fight. But the Kaiser – what's he done to me? What's Guernsey to him?'

The couple's eyes locked together. George and Perotine were reduced to onlookers.

'Here,' Perotine tried to break the spell. She presented George with a bunch of mixed yellow flowers. 'Take these back to your mum.'

'Ah,' he said. 'But you spent your time picking them.'

'Now I can pick more. There's plenty.'

'*Merci bian*,' he said.

'You won't remember, but I'm sorry about the dandelions,' she said. 'We were just children back then.'

'Oh, that was a long time ago. Forgotten it.'

'It was sweet, but…' Perotine gave him a smile. There was compassion in the world, after all.

Artie broke away from his glaring contest with Edith. 'Brother George, flowers from a young lady!'

'They're for Mémaen. We'd better get them back before they die.'

'Yeah,' said Artie, passing a final glare at Edith.

The brothers turned away, but Edith swung her arms as they did. 'Quick march!' she commanded, 'left, right.'

Perotine slapped Edith's arm with the back of her hand.

'What?' demanded Edith.

'Stop it,' said Perotine. 'You can tease too much. You don't appreciate what you've got, you.'

Edith watched the boys retreat up the hill. Artie strode out at first, then paused to let his brother catch up, then slowed to match his pace. A holly bush concealed them briefly, and then a field bank shielded them from the waist upwards. The hedge along the bank rose gradually to block them from view entirely. That's how it could be, watching Artie march away. Edith felt a sense of loss and it worried her.

Later that week, after their supper of cabbage soup in the dower cottage, Edith's mother brought a *Press* round from Uncle Tom. As they sipped tea, she rattled out the latest list of the fallen with a strange kind of glee.

'*Cor*, the Bailiff's son too? The new Bailiff, that is, Mr Ozanne. His son was killed. What is it all coming to when the Bailiff loses his son, even?'

Edith did not know the Bailiff, or his son. She did not move in those circles. At that moment she imagined her mother reading out news of Artie's death and realised the folly of her teasing. She had never meant him to actually go to war and there was a horrible possibility that he might just do that out of injured male pride, or possibly even to spite her.

'There's another letter about them shirkers…' her mother began.

Edith took a shawl and went out into the evening.

Chapter 18

There is a word in Guernesiais pronounced *boucaller* and that was exactly what George looked like he was doing. Mooching. He was very good at it, he'd spent a fair chunk of his life doing nothing in particular but making it look like activity. As Edith hurried down Le Préel, she saw him up ahead, idling where elm branches arch in from either side of the road to form a tunnel. A family of rabbits held his attention until Edith caught his eye.

'Wharro, Edith.'

'George Bazin, just the man!' she said.

He grinned. How that boy's face lit up when he saw her!

'Is Artie at home?'

'Should be.'

'Could you send him out to me?'

His glee subsided when it was clear she wanted to see Artie, not him. 'Of course,' he said.

'I'll wait by the *abeurvaeure*.'

Built of biscuit-brown granite, the *abeurvaeure* channelled a stream into a watering place and was carved with the names of the great men who'd had it erected for the good of the parish. Edith found a smooth seat and sat down. She smiled as George hobbled off. The boy was besotted with her, it was clear. He'd jump off a cliff at her command. What of his brother, though? That remained to be seen.

Artie appeared within ten minutes. The sun was going down and had already buried itself in cloud.

'Hello, Edith, George said you wanted me.'

'I said I wanted to see you. It's not the same as wanting you.'

'Aw, Edith, you're one who likes to tease.'

'And it's cruel of me, I know. And it was cruel to tease you about the army. Let the others go if they want to. We need the Militia, we need men for God's sake. What's the island going to be like if you all join up? We'll be old maids by the time you come back, spending our pretty years knitting socks and writing long letters. Then when you come back we'll all be grown fat and ugly.'

'You'll never be fat and ugly. Not even when you're as old as the Valpied sisters.'

'You're a gentleman, Artie.'

He took her hand and kissed it. 'And you, Miss Mullane, are a lady.'

'So we won't talk about the army any more,' she said. 'If you want orders, your orders are to stay right here, with me.'

Artie gave a little salute. 'Yes, ma'am.'

Such a secret could never stay secret for long. The very next evening, Marie Bazin was serving supper in the kitchen of the Big House. Uncle Jack was there, as usual, with Artie and George, and their father. Perotine's flowers were in a jug on the windowsill but beginning to wilt.

'This family needs more women,' Marie grumbled. 'Look at the work I have to do, and you four just sits there.'

'We're working men, Mémaen,' Artie said. 'And we're defending the Empire too.'

'Defending the Cobo Hotel more like.'

Artie's mind was elsewhere. 'Should have had daughters, you,' he said carelessly.

The room froze. His mother's glare cut into Artie until he bowed his head over his beanjar and concentrated on eating.

His mother recovered her composure, but her tone was hurt. 'I miss your mother's help around the house, Henri. Old as she was, she never shirked.'

'Artie's got a sweetheart, him,' George blurted out.

'George!' Artie snapped.

'Soon as they're wed, she can help you out,' George added sullenly.

'So who's this girl, Artie?' Marie asked sharply. 'Not one of those French girls working over by Pierre's place?'

'No one special,' Artie said, although his pride could not stay hidden.

'Out with it, lad,' his father said, smiling broadly. 'Sooner we meet her, the sooner she can be scrubbing out the *bashins* with your *mémaen*.'

'Edith Mullane,' George stated.

'Not Edith Mullane!' Marie almost shrieked the name.

'*Doublié dé laid!*' Artie cursed his brother.

'Language, Artie!' Henry corrected.

Artie continued to attack George. 'You a spy for the Kaiser as well? Want to tell all our secrets?'

Marie wrung her hands within her apron. 'Not Edith Mullane? That skinny redhead who lives to the Bailiff's Cross with that mother of hers, who was Ruth Le Page? She was never no good that one, even before she moved to the Vale with that Irish lout. He's Catholic, she's Chapel, what's that all about? Got what she deserved in the end. He ran off with some foreign girl. French she was.'

'Mémaen, that's not Edith's fault. Her mum's raised her on her own.'

'Still, it's family that counts, Arthur Bazin. Family is important, and what family she's got isn't worth two doubles.' She snapped her fingers. 'I hear she's on the parish most months. Think twice, my lad. Find one of the nice local girls, or one of those fancy young ladies you meet in the bank if you must, but not an Irish trollop.'

'She's as Guernsey as… his bloney Guernsey!' Artie jabbed a quivering spoon towards George. He stood up, angry. 'I'm going to get off this island one day. I might marry an American, or a Zulu princess from Timbuktu; I don't have to marry a Le This or a Le That because you knew her mother and she could make beanjar as good as you—'

'Artie, don't shout at your mother!' Henry tried to intervene.

'As for you…' Artie dug his spoon into his beanjar and flicked a huge dollop at George's breast. The splat was spectacular.

'Artie!' yelled his father.

George stared at the mess of beans, pork and gravy on his Guernsey, too surprised to react. Artie spun round and made for the back door. His father was shouting after him, but his mother had turned to berate George.

'You useless lump, you! Clean up – and don't you go telling tales.'

Nothing cements young love more firmly than the disapproval of parents.

Two days after he had thrown beanjar at his brother, Artie sat with Edith on the chairs in Candie Grounds. He was in his khaki, but the Militia bandsmen were in full scarlet dress. 'God Save the King' played and the crowd sang with gusto. The rest of the programme had the military, patriotic flavour which had become so popular; 'Rule Britannia' and 'The British Grenadiers'.

Artie tapped his feet, mentally marching to the tunes. Edith gripped his hand. After the concert, she took his arm and they wandered into the Lower Gardens. An old soldier came towards them, with medals pinned to his Sunday suit proclaiming service in Queen Victoria's wars. Greying and stooping, he smiled at the young private and made a cup-handed salute.

Private Bazin returned the salute with a grin.

'You do look smart,' said Edith. 'But I'm so glad you're not in the Regulars. I couldn't stand watching you march off down the road. You know that my dad left us, walked out when I was twelve years old? Never saw him again. If he'd done something heroic perhaps it wouldn't have felt so bad.'

'My grandfather died on a shipwrecked steamship, the *Stella*, saving people,' said Artie.

'Yes, something like that. Something we could tell people about and feel a little bit proud, even though we're sad inside. You must have heard what happened to my dad, the whole island knows.'

'I heard he ran off with some woman?'

Edith glanced at a bench and tugged him towards it. The bench stood in a patch of sunlight and they sat side by side. She gripped his hand, sighing loudly as if about to recite a poem.

'Right, I was twelve, as I said. We were living to the Vale. My dad was a quarryman – like yours, in one of the big quarries there. He'd come over from Ireland for the work. I think he'd been in England a while too before that. There's not much work in Ireland, so they say.'

'Funny that so many people want to come here – the

French, the Irish, the English. You'd think it was all a bit small for them.'

'Well it's small for me, that's for sure,' she said. 'And my mum. When she met my dad, she'd been engaged to someone else. A farm boy, some cousin. It's a small place enough without marrying your cousin. Well, she threw him up for a wild red-haired Irishman. He was going to show her the world, but all she got to see was the Vale.'

As she talked of travel, he realised that the narrow green haven of the Lower Gardens, with its statues of Pan and exotic shrubs and great gingko tree was less like Guernsey than anywhere else on the island. Specimens from elsewhere had been planted and nurtured for the benefit of those who would never see the faraway lands where the seeds were born.

'Then one day he was gone,' Edith continued. 'I didn't understand at the time, but he just didn't come back. He and Mum used to argue all the time, but everyone's parents argue, don't they? He took all the money from the jar, packed his things into bags when my mum was shopping down at the Bridge, then he was on the next mailboat and away.'

'Do you know where he is now?'

'No – and I couldn't care less, me. What a place to live, eh? St Sampson's hasn't had a bridge for a hundred years but everyone still calls it the Bridge. I hoped Dad would come back and take us all away with him, but he didn't. We went to live with my auntie in Town, but Mum and her sister, they don't get on, so we ended up in the Castel. My sister Leila stayed behind because she needed a job and my aunt needs a skivvy around her guest house. She wanted me to stay too, to keep me on the right path, but I wouldn't. At least I'd have been in Town, but my aunt would just ram scripture down my throat and I couldn't take that.'

'I'm sorry.'

'Don't be sorry, that's just life. *Toute chaose à sa fin*, as Adèle says. See, there's me using the country words; I don't speak much patois, you know? I try not to – I actually try not to, is that bad?'

'No, no, speaking proper is the way to get ahead,' he said, choosing his words deliberately.

'I understand the patois enough,' she continued, her voice ever so subtly changing so that indeed she spoke more correctly. 'What with Adèle as a friend – and others before her – but no one ever taught me. Mum and Dad used to argue in English, but I guess Dad must have learned enough Good French to get that harlot to run off with him. She was a maid working for my aunt, which is how they met, so the story goes. It would sound exciting and romantic to be whisked away like that, but in real life it's so... disappointing.'

Artie squeezed her hand.

'Don't you find that? That life's disappointing? That all the good things you hear about happen to other people far away and a long way off? In books, or in the papers. Or it's a friend of someone's friend who did it?'

He needed to reassure her. Artie needed her close by him, not dreaming of elsewhere.

'Good things happen here. Life could never be better. There's a million men hiding in trenches right now dodging shells who would give anything to be right here with you.'

She laid her head on his shoulders. 'Promise me you'll never run off with a French maid? You'll never run off at all – and if you do, you'll take me with you.'

The gentle pressure on his shoulder was an irresistible force. 'I promise,' he said.

CHAPTER 19

Artie was passing the parlour door in the Big House when his mother called his name. Pushing open the door he saw his mother in her usual chair beside the fire, and his father sitting opposite, reading the paper and toying with an unlit pipe.

'Henri,' she called her husband's attention. She always used his original name, and they always spoke Guernesiais together too, as if it were their private armour against a changing world.

His father looked up, making a sound as if startled. 'Aha?' It was one of those coded messages used by man and wife and this one said *you broke my concentration*.

She inclined her head towards Artie. 'It's time.'

The paper was folded and the pipe set aside to show an announcement was to be made. 'Artie…' he said.

Marie Bazin took over the narrative immediately. 'You know what the doctor said to me after George was born? He said I'd never have another baby.'

She carried a strange, hesitant glee on a face that had seen too many summers pinching her eyes against the sun and too many winters being scoured by wind and rain. She patted her waist for effect. 'I've been feeling strange, and I wondered what it was.'

Artie felt a strange, dizzying sensation. 'No.'

'I think so. Two or three months I've felt like this. I thought it was the changes, as my mother would have said.'

'Marie!' her husband chided.

'Hush, he's a man. He'll have a wife of his own soon enough and the more he understands the easier it will be for the both of them.'

Artie shuffled his feet, not knowing what to say, deeply embarrassed.

'I know everyone will say I'm too old, but my cousin Emily was forty-seven when she conceived her last.'

'Well,' he said, absolutely lost for words.

'It will be a girl this time,' she said, with a smile. 'I lost my girl, as you know, so God has sent me another.'

'Marie!' her husband cautioned, but she would not be quietened.

'Late babies are usually girls, you can ask anyone.'

'It's not something that troubles men too much.'

'Well this is going to trouble you, Henri Bazin. I won't be able to do so much around the house in three or four months' time, so you men need to be ready for that. There will be a new mouth to feed and I'll need a crib. It's a good job we're in the Big House now.'

'And George?'

'You tell George, eh? Quietly, when you're off having one of your adventures. He might be upset, you know how he is.' She carried an almost serene look as her news was at an end.

Henri Bazin put his pipe into his mouth, still unlit, and sucked it with a thoughtful sound. He raised one eyebrow to his son, and then raised the paper to read once more.

Artie was stunned by the news. Plenty of their neighbours had big families of six, eight or ten children and most of these had survived to adults. He had at times envied the gang of Ogier boys or the motley crowd of Adèle Le Page's sisters and brothers, but he had become accustomed to the two-man team. Henry and Jack would be followed by Artie and George.

Edith did not approve either. 'It's too late in life for them to be raising babies,' she said, after working through several expressions of shock and surprise as they walked one of the tree-shrouded lanes.

'It's not something I want to think about,' said Artie.

'Babies?'

'No – parents having babies.'

It was an uncomfortable thought that parents could enjoy love too.

'I know what you mean, but I'm completely used to parents doing unsuitable things,' Edith added. 'For instance, my mother has a new "friend". And I hope to God there are no babies involved there, or I'll just die.'

'A man friend? Who is he?'

'Oh, this farmer, to St Martin's.' Edith wafted a hand vaguely to the south-east. 'She met him down the Markets last week. She keeps telling me what a big house he's got. And land. My mother and land and property, *là*! Have you read Jane Austen?'

'Who's that?'

'She writes books about young women seeking to better themselves. My mother could have written them – or been a character in one of them.'

'I don't read books any more.'

'I thought you had a dark secret desire to become a teacher?'

Artie looked off into the distance, over a bright green field and dusky treetops to the barely perceptible line where sea met sky.

'Yes, well, that was before the war. I'm looking at ledger

books all day at the bank, and I can't just sit reading when I'm supposed to be on Militia duty.'

'But don't you find books help you travel?' she said dreamily. 'To other places, other times, to be other people?'

'I don't want to be other people – who do you want to be?'

'Myself. Just not here, living in the parish – or on the parish.'

'That will stop if your mother marries a farmer from St Martin's. One with land.'

'Yes, I suppose some good will come of it.' Edith paused and looked over a gate southwards towards the upper parishes. 'I'll have to move up there, you know.'

'It's not the moon.'

'No, but it's more than a short walk. That said, I'll be working in Town this summer, even. My sister Leila is off to England to work in a factory so my aunt is short a skivvy and, well, it's better than picking tomatoes. It fairly ruined my hands last year. And the sun! I don't have that country colour like Adèle.'

'Town? That's good. I can see you when I take my break at lunchtime.'

'Some days,' she said.

'Or before I come home, if we can't manage lunchtime. And Fort George is close by Hauteville; I'm there most weekends.'

He reached out and held her by both shoulders and kissed her gently. 'Our mothers don't even need to know.'

The new baby would be a girl, George was convinced. He often thought about Drusille, the sister he had never met, and how she would have grown into a woman, and wondered whether they would have been friends. Now he would have a sister, at last. It was almost as if Drusille were coming back to them, as if she had been waiting in heaven for a chance to return.

His father was not working at the quarry that month. The war had brought a sudden end to street-laying and bridge-building in England, so the demand for Guernsey granite had dropped like the proverbial stone. Henry Bazin claimed there was 'plenty to do' in the greenhouse and the vegetable patch, which was almost true, and quarrying usually tailed off at that time of year anyway as the quarrymen traditionally found 'plenty to do' in the summer. He was drinking tea and looking for parts of yesterday's paper he had not yet read.

'So, Pépaen,' George said. 'It's going to be funny having a sister.'

'Funny? And who says it will be a sister, eh?'

'Mémaen says so.'

Henry Bazin gave a harrumph.

'It will be nice, because I never met my sister. She'd have been my big sister, Drusille would.'

His father stopped reading. His hands tensed on the newspaper, making the slightest scrunching sound.

'I'd like to have met her. You never talk about her, you and Mémaen. Why's that?'

'We just don't. The dead are dead, and it's best to leave them lie.'

'But you talk about Gràn'père, both Gràn'pères, and—'

'George!' Henry thrust down the paper and glared at his son. 'We don't talk about her, ever! Don't pry. You're just a boy, you don't understand.'

'What did she die of?'

'Accident,' his father snapped, then wagged a finger. 'You're not so big I won't knock you down. Now you never talk about her again, especially not to your mother.' He mellowed. 'It will upset her, upset her badly. Now get off and find some work.'

George went outside into the morning sun. The lane was quiet, as usual, apart from the caw-caw of a crow, followed by the screech of a seagull. A few moments later a songbird started up, but George could not see it. Their cock crowed twice. Artie came out of the house in his suit, wearing a flat cap but no coat.

'Morning, George.'

'Can I walk to the bus with you?'

'You going to Town?'

'No, I just want to walk.'

The brothers walked towards the Cobo Road and the horse-bus stop.

'Mémaen says we're having a sister,' George said.

'Yes, that will be nice.' Artie gave the impression of having given it little thought.

'Do you know what Drusille died of?'

'What? Little Drusille, our sister?'

'Yes, I asked Père and he near shouted at me.'

'Blames himself, I reckon. She drowned, down La Grande Mare somewhere. In the Mare, or one of the *douits*.'

So that was why the old woman had laughed at him. The whole parish must know – everyone but George.

Artie continued. 'They never talk about it, so I asked Uncle Jack one day. He said how badly they took it, how it cut them up. It was just before you were born, so life moves on. What's done is done, *mon viaer*.'

That night, George dreamed of a girl, a sister, a new sister. By day, he also dreamed; of Edith, who would be a sister of sorts if Artie ever got around to marrying her. Also, inevitably, there was the other.

George spent most of that summer on his own. Artie always seemed to be at work or with the Militia or down the pub and Mémaen would retire early to bed. Edith had moved to St Martin's, and more and more of the young men seemed to be vanishing to France or further overseas. Jack was with Helier de Carteret out rebuilding walls and fixing barns after the winter storms, so George was alone with his stone and his cold obsession.

And when he was alone, she would come. A point came where he dared not put back his glasses after a session of close work because he knew she would be sitting on a wall behind him, or darting between the sunbeams in the orchard.

This was not the carefree running of summers past, it was the dodging of the hunted, the hiding of the one who is afraid to be seen. When she sat, she glowered. She was troubled, she signalled danger. Zeppelins? Submarines? German spies? What was it? George must watch and take special care.

At night he could not see her, but suspected she whispered into his sleep. He wondered what she was doing and where she went. George longed to know, but ignorance is the basis of faith. Did she vanish entirely or did she dwell in some hidden realm beneath the dolmens or the fairy cave? Was she a spirit of air that lived on the wind, or a spirit of water that returned to the waves each night? Or did she, like little Drusille, sink cold into the still pools of La Grande Mare and dissolve in its mists?

CHAPTER 20

Summer work meant the women no longer needed to go begging to the *Procureur des Pauvres* for support, but at times Edith felt destined to carry on the family trade. Taking in washing and sewing were the latest means to avoid destitution. Mother and daughter sat across from each other well into the evening, working at their sewing while there was daylight, one either side of the cold fireplace. Just behind Edith's head hung the washing. They had moved to St Martin's, but not to any mansion. 'Uncle Frank' had not so much land as imagined and the three of them occupied two rooms on the first floor of a wing behind a farm. Cows moved around downstairs. The main room served as kitchen, dining room, lounge and scullery and made up as a bedroom for Edith.

A wooden-cased clock ticked on the mantelpiece. One tick came slightly faster than each stitch. Edith was attaching a collar to one of Doctor Chapell's shirts. 'Uncle Frank' was in all likelihood at some pub.

'So who's the young man I hear you've been seeing?' her mother asked.

'Arthur Bazin.'

'Marie Allaire's son? The tall one? He's a catch, goes to work in a suit. What's he do?'

'He works in a bank in Town, on the High Street,' Edith sighed, with a little grin of pride.

'They live to the coast, eh?'

'Halfway there, down a little valley.'

'Round past where Uncle Tom used to work?'

'Yes, but he's not my uncle.'

'Not as far as that big mansion what the admiral had?' her mother continued. 'And past the run-down place where those wicked Valpied sisters live?'

'I imagine so.'

'And Marie Allaire's husband's brother lives there too? Now that Jack Bazin, he'd be a catch.' Ruth Mullane stopped darning and looked off into space. 'He's unmarried, and he's got a trade.'

'He's ten years older than you are, Mother.'

Mother brushed back her own hair, as if in front of a mirror. 'He's smiled at me more than once.'

'He's in business, he smiles at everyone. They make tombstones, he's looking for customers.'

'Hey, my girl, I'm not halfway to fifty yet.'

Edith smiled. Her mother's vanity alternately amused and appalled her.

'Still, there's got to be a reason Jack Bazin stayed unmarried,' Edith mused. 'Thwarted love is my bet. I bet there was some girl he fell madly in love with when he was young and she threw him over for another, and he vowed never to love anyone else so long as he lived.'

'That's twaddle. He's just not met the right woman. I reckon he's shy. He's been building his business, him. One day... he's got a nice big house.'

'Artie lives in the Big House now – his uncle Jack has the cottage.'

'Là! Imagine if we could move in there!'

Edith's heart froze at the word *we*. She was not embarking on a joint enterprise.

'They call it the Big House, but it's not so big. I've never been inside, but it wouldn't feel much bigger than what we have here once you fit all that family in.'

Her mother began to sew again. 'Marrying a banker, eh?'

'I said nothing about marriage. I'm only eighteen.'

'I was just eighteen when I bore your sister.'

'Yes, well, that's you.'

'You'll have to bring him to meet me.'

'Here? Not in a thousand years.'

Her mother glanced around. 'We could tidy up.'

'It's still…' Edith waved her hands at the laundry.

'Or you could get him to invite us down to tea…'

'No. He hasn't asked me yet, and I'm in no hurry to marry. I've already darned enough men's socks and washed enough shirts to last a lifetime.'

Ruth Mullane looked hurt. Her own fortunes had followed a downhill spiral, so she took special interest in the lives of others.

'So many young men are joining up, though,' she said quickly. 'You have to marry him before he goes too.'

Edith froze in her work. 'You mean in case he's killed?'

'Didn't mean that at all. And I tell you what's a pity too – that Marie Allaire is having a baby by all accounts. At her age.'

'It can happen,' Edith said. 'If you're not careful.'

'Still, it means another portion, eh? Your Artie won't get so much now. Unless it's a girl and they can marry her off. Still I daresay it might be you bringing the young 'un up if nature is unkind to them Bazins.'

'Stop it, Mother! Stop planning my life.'

'I just want you to have a good life. Not make my mistakes.'

'I'll try very hard. Step One is not to fling myself at the first man that comes along.'

And not have babies, Edith decided silently.

Edith and Artie found fifteen minutes to share one of the benches near the tram terminus on the Esplanade. By chance George was also in Town, and he waved at them from over by the harbour.

'Why doesn't George get rid of those glasses?' Edith asked.

'They're his lucky glasses,' Artie said.

'Lucky? George? Who is perhaps the most unlucky man I have ever met, with his wobbly leg and his terrible eyesight. He'd have no job if it wasn't for the war, for sure. And he'll never marry, even.'

'He was always sweet for Perotine.'

'She wouldn't have him if you all marched off to war and George was the last man left behind. She'd sooner go join the convent – she told me that once. So how is he lucky?'

'Well, perhaps lucky is the wrong word,' Artie said. 'He's more like superstitious.'

'About his glasses? Seven years' bad luck if he breaks them?'

'He already has broken them – that's the point. He thinks they…' Artie stopped himself.

Edith looked expectant. 'Make him look handsome? Make him look like… ah… inter-lectual?'

He was silent.

'There can't be secrets between us.'

'Promise you'll never tell a soul if I tell you?'

'Oh, I swear. What's to tell?'

Artie took a deep breath before betraying whatever confidence held him back. 'I can share a secret with you. It's not like a secret told to anyone else.' He paused, as if doubting those words. 'George thinks he can see a woman, a pretty girl, following him. Reflected in his glasses.'

Edith let her jaw drop open. 'What?'

'Ah, it gets worse. She tells him the future.'

'Sweet Jesus and Mary!'

'Don't… don't tell anyone, please, his life's hard enough. It's been an obsession with him since he was little. I reckon he's got worse since the war started.'

'He needs to grow up,' Edith said firmly. 'Shame the army won't take him. He should just throw them glasses away and get in quick with one of those plain girls who're pining for the men who have gone off to France.'

'You try telling him.'

'I will,' she said.

The boy with the enchanted glasses was leaning on the blue railings beside the new harbour. As usual he was wearing a navy-blue Guernsey which had known better years, and a shapeless cap. Edith stood up just as one of the electric trams came clanking into the terminus. She had only been on the trams a handful of times, and found it a thrill. Electric trams seemed so out of place amid this world of horses and handcarts, or perhaps it was now the horses and carts that were out of place. She waited for the Number 5 to pass then strode across to George. Now was the time to test his devotion to her.

'Wharro, Edith!'

'George! You come to Town to buy some new glasses?'

'No, no, I'm looking for a boat.'

'You need new glasses,' she said kindly.

He touched them instinctively, defensively.

'These need to go.'

Gently she took them in both hands and he relaxed and allowed her to remove them.

'See, you're quite handsome underneath.'

In a way he was. He had Artie's wide, honest face, but his cheeks were reddened by the sun and made brighter by his pale eye sockets. Already these were rimmed about by creases from years of pinching his eyes to see.

'You don't need these old things.'

'Ah, but,' George stammered. 'I can see you fine now, Edith,' he said. 'Fresh and clear as anything, but nothing beyond.' He paused and gazed at her. 'Then, I don't want to see nothing beyond.'

'You old charmer, George Bazin! See, look, they're cracked. One day the glass is just going to fall out into your hand. You need a nice modern pair, now you've got a job and some money.'

He grimaced.

'Charm the girls. There are plenty to spare now.'

George asked for the glasses back and he put them on, bashful. She prodded his chest. 'You can do it, George. You were brave enough to volunteer for the war, so you're brave enough to do this too. For me.'

CHAPTER 21

Oh, she was angry! George awoke in the night. Who was angry? Edith or the spirit? Poor cold Drusille, or the unborn sister? It was high summer and he was sweating.

He went to the window and pulled the sash full open and let the night air in. Moonlight flooded the lane and the field opposite. He could see no detail, no fine shadows or shafts of light. Nobody moved and there was no sound except perhaps for the distant shifting sea. In order to see the beauty of the still night he would just have to reach for those glasses. Ah, but that is what she wanted! She would be out there, between the moonbeams, waiting for him.

'Bloney fool,' he cursed, closing his eyes and screwing his fists into them. 'Bloney fool!'

Cider and beer had made him drunk a few times before now. He had tottered home on those nights barely knowing the way, and all kinds of fears and fantasies had swirled around him. Now he was not drunk, but maybe he was going mad. Yes, he could feel a darkness creeping into the back of his mind that threatened to drag him down. Being insane would be the ultimate escape; just follow the dark as if it were light in a tunnel, then everything would be fine. He would sink into the well of night. No need to worry, any more.

This had to end.

After church that Sunday, George made an excuse to linger. He often walked among the headstones, admiring the old carving and frowning at work he thought inferior, so no one thought it strange. No stranger than usual, that is.

The rector emerged after all his business was concluded and all the parishioners departed. George moved to intercept him as quickly as he could.

'Rector.'

Deep in thought, the Reverend Mosley was startled. 'Ah, eh, George Bazin?'

'Rector, I have a question. A serious question, to do with angels and spirits and things like that.'

The man of God frowned. 'Well, my wife will have a pot of tea waiting for me – I'm parched as the desert. Will you join me?'

George walked down to the rectory, passing pleasantries and thinking it was usually the posh people of the parish who were invited to tea with the rector. The rectory was halfway down Rectory Hill and he edged inside uncomfortably, wondering if his boots were muddy or his suit was dusty. He was offered a chair in the kitchen, which was tidier, less crowded than at La Vallée. The rector's wife seemed surprised to see the young man sitting there. She sensed the intimate nature of his business and left immediately she had served tea with some French biscuits on a small plate set between her husband and his guest.

'So?' asked the rector, his face neutral but expectant.

'Don't think me a madman,' said George. 'But I keep seeing an angel.'

'An angel? In what, a vision, a revelation, what?'

'Least she could be an angel. I daren't think what else she might be.' He quickly took a sip of tea. It tasted thin, and sweet after he had poured in two spoons of sugar.

'So it's a female in this – what – apparition?'

'Yes, young, yet maybe not young. It's hard to say, I never get a clear look at her.'

George thought it was time he took one of the fancy biscuits and did so, taking the tiniest of bites so as not to create a mess of crumbs.

'My reading of the Bible teaches me that angels of the Lord have the faces of men,' the rector said.

'Is it?'

'Yes.' The man of God became thoughtful. 'Have you suffered this vision often?'

'It's not a vision, she's really there – just behind me.' George waved his biscuit over his right shoulder. 'She sneaks up behind me. I don't know how often, it's happened every now and again since I were seven.'

'I see,' said the rector, nodding with his brows creased. 'And the subject of your vision is this young woman, and not, say, an image of yourself?'

'Me? No! I couldn't see myself – that would be daft.'

'Quite,' said the rector. 'I ask, because you must have heard the stories, the old wives' tales, the old superstitions that still linger out in the country? Stories of people who profess to have seen themselves, off down the road or walking through the garden.'

'No one's ever told me that.'

'No, no, but they wouldn't, not these days. But the story goes that the people who have seen themselves in this way are deeply sick and they die shortly afterwards. It's nonsense of course, it probably comes from having a high fever, but you don't look like a man who has a high fever.'

'No, I'm fine, I'm fit,' said George. 'So could she be a ghost? Following me, haunting me? But if she is, she's a good ghost, because she always comes when something important is about to happen.'

The rector shrank back in disbelief. 'Important in what way? Offer me an example.'

George found a good example, one he'd never shared before. He explained he had been fourteen or fifteen years old. He couldn't remember the exact date, but it was three years or so in the past. He was fishing beneath Grandes Rocques and noticed he had company. By then he knew she did him no harm and would vanish if he looked for her, and only when his mind was elsewhere would she appear. The less he was expecting her, the more likely she was to come, hair flowing over her formless shift.

'She reminds me of one of those angels in the churchyard, or one of those paintings up on the church roof.' This had always been a comforting thought.

On this occasion, his guardian seemed distracted and had chosen a high point on the rocks, shielding her eyes and looking north to the Casquets as if searching for a ship. He looked that way too. George was too young to remember the loss of his grandfather on the steamship *Stella* but the family often talked about it. With the aid of his glasses he could just make out the dot of white that was the Casquets lighthouse. There was a fishing boat out in that direction, and a steamer making for the Little Russell, trailing black smoke. What was she looking for? It was a clear and calm spring day, without a hint of malice in the seas.

A thought gripped him. She was sensitive to danger and to tragedy. What of that steamship? George watched it closely until it disappeared behind the top of the island. Back home he asked his father anxiously if there had been a shipwreck, and his father said no. Two days passed before George came in from helping in a vinery and his father told him the story he had heard about a ship coming to grief off the Casquets.

'Was people drowned?'

'Just cows, I heard. Lots of cows drowned it said in the paper, but the sailors were safe.'

So the spirit cared for cows, as well as people, or so George thought for a few days more until they were sitting down to supper.

'Did you hear?' Father said as he buttered his bread. 'That big ship went down, the *Titanic*. A thousand or two thousand people drowned. It was only off Alderney last week, all lit up at night on its way to America. Still, it's gone down, and Guernsey people on board even.'

'Who?' asked Mémaen. 'Do we know them? You can't tell a story like that, Henri Bazin, then not tell us if our friends and relations are on the boat.'

'Well, there's a quarryman from up Port Grat, one of the Duquemins. What's he doing on a big ship like that full of rich folk? Then that boy preacher, Mr Nicolle's nephew, the one who preached at the Cobo mission. He was on it too.'

'Where did it sink?' George asked, anxiously.

'Way out in the Atlantic somewhere. Hit an icy rock and sank, just like that… a terrible tragedy. It's in the paper today. Lots of rich people and famous people gone down with the ship. It's just like our *Stella*, yet ten times worse.'

Leaving his supper unfinished, George ran out on his own, hardly noticing the thin rain. He ran or hobbled all the way to the high rock of the Guet. The wind threw rain at him, then eased. Racing cloud filled the sky and out to sea, grey slanting shadows marked where rain squalls trailed from the ragged skirts of the clouds. He looked north over Cobo, and beyond to Port Grat where families must be waiting for better news.

In the raindrops he could see her face a dozen times. She was nodding, grim-faced. He was sure then that she had watched the great *Titanic* sail westward. Using her fantastic sight she had seen further than he had been able that day. He felt sorry for her. Trapped in bubbles of water and glass she could only observe the tragedies of the world. She could say nothing, do nothing, even when she knew that something terrible was about to happen.

'You saw it!' he called to the wind. 'You saw it!'

One day he would learn the skill to interpret what she meant. One day, *he* would be able to see into the future. He turned back to look at the sea once more. 'Those men, Duquemin and the boy preacher, were they drowned or saved?'

He thought he saw her smile. A week later, he knew he had seen a smile; he was certain. Keeping his ears keen for chatter, he heard that both men had indeed survived, although a dozen Guernsey lives had been lost. This was power, this was real power.

The rector blinked. After a moment he quoted, 'Woe to the foolish prophets who follow their own spirit and have seen nothing!'

'Eh?'

'Ezekiel. I forget the precise chapter and verse but I have had cause to bring the words to the attention of several women of the parish; never a man. Do you know your Bible well, George Bazin? There are many injunctions against sorcery and soothsaying and divining the future. Only God know what lies ahead – do not put any faith in imagined omens.'

Rebuked, George fell quiet.

'Is there anything you would confess? Is there some crime, or other evil you have done which demands that your spirit be cleansed?'

'No, no.' He thought wildly of everything he had ever done, guilty for every white lie or furtively stolen apple.

'Everyone speaks… well of you.' The rector shaped his words, for they were not true except in the sense that he knew George was not the sort to commit evil. 'And your family, too, are well respected.'

'My family?' he blurted. 'They've not done anything!' As he said this he started to doubt his words. Perhaps the sins of one generation would come back to haunt the next. 'My *gràn'père* was a hero!'

'Yes, quite,' the rector continued. 'So I do not know how this idea has got into your head.'

George removed his glasses. 'It's me glasses. She only comes when I wears my glasses. But then that's most of the time when I'm awake and not doing close work. She's always over here, over my right shoulder.'

The rector took the spectacles gingerly from George's hand and inspected them. 'You've chipped them.'

'That was done a long time ago. The day I first saw her.'

The rector wobbled them around in the light before his own eyes. 'I see.' He laid down his hands, but did not release the glasses.

'Well, George, these are difficult times for us all. We might all worry about what lies ahead, and then when something ill happens we look back and remember yes, we saw a crow or a black cat or a shape in the tea leaves. You're still a young man; your imagination is getting the better of you.'

He handed the glasses back. 'Buy new spectacles, if these carry bad memories.'

George had resisted suggestions of replacing his glasses as smaller children resist the confiscation of a favourite toy or blanket. His mother had suggested it as soon as he found steady work with Jack. Artie was always saying it, then Edith and now the rector had delivered God's judgement too. Perhaps it was true that he was drifting into sin and darkness by superstition, but it was Edith's opinion rather than tea at the rectory that carried most weight in persuading him that he no longer needed illusions. Now he was a man, he did not need an invisible companion. He'd buy new glasses – and Edith would be impressed.

Expensive and heavy, the new spectacles felt awkward to wear after his trusted old pair. Looking at his reflection in the optician's plate-glass window, he juggled them on his face. An unfamiliar George looked at an unfamiliar world.

The old glasses went into a cigar box where he kept a few other childish souvenirs, and that box went beneath his bed. As he closed the box, a part of him seemed to have been left behind, but he felt a strange satisfaction. His childhood was behind him; he was free.

CHAPTER 22

E dith spent the sunny days inside her aunt's guest
house in Town, cleaning. Some tourists still came here
from England as a place to get away from the war, and
rest-cures were still in vogue. Yes it was said that German
submarines lurked offshore, but that only added to the thrill,
and the mailboat captains were becoming regular heroes for
dodging them. Some men came on business, or to do various
work for the British Government, perils or not.

She hated cleaning and was jealous of the people who
could simply pack their cases and leave on Friday, but at least
she was within sight of the harbour. Each day the mailboat left,
she imagined herself on board. Some of the men who came to
the guest house brought their wives, but one day there would
be a handsome doctor, all on his own, come for solace and
rest. Then he would spot this flame-haired chambermaid,
who was not born to be a chambermaid. It would be love at
first sight and he would whisk her away to his smart house on
the fashionable side of London. They would be married in the
spring and invite all the grand people who he knew through
his practice.

Unfaithful daydreams pushed Artie aside, and when she
reflected on this she was ashamed. Then again, why should she
be? Artie seemed ever to be at work or on duty. She no longer
went to the Castel church, and had to manoeuvre around her
aunt to conspire to meet her beau even when he had time
off during the day. By night she was in St Martin's, sharing

a smelly loft with her mother who was pleased as anything at living rent-free; 'Uncle Frank' received his rent in a different way. Edith vowed she could never be slave to a man like that, so after the thrill of boy meets girl, was that all the future held for her and Artie Bazin?

One weekend in August he took her dancing at St George's Hall, and for once her faded dress did not let her down as there was a wartime mood against extravagance. Even the dance was disguised as a benefit for the soldiers' relief fund.

This was it – she had arrived. This was the pinnacle of all Guernsey had to offer – St George's Hall, just off the seafront, not quite on the north edge of Town. It was a plain establishment, quickly adaptable for meetings or dancing or the new craze for roller-skating. *This is it,* she thought, feeling tears in her eyes. *This is as good as life can get.* As they fumbled through the waltzes, Edith knew Artie grew happier with each moment they were together. His thoughts were moving in a different direction to hers.

Courtship, marriage, babies, housework, more babies; her pretty years would fade, and she'd grow old like Marie Bazin or deny reality like her own mother. Infirmity, sickness, regret, wasted dreams – all whirled through her head as she danced. Those romances she read ended with the glorious wedding, but what happened after 'happy ever after'? She loved him, she loved to hold him, she loved to kiss him, but *there would be babies*. And then her slow slide to the grave would begin.

She had to tell him. She had to tell him, or she would burst.

'So!' he declared as they walked along a breezy seafront back to the centre of Town. 'Give us a kiss!'

'People will see,' she chided.

'We've been courting for a year, on and off.'

'Really, a whole year?'

She wasn't coming any closer for that kiss. 'I didn't tell you my big news,' he said. 'They've made me a machine-gunner. And I'm promoted corporal.'

'That's good – does that mean soon you'll be an officer?'

'No, they only make you an officer if you have money, or have gone to the college. My friend Edwin is going to be an officer – they're sending him to England.'

'England? This bloney war is pulling everyone away from the life they used to lead. So, you know what? I figure it can pull me away too. Some good has to come out of it.'

'What?'

Edith drew breath as if about to say something momentous. 'Look, Uncle Frank doesn't own the farm in St Martin's, far from it, he just works there. So much for the land and the money! He's moving to England.' Quickly she plunged on. 'Well, Mum says he is, so we can hope. He's going to look for work on a farm – they're really short of men now – and he's got this thing with his eyes that means he can't enlist. And Mum says we can work in a munitions factory like Leila does. They're paying good wages making guns and things.'

'But you're not going too?'

'Why not?'

'You can't... well...'

'I can get a job, a proper job.'

'But in a smelly factory?'

'My sister does it. And it's better than skivvying or begging from the parish.'

'But what about me and you?'

'Oh Artie, I know, but I can't stay here, I just can't.'

'But I need you, I'll miss you.'

'You'll find someone else – Adèle is just waiting for her chance.'

'Adèle? I don't want Adèle.'

A few paces closer to the point of no return, she found another line of attack. 'I daresay your mum will be happy with me out of the way. Bad Irish girl.'

'No, no, Mémaen will come round one day. She just needs time.'

'And I need time, and you never have it.'

'Well, I'm sorry but there is that bloney war going on over there. What with the bank and the Militia… I love you, Edith.'

'Don't!' She held up her hands to block his affections. 'Don't tie me down, don't force me to stay here. I won't be staked out in a field like a cow.'

'You can't leave! You can't honestly leave. The island won't be the same without you.'

'Yes it will. It will always be the same.'

'Not true,' he insisted. 'They never had electric trams when my father was little, nor Zeppelins. You'll see, when the war is over there'll be airships flying between here and England, carrying passengers instead of bombs.'

'When the war is over,' she sang. 'How many times have I heard that? All those girls tonight, sitting around without partners, mooning for their sweethearts, it makes me sick to the stomach. And the love thing, it's like an infection. When I'm gone, you find someone else, right? Don't pine for me. Don't go off and volunteer for the war just to forget me.'

'Just might,' he said gloomily.

'Don't, Artie, don't even tease!'

At the bottom of the Avenue, she stopped in the roadway and gripped his hand. 'It's not that I want to leave you.'

'But you will,' he stated.

'We can't stop what's happening, it's the way the world's going. I'm sorry, Artie, I'm going to miss you, but I have to get away.'

'So this is à *la perchoïne, ma chière*?'

'That's one phrase I won't be sad never to hear again.'

'Don't hate the island, Edith; it's what you are.'

'It's not what I am! And I don't hate it, I just want to be *someone*. And I'll never do that here. I want to travel the world.'

'Like your father did?'

That hurt.

'And what of you?' she snapped back. 'You said you wanted to get away.'

'No, I want to go *to* somewhere. Not just escape. There's a difference, you know. It's like you leaving me, but you're not leaving me for anyone else, you're just going for the sake of going.'

Edith released his hand. 'You don't need to walk me any further, thank you. I know my way home. Goodbye, Artie.'

So that was that. Love was a cruel general that disarmed you before plunging you into battle. Edith walked away swiftly and he felt a loss he'd never known before.

CHAPTER 23

Between the fort at Grandes Rocques and the horseshoe bay of Port Soif is a small inlet called Port des Malades. Thrust into the sea between the two bays is a pinnacle of biscuit-brown rock. The sea surges on three sides, deep and blue. Only on the highest tides do they reach around the rock and cut it off from the land. Hanging on to that last moment before clambering to safety is a game best left for a fine summer's day.

Artie stood on the very apex, hands on his hips like some great mountaineer on the Matterhorn, although he was scarcely fifty feet above the sea. George cowered in the shelter of the outcrop, wary of that last climb, the sheer drops and the wind that surged from the west even on a cloudless day.

'Smell the air, George!' Artie called. 'All the way from America!'

George stood up and took a deep breath.

'Last people to breathe that air were Americans in their big cities. Or Red Indians.'

George smelled salt, seaweed, but little more. He checked for a hint of woodsmoke from campfires, of fat cigars, of exotic spices, but he could only smell the sea.

'I'd like to go to America,' said Artie. 'Sail there on a big ship.'

'Like the *Titanic*?' George said grimly.

'One that doesn't sink. When the war's over and there's no submarines out there.'

Just to the south, on the next headland, was the granite fort built to fight off Napoleon. 'Seems like there's always another war,' said George.

'Yeah, but we wins 'em all, eh, George? See this, climb up!'

Easy to say, but his leg was untrustworthy. George glanced down at the drop behind him, then up at Artie. He was wearing his new glasses, and from the corner of his eye he saw nothing and no one behind him. Nobody to warn him of the danger, nobody to stop him falling, no one ready to catch him if he fell. Courage was needed to face the future. Every day of it, every step he took was up to him to get right. George began to climb upward, rock by rock, and reached for the hand offered by Artie.

Endless, tireless waves filled the horizon.

'See what the teachers told us about old Admiral Saumarez, who lived down the lane from us. Back in the days of pirates and sailing ships, the old admiral was out there, with his little fleet guarding Guernsey. Then up comes the Frenchies, big ships, with lots of guns. Well he was trapped, wasn't he? So he sends away his slow ships but he stays behind to keep the Frenchies busy while the others escape.'

Artie used his hands to point out each chase and tack in the story. 'So, he's outnumbered, and getting surrounded. He can't go south, he can't go north and he can't go west. If he does, they'll sink him. If he sails east, bam! He's on these rocks and sunk.'

'What did he do?'

'Well he was a Guernseyman. And his crew, some of them were Guernseymen too. And he looks and sees his house up there and talks to his crew and they can see their own houses, so they know just where they are. So he sails this way, with the Frenchies chasing him.' Artie pointed northwards. 'See them rocks?'

149

Here and there, a mile or so offshore, lay the fangs of rocks and reefs given the names Suzanne, Les Grunes and Le Grand Saut Rocher. Spumes of surf signalled destruction for any ship venturing their way.

'So, the old admiral sails right between them. Well, them Frenchies don't know these waters and they could see the rocks and they reckon the admiral is mad and going to be fish food in minutes so they turn back. The admiral slips through the rocks and he was away, laughing at them!'

'Did he escape?'

'He did – and he did lots of other brave stuff, which I've forgot, but that's the way the teacher told it.'

George looked to sea, imagining the sailing ships of old, their great towering masts straining under full canvas as they played catch-me-if-you-can in and out of the cruel rocks. The world was a kind of drawing slate, where a scene would be sketched, and then quickly erased to leave just the slate and the story of what had once been.

'You should be a teacher, Artie. The way you've always told me stories like that.'

'I will, one day. I've made up my mind. When the war's done and we're all back to normal. I'll be old enough then, and I'll get someone like Mr Torode to write to the Education Committee for me.'

'Will you marry Edith then?' George asked, not knowing what he wanted the answer to be.

'Hah!'

'Where's Edith to, anyways? We never sees her any more. I though you two were all set to be married?'

Artie exhaled heavily. 'Teachers only teach you so much. The big lessons come after school is done. This war is changing everything.'

'Not round here.'

'Even round here. There's no shells falling in the Castel, for sure, but it's not the same place it was a year ago. Everyone Edith meets fills her head with plans to get away. First she's going to be a nurse, then go work in a factory, anything but stay here. And now, I hardly see her at all.'

'Is that why Adèle keeps calling round?'

Artie just stared at the horizon.

'Adèle Le Page, dear Adèle Le Page. Mémaen says she's a "sensible girl". She knows one end of a cow from the other, and she'll make a perfect Guernsey wife. And Edith? Well, she's flighty.'

'But that's what's good about her.'

'Is it? Mémaen warned me about her, and Mémaen knows best.'

Artie picked a small stone from a gully in the rock and flung it out to sea. 'Edith is flighty, and she's going to fly.'

George was saddened by Artie's news. Of course he was sad for his brother's loss, but it was his own losses he felt more keenly. Edith was gone, and his old friend was gone too. All around him the world was clean and fresh and clearer than it had ever been through his old lenses. If the rector was right about the sin of foresight, then he had done good by purchasing those new spectacles. If that spirit girl was somehow evil, the work of the Devil, she was banished now, trapped forever within a glass prison, and then that glass hidden in a box in the dark beneath his bed, even. No more messages would come from the other side.

She was trapped. The thought made his mouth dry. She was alone in utter darkness – just like little Drusille in the graveyard. The glasses had been replaced just as Drusille would be replaced by the new sister.

Without intending to, George came to stand at the inland edge of La Grande Mare, close to the spot where he had slipped and mired himself. The war was a year old and death had become so much a feature of life. Chipping at his stone, he carved the few words that summed up a lifetime. He hoped those souls were happy with his work.

But do not ghosts want revenge? Do they not come back to haunt those who have wronged them? The Grande Mare was as much farmland as true marsh these days, but somewhere, down here, twenty years or so ago, a little girl had drowned. The police might have come, and a priest too. It may even have been in the paper. He imagined the anguish of his mother, and his father. He imagined how good, solid Uncle Jack would have comforted them. He imagined the nasty gossip from the Valpied sisters, the sly looks and the nudges and the whispers in the back pews of the church after Drusille was buried. Drusille's death was a sad story, but it felt like a story badly written.

It was time he went to work.

'Was wondering where you'd got to,' Jack said as he came into the yard. 'These headstones won't cut themselves.'

'I was down by the Mare, thinking about Drusille.'

'Who?' Jack looked perplexed. 'Oh yes, the little one, yes, yes.'

'Do you remember Drusille's funeral?' George asked.

'Of course.'

'Tell me about it. The whole parish seems to know the story but me.'

'You don't want to hear all that?'

'I do. Truly I do.'

Jack nodded thoughtfully. He took a breath, a bit like Artie did when launching into one of his tales of long ago. 'It was soon before you were born,' Jack began. 'Your *mémaen* was – well – I never saw a woman look so beside herself. One baby gone and another just about to come. Your father had hurt his back in a fall and was out of work, I was just getting by, your grandfather at sea all the time… dark days.'

'You never made a headstone for Drusille.'

'Well, I wasn't a mason then, and we had no money. And you didn't for little ones, even.'

'Mmm.' George looked thoughtfully into the distance. 'What was she like? My sister?'

'She had a pretty round face, like your ma. Blue eyes. In other ways she was like you too,' said Jack. 'She had the same problem walking – worse than you, even. I wager she'd never have come on as well as you have. Other things were wrong with her too: her heart, her chest – I'd be surprised to see her with us today, even without the accident. It was a blessing, in a way.'

'She drowned? In a *douit*?'

'No, in one of those little pools down the Mare. It's dried up now, turned to grass for most of the year. Your mother took it very bad, but your father was a rock. Good solid man, your father. I know he's not had my share of luck…'

George was not going to be deflected. 'How does a girl who can't walk drown in a pool, all the way down the Mare?'

'Ah. That's why your mother took it so hard,' Jack said, with a defensive tone. 'It was one of the first fine days that year and they were – I don't know – picnicking by the dunes.'

'I was born in April, on Cuckoo Day they tell me. So when did Drusille die? March, February?'

'It were well before Easter,' Jack admitted. 'It was bitter cold when we buried her.'

'So they were not picnicking then?' George challenged.

'No, not picnicking for sure. I wager they were walking, taking the air or something,' Jack blustered. 'Your father couldn't work; they did that kind of thing to pass the day while he got better. My guess is they were so used to her not being able to run off, they turned their back on her. Your parents were still young; they thought the world of each other.'

'Run off? I never ran until I was seven.'

'It's a way of speaking.'

'Crawled off? Rolled off? Carried off by the *pouques*?'

'George, what's this all about?'

'They never told me anything about Drusille.'

'Well you don't. Things that hurt are best left to lie.'

'Sink,' said George.

'Eh?'

'Left to sink.'

George stayed in the yard only as long as he needed to. He found his hands were trembling as he tried to work the stone. He made one false cut, cursed, and laid down his chisel. That slip would take some correcting, and today was not the day for righting errors. Some of course could never be put right.

Barely noticing the light drizzle, he worked his way back up to La Vallée, more determined than he had ever felt. This must be the way the Tommies faced battle; setting aside fear, looking grimly ahead to that deadly horizon; steadfast in their purpose and unstoppable.

'How are you, Mémaen?'

His mother was at the sink and turned as if surprised. 'George,' she said. 'You startled me.'

For a pregnant women, she hid her belly well. If anything she looked even thinner than before. George knew she had been sick a few times, but everyone said this was normal in her condition.

'Are you well?' he asked again.

'Oh, you men, thank your stars you'll never know what it's like to be a woman! But I'm fine today – and you? You're back early, is there no work?'

'I was thinking about the baby.'

'Worrying more like – you should see that look on your face.'

'What happened to Drusille?' he asked bluntly. There was no simpler way of putting the question.

Marie had been pale of late, and now she became paler.

'I've been down by the Mare, thinking.'

'Don't think,' she snapped. 'Things are passed.'

'It would have been really hard for you and Père to look after a new baby and Drusille as well. With no money, and Père being off work, and Drusille needing all that care like I did. Doctors' bills, special shoes, spectacles one day no doubt.'

His mother stared at him, a glint in the corner of one eye.

'So God took her away,' he said. 'And you didn't have that problem any more.'

A tear ran down one cheek, then another. Her eyes were deep brown pools of sadness.

'And I thinks, if God hadn't done that right when He did, you would have had two of us cripples to look after. And sometime that year you'd have gone to the Mare, and it would have been useless baby George who crawled into that water to be drowned.'

'Wicked, wicked, wicked...' she panted.

'Isn't that so?'

'No, no. You don't understand!'

'I think I do.'

'You don't understand...' His mother sobbed. 'Everything

we have done… everything to bring you and Artie up proper. And this is how you pay us back…'

She drifted past him into the hall.

'Mémaen!'

His mother clumped up the stairs one by one and closed her bedroom door.

George found that he was crying too.

CHAPTER 24

As summer passed, something grew within Marie Bazin's womb, but it was not a baby. Instead of becoming fat, she was losing weight. Her sickness did not come in the morning, but after she ate. Thin, grey, older than her years, she continued to care for her family while the men watched her fade, powerless. Some months after proudly announcing her pregnancy, she admitted it was something else.

'Doctor Chapell comes round whenever he can,' Artie said.

He sat in near darkness within the single room where George was living. It was the only habitable part of an old cottage close to Kings Mills, which he rented from Perotine's father for no more than a promise to keep it from falling down. Some years back, one of the Guille relatives had died without an obvious heir, and half a dozen members of his family – and their advocates – had been squabbling over the cottage for longer than seemed sensible. Meantime, the cottage was returning to dust.

'Doctors are so expensive,' Artie continued. 'And there's nothing they can do.'

George shifted on the bed–cum–sofa he had built against the wall that week his father had set about him with a belt. He would not fight back against his father and he could not run, he simply blocked the blows until his father had exhausted thrashing and cursing him for killing his mother.

'Is Mémaen dying?'

'She has a cancer, down here,' Artie patted his belly. 'I don't know how she caught that – it's a woman's illness, I think. Or so the doctor said.'

'So can he make her better?'

'No. He can't do magic. When your time's come, it's come.'

'She can't just die!'

'They've taken her to the Cottage Hospital, to keep her comfortable. You can come and see her tomorrow. I've talked to Père. I've told him it's not your fault. Whatever you said to her…'

George had not told Artie what he had accused his parents of doing, and they had clearly not shared their denials with him either. Jack had been silent on the matter as they worked in the yard – deliberately silent, betraying that there was something he might say but would never actually say it.

'Did you bring it?' George asked.

Artie handed over the cigar box. 'There's nothing in there,' he said. 'Just your old things. I don't know why you want them.'

'I like old things. This old cottage, old stone to carve, old tombs to visit, your stories of Guernsey in the olden days. I don't like the new world and its wars, the hospital doctors who can do nothing more than Mrs Lake and her potions. The way people just leave…'

Artie sighed. 'Come to the hospital tomorrow. Mémaen wants to see you, and Père can't deny her that. I'll talk to Père again about you coming back to the cottage. Family is family, Mémaen always said that.'

Once Artie had gone, George sat until the light had almost gone from the window. Over on the sill, reflecting the last rays of sunset were his new glasses – useless things! He had been blinded by them, else he'd have seen this coming. He could have done something, warned Mémaen that it was not a baby but a cancer.

George was not his own master and he knew it. Common sense had trickled away over these weeks living the life of an exile. Reverently he took up the cigar box, and out came the old pebble glasses. He delayed putting them on, fearing his own foolishness. A man should not need fairies to maintain his equilibrium, but his father had beaten him like a boy. When he was finally a man, the glasses would go away for good. Fingering the frames, he slipped them on. The glasses hardy fitted, but he could bend them – he could have new wires fitted to the side! He trembled. What if she did not come back? What if she resented him for abandoning her? Night closed in and cold reached into his soul.

Marie Bazin sat like a ghost, half-upright in bed, wearing her best nightgown. The dark good looks of her youth were gone and a small, greying, skeleton woman remained. Henry sat beside her, holding her right hand while George shuffled on a chair next to him. The hospital offered scant privacy with its row of iron beds, the coughing and complaining patients.

'Georges,' his mother said in patois. 'I thought you bought new spectacles?'

He said nothing. He couldn't let his last words to his mother be a lie.

'You forgive us, George,' she said. 'Forgive us for being angry.'

'Yes of course,' he blurted. 'I'm sorry…'

'Henri,' she said, dreamily. 'Will she forgive us?'

'What?'

'Bury me with Drusille.'

'No, I don't…'

She gripped his hand tighter. 'Bury me with my little girl. She'll have been lonely.'

A tear ran down Marie's cheek. George removed his glasses to stop them misting and closed his eyes. He did not want to see his father cry too.

'Promise?' was her final word.

Her husband continued to speak, but Marie closed her tired eyes and her breathing became shallow. Soon it was barely perceptible and she slipped from the world without further struggle. Henry held her hand until it was cold, then kissed her forehead. He glared at his son, and turned away. George trembled to approach his mother, who might no longer even be his mother, and kissed the fading warmth.

Henry Bazin walked down over Candie and into Town, with George some yards behind. His father looked as though he had left half of himself behind. Finding a wall to lean against, opposite Artie's bank, he lit his pipe and gazed into space.

George said nothing, simply looking this way and that in his too-small glasses, watching the townsfolk busying by. Each was fired by their own urgent task – to deliver a parcel or unload a wagon or buy patent powders. A two-wheel cart struggled up High Street – narrow and canyon-like, with shops and their tall gables on each side. It held empty churns which rocked to one side as the single grey horse made its turn up Smith Street towards St Paul's Church. George made note of all these things around him that he had seen many times before, yet never taken the pains to study. And his mother was still dead.

When the bank closed, Artie came out, buttoning his coat

over his suit. He almost walked straight past the crushed man and his wounded brother without recognising them.

'Pépaen?' Artie arrested his march and came to join them.

'Your mother is dead,' Henry said.

Artie gave a sigh and nodded. He must have known, deep in his heart. All three went home by the horse bus, George sitting behind the others. His father made no comment when he alighted on the Route Cobo and followed them back to La Vallée. Jack had lit the parlour fire in the Big House and was stoic as his brother told him the news with a halting voice and a barely disguised sob. They hugged each other, and went outside. Artie followed after a few minutes. Alone, George took his mother's rocker by the fire, his owlish side leading him to wallow in morbid thoughts. He took off the glasses, wiped them on his shirt tail out of sheer habit, and then replaced them.

The world was the same, yet not the same. He glanced right – she was not there. Perhaps it had all been a childish game after all. He became distracted, began to doze. Awaking at the sound of a cracking log, he knew he was no longer alone. Dancing in the reflected flame was a familiar shape, all gay at her return. George was forgiven and, perhaps, he too should forgive.

George moved back into his room in the cottage without provoking a single comment from either his father or uncle. He left the house early the next day, taking a piece of bread instead of breakfast, walking to Jack's yard and picking up his work. He was putting the finishing touches to a gravestone for Alicia Patricia Everett, née Le Patourel, 87, giving it extra care.

When Uncle Jack arrived, he came over to watch him work. 'You all right, mousse?'

'Yes,' he said.

After a pause in which it was clear George would not say more, Jack spoke again. 'You should carve your mother's headstone, George. She'd like that.'

He nodded slowly. 'English or French?'

'English. She was always keen that you speak English.'

'Do you think they speak English in heaven?'

'If I knew that I'd be a rich man. Hebrew, I'd guess. Or Latin, like the Catholics use.'

'Will Mémaen have to learn Latin, then?' George was not asking a real question, just working over the idea of heaven in his head. Up there, everyone must speak the same language, and everyone must be as fit as they were in the prime of their lives. Gràn'père the hero would be there, with Gràn'mère, and both Gràn'père and Gràn'mère Allaire whom he had never really known. It was a warming thought that the unknown sister would be waiting for her mother to hug her once more. Alicia Patricia Everett would be there too, watching him perhaps as he recorded her cherished memory in Purbeck stone. He would do a good job for the dearly departed widow, but his mother's stone would be as perfect as he could make it.

'We've a good piece of granite laid by,' said Jack.

'No,' said George. 'Can we find some marble? It will carve better than granite and last longer than Purbeck.'

Jack sighed. 'Well there's a war on, so it won't be cheap, but I know where we can get some.'

Before he had chance to start work on the headstone, there was a funeral to face. The gravediggers were already at their work behind the Castel church when George arrived to check their handiwork. Sufficient room had been left in Drusille's plot so that her parents could one day join her. Arms crossed across his Guernsey, George stood close by. The two gravediggers glanced at him.

'Do you enjoy watching men work, you?' asked the verger.

'Just take care of my sister,' George said, firmly.

Drusille's little coffin had been buried at a shallow depth, but two decades had turned it into blackened matchwood. The rector stopped by to see that it was placed gently on a plank, lifted and covered with a rug while the men worked. George looked away lest there was a glimpse of a little arm or toe projecting from the box. Within the upcast soil he saw grey-white fragments the size of chicken bones. These graves had disturbed older graves which in turn had disturbed graves older still. Humans were in the very fabric of the soil – as if the island was made from its people.

Chunks of brick or tile from goodness knows what age were thrown on to the spoil heap as the men dug deeper. Maybe the mythical castle of the Castel truly lay here, buried beneath the generations. An immovable piece of granite or masonry, or even the bedrock of the island itself finally stopped the spades going any further. After a rest, the men gently lowered the rug-covered box back into the depth and covered it with soil, leaving room enough for two coffins above.

George was wearing his old glasses, not quite misted by tears. He could see the dark hole yawning. One follows another into the ground. It was a horrible, morbid thought. He must carve the name of Marie Bazin well, so that it lasted beyond mere memory itself.

CHAPTER 25

T he rain came thin and cold and ran off the statue of the *Gràn'mère* like tears. George and Artie, Henry and Jack carried Marie Bazin's coffin from the church to the burial plot. They moved slowly, more slowly than solemnity demanded to keep in step with George's pace. Marie Bazin was soon buried and gone.

It had once been unusual for women to attend funerals, apart from the closest of relatives, but the war was changing even the deepest customs. Edith Mullane had stayed at the back of the congregation, mixing with a good many friends and neighbours of the departed. Marie Bazin had been well liked and had several dozen close relatives within walking distance of the church. More would come to the house after the funeral. It was chance to take stock, see who was left, be satisfied that you were one of those still breathing.

Unlike the Irish, Guernsey people did not go in for an exuberant wake. Hospitality extended to tea back at the cottage and one of the Allaire relatives had dropped off a quantity of *gâche* and Guernsey biscuits knowing there were now no women at La Vallée.

Artie expressed surprise when Edith came up to him after the service and touched the back of his hand.

'Edith!'

'I'm terribly sorry about your mother,' she said.

'Thank you.'

'I never got to meet her. Not properly. Everyone said she was very kind.'

'She would have liked you,' Artie said.

Edith nodded energetically, knowing that Marie Bazin would have faced a mountain of prejudice to climb first. 'I would have liked her, I'm sure. My mum was at school with her.'

'I heard.'

She forced a smile. 'I don't think they liked each other.'

'No. I gained that idea too,' he admitted.

After the quiet of the church, the mourners who emerged created a hubbub of conversations. Most talked about the Marie Bazin they had known, how she had entered their lives and how she had affected them. Letting the crowd pass, the young man and young woman fidgeted in the drizzle, neither sure where the future was heading.

'I thought you were to England,' Artie said.

Oh, if only! 'No,' she said. 'Not yet. I thought I'd come along because I always felt your mother stood between us and I wanted to...' She found it hard to explain. 'Forgive... I don't know.'

'Will you come back to the house?' Artie asked. 'Or is it the wrong way for you? Or too far to where you're living now? I must confess, I don't even know where that is.'

'Oh, still exotic St Martin's.' Edith began to walk and he matched her pace. 'It's exactly like the Castel, except we see the sunrise instead of the sunset. They've even got a *Gràn'mère* by their church gate.'

She paused by the statue. 'But theirs is better. It's still got a face.' She touched the smooth stone where a face may once have been. 'Your preacher should get George to carve her a new one.'

Artie found a smile just for her, on a day without smiles. Mourners began to disperse from the church gates. The senior Bazin brothers were in conversation, heads bowed, hands in the pockets of their coats. Artie offered Edith his arm and they followed on.

To the steady drip-drip of raindrops from overhanging trees they continued walking towards the west, leaving Marie Bazin to fade into reminiscence.

'Uncle Frank's gone to England,' she said. 'He's going to send for us, as soon as he's set up.' She made a show of crossing her fingers. 'My mother's plans have a habit of unravelling.'

His grip grew ever so slightly tighter, and suddenly Edith recognised her life risked slipping backwards. She stopped, bringing Artie to an abrupt halt. She let go of his arm and half turned back towards the church.

'I thought you were coming to the house?'

'No – I've never been before and it wouldn't be right now. We both know what your mother thought of my mother – and me – so it wouldn't seem proper just to march straight in the day she's buried.'

Edith stepped away from him. 'I'm truly sorry,' she said.

A rare southerly wind whipped the Little Russell channel into green, white-capped waves. A high tide drove them against the castle breakwater where they exploded in spray that carried higher than the bastions and fell into the harbour itself. Edith had come down to shop in the Markets for her aunt. It was one of those lunchtimes when she could have contrived to meet Artie Bazin, but she had burned that bridge now. A cargo ship edged cautiously from the harbour, nosing into the waves. Its bow lifted as it hit the first and then fell to meet the next. It was leaving, but Edith was not.

Someone else was watching the ship. It was George Bazin, standing at the edge of the quay in front of Prince Albert's statue. The boy had an endless capacity to find interest in the mundane and be transfixed by it. How many hundreds of boats had he seen heading out to sea? Yet George watched the ship in great wonder, like a tourist would.

'Hello, George. Your new glasses look very smart.'

She had seen him on odd days wearing his old baby glasses, but today he was wearing the new ones.

'Wharro, Edith,' he said. Whereas Edith wore a long dark coat against the wind, George had simply put a second Guernsey on over the first. 'Hello,' he said, as if in translation or unsure she'd heard him.

'What brings you this far from the parish?' she asked.

'I'm buying a boat. John Tostevin is off joining the navy so won't be needing his boat, so I'm buying it. Well, Père and I are sharing it and Uncle Jack's lending us the money. We'll go for spider crabs and chancre off the west coast. Mackerel when they're running, bream, bass. Prices are way up since the war started, and there's less work for Père now and he's not fit for the Militia no more…'

She smiled as he babbled. If Europe had been populated exclusively by George Bazins there would be no wars.

He paused. 'You're still here,' he said in wonder.

'Why wouldn't I be?'

'Artie said you were to England with that farmer and your *mémaen.*'

'No, well, that farmer was really just a farmhand and he's gone without us and we've heard nothing since.'

She pointed at the cargo ship struggling against the waves as it moved south towards Jersey.

'The story of my life is written just there,' she said.

'Somebody else heading over the horizon, and me staying right here.'

'You wouldn't want to go to Jersey,' he said in disdain.

'No, I don't want to go to Jersey,' she said.

'Nor France, with the war on.'

She felt a raindrop sting her cheek.

George looked at the sky. 'Thought it would rain,' he said, raising a hand to catch another drop. 'Does Artie know you stayed?'

'No, I haven't seen him since your mother's funeral.'

'Been busy, our Artie. I reckon he's missed you though. He's been all quiet. He's been out drinking with Père, or with that Mr Brown from the bank.'

'Has he? He's not calling on any of the spinsters of the parish?'

'Not him. I reckon you hit him right here,' George thumped his left breast. 'Like a sniper.'

The rain was starting to strike with more determination. 'I'd better get to the Markets,' she said. 'You get under cover, you'll get soaked.'

'Caw, fisherman, me,' he said. 'Don't mind the rain. I've got to wait for John Tostevin.'

'Give my regards to Artie.'

'Will do. Glad you're still here, Edith!'

She went over to the Markets and fulfilled the shopping list. Coming out, she took one look at the rain and decided to linger under the Arcade in the hope it would stop. Running across Market Square towards her came a young woman in a dark uniform. As she came under cover, she slowed to a halt and smiled. Together they watched the rain splash into the cobblestones, and started talking. Her name was Violet, and she gave Edith an idea.

CHAPTER 26

Edwin Brown had joined Artie's bank just after the New Year of 1915. Despite his English name, he came from a local family, although some would say that because his ancestors came over with the garrison in the eighteenth century he did not have the same pedigree as the Brehauts and Le Marchants who had been here since Norman times.

He had been sent to school in England, and had lived with relatives in London since the war started. His family was well-to-do, and his father knew someone who knew someone who secured him a position at the bank in Guernsey. Edwin did not come in as just another clerk.

Short of friends when he arrived, he had latched on to Artie Bazin, not as yet another of his gang of parish lads, but as a true comrade. They could share a joke about the stiff Mr Jepson and swap newspapers during the lunch break.

Cruel people said that Edwin had been brought back to skip the war. It had become the practice in England to pass white feathers to fit young men not in uniform, and now there were even whispers of conscription. The cowards, the shirkers and the socialists who had no care for the king's war would take their place side by side with the heroes. If he had stayed in England, Edwin would have had little choice but to join the forces.

'Honestly,' Edwin said as they sipped tea in the rest room. 'Can you see yourself as a soldier?'

'Yes, suppose.'

'But of all the careers in the world? Soldier? Marching, shooting, waiting around, paid a pittance, no young ladies to brighten the day?'

'No, not put like that.'

'Exactly. We're trying to fight a war with shop boys and farmhands who fancy trying their hand at soldiering. And the Germans must be doing the same, and the French. Think of all those waiters and chefs suddenly pushed into uniform. Commanded by men fresh out of school who've never even run a corner shop, let alone a battalion. No wonder it's such a bloody shambles.'

'I never thought of it like that.'

'Could some Tommy Atkins just march in here and do your job?'

'If he had neat writing… and if he could do his sums… spoke politely to the customers.'

'And, and, and… answer: no. So how come a trained, well-educated bank clerk can suddenly become a soldier? Everyone should do what they do best, that's what I think.'

Put like that, Artie had to agree. The original regular army – the Old Contemptibles – had been all but destroyed at Ypres, and the first wave of Kitchener's volunteers was being whittled away at Loos. The battlefront was locked rigid somewhere towards the Belgian border and it was rumoured that even the English shells didn't explode when they ought to.

Leaving the bank one Thursday in October, Edwin drew Artie's attention to a smart young woman in uniform standing outside Boots the Chemist.

'I say, look at her.'

Artie had to look twice before he recognised Edith Mullane, newly fitted into a dark uniform with her hair drawn up into a cap. She smiled.

'By, she's looking our way!' Edwin said.

'She's looking my way, you mean.'

'So, who is she then?'

'Edith Mullane. We… we're good friends.'

'Aha, dark horse, Bazin. Introduce us.'

'Edith!' Artie called.

She came forward to meet them halfway, where Smith Street met the High Street.

'Surprise!' she said.

'What's all this?' Artie pointed to her uniform.

'Conductorette,' Edith announced. 'On the trams. Started yesterday,' she grinned proudly. 'Like my uniform?' She performed a twirl as if she were a stage performer.

'You've cut your hair.'

'Only a little.' She removed her cap and showed a neat bun. 'I do it up just so. And who's your friend?'

'Edwin Brown, at your service, ma'am.'

'Oh he's a charmer!' Edith laughed.

'They're never letting women drive trams?' Edwin said.

'Not driving, just conductoring. Too many men going off to fight, see?'

Artie and Edwin shared a glance. As more men volunteered for the forces, the weight of guilt increased on those left behind.

'We were just talking about that this morning,' Artie said.

'Don't you dare!' She wagged her finger to warn him. 'That cousin of mine from the Vale: Jim? Whose flouncing we went to? He was killed, him, fighting with the Irish out in France. We heard just this week.' She paused. 'I always hated him, which seems horrid now. So you stay here, if you've any brains and you want to keep them in your head.'

Edwin jutted out his square jaw and nodded agreement. 'Wise words, wise woman.'

'So, you're still in Guernsey?' Artie asked, with just a glance at his forward friend. 'What happened to the big plan to escape the island?'

'I'm going nowhere,' she said firmly. 'Except, to be sure, I'm going to the Bridge and back six times a day.'

'Let's have tea,' he blurted. 'There's that café down by the Albert Pier.'

'There is. Well, I finish early on Friday.'

'Aw, Militia bomb practice,' he said.

'Saturday?' she suggested.

'Fine – how about noon?'

'Noon it is.' She replaced her cap firmly. 'Good day to you, Mr Brown, Artie.'

Edith looked very good in uniform and the men stood and watched her recede down High Street.

'If she had said no, I'd have jumped right in there, old boy,' said Edwin.

Artie looked at him sharply. 'Any man who gets between me and Edith better watch out, *mon viaer*.'

Edwin's words worried him. At first glance, Edwin was too smart and too rich to go chasing a penniless girl like Edith, but not every man was so choosy. Artie must go all out to win Edith or someone else would beat him to it.

For all his philosophical objection to citizen soldiers, Edwin Brown had joined the Royal Guernsey Militia soon after his arrival. Naturally, a word in the right ear and he was down for officer training. It was just grooming for management, he told Artie. A pip on the shoulder never did anyone's career any harm. One day, he'd put a good word in for his friend.

Officer training might be a long way off for Artie Bazin but he was learning a thing or two about tactics. If opportunity presented itself, a man had to strike. An advantage did not last for long and the meek seldom inherited anything, let alone the Earth. Artie did meet with Edith that Saturday, and it was a sober Edith, a grown-up Edith. Add a uniform and the flighty girl was gone. They chinked teacups.

'To the future,' she said.

'Shall we start again?' he asked.

She pointed a finger at him. 'You know, you need to start asking the right questions.'

'Which are?'

'You work it out.'

Artie was on Militia duty overnight at Fort George, but on Sunday morning won leave to go to church. It was a fine day for so late in the year, with less wind than of late. With a dozen others, mainly St Martin's men, he walked through the back lanes as far as their parish church. By the time the Militiamen reached the gate, only six remained, the rest having turned aside to various chapels along the route.

There was indeed a *Gràn'mère* by the gate at St Martin's Church, with carved face and necklace still defying the years. Artie removed his army cap, unbuttoned his greatcoat and went in with his fellows to sit on a pew near the back. Several pews forward, red-gold hair fell from behind a white-and-blue bonnet.

He'd worked out the question.

After the service he nipped out smartly, urging his comrades to leave without him. He took up station beside the door like a sentry a few moments before Edith came out in company with some older woman.

'Edith.'

The older woman paused mid-anecdote and met the challenge in his eyes, but Artie tipped his cap and she drew back with only the slightest loss of poise.

'Artie, my,' Edith said.

'Miss Mullane, will you walk with me?'

The route she led him along was not direct. Instead they walked towards the sea for a good twenty minutes along the lane which aims for Jerbourg point. All the time they talked, of their lives, their families, their friends. When the sea came into view on their left, the couple turned off into a field where an old granite gatepost lay ruined, but formed a perfect seat for two.

For a few minutes they were quiet. Artie took her hand and she did not resist. Deep blue, the Little Russell stretched below them. Beyond they counted Jethou and Herm, Sark then France. Jersey seemed much closer than it should, a blue smudge to the south. Even Sark reared huge with the sun throwing shadows across its brown cliffs.

'How could you leave all this for a city?' he asked. 'For factories full of smoke, making bombs?'

'A city with dancing halls and electric theatres.'

'And Zeppelin raids,' he said.

'A million people live in London.'

'And every one out to rob you or cheat you, I'll bet.'

'Yes, but I wouldn't meet aunts and cousins every day in the street.'

'Family is good, Edith. That's what my mother said, before she died. You can't beat family.'

'You can beat my family.'

'So join mine,' he said quickly.

Edith's chin was trembling. He feared she was going to say no, or burst into tears, or slap him. Did she want him? Truly?

'You askin', Arthur Bazin?' she challenged.

'Yes. I figure we'd best get married, else you'll go away,' he said. 'Would you like to be Madame Bazin? Will you marry me, Edith?'

She grabbed him by the shoulders and kissed him three times. 'Yes, yes, yes.'

His cap fell off, but he let it lie and gave her a huge hug. '*Cor*! Thought you'd say no for a minute, and I'd feel really stupid.'

'Artie, no. It will be wonderful.'

'You'll come and live at La Vallée, and we can have my room in the Big House. George can stay in the cottage with our Uncle Jack. Can't see either of them getting married, so the cottage will do for them.'

'Married?' Edith giggled and let him kiss her again.

This was glorious. All was right with the world and who cared if Europe fell apart, so long as Guernsey survived and there was a place for him and for Edith!

'Well, there'll be plenty of time for all this,' she said after a moment, and stood up, straightening her coat. 'That stone's cold!' she exclaimed. 'Come and see Mum, she'll be pleased as punch. She's been marrying me off to every other man who walks down the lane. This one's got so many vergies of land, and this one's a doctor's son…'

'I'm none of that.' Artie picked up his cap swiftly, and then vaulted over the gate and helped Edith over. 'I'm not rich or anything.'

'But you will be, Intermediate School boy. No quarry for you, no picking tomatoes or chasing fish about. You'll be in your suit in your office. And I'll wear a hat with a broad brim like that English bank manager's wife and I'll be a proper lady and stop saying 'bloney' this and 'bloney' that.'

'You will too.'

'And we'll have two boys and two girls, and they will all go to the Intermediate – no, to the colleges – and find perfect matches.'

'*Cor*, girl, you've planned our life.'

'You have to plan. Then you're ready for what comes round the corner.'

He squeezed her hand. 'Now, show me the way and I'll walk you home.'

'*All* the way home?'

'At last.'

Artie and Edith walked arm in arm all the way to a farmhouse down a lane where Artie had never been. A long, lime-washed wing ran back from it, with a set of granite steps leading to the first floor.

'We're here,' said Edith. 'You must excuse the place, it's fairly horrid.'

When Artie had walked her down to the old dower wing by the Bailiff's Cross, they always parted some way short. Today they paraded straight up the steps. Edith's mother opened the door before they reached it, a barely suppressed gleam of delight on her face.

'Mrs Mullane?' Artie said.

'Come in, come in!' she said. 'I've got the table all set. We don't have much but you're welcome, I can set another plate. You're Arthur Bazin, aren't you? My, you look smart in that uniform, doesn't he look smart, Edith?'

Edith nodded, smiling nervously; embarrassed maybe. Artie took one glance at the laundry-hung room, found his courage and squared up to Edith's mother.

'Mrs Mullane. I would very much like to marry your daughter.'

CHAPTER 27

A betrothal party might have been held in better times, but Ruth Mullane had no money and Henry Bazin had little more. Jack bought in some cider and bottles of beer to La Vallée and enough relatives were summoned to fill the house and bring cake and bread with them to make a jolly affair.

Edith liked Jack – as did everyone she spoke to. He took on the task of showing her mother round the pair of houses, their kitchens and parlours, the dairy and the yard. Jack carried a wry smile on his face as if he'd met many a shrewd operator in his time, and knew one when he saw one.

'Do you like cooking?' Edith heard him ask.

'When I can,' her mother replied.

Elbow to elbow the relatives passed on their best wishes. Edith positively glowed with happiness and Artie's grin never left his face all night. The spirit of mourning was driven from the houses and a new woman prepared to take the position of mistress.

One chink remained in the bright clear future she had imagined. She spoke quietly to Artie as soon as space allowed. 'You know my mother is wanting to move in?'

'Um, I guessed she would,' said Artie.

'I hoped she'd go to England with that farmhand.'

'That was never going to happen, was it?'

'No. She has a history of latching on to men just as they

are leaving – and they let her, knowing they can soon leave her behind.'

'Still, you wouldn't want to wash and cook for all three of us, would you?'

'No, there is that. Your Uncle Jack is sizing her up right now, but she thinks it's her that's doing the nosing around.'

'*Ma chière!*' her mother came back into the room and gave Edith a hug. 'And my new son!' She hugged Artie too. He gave the politest, gentlest hug back.

'Your Uncle Jack is a good man,' she said. 'Showed me all round and my, what a big house. If you think of them both as one house, which I do.'

'You'll come and live with us, won't you, Mum?' Edith said, tight-lipped. There was of course never any question.

'Oh, of course. That's so sweet of you to ask.' Her mother gave her another hug, then a kiss on the cheek. 'We've got to leave the farm next month even, and I wouldn't want to go back to Marguerite's. You can ask for too much Christian charity.'

In the kitchen of the cottage, a plate of *gâche mêlaïe* seemed to have been forgotten and George was methodically clearing it, deep in his own thoughts. Edith took the daintiest piece left.

'You look sad,' she said.

He avoided her eyes. 'No,' he said, pushing another piece of the apple cake into his mouth. Talking around the cake he said, 'I'm glad you're coming to live with us, Edith.'

'You're glad I'm marrying Artie?' she asked, firmly, to assert that this is surely what he should be glad about. 'We're marrying at Christmas – none of this long betrothal nonsense. So yes, we'll be living here, and my mother's coming too.'

She waited for a response.

'To make room, your father's moving next door with your uncle…'

'And I'm pushed on to the green bed in the parlour.'

'The cottage parlour, yes.' She felt a little guilty evicting George from a proper bedroom, but she had never had a room of her own. 'Artie says it's barely used…'

'I'll be next door,' he mused. 'You'll be next door.'

Finally George looked her in the eye. 'You know I nearly had a sister once, but she died? She'd be about two years older than you are.' George grinned brightly. 'I likes having you here, Edith. You'll be the sister I never had.'

PART 2:
DIEX AÏE

CHAPTER 28

Chip by chip George carved out the date 1916. He had formed a new lintel for a house that was being extended backwards to double its depth. Either side of the date, he carved the initials J and C for the owners.

At La Vallée, the winter passed in a whirr of novelty. Ruth Mullane set to with a will to impress, endlessly enraptured by the side-by-side complex of house and cottage. Never strong-willed, she allowed Edith to take the lead in planning the cooking and the shopping without as much as a discussion. All the men fell in behind, so that within a few weeks of becoming la Missis Bazin, the eighteen-year-old girl was running both houses with a flair that would even have impressed Marie.

In so many parts of the world, the war raged on. Safe in the Castel, George continued to learn the ways of stone. Safe, yet eerily unsafe. When the future lurks unseen, sane men can do no more than proceed oblivious, and deal with crises as they occur, but George knew that his future was not unseen. He need only take the step of removing that box from where it now rested beneath the green bed and slip on the glasses. His far-sighted friend would be at hand if only he reached for her. Over the years he had grown attuned to her attitude, if not always to her meaning. Surely she would be able to warn him if one of his friends and relations were in danger, so he could pass on the warning in time.

No, of course, it did not work like that. He had never known the meaning of her warnings until after the event. All he could do was prepare himself. Choosing to remain blind to what was coming, he worked on the headstone with care. Another young man had died for peace.

He heard his uncle crossing the yard behind him, making for the gate with purpose in his stride.

'Jack!' he called, popping his new glasses on to bring his uncle into focus.

Jack paused, frowning.

'I'll be finished soon. Shall we move this stone straight up to the church today?'

'No,' said Jack. 'It can wait until tomorrow. I'm in a bit of a rush now.'

He was wearing his working clothes, but looked a little smarter than he might be on a working day.

'I've got to go to Cobo to do a job for Mrs Patterson.'

Mrs Patterson had been married to a man in the colonial service, Jack explained over dinner that night. She had not taken to the climate in India and had shipped back to England with a plan for their future. With the money her husband sent home, she bought a guest house nestling under the Guet and overlooking the sea at Cobo. This would be their home when Mr Patterson retired in a few years' time, and would also provide an income. Guernsey was in any case a cheaper place to live than the genteel towns of England and his pension would stretch further. As it was, Mr Patterson died of typhus in Hyderabad and never got to see the house. His widow donned black, but had set herself to complete the plan.

Not all the locals liked the English incomers buying up the best houses in the best positions, but even the grumpiest welcomed the money they brought in. Jack had gone round to help fix her front wall that had been badly smashed by an unusually fierce rainstorm. After that it seemed to his brother and to George that Jack was called round to fix a great many things.

As fighting on the Western Front erupted into the worst carnage the world had ever seen, Guernsey stayed at peace when summer came. One Sunday George stood on the top of the beach at Cobo, his wooden fishing boat pulled high from the water and turned keel upwards. He was painting it a fresh coat of blue. Out to sea he could see a convoy of grey shapes streaming smoke from every funnel. From the south came what at first appeared to be a seagull. It was seagull-sized and travelled at seagull speed, but the shape kept growing and it was moving in a direct line, not weaving to and fro as gulls do. The flying machine droned closer, appearing to be a brown rowing boat suspended from two tiers of rigid wings. His breath was taken away by the sedate beauty of the thing as it coursed north along the coast, ignoring the wind and defying gravity. Men must be aboard the flying boat, looking down at the earth as if they were gulls. This truly was the century of marvels.

In the yard behind the cottage, Edith heard the noise when she was pegging out the washing, and looked up. It took her a few moments to work out what she was seeing. People had talked about aeroplanes and they had been described in the papers but here was one for the very first time. She wanted to wave it down and ask the pilot to carry her away, to carry her and Artie far over the horizon to the New World where there was no war.

Artie saw it too. He was up on L'Ancresse Common learning to fire a new type of light machine gun. All the Militiamen stopped and watched the seaplane go by. A target was painted on its side in red, white and blue. One of the men playfully aimed his rifle.

'You'd never hit it, lad,' warned the sergeant. 'They look slow from down here, but they fly faster than the wind.'

Artie followed the plane with his finger. If that were a German aeroplane *he would never hit it,* not even with his new Lewis gun. Yes, the aeroplane was a marvellous thing, but this technology opened up a whole new world of terrors.

The Battle of the Somme raged all summer, and the last brave boasts died with the news. Two dozen islanders fell in the slaughter and Len Batiste, the stonemason's apprentice, would never return to the Castel. He'd been shot through the head by a sniper's bullet and killed instantly – or so his mother was told.

'It means that it's your job, now,' said Uncle Jack as he walked to work beside his nephew. 'For as long as you want it. In truth, you'll make a better mason than Len ever would, rest his soul.'

'Saw his mum yesterday, in the lane,' George reflected. 'She looked away from me, like it was me that killed him just to get his job.'

'Don't think ill of her. He was her only son, and her daughter is to England with the Salvation Army nurses so she's all alone up there. It's a bad business, George.'

'The paper said over a thousand men were killed…'

'A hundred thousand in the first couple of days,' Jack stated.

'W…?'

'Yes – that's about two… three times as many people live in Guernsey, counting women and little ones too. All in one battle, and it's still not over. We've got to win this war, it's got to be worth all this suffering. If I was young enough, I'd go myself if I thought I could make a difference.'

'And me,' said George. 'But they won't have me.'

'They'd have your brother like a shot.'

'Don't talk Artie into enlisting!' urged George. 'I know he thinks about it from time to time. A lot of his friends have gone and the girls tease him. Even Edith.'

'Surely not Edith, not now she's married him? She doesn't want to be a widow as soon as she's a bride, eh? Artie's best off here, with the Militia – and if he ever asks, tell him I said so, and he's to pay no heed to what the silly women say or those old fools who write to the newspaper.'

So the Great War dragged on into its third autumn and Jack was proved wrong about the demand for headstones, as men were being buried where they fell. Only a few bodies came back to the islands, chiefly those of men who had died in hospital in England. Chipping their names was as close as George thought he would come to the war.

CHAPTER 29

Within the master bedroom, Edith had learned why her mother was so drawn to men. Kissing in the dunes was one thing, but hugging Artie's naked body close to hers transported her away and beyond. She discovered the kind of sin the preachers preached about, and knew why they frowned so hard. Love – and lust – could rule the world if left unchecked. No need for church or governments or wars when there was love in all its frantic fulfilment.

Artie eased out of her, took his own weight and slid down the bed beside her. Dawn was fresh in the sky outside and the bells rang out a Sunday. She snuggled back close to him, and dug one finger into his chest playfully.

'I know why you want to be a schoolmaster,' she said.

'Why's that?'

'Because you like being in charge. You like being on top…' She giggled and he smiled. 'You like people doing exactly what you tell them to do.'

'I didn't hear you complaining.'

'Cheeky,' she said.

'In truth, I like finding things out. And then I like sharing what I know. I spent all my childhood looking after George. Then I was… I don't know… section corporal to all the local lads who needed to be organised to play football, or hide-and-seek or *djablle*.'

'You're our local hero, you. But are you serious about becoming a schoolmaster?'

'Sometimes – the bank can be so boring. Some days I wish I was out in the sun, breaking rocks with my father or helping George and Uncle Jack with the tombstones. Man's work, you know? But one day, if I stick the bank out, I'll be like Mr Jepson who is in charge of the clerks. I can buy us our own house, not just wait for Père to die and take half portions with George.'

'Can we live in Town then? Sell your portion and buy one of them modern houses in Town?'

'Why not?'

She paused, having prepared her next speech after some days of thought. Edith had been mulling over a plan for several months, even before she agreed to become Mrs Bazin. A naked woman in close contact, with one leg wrapped securely over her lover, is a persuasive thing.

'Does your bank have an office in London?'

'Branches everywhere, all over England.'

'I bet a lot of their men have gone away to war.'

'There's a whole regiment of them joined up together.'

She pursed her lips. 'Here's an idea. Suppose you asked that Mr Jepson if you can go and work in London? They might have a higher position for you that pays more money. In London we could really move on – you'd work in a big branch.'

'London? We're only just married, and you're settling here so well.'

'You always said you wanted to travel. So here's a start.'

'But there's George, and Père, and Uncle Jack.'

'I didn't marry George, Père and Uncle Jack. I bet those London banks are short of men now, just like Jack needed George when the war started.'

'Filling dead men's shoes feels dirty.'

'But it's happening every day. See me on the trams – when did they ever let women do work like that? Next we'll be getting the vote.'

'Yeah, and then I suppose we'll get lady jurats and lady deputies too,' he said cynically.

'And why not? We've got brains. All you men seem to do is start wars and go off and get killed in them.'

'All right!' he laughed. 'It's not such a bad idea. Had it once or twice myself.'

'Someone's going to get those jobs, so it may as well be you.'

'I'll ask. They can only say no. Sounds like they'll give 'em all to women otherwise, eh?'

Artie delayed asking the question for as long as he could. There was a Militia exercise, and then the bank was short-handed when one of the managers was recalled to Head Office, then Mr Jepson caught flu, then Artie simply forgot. Yes he wanted to be with Edith, but she was with him now. Transplant the house anywhere and they would be together, so why move at all? He did not say this to her directly and she only raised the issue every week or so through the spring, during which time a new reason arose to explain why he had done nothing.

By May, the British government saved him the need to find any more excuses and dashed la Missis Bazin's hopes of moving to London. Conscription was extended to include married men. If they carried out Edith's plan, Artie would likely be conscripted into the army. There would be no glittering career in the bank, only the glitter of bayonets. Edith threw a saucer across the kitchen when he told her, and it broke. She stormed out of the house to the crest of the hill and stood looking westwards to the distant sea horizon. Life was so unfair!

Artie followed her and laid one hand on each shoulder, whispering in her ear.

'Never mind,' he said.

'Bloney war,' she said.

'There's worse happening,' he said. 'Worse things than just stopping us moving away.'

'Yes,' she said, without conviction.

'It's bound to be over soon,' he tried to comfort her. 'With this conscription, the English must have a huge army now. A million men or something.'

'Yes,' she said.

'We'll sit it out, save up a bit of money.'

'All right, we'll sit it out. But no babies,' she said firmly. 'I'm too young for that. I know they gave us the Big House thinking we'd be making babies straight away, but we have to wait. They'd throw me off the trams and we wouldn't have two doubles to rub together again. No babies, absolutely not, until the war is done and we've made our plans.'

'But...'

'It doesn't mean you can't touch me. We just... take care, that's all.'

'Fine,' he said.

Fit men who had stayed at home began to feel lesser men than those who had volunteered and gone to fight in France or elsewhere. Inside the bank there was a tension each time a newspaper was opened. Someone would utter a little cry, a gulp, a sigh of disappointment as they spotted a certain name. It had once been a novelty when the exploits of a friend or neighbour made the paper, but the drip-drip of wounded, missing or dead became dispiriting. The casualty of the day was a hard thing to anticipate: one friend-of-a-friend-of-a-relative would be listed, sometimes with a photograph. Edwin Brown read the English papers, and was particularly dry-mouthed when the lists grew long, as almost all his class from his public school had become officers in one branch of the services or another.

One lunchtime as that summer ground on, he was smoking a cigarette in the High Street, white-faced and looking at his shoes, not daring to look anyone in the face.

'You all right, old man?' Artie asked.

Edwin nodded.

'Lost someone?'

Edwin nodded again. 'A few.' He frowned and pursed his lips. 'My rugger captain, my old fag, a couple of the masters. Danny and Albert from university – both in the same list today. We used to share digs.' He looked off into space. 'Frankly, I've lost count. We don't know how lucky we are living here. Being able to just… watch.'

'Is it time to go?' Artie asked.

'No,' Edwin said, but his eyes betrayed indecision. 'Only a madman would go now.'

For all Edwin's mixed emotions, Artie knew the watching was nearly over. He'd been reading *Press* accounts of discussions held at Government House, and on the floor of the States Chamber. Every taproom and parlour began to pick up the drift of the argument. Guernsey was 'doing its bit' for sure, more so than most places, but the bravery of its sons was almost invisible. A sailor here, a signaller there, half a dozen soldiers in far-off places nobody had heard of, a few engineers beavering behind the lines, but it was not enough. Those in authority on the island wanted the name of Guernsey to appear in dispatches, even on the front pages of the newspapers.

The Lieutenant Governor was an old soldier who had

won the Victoria Cross, and he came up with the solution. Sheffield, Bradford and even the Bank of England had formed their own regiments, so the answer was obvious. There would no longer be any need to join the Irish. Guernsey was to have its own regiment at last!

Just before Christmas, the order was read out when Artie's company was on parade at Fort George. The Militia was suspended for the duration of the war and its men enrolled as one into the Royal Guernsey Light Infantry. Hundreds of years of tradition were at an end and islanders could now be conscripted into the British army.

As soon as the company officer had finished reading, he offered to answer questions. Artie was the first to speak up.

'So what does it mean?'

'What does it mean, *sir*,' the major corrected. 'You're going to have to remember to call officers "sir", Corporal Bazin.'

'What does it mean, sir?'

'The Royal Guernsey Militia is suspended. All the officers and men – that's us, boys – are now in the Royal Guernsey Light Infantry. *Et bian, mes soudards!* Like it or not, we're going to war.'

CHAPTER 30

'Resign!' Edith shouted. 'Get out now!'

His news stunned her. Such unfairness could destroy her reason. Artie's call-up papers had arrived on Christmas Eve.

He stood with his Militia greatcoat still dripping rain on to the kitchen floor. She had known that something was wrong as soon as he came in. The night was dark but the news darker. She laid her hands on both wet sleeves of his coat, appealing to him.

'Just resign, please.'

'I can't, it's law.' He gently freed himself of her arms. 'They'd throw me in prison, or maybe they'd shoot me.'

Button by button, he started to unfasten the coat, still shocked himself.

'But you're not a soldier, none of you are soldiers. Maybe I can see you, yes, Mr Hero of the Parish, and that Edwin of yours, but what about poor old Pierre Du Port – he's a grower, what kind of soldier is he going to make? And all the others, just boys and farmers? I can hear the Kaiser laughing from here.'

'The law says we're soldiers, so we're soldiers. We all are, all my mates, Dippo too. Like it or not, as our officer said.' He shook off the coat and went back to hang it on the peg by the door. It was an alien thing, this uniform he was wearing, and now it meant so much more than it had a day before. He went back into the kitchen to face her, to defend something indefensible.

'And all our plans!' she said plaintively, 'everything we were going to do.'

'Old Jerry doesn't give two doubles for our plans. Don't that make you angry? Doesn't that make you want to go and fight him?'

She was holding back the tears. Just a glint came to her cheeks. 'When are they taking you away?'

'Not yet. We've got to train, get new uniforms and the like. War's likely to be over by then.'

'Oh yes, when the cows perch in trees.'

He sat on a chair and untied his boots, trying to find a positive note to ease his wife's anxiety.

'Edwin Brown's back from his officer course. He's says with me being Intermediate School, I might get a chance next year.'

'Officer?'

'You'd like being an officer's wife.'

'So long as he's a live officer.'

Christmas could have been a sober affair after the sudden change of events, but Ruth Mullane did not enjoy being sober for long. It was in fact the merriest Christmas La Vallée could remember, even if the jollity was forced. Artie marked the season by growing a moustache. It was part of the regular army uniform, he said, and most of the men either had them already or were busily cultivating the look. Edith found the tickle strange when she kissed him, but noticed how it made Artie look older, taller, wiser and more formidable.

Guernsey's new regiment remained in Guernsey, but many local men were already scattered across the globe fighting for the Empire. So the pattern of 1916 continued into 1917. It was a rare edition of the *Press* that did not carry a short column on a local man who had been promoted or awarded a medal, or was a casualty. The killed were most often from the Vale or St Peter Port, serving with the Irish or the Artillery. Some were sailors, drowned. Others were off in Palestine or other improbable places, falling to illnesses such as malaria and dysentery unheard of at home. Those listed 'missing' in 1916 were now grudgingly being declared dead. Edith found the word deeply upsetting. She imagined a young man lying wounded on a grey empty battlefield with smoke drifting across it and everyone else gone. She imagined his cries for help and how these would fade as he realised he'd been forgotten. The man too would fade, out of sight, then out of memory with no preacher to say a prayer, and no George to carve a tombstone.

For those left behind, or still waiting to see what the year would bring, life on the island changed in subtle ways. Band concerts had a military air, and dances were not deemed frivolous if they were held with a charitable aim; to raise money for comforts of the troops or to help the wounded. Islanders had been used to seeing the garrison or the old Militia around Town, but khaki uniforms were now so much more in evidence. The patriotic posters, the knitting drives, soaring prices, half-empty shops and the women in black reminded everyone that this was total war and that no one would be untouched by it.

With a chill wind in the air, Edith met Artie in Town, where the Albert Café made a handy meeting place. He was in his Militia uniform with its old badges, as the new ones had still not arrived. She was in the uniform of the conductorette, smart and efficient and more beautiful than ever. It was her twentieth birthday and a half-hour at lunch was all the time they could spare.

He pushed a slim package between the teacups and seed cake. It was wrapped in red crêpe paper.

'Oh Artie!' She quickly unwrapped an ivory comb, backed in silver. 'It's lovely!'

'Your hair is so magnificent, I should have bought a gold one.'

'Oh no, this is just perfect.' She played with it in the light, and was about to try it but her hair was bundled up inside the cap and she would have no time to re-arrange it.

The door opened and a young man came through, ushered inside by an older woman who must have been his mother. Her dark coat looked expensive, with a black fur collar. She held the door open for the young man and instructed him which table to take. She talked to him like a mother talks to a child, or in the way some people still talked to George. He moved slowly and uncertainly, yet was easily Artie's age.

People stared. In the centre of his face was a mask held in place with straps. It was skin-coloured but not the colour of skin of anyone Edith knew. The moulded nose had slits through which the poor man could breathe.

He has no nose, Edith thought. She glanced away just as the mother's glare cut sharply through the stares. *He has no nose*. At home he would take off the mask to reveal a gaping hole and a cheek torn away by bullet or shell. Edith felt sick. She grasped Artie's hand tightly.

'Hey! What?'

'I want to go,' she said. 'I need some air.'

'What about your tea?'

'I want to go now.'

Outside she walked briskly back towards the trams.

'Edith?'

'Sorry,' she said, almost in tears. 'Sorry. I just thought… that poor boy.'

'Oh, that's one of the Careys from Town… ah… Thomas. He used to come into the bank. I've seen him around. He's a bit shell-shocked.'

'He's got no nose! How do you live without a nose? How can you ever go out in public without people staring?'

'At least he's alive. He must have been really badly wounded, but the doctor's saved him.'

Edith laid both her hands on Artie's chest. 'That could be you – I had this horrible thought suddenly that it could be you without a face or without legs…'

Artie gripped both her shoulders. 'Stop it! Don't think like that. The boys out there have had some bad luck, that's all. We'll win the war soon, you'll see.'

'I don't want to be a widow, Artie. And I'm not strong enough to do that.' She jerked her head back towards the café. 'Lead you round like a baby, seeing everyone stare. If you had no face, if you were hobbling around like George does, I don't know what I'd do, I don't know how I'd cope.' Panic was in her voice.

'You'd cope fine,' he soothed. 'And it's not going to happen anyway. They're not going to send us out there any time soon; we're still training. It's like you said; we're not real soldiers. Half of the boys can't speak English and them snooty generals don't trust us. It will be months yet before we go, if ever.'

Yet it no longer felt like months. Edith joined what had become a Bazin family ritual, mounting Jack's cart to attend great public occasions. Each time, the combinations changed. Marie was missing now, but grief had been replaced by a respectful memory of the woman she had been. One day in May, Edith sat in the cart with her mother and Jack, with George driving. The men had brushed the stone dust from the cart and laid out old rugs to sit upon. Henry Bazin climbed aboard the cart at the last minute, after making a big show of how he was too busy to watch parades and listen to speeches. He addressed all these grumbles to Jack, loudly, as he still said as little as he could directly to George.

Edith wondered what had passed between them, but Artie wouldn't say. Her new brother was no less strange even for knowing him better.

At Cobo they collected Mrs Patterson, who was wearing a broad beige hat that overshadowed Edith's grass-green hat she had bought from Creasey's, and the straw affair worn by her mother. The coast road was tortuous but the sun was at their backs and the sea a livid shade of blue. Glasshouses glinted in the sun.

The Vale church came into view, perched on a *hougue* beyond what used to be a channel separating the Vale from the rest of Guernsey. To the left was Grande Havre, to the right the Vale pond and on the road in between they nosed into a procession of carts, horses and a regular crush of people on foot heading north. Motor buses were crowded beyond capacity and groaned forward slowly in the jam. L'Ancresse Common was a dune-scape of rough grass and furze breaks which had proved to be the perfect place for exercising Guernsey's regiment. Trench lines had been dug for practice, then stormed for practice. The forgiving sand of the Vale stood in for the poisoned mud of Passchendaele.

It seemed most of the island had turned out. Never before had Edith seen so many people. A fair slice of the menfolk was assembled in khaki, ranks upon ranks of them, well over a thousand. The dignitaries were dressed for the occasion; officers in service uniform, jurats in purple robes, clergy and deputies in black. The band played and crowds craned their necks to watch. The RGLI was to receive its colours, newly sewn by the gentlewomen of the island. Edith tried to see past the old men and the other ladies' hats to see Artie, and there he was! Slightly taller than most of his comrades, he stood proud and straight with a corporal's stripes on his sleeves. If only war could be won by marching and parades, it would be such a splendid business. She would follow the colours anywhere if this was all that soldiering entailed.

On the day of the parade, Artie truly felt taller than a normal man. It was now his personal mission to save Guernsey, the king and the Empire from Teutonic domination. All his mates were with him, tough quarrymen and smart bankers. The pick of the men from the best island in the world. No foe could stand against this Common-full of heroes.

Edith the conductorette continued to fill the shoes of some man who might or might not ever return from the war. Tired after a long day on her feet, up and down, collecting fares, calling out the halts, she stepped down from the tram. After this she would still have to walk home, there being no tramline to the Castel. From time to time people commented that a married woman ought to be at home, making the house ready for when her husband returned from work, but the world was not what it had been at the start of 1914 and never would be again. Artie would be at Fort George with the battalion, but George and the old men were waiting for her. Not that Henry was truly old, but since his wife had died he had taken on the air of a man whose best years were behind him. His determination not to talk to George was turning into a habit of not talking to anyone. Jack, by contrast, was acting like a rooster in spring, strutting down to that Mrs Patterson's at any opportunity.

Thank God for Mother. Edith was surprised to be thinking that. Ruth Mullane cooked and cleaned as she ever did, earning her keep in the side-by-side Bazin household. Right now she would be seeing to the fire and cooking up the supper. Edith smiled as she trudged uphill. It would be like this to have servants, she mused. Fire ready, meal ready, table set.

One day there might be a baby, but not yet. Not until the war was over and they were set up, perhaps when she was twenty-three. Their agreement stuck and Artie had the sense to play the game too. Ruth Mullane could be shamelessly frank after a couple of gins and had taught her daughter a thing or two about avoiding babies.

As usual the driver had let Edith alight at the terminus rather than go back to the tram sheds when the tram went off service. She walked Fountain Street, aiming for Trinity Square, followed by the steady uphill trudge of Victoria Road. Coming the other way from the back of the Markets were two figures. It was only early evening, yet a man and a woman were swaying drunkenly, arms locked as if to support each other.

One was a sailor – a French sailor, quite short and round. Draped around him was a woman with frizzy hair. The woman glanced Edith's way, looked down, scowling, and then brought her head up with a broad smile.

'Hello,' she said cheerily.

An unmistakeable tang of alcohol shot out with the words. 'Mother!'

'Edith, dear. This is my friend Marcel.'

Marcel the sailor released her mother. His face was ruddy and his moustache hid most of his mouth. His accent was heavy, even heavier than that of people from Torteval. 'Ruthie, who this beautiful woman?'

'This is my Edith,' she said proudly. 'My daughter.'

'Don't daughter me!' Edith snapped. 'Why aren't you at home, looking after the men?'

'Aw, Artie's on duty.'

'And George? And Henry? And Jack?'

She waved a hand. 'Oh, men, they'll be all right. They'll probably go to the pub, have a pie, them.'

'And how many pubs have you been to?'

Her mother's manner changed instantly. 'That's none of your business, my girl! And don't get preachy like your aunt. You like a drink when it suits you.'

'Not at six o'clock in the evening.' She glanced at Marcel. 'And I don't pick up sailors. My God, that's original isn't it?'

'Edith!'

The conductorette stepped out into the roadway and strode past her mother. She shook off a grab at her arm.

'I'll tell the men you won't be back.'

'You'll do nothing of the sort!'

Tears in her eyes, Edith kept striding, striding away.

'Edith!'

She regretted ever having agreed to her mother moving into La Vallée. It had been a stupid idea, stupid and soft. For the next half-hour she seethed as she climbed out of Town, strode down the road called the Rohais, then up past the church and down again to the west. It began to rain, a thin rain that worked its way inside her clothes by stealth.

George was standing in the kitchen. Having lit the fire he was now busy making a mess on the sideboard with a knife and an onion.

'Wharro, Edith.'

'I'll do that, George,' she said curtly.

He stepped aside. 'Where's your mother? We was worried.'

Edith went back into the hall to hang up her coat without

answering, and then came back and pulled open the pantry door. 'Corned beef and potatoes?' she asked, partly to herself.

'I chopped an onion.'

'That's a start.'

'But your mother…'

'Where's Jack?'

'Mrs Patterson's for supper.'

'Your father?'

'Pub.'

'Wish I was in the bloney pub. So it's just me and you again, eh?'

'Yes. Still it's not so bad,' he said brightly.

She gripped a potato in her hand as if it was a bayonet aiming to slit his throat. 'Not so bad? How can things get worse, George? Tell me.'

'Was a nice day till it rained.'

With a howl of rage she threw the potato at him. It was not well aimed and he ducked easily.

'Edith!'

'Go into the parlour, sit down, read the paper and I'll make supper. I'll get changed then I'll start.'

'I can help.'

'Go!'

Ruth Mullane came home without ceremony. She slipped quietly into La Vallée just before midnight, and the next morning set about life as it nothing had changed. Edith saw her slip into the scullery with a basket of washing. Henry Bazin saw her too – striding across the yard, unlit pipe in his hand. Edith saw the rage on his face and made to follow him.

'My wife was right about you,' Henry's voice boomed from the scullery. 'You move in here, making like it was your home. Lording it. Eating our food…'

'I do my bit.'

'You're not a shadow of what my wife was. Look at this place.'

'Well, that's Edith. She's the mistress of the house now, isn't she?'

On cue Edith reached the door, finding it blocked by the angry quarryman.

'Blame your own daughter, would you?'

'I've got things to do.' Her mother tried to push past him and escape from that tiny room. 'Let me be!'

'Henry,' Edith cautioned.

'The whole parish knows her antics,' he said. 'French sailors, is that what you want for your mother?'

Ruth butted in, unwisely. 'You speak French, you all speak French out here.'

'But we're not French, and we're decent people.'

'Oh yes, oh yes. What about your brother carrying on with that widow?'

'Nothing improper in that. They're not drunk all the time.'

'You can talk, Henry Bazin! How many nights a week are you down the Cobo? How can we keep house and home together when it all goes on Vimiera cider and Randall's ale?'

He raised his hand.

She shrank back. 'You wouldn't!'

'Henry!' Edith warned.

Henry lowered his arm and took a step back. 'No,' he said. 'I wouldn't soil my hand.' He stepped outside and allowed Edith space to slip into the scullery.

'You're back then?' Edith challenged.

Her mother shrugged.

'Until the pubs open,' Henry growled, then walked away.

'Well?' Roles were reversed and daughter was scolding mother.

'Marcel only came here for a month,' Ruth Mullane began her defence. 'He's helping with the seaplanes, him. He's a petty officer.'

'Whatever that is. Is that good?'

Ruth rubbed her hands together anxiously. 'Well,' she said. 'The good news for you and the brute Bazin is that you don't have to worry about me any more. Marcel's asked me to go with him.'

'To where?'

'To, to… well, I can't remember the name, but it's that navy place in France. It's that big base, where Marcel is based.'

'Are you getting married?'

'We might.'

'So you're his mistress? Or are you his whore?'

She expected rage from her mother but instead heard only a desperate panting. The rubbing hands turned to wringing hands. '*Chière*, don't think badly of me.'

'Ha!'

'It's for the best. Them Bazins don't want me here. That one'd have beat me if you hadn't come by. He's still pining for his wife and no other woman is ever going to be good enough for this house. You remember those words – it will be you next.'

'So you're just leaving?'

'In five days.'

'Mother – it will end horribly.'

'Why should it?'

'Because it always does.'

'This time is different.'

'But you're not different. You can move to this big French base, but you will still be you. And you can't even speak French.'

'I can a bit. *Un petit peu*. It's not so different to how they speak down in Torteval.'

'Well, have a *très* jolly *bon* time. And don't forget there's a little war going on over there. It's been in the papers, in case you were too drunk to notice.'

'*Chière!*'

Edith turned and made back to the house. She would turn her back on her mother, not the other way around.

As things turned out, Marcel the French petty officer was as good as his word, despite being French and despite Ruth Mullane's long history of poor judgement. After five days of silence punctuated by arguments, Ruth Mullane left La Vallée on a cart carrying a suitcase and a valise. Edith came to the front gate and made a show of waving the pair off. She fully expected her mother to be back within a week, weeping and contrite and completely penniless, if not stricken with some horrible disease and carrying a bastard. At first she was angry, then relieved, but once the cart had vanished behind the trees she felt alone. For years and years she had wanted to be free of her mother; now it was a reality the thought frightened her.

'True mistress of the house now, Edith,' said Jack, with a wink.

'Edith will do grand,' said George, beaming.

Henry was not there to add extra weight to her burden. Barely twenty years old, she had four fully grown men expecting her to mother them.

'We'll get a girl in,' she declared. 'Adèle's sister Alice is looking for work. We'll pay her half what I get paid on the trams. You can all chip in.'

Jack was going to question her but she forestalled him. 'I'm Artie's wife, I'm not your domestic.'

CHAPTER 31

After the parade at L'Ancresse it was back to the monotony of duty for Corporal Bazin; watching for an enemy that might never come, waiting for an order that felt more likely each day. Of course, his brother had tried to volunteer for the RGLI, but even after all the slaughter of the Somme and the struggle for little Guernsey to field an entire regiment, the king would only have fit men. A company of quarrymen had also gone out to support the army, but if the whole parish was emptied brother George would be the last to be called.

Artie was still granted hours and whole days free to spend with his family, and nights to see Edith, but few chances remained for him to be that all-knowing big brother. He suggested George should come down to the harbour, where the French were building a seaplane base. Out on the castle emplacement, the model yacht pond had been drained, and in its place a skeleton of wood was arising. Artie stood by in his new uniform with the Light Infantry bugle badge and GUERNSEY shoulder title, all matter-of-fact as he pointed out the seaplanes to his brother. He was still the teacher, and George still the willing pupil.

Two of the seaplanes were moored in the harbour. Another was out in the Russell, wallowing in front of Jethou. The seaplanes were boat-like things, with a pair of wings stacked on top held up by struts and braced by a lattice of wires, much like you would rig a sailing ship.

'I saw one flying, last year,' said George. 'And more since, but further out to sea.'

'They hunt submarines,' explained Artie.

'Have we got flying boats like this? The British?'

'Plenty; there was one here a few weeks back.'

'And the Germans too?'

'Yes, bad luck. And they've got the Red Baron,' Artie growled. 'The terror of the skies.'

'I've heard about him,' George said. 'He paints his aeroplane red.'

'So everyone can see him coming, and everyone knows it's him. Like a knight of old painting his shield,' Artie said, injecting romance when he knew that truly there was none.

'I'd like to fly,' said George.

'Not me!' said Artie. 'Not with the Red Baron about. I don't want to fight in the sky, up on me own. Better to be on the ground, with all my mates around me.'

Herm and Jethou lay anchored across the Little Russell. To the south it was just clear enough to see Jersey, and on the eastern horizon lay France. Keep walking east from that shore and sooner or later you would find a war.

'Artie, could you kill a German?'

'Course, easy.'

'No, but really kill him if he was standing just over there? And what if you shoot him and he's not quite dead and he's badly hurt?'

'Then we finish him with the bayonet.' Artie made a thrust. 'Yah!'

'But if he was only slightly hurt, like shot in the arm up here. Would you just let him run away, or take him prisoner? Because he'll have a brother at home like me, and a *mémaen* and maybe a sweetheart or a wife…'

'George, what is all this?'

'Germany is a long way from Guernsey. Why go to fight in France? The Germans are never going to come here.'

'Ah,' said Artie. 'But if they capture France, then that there land will be German.' He pointed to the left of Sark to the barely visible line on the horizon. 'Then Guernsey is next, and you'll have to learn to speak German as well as English and the Good French. And we'll all be eating sausages.'

'I like sausages.'

'Me too, but that's not the point. I've got to go to France, if they order me to. Likely they'd shoot me if I said no. Anyhow, I want to see it. This is all I know. We might go to Palestine, or Turkey, or somewhere else.' He jerked a thumb back over the Town. 'I've never been anywhere.'

'You've been to Jersey.'

Artie glanced briefly at the pencil smudge off to the south-east. 'It's not so different from here – except it's full of *crapauds*. There's a town and a harbour and a castle... and *crapauds*.'

'And you've been to Sark.'

'No, it was Herm. And Crevichon, of course.' The conical stub of rock was just distinguishable between Jethou and Herm. 'Remember when we went out with Uncle Jack before the war, when he went to see if there was any stone worth having?'

That was the furthest George had travelled.

'You remember – Jack told us how they made St Paul's Cathedral in London out of Crevichon granite?'

'Yes – it must have been much bigger before that,' George observed. 'And does that Prussian prince still live to Herm?'

'Who, Prince Blucher von something? He went back to Germany, him, when the war started. Then he died even – it was in the *Press*. Lucky, else I might have had to shoot him one day.'

Artie realised what he had said. One day, he could be standing on this very same spot after the war was over. George would ask how it was, and Artie as usual would tell his stories. But what if he did kill a German, what would it be like? How would he feel with another man's blood on his bayonet, or to see one cut down by his Lewis gun? Or a whole troop of them, in a line, falling one by one? There were Quakers refusing to fight and being called cowards, but they claimed they had a moral objection to killing and the Bible said it was wrong. Yet the preacher at church said God was on our side, so how could killing Germans be wrong? A lot of the boys had shared whispered worries between the bravado, but sentiment was being trained out of them. Artie would kill when he needed to, but then the killer would need to come home, cuddle his wife, eat with his family and become a normal person again. There might be some stories he could never tell anyone.

In the morning that came too soon, Artie lay with his head snug in the valley between his wife's breasts. Raising it slightly he kissed the closest flesh, then snuggled back. The air was so hot they hardly needed a sheet, let alone a blanket.

'I'm going to miss this,' she said.

'Being with me?'

'Of course, silly. But I'll miss this especially. I like to cuddle up close. Don't think I'm slutty, I just love being this close to you.'

She squeezed his shoulders, and then slid one hand down and squeezed a buttock too.

'You're a prize wife.'

'So you should exhibit me at the summer show, with all the prize Guernseys. If you win a rosette, you could pin it to my ear.'

'I didn't mean that! You're just the best.'

'The best deserves the best. You know when I said I wanted to get away, and you said I needed somewhere to go?' she said.

'Mm?'

'Well it's here, with you. This is where I want to be.'

'See, Guernsey's not that bad.'

'No, no, in bed, with you, in our home. Doesn't matter where in the world that actually is. But when you're done soldiering, promise we'll go to London and you'll get one of those bank jobs.'

'We will too.' Artie had surrendered to the inevitable. 'Mr Jepson is going to write a letter for me, and Edwin Brown says he'll get his father to write one, even.'

'See, friends in high places. We're going somewhere.'

'*Ouai*, France.'

He pulled himself upright, accompanied by a theatrical groan. Mr and Mrs Bazin had spent the night pretending that the order had not come, that they would continue living their quiet lives untroubled by the war.

'It can't be that time,' she said.

'It's well past that time.'

'I never got you breakfast.'

He kissed her. 'There's things better than breakfast.'

Once Archie had gone, Edith cried. Allowing herself that weakness for half an hour, she cleaned up her face, dressed, and went to organise the remaining men.

Henry Bazin, George, Jack and Edith found themselves a good position on the sea wall, overlooking the quayside on the White Rock. A crowd soon grew around them, come to see the RGLI embark for England. At the head of the battalion came the band – even from the White Rock it could be heard making its way through Town. Crowds lined the route all the way down Fountain Street, all along the waterfront, and all along the quayside to where the steamer waited.

At last they came, playing 'The Light Horseman'. Heading the parade was Joey the donkey, the regiment's mascot dressed up in an embroidered blanket of Guernsey green. Stubborn old Guernsey had to have a donkey for its mascot: small, grey and unassuming, faithful and plodding, hardy and tough, slow to anger but ready with that vicious kick when its patience snapped. Behind the band strode the officers and the standards, and then the troops in khaki marching in fours. George pinched his eyes to spy Artie, but Edith saw him first.

'Artie!' she waved frantically, but if he glanced her way he kept his head straight to the front. He was marching smartly to the tune, right arm swinging, left arm carrying a rifle at the slope. Six or seven hundred of Guernsey's finest young men came to the halt by command.

Tears rolled down Edith's cheeks. Cheer, cry, wave, be proud, be sad, be brave; so much came at once she felt like she would burst.

George's glasses had misted. For some reason he was wearing his old ones. Beside him, Henry Bazin had a glint of wetness in his own eyes. All along the waterfront, pride mixed with fear.

Commands were issued, the soldiers broke ranks and filed up the gangplank on to the ship. Then came the wait as the steamer prepared to leave. The crowd became restless, wanting the tension to be over, wanting the excuse to give one last cheer. Energy began to seep away, enthusiasm ebbed. Children began to wail. One or two families started to walk back towards the shore.

'There's Artie!' Edith said. She had clutched a white

lace handkerchief ready for the moment, so now waved it frantically. 'Artie! Artie Bazin!'

A distant figure in muddy brown waved. All the men were waving, but this waving arm was special. At that moment the ship rumbled into life, its cables were cast off and it began to move sluggishly into the harbour pool. Belching black smoke it carefully made the turn in front of the castle so that it was pointing seaward. Slowly gaining speed it headed straight between the pier heads, its bow pointing to France.

The crowd roared. Cheers went up: hip-hip-hooray. Flags, hats and hankies waved. Men yelled encouragements, women screamed best wishes and children sat on the shoulders of their grandfathers. A generation vanished over the horizon, to England, then to war.

CHAPTER 32

Half the men on the *SS Lydia* had never left the island and many spoke no English at all. Artie was surrounded by this great khaki crush, hearing both proper English and Guernsey English, Guernesiais, the Good French and mixtures of one peppered with another. True Guernseymen mixed with the English, the Irish and the half-French who called the island home. It was hard to believe this pack of ordinary men would one day be asked to fight.

Artie had never been on a steam train before, and neither had Pierre Du Port. Sitting opposite Artie in the third-class carriage, the grower who was now a machine-gunner had a fixed grin on his broad face. England was big and green, with lots of trees. Guernsey doesn't have proper woods of the kind described in children's tales, just little clumps of trees in places it is too awkward to farm. Even down The Forest there was no forest. Over the shoulder titles of his colleagues, through the thick blue cigarette smoke, Artie glimpsed the country they had come to fight for.

London was one of those places that existed vividly in his imagination before he saw the reality. A vast railway station was full of smoke and noise and more activity than Artie had ever seen. Its arched glass roof was like a cathedral and the sound and bustle overwhelming. The battalion formed up in the street outside, with London bobbies keeping the carts and motor taxis clear. Tall buildings made the streets feel like ravines, reducing the sky to a slit. Artie took his place in the

214

ranks – the taller men were always in the right-hand file to make a better show. At the order they were off and the Royal Guernsey Light Infantry marched through the capital. This was turning into an awfully big adventure.

Edith's adventure was the tram ride north, through the industrial wasteland between St Peter Port and St Sampson. The great quarry yawned on one side of the track while a stone-breakers' yard lay on the other. Most of the quarries were quiet now, with the men away and the market for stone vanished. At some point in time, she reasoned, all the granite would be gone anyway and the island would be just holes and piles of waste. The likes of Artie's father would have no job and what then? Tomatoes perhaps would be the future, if there was enough land between the holes still to grow them once the quarrymen were done.

When she returned at the end of her run, there was a great to-do at the tram terminus in Town. A little girl had been run over by the Number Eight at the Salerie and very badly hurt. Violet, the conductorette on board, had been sent home in a state of tears. At first, rumour said that both the girl's legs had been sliced off, but later all heard that she was dead. Edith took a drink with the other tram girls at the end of that day. Violet joined them later, drinking brandy fast and smoking Muratti cigarettes. Her Number Eight had become a killing machine, joining the dreadnoughts and the Zeppelins and these new 'tanks' the paper was talking about.

Both George and Henry frowned at her when she came home, long after dark, less steady and sober than was truly respectable. She sensed their disapproval and did not pause to explain or seek pardon. They would not understand.

Nobody mentioned it the next day, and she avoided looking

the men straight in the eye until it was clear the matter would be left to rest. This episode was exceptional and they must know it, but her mother had set a precedent and she took care not to repeat it. Most weeks, Edith's distraction was visiting the library, so she could fill her lonely hours at La Vallée by reading. For a while she became Jane Eyre or Bathsheba Everdene, finding romance and ultimate redemption.

George showed no great interest in books, unless they had maps or pictures of great buildings in them. He was one for the newspapers or magazines that talked about the mechanical wonders of the world. One evening he sat with Edith, one either side of an unlit fire, George hunting through the war news in the paper.

'America has joined us now,' he said.

'Yes,' she replied, not looking up. She was seated in Marie Bazin's old rocker, sunk into one of her thick novels.

'I looked at the map book – America's a huge country compared to Germany and they must have a massive army,' he said. 'It's only a matter of time before we'll win now, and Artie will be home again.'

All the men had turned into war experts by now. Surely, if all those experts who understood the maps and the politics and the strategy met together they would be able to end the insanity. Perhaps nobody had a vision beyond something called victory.

Edith raised her eyes from her book. 'Do you still have dreams, George? About the pretty girl?'

'No. That was back when I was little. And they weren't rightly dreams. I figure it was just my glasses, the old ones. I chipped them and afterwards there was a glint in the glass what looked like a woman. That's all it was. I made it a game, I guess.'

'Because all the other girls called you names and chased you?'

'Could be.'

'I'm glad you don't see her any more.'

'So am I.'

'I wouldn't want to think we're being spied on by some strange woman.'

'No.'

'I never believed these stories, the old wives' tales,' she said. 'The sort of nonsense my mother used to tell me, about *pouques* casting spells and *varioufs* howling at the moon.'

They talked for some time, about things past and things that might be. America had joined the allies and the war would be won and George no longer glimpsed the raven-haired woman who foresaw doom. He told Edith that he was happy she was with him at La Vallée, and for once she found it comforting.

Kent was a homely county, a bigger version of St Andrew's parish, with rolling hills, fields of garden crops, small farms and churches. It was a sunny place, with less breeze than the Castel, and was often hot and still in the afternoons. The 1st (Service) Battalion RGLI drilled at an army camp somewhere near Canterbury, which was a cathedral city. It was not as huge as London, but still on a different scale to anything Artie had known.

Training was by sections, then platoons, then whole companies. It needed two men to carry a Lewis gun for any great time, and more to lug its ammunition. Modern technology was both heavy and complicated, so Artie and Pierre had been natural choices to form the core of the machine-gun section. As they trained, the officer repeatedly told the other men how they had to protect the gunners and keep them supplied with ammunition. Artie learned his role by heart, stripping, cleaning and un-jamming the gun until he could do it in the dark, in the rain and after a long run up a slope.

'Corporal Bazin!' Lieutenant Warry called him over and asked him to sit on an ammunition crate. Warry was still short of thirty, a lean, educated man.

'Sir?'

'What did you do back home? Office work, wasn't it?'

'Bank clerk, sir.'

'Yes, yes, I think you served me once.'

'I did too, sir, a few times. Your family are growers, aren't they?'

'Fruit exporters actually, but they're not exporting much fruit these days, sadly. Now, you were at the Intermediate School? Do you have good certificates?'

'Good enough for the bank. I thought about being a teacher one day, but the bank is a good place to start off. My Edith and me are thinking we might move to London after the war, so I could work in one of the City banks.'

'You'd get a better position if you were an officer.'

'Officer?' Artie had shared this fantasy with his wife, but was surprised by the suddenness of the proposal.

'Look, Bazin, when anything is going on with the lads, you're at the centre of it. One of my fellow officers referred to you as being the ringleader, but in fact I think you're simply a leader. What the military textbooks call "a natural leader".'

Artie had seldom thought of himself that way, but after a moment's reflection realised it was true.

'Now, the British Army is a bit "who your father knows" and "what school did you go to", but all that's falling away with the war. Good officers are what they need, not Eton schoolboys who know their Homer. And after the Somme and Passchendaele they're running out of Eton schoolboys. So, can I put your name forward for officer training?'

'Yes, sir!'

'It won't happen straight away of course. We've got officers coming out of our ears at the moment – local men are transferring in from other regiments just to be with us. You'll have to wait until after we've been in the field for a while, so they know you've seen the elephant.'

'Elephant?'

'Sorry, it's an old saying... Well, don't worry. Christmas, perhaps. We'll bring out more boys from the Second Battalion, then send you back to Fort George for training in exchange.'

Christmas! The July sun beat down and winter seemed so far away, but last Christmas he had only just joined the army, and the Christmas before that he was newly married. Those months had passed in a rush.

'Our Edith will be proud.'

'I bet she will. I'll start the paperwork moving.'

Tourists love to visit islands, but islanders by and large have a twitch to get away. It is not the leaving that is so special, but the return. To come back, after seeing the wide world and braving adventures. To bring back treasure, to boast and tell tales. A small, comforting place called home awaits the traveller when his travelling is done. So it had been with Gràn'père Bazin, and now it was with his grandson.

The family received Artie's letter only the day before he arrived home on the mailboat. The Guernseys were given leave in small groups and his turn came at the beginning of September. Despite an early bout of bad weather, the autumn gales proper were still a couple of weeks away so he made a good crossing.

Before the boat docked, he could see the familiar group by the familiar cart. Artie strode down the gangplank, already a conquering hero. His face had turned as brown as if he were a quarryman, not a banker. He gave Edith a hug, then his father, then George.

'Where are your stripes?' his wife asked.

'Ah,' he said.

'They're not making you an officer already?'

'No – not yet.'

'So, what about your stripes?'

'Aw, lost them for a bit. These drunk Engineers made fun of our boys in the pub. Said we couldn't talk proper English.'

'Oh, so you started a fight?'

'They started it – we finished it.'

'As if there's not enough Germans out there?'

He shrugged. 'Lieutenant Warry said he respected me "for standing up for the regimental honour", but then he takes my stripes just to make an example of me. I'll get them back when we go to France.'

Her face was so pale, yet she lost what colour she had. 'When's that?'

'Dunno.'

He had a fairly good idea, but was not going to share it. Artie helped Edith up into the cart. He tipped his cap to Mrs Patterson, and climbed up beside his wife.

'So no fighting yet, Artie?' Jack called back as the cart rumbled forward.

'No, we're just at this big camp in Kent. Just training and marching. I don't think the generals think we're up to it. We're just Militia, peasants who can't speak the king's English.'

'Well that's good,' Edith said.

He grinned at her, glancing over her shoulder at the harbour cranes, the wide pool and the squat castle. For all his yearning for adventure, it was good to be back. Edith looked prettier than ever, her face peeking from beneath the white bonnet. A worry was crossing her face.

'I bet you've lost your chance of being an officer,' she huffed.

'No, Lieutenant Warry put the papers in before we had that set-to. I just hope no one tells the nobs about the scrap.'

'You need to grow up, Arthur Bazin! It would be good if you were an officer. I could look those snotty women in Town in the eye.'

'Pay's good too,' he said ruefully. 'I could buy you some new things. And after the war, well, I'll have learned something more useful than how to fire a machine gun. We will go to London, just like you want to. We marched right through the city, even. You should see it, Edith – shops and cafés and theatres. And George, the buildings – they're great big things with carvings and writing way up high. If you lived in London, you'd have work forever.'

George and Jack part-turned to hear what the adventurer was saying. He told them all about the capital and the parade through the city, as quaint, sleepy Guernsey passed them by.

Everything is so small, Artie thought. For all his talk of moving to London, *I like small.*

A week's leave passed quicker than any normal week. At the harvest festival, the Castel church was packed with parishioners and troops on leave, and those destined to stay behind. Some professor from England read the lesson based on 2 Corinthians 8:15 whereby, 'He that gathered much had nothing over and he that gathered little had no lack'. It was time for the reaping, and for giving away what you treasured.

Edith said she would not come to the White Rock to wave Artie away at the end of a week that was ever so short. She had done that once, and too many parades and too many farewells must rub in the truth too deep. So she said farewell quietly after rising early to make Artie's breakfast. She leaned close and kissed him. She said something about his moustache tickling. He hugged her tight, and then kissed her again. Letting go slowly, he picked up his kitbag and went out of the door.

George was waiting outside. Their father and Jack had said their farewells over breakfast. From the end of the path, Artie gave a wave to Edith, who was half-hidden in the dark of the hall. She turned away before she closed the door.

The brothers walked at George's pace to the end of the lane. 'Look after her, George.'

'I will.'

'Père's not as fit as he was. The quarrying fair wore him down, but not having any quarrying is wearing him down more. And losing Mémaen just drained him. Jack's much the tougher of the two, even though he's older. So, look after them, you.'

'I will.'

'I'm going to try to write. I don't know how many letters they will let me have if we go to France, or what I'll be allowed to write about, so I'll send them all to Edith at first. She can read you the interesting bits. I never saw myself as much of a writer but there's not a lot else to do once you're in camp.'

'Wish I was coming with you.'

'I wish you were too. Brothers should stick together.'

Pierre Du Port was waiting at the end of the lane, dressed

identically to Artie in khaki greatcoat and flat cap with kitbag by his side. Artie had new brothers now.

George stopped. 'Get a Hun for me.'

'I'll bring you back a spiked helmet as a souvenir.'

'Yes, do.'

'À *la perchoïne*.'

'À *la perchoïne*!'

Artie felt his throat completely dry up. He slapped George on the shoulder and turned away.

CHAPTER 33

By ship, and now by cattle truck, the Guernseys drew closer to the war. Artie looked through the gaps between slats of the wooden carriage as it made its way across France. *It's so huge,* he thought. *Too huge for us.* For a night and a day he watched the scene pass by as pages flicked in a picture book. Fields, farms, woods, distant church spires and country lanes not so different to those back home. The world must be an enormous place if this was just one part of France, and his island seemed a terribly tiny dot compared to all this space. A man could even be frightened of so much space.

It rained in Belgium, and it seemed to rain all the time. Not a fresh rain that comes from the west over Vazon, but a vertical, soul-drowning cold rain. Army tents were little comfort, beset on all sides by mud and the threat of being washed away. Artie thought he heard distant thunder over the rain. It came and went, this thunder from the east. Only when he heard it again on the second day in camp did he realise that this was the sound of war.

One day ran into the next. When the rain eased it was replaced by a new and unexpected nuisance – German aeroplanes. A dull thud followed by a longer rumble, echoed from the far side of the camp, closely chased by another. Dynamite was used in the quarries back home to loosen the stone, so Artie had long known the sound of an explosion. He came from his tent, saw something from the corner of his eye and just caught sight of an aeroplane high above him before it turned and vanished into a cloud. The Guernsey boys were tense for an hour, then after a second bloodless attack from the sky they shrugged it away.

Corporal Bazin was given his stripes back. His war began by repairing roads and ditches amid a landscape ruined by battle. He gazed out across fields swept by the tide of war. When that tide had receded, it left pools of water, churned earth and rusted wire. No building still stood that could be called a building, and every tree had lost its branches, reduced to ghostly spikes sticking from the mud. No birds sang and only opportunist weeds gave any hint that this had once been farmland. For all the old soldiers' tales of trenches and mud he had heard before reaching the front, this blasted shell-scape was shocking to behold.

Roads were important, said the officers. The Germans were some miles to the east, yet liked to fire shells at this road to harass those who dared travel along it, and ultimately to pound it into un-crossable mush no different from the ground to either side. The Guernseys found the latest shell holes and filled them with dirt and gravel, so the road would remain worthy of that name for another day.

A dull 'crump' brought work to a stop. The whole platoon watched a spout of brown rise from the ground one or two hundred yards away then watched it fall back. A faint shock of air wafted over them, little more dramatic than a sudden squally breeze. One minute later came another, off to the right. German gunners were groping for that road, blindly but methodically, using maps and rulers and basic maths. After the third shell had missed its mark by a good quarter-mile, work resumed but it was not as carefree as before. This lazy shelling stopped after a while, but everyone knew it would start again in time. All the men had played crown and anchor, seen wages lost in unfair runs of bad luck and watched others rake in piles of money after a single bold gamble. Now they played a different game. The laws of chance said that sooner or later the distant gunners would strike the road and men would be hurt. Although the true fighting had not even begun, it was only a few days before Major Davey was killed by a shell.

Day by day, the mood slipped. There was nothing heroic about being killed clearing out *douits* or filling in potholes. And the weather was always wrong over here – too hot, too cold or too wet. Woollen uniforms were soaked by the rain, over-hot when the sun came out, and seemed to let the wind blow straight through. Artie and a dozen men continued to work on the road, straight as La Route Militaire up the Vale, but so cut about by shell craters, ruts and potholes that it was hard to see where the road ended and the ruined countryside began. Filling holes did not feel like soldiering, and the major's death touched them all.

Graves lay by the roadside, in ones and twos and in dozens. As he worked, Artie noticed a fresh rectangular pit had been dug a few yards to the left of the road. A wagon lumbered from the front line fairly packed with khaki bundles. Hands trailed from a heap in the back of the wagon and Artie turned away from the sight. Four men took down the bodies as if they were no more than sacks of potatoes and dropped them into a pit side by side, one followed by another. Artie expected prayers and a bugle after the earth was thrown back, but there were none. The grave party simply lit cigarettes when their job was done and then moved back to their cart with hunched shoulders – bored, as if they did this often. This was no war of scarlet and glory; it was not Sir Isaac Brock storming the Queenston Heights, nor John Gaspard Le Marchant charging at the head of his dragoons. It was a war of holes – holes to fill, holes to hide in, holes to attack, holes to be buried in. And everything was brown.

At the end of another tiring afternoon of labouring, he stood with Pierre Du Port and Lieutenant Warry at the edge of the road they had returned to usefulness. A pair of English officers had stopped to talk to three of the Guernseys some way down the road. They pressed on towards the lieutenant. Both men wore red armbands and sported red bands around their hats. One was a major.

'Are you the Guernsey lot?' he asked as Lieutenant Warry saluted.

'Yes, sir.'

'What are those men back there jabbering at? What language are they speaking?'

'Guernsey French, the language of our Norman forefathers,' Warry said in his crisp, educated English.

'What? Good God, how are we supposed to win a war with men who can't speak English?' He turned sharply to Artie. 'Do you speak English?'

Deliberately Artie said '*Chiq tu dis?*'

The major's moustache twitched.

'Good God.' He turned to Warry again. 'Where's your battalion headquarters?'

Warry told him and the two Englishmen stomped off.

Lieutenant Warry eyed Artie. 'That was an interesting defence of an impossible position, Bazin.'

'Who does he think he is, Lieutenant?'

'Headquarters staff. He'll be tucked up safe in a nice chateau tonight. It's not like the old days when generals led from the front. I felt like saying "we bleed just like you Englishmen", but then my mother is English and we've enough with the Germans on our plate to start fighting 1066 all over again.'

Soon there was talk that the real fighting was about to begin. Men of the RGLI were taken by train from Belgium into France to a new camp. Lieutenant Warry changed his officer's kit for the equipment of a private and began to carry a rifle. Old sweats had told him this was the best way to avoid being singled out by a sniper. It was learn fast or die, the veterans said, so the newcomers learned as fast as they could. There was no more digging of ditches; it was march, train, run, shoot, and follow orders – always orders. At least there was sport most afternoons and Artie liked his football.

The platoon marched to a field well behind the reserve lines, and was told to break ranks and rest while the officers talked. Shielded from eyes in the air by a line of trees were six huge green metal rhomboid boxes, each the size of a shed, and each with a number and name painted on the side. All the numbers and all the names began with the letter C. Pierre Du Port and Artie had a love of machinery, so they strolled across and tapped the solid metal.

'Water tanks,' Pierre said. 'That's what I heard they were.'

'It's a land-ship,' said Artie. 'It's got an engine, like a train or a motor bus. Look, it's got cannons.'

He stroked the tube projecting from a sponson on the side of the vehicle. Next he spotted the barrel of a Lewis gun projecting from the back of the sponson.

'And machine guns. *Cor*, it's like a fort. It's a battleship on land, for sure.'

'Oi!' called a voice.

The man was clad in brown overalls and his face and hands were blackened.

'Don't touch Cynthia.'

'Is this a land-ship?' Artie asked.

'Tank.'

'Said they was tanks,' Pierre chipped in.

'And they're going to smash the Huns,' said the tank man, grease-smeared and smelling of oil. 'We don't have to worry about bullets and machine guns.' He slapped the metal. 'We pass through barbed wire like it was only bits of string.'

'Six of these will be really handy,' said Pierre.

'Six? We've got hundreds, mate. Trains full coming up every night. This is going to win the war, lads. You sound like you're from down the west. Cornwall? Somerset?'

'Guernsey – Royal Guernsey Light Infantry.'

The tank man screwed up his chin, as if he'd never heard of Guernsey. 'Well, mates, after we go in, you just follow on behind and take the prisoners. If there's any left to take.'

Artie allowed himself a smile. Maybe he had joined this war at the right time. Maybe the British were on the point of final victory. Nothing could stand against such a monster.

Artie backed off. 'Best of luck with your tanks.'

'Best of luck, Guernseys. See you up the Hindenburg Line.'

Diex Aïe. Artie pondered the regimental motto for a moment. Maybe God was truly helping them now.

CHAPTER 34

The cat was out of the bag, as the saying went. No announcement was made that the RGLI had shipped to Flanders, but soon it was a secret to no one. Major Davey had been killed in the middle of October. George read the story aloud from the paper when he was with Edith in the parlour of the Big House. Edith was listening but saying nothing, knitting industriously at the other side of the fireplace. A shiver went through him. The Guernseys must really be in danger if such a senior officer could be killed, just like that. So much for people saying they would never be allowed to do any real fighting. More than ever he wanted to be there with Artie, because although Artie had always stood over him, protecting him, he felt that in his way George protected Artie too. As someone who once thought he could see the future, George felt blind and naked.

The next evening, Edith was preparing the meal, peeling potatoes in the sink. Now the price had doubled to a shilling a bag she would peel just one for each of the men and a small one for herself. She'd even keep the peel to use as pie-topping, a cheap and quite nasty alternative to real pastry. With loaves reaching nine English pennies and sugar rationed, they were all going to be a lot thinner by the year's end.

Her brother-in-law came into the kitchen and said hello.

'George, what happened to your glasses?'

He was wearing the old ones for the first time in many months.

'Ah, I just put me old ones on by mistake this morning.'
She went back to her peeling.

The following day, when she came back from the tram, again she noticed the glasses.

'George. Are you getting more forgetful than usual? You're in the baby glasses again.'

'Yes, the others need mending. I'll see about them later this week, next time I'm in Town.'

'Will that be expensive?'

'No, no, shouldn't be.'

George Bazin was a terrible liar. He did not look her in the eye as he spoke. Later, as she was busy about the Big House, she chanced to look into George's room. In what seemed to be an endless game of musical bedrooms, he had moved upstairs into the room Ruth Mullane had vacated. George had left the door open and sure enough, the newer spectacles lay on the dressing table. Her spine tingled, her heartbeat began to rise and she felt an unusual fear. She went over and inspected the glasses. Other than for a few little scratches, they were undamaged.

November came, but the customary winter work in the quarries did not come with it. Men were scarce, though, and George was more skilled than most who remained so he was still cutting and shaping stone. Severe gales at the end of the summer had brought plenty of work for the stonemasons, with walls damaged and even roofs down. He stopped work on the granite he was roughing out as a quoin, and walked over to the bench where Jack had left him a mug of tea. Taking the tea out into the chilly air, he put on his glasses. Sea and sky were grey and even the air tasted grey. The wind carried a wet feel, bearing low swooping clouds and threatening rain. George sipped the tea and his glasses fogged.

She was back! Distant, dark; brooding like the tail of a cloud that drags rain over the sea. Still and menacing, she frowned with intent to sear his soul. He felt that chill familiar from childhood and never forgotten. George sipped his tea and looked across the Mare, trying to be rational. So there was bad news on the way – it was always so when she came to him in this manner. He took another sip. If only he could warn Artie. Then again, the danger might be closer to home. Henry Bazin had seemed to fade once Artie marched away. Maybe it was the cough, maybe the loss of his wife, but his father was not the man he had once been. Perhaps at last, the time had come when George could actually act to avert tragedy.

Her warning made George restless. He walked around house and cottage noting every conceivable threat or danger. Next, he set about rectifying them. Edith quickly lost patience with the frenzy of fastidious precautions.

'George, for goodness' sake, Alice cleaned this floor once today!'

George waved the broom. 'Dust will make Pépaen sneeze – he's not been well.'

'Dust! Leave the chores to Alice. And the rug, why is it in the middle of the room?'

'Well, sparks from the fire could catch light, then burn down the house while we're all asleep.'

'George, you are mad. I wish Artie was here to see what an old woman you're turning into. And you're wearing those bloney glasses again!'

'So I am.'

'Aah,' she said as if all became clear. 'I know your game, George Bazin! I thought you'd grown out of all that *pouque* nonsense? Take those glasses off and leave them off, they look ridiculous on a grown man. They don't fit and they're cracked and they make you look cracked.'

'They're just my lucky glasses.'

'Well you don't look like a man who is lucky. In fact you look like a man who's just lost a fortune. Not a smile, not one of your little jokes or stories for days. You don't even look me in the face.'

As if to prove the point, he glanced at her and looked away.

'But you do look at me, when you think my back is turned, and I've seen the way you look at me and I don't like it. You watch me – I've seen you watching me.'

It was true, but he would never admit it. 'I just want to look after you – something bad is about to happen, to you or Père, or Artie…'

'Artie? What about Artie? What have you heard?' She came across and shook him. 'What have you heard?'

'Nothing. I've heard nothing. I just feel…'

'You've seen a bloney fairy in your glasses!' Edith pushed herself away from him and covered her face with a hand. 'Oh my God, I'm sharing a house with a madman.'

Henry came in. 'Who's a madman?'

Edith pointed a silent finger at George.

'George, what have you been doing?' Henry growled. 'Touch Edith and I'll knock you down. You're not so old that I can't show you who's the man around here.'

George stepped back – he had not forgotten that strapping.

'He didn't touch me,' Edith said. 'It's just… he's a storm crow. Bad tidings and evil omens, it's all stuff and nonsense fit for the Valpied sisters, not me.'

'I said nothing,' George blustered.

Edith snapped her fingers. 'Right, this is what is going to happen. It's too far to walk back from Town, now it's dark in the afternoon and the weather's gone foul. When I'm working, I'll stay over at Aunt Marguerite's.'

'Edith, you can't,' said George.

'You called her an old witch,' said Henry.

'Pious and stuck-up, yes, but she's in Town and she's family. She's always got empty rooms these days. I'll be fine if I mind my p's and q's and don't swear in front of the paying guests.'

'But who will cook us supper?' moaned George.

'Cook your own bloney supper. Get Alice to do it. I've got a job, and it's war work, so I'm playing my part just like our Artie is.'

The men looked at each other and Edith swept from the room.

'Edith, please,' begged George, following her into the passage.

The wagging finger came back. 'Not another word,' she hissed. 'I'll keep your secrets, for family's sake, but just see if they don't lock you away in the asylum for your jabbering about ghostly women who tell you the future.'

'Wish Artie had never told you.'

'Well he did. Now grow up, put your proper glasses on and join the real world.'

'And will you stay?'

'No, no, not another day.'

Edith did not enjoy staying at the Mon Repos guest house with Aunt Marguerite. Business was bad, due to the war, and Edith's sister Leila had not been replaced once she had gone to England to do war work. Marguerite never missed the chance of offering a little chore that Edith could help out with. One day it was the fire, the next a bit of cleaning, the next a little laundry for the one guest. Edith was also expected to pay for her board, even if her aunt had ceded a heavy discount with a great show of charity. This she chose to raise in conversation every day or two, just to remind Edith how Christian she could be.

Still, it saved Edith two hours of walking each day or the fares on the horse bus when she managed to catch it lucky. She was not forced to cook for a trio of men and when the day was over she could find a corner and read quietly. Marguerite was also a reader, but of late preferred the Bible or the life of some saint or missionary. She raised her eyebrow at Edith's romances, but at least both women could read in peace.

Christmas was on the horizon and Edith wondered if some soldiers would be sent home. One year there had been no fighting at all, and the English had played football against the Germans. Support committees were busily making up Christmas boxes for the troops, so Edith set out to find little things she could parcel up for Artie. His one letter so far had complained about the food and the wet. She did not greatly approve of smoking, something she had inherited from Aunt Marguerite, so was not tempted to stuff the package with pipes, tobacco and that kind of paraphernalia. Edith decided to knit him a balaclava helmet in leaf green to help him blend in with the countryside and used the rest of the wool for some socks. Woollen gloves soon became cold and soggy in the rain, so she was saving up to buy him a good pair of sheepskin mittens.

On her day off from the trams she walked down to the Markets to see what else she could send to the front. Chocolate perhaps, if it was well wrapped. In Le Riches store she spotted the ideal gift – a plum pudding in a tin. As she counted out her money, a well-dressed couple and a young man in an officer's uniform were next in the queue behind her.

She turned to leave.

'Good day, Mrs Bazin.'

It was Edwin Brown, Artie's colleague from the bank. 'Mr Brown?'

'Call me Edwin, please. Oh, this is my mother and father. Father, this is Mrs Bazin, my friend Arthur's wife.'

His father nodded stiffly and his mother gave the weakest of polite smiles.

'Well, I'm not one for shopping, so how do you fancy a spot of tea?' Edwin said.

'Ah?' She was taken by surprise by the suggestion.

'Mother?' he asked.

'Well, we have a very busy morning...' his mother started to say.

'So, I shall escort Mrs Bazin myself.'

'Very well, but leave space for luncheon.'

Edwin raised his eyebrows as they left the grocers. 'Mother still thinks I'm seven years old. The king's uniform may as well not exist. Dreadful weather, isn't it?'

She glanced skywards. 'Yes, I hope it's better in France. I'm just buying a few things to send to Artie. Shall we go to Le Noury's?'

'Fine – have you heard from Artie?'

'Yes – once. He must be too busy to write.'

'There's been another big offensive at Passchendaele, he could be in that.'

'Oh, do you think so?' Edith crunched her handbag in tension.

'Well, perhaps not – let's hope not,' Edwin spotted her alarm. 'Just about all my friends are out there – those who are left. The battalion are just training, training, training by the sounds of it. So, if we pop into that tea shop in the Arcade you can tell me what you've heard and I can swap my news too.'

It was only a short walk to Le Noury's. Edwin ordered a pot of tea for two and some buttered scones. Edith glanced at his shoulder title.

'Why aren't you in France with the others?'

'I'm in the Second Battalion. It transpires that we've got too many officers, because lots of Guernsey chaps have transferred back from other regiments. I can only go to France if I resign my rank, which seems a bit silly. So, I'm stuck back here training up replacements.'

'Who are they replacing?'

'You know. Chaps who're sick…'

'Or dead?'

'And chaps who weren't up to going in the first place,' he said hurriedly. 'It was all a bit of a rush back in June. Some of the first wave were too old, some not really fit and so on, so we'll be bringing them back. And as for me, I've been officer training in England.' He tapped his shoulder pip. 'Second lieutenant.'

'Là, an officer. They talked about making Artie an officer.'

'He's what, a corporal already?'

'Yes,' she said. 'And a machine-gunner. Fancy that, all the book-learning and he ends up a machine-gunner.'

'But after the war, all the officer training will come in handy. And being a corporal,' he added. 'A trained leader of men. It will help us rise in the bank.'

'You don't need help,' Edith said. 'Doesn't your father own the bank?'

'No, he's a shareholder, which means he owns a little bit of the bank.' Edwin teased a currant out of his scone. 'It's like he owns this currant and other people own the rest of the scone.'

Edith was delighted by the scone-as-bank demonstration. 'Still, it's better to own one currant than no currant at all.'

'And one day, with hard work, I'll have a currant of my own.'

'And inherit your father's currant? So you'll have two.'

'In no time I'll have a whole scone!'

CHAPTER 35

As November passed, the Guernseymen learned to love the tank. Again and again they practised following them, and storming trenches in fields turned into model battlefields. It was a kind of sport and Artie loved it. He and Pierre would run across those fields with the great Lewis gun swinging between them, the rest struggling to keep up with satchels of ammunition drums. Artie in fact was strong enough to lug the gun on his own for a short while, either over his shoulder or across his chest. Now he saw the sense in all this drill. The boys were a machine not so different from the tank. Lieutenant Warry was the driver, all the boys were wheels or cogs to make it go and Artie was the weapon. They practised so they would do it right when the great day came. Craftsmen who had worked wood or stone at home learned the craft of war, fishermen learned to hunt men, farmers grew to know the importance of good ground.

One dank, dark, November night, the Guernseys marched in silence. For hours it was march; stop; whispered orders; and then march on. Someone must know where they were heading. The countryside was clean, almost untouched by war, quite unlike the wasteland they had left further north. Before dawn they were crouching in a well-made trench; wet, tired and hungry. Artie ate what he could, but noticed that Pierre ate nothing. Tea was welcome and came loaded with real sugar.

One bird began to sing. Back home, Artie would have said it was a thrush, *énne graïve,* but was not sure if they had thrushes in France. The bird must know it was getting light. Some men glanced at their watches every few moments, as if to slow time to a stop.

Up on the ridge beyond, Germans were sleeping, making coffee, stretching themselves ahead of another tedious, uneventful day. These were no hardened Prussian grenadiers, but men already weary of war with their shattered ranks padded out with boys fresh into uniform. This was a quiet part of the front, their generals had told them, a place they could rest secure behind that triple barrier of concrete and wire which was the impregnable Hindenburg Line. Many had only moments to live.

'Seventeen minutes past six,' one of the officers whispered.

'I make it twenty past,' said another.

The earth shook and the sky was torn apart. Artie covered his ears against the sudden thunderous noise. Cannons, guns, howitzers and mortars of all descriptions sent screaming death towards the enemy. The Guernseys blocked their ears instinctively, but one by one they eased their hands off, accepting the tumult of war all around them.

'Glad I'm no German,' said Pierre.

Gone were the days when the British politely gave the enemy a week's warning of an attack with a leisurely, futile bombardment. A hurricane of shells struck at the click of a second hand, shocking and stunning those it did not kill.

Nobody looked at watches any more. Other sounds could be picked out between the artillery. Heavy machine guns played like the Devil's piano, hammering out the same note repeatedly, on and on without a pause. Another sound was heard, an unearthly rumble, mixed with the squeak and squeal of machines. It was as if the earth were opening and the beasts of the apocalypse were venturing forth.

'Tanks,' said one man. 'Listen to them tanks, hundreds of tanks.'

'Wish we was in tanks,' said Pierre to Artie. 'Think about the target shooting we did on L'Ancresse. We're behind sandbags lying down and shooting at those targets. How many shots did you hit with?'

'Eight every ten.'

'Me too. Just thinking about them Huns up there. They're behind sandbags yet looking down at us. When we gets out of the trench and goes up the hill, it will be like target shooting for them. Maybe they'll get eight out of ten too.'

'It's not like that here,' said Artie. 'We Guerns aren't just target boards. We ain't so easy to kill.'

'I was talking to a corporal who'd been on the Somme. He said there was whole regiments shot down in minutes, even. Just like targets, one after another.'

'People talk, people make up stories. If it was that bad, would our officers lead us into that? Course they wouldn't. Listen to them shells. Is any man with any sense going to wait around with that coming at 'im? Anyway we've got tanks. You can't shoot them.'

'Wish we was in tanks, us.'

More than two hours passed. Day came with a grey light, where misty rain mixed with the smoke of battle. The noise of war had lessened, moving into the distance. The officers went away to talk. When Lieutenant Warry came back, he pulled the platoon close to him in a tight knot.

'Right, boys, our turn next. We've been through this before, but here it is again. There's these bridges our Division has to capture. The English and the tanks will have taken the first Hun trenches. We're to pass through them, take the second trenches and the wood.'

'What wood, sir?'

'You'll see it – just follow me. After the wood there's a canal and a village, which is where the bridges are. We're on the left, the rest of the battalion is to the right of us and the Middlesex lads next across from them. They're going first. Any questions?'

Someone spoke up in Guernesiais. *'Tchi qu'i faout faire?'*

Then someone else, less polite, asked why they were just hanging around. Soldiers always grouse, but the next few minutes could mean life or death for them all.

'Bazin!' Warry caught Artie's eye. 'Translate into patois.'

Artie turned about and summarised the plan in a mixture of Guernesiais and Guernsey English, with plenty of hand actions. The men quizzed him, and he cross-checked with Warry, who was growing nervous and impatient.

'Just follow me,' he said.

Warry moved off and the men followed, weaving their way forward through zigzag trenches higher than their heads. At the front line they sorted into platoons and sections, checked equipment, gave each other tight smiles, pats on the shoulder, words of encouragement. Lieutenant Warry went up a ladder and Artie followed him. Pierre passed up the Lewis gun and came up by his side.

Artie turned to face the Hindenburg Line, braced for the bullets that did not come. He saw a gently undulating landscape before him, shrouded by mist and smoke. As a battlefield it looked strangely empty. He waited for Pierre to take the other carry handle on the heavy gun, and began to march swiftly uphill. From a slit in the earth, the battalion emerged. Muddy green-brown figures moved across the muddy green-brown winter fields. Hundreds of men could be seen now away to the right, but hardly anyone to the left.

Pierre's shoulder title caught his eye. GUERNSEY.

Half the island is here, Artie thought. *Almost every man I know.*

He felt pride, he felt a thrill.

I wish George could be here. Him and his invisible friend.

In extended line, the infantry moved up the gentle slope. Mostly they walked, sometimes making short dashes. Officers shouted that they should keep together, keep up the pace. All the shooting and shelling was up ahead and every now and again a dark rhomboid shape could be seen lumbering forward, or halted spitting flame. Overhead, the impossible aeroplanes swept towards the enemy like vengeful angels. It was easy to think this was a dream or a fairy-tale world, or that this was reality and the quiet green island was a half-remembered childhood fantasy.

Dark scrapes on the grass showed where shells had fallen. Wet raggy bundles showed where men had fallen too. Pierre paused for a moment and bent beside the first body. The man lay on his face and seemed completely unhurt, only sleeping. His shoulder title read MIDDLESEX. Pierre stood back up and moved on.

War seemed very easy that morning. The formidable Hindenburg Line had been turned into a shambles of twisted and flattened wire, pounded and abandoned bunkers. Artie gave the mangled enemy bodies no more than a glance. The battle here had been between metal and flesh, and metal had won. A gaggle of grey-coated men were being herded downhill by a pair of jaunty Londoners. The Guernseys glanced at their defeated enemy, picked their way through the wreckage and moved on.

Artie began to relax. He could march all the way to Berlin in this manner, simply following the tanks, lugging his gun and with no need to kill anybody. Casting glances at Pierre to keep up his spirits, he followed the lieutenant through a shallow valley. Over to the left was a steep, comforting wood. With all this mist and smoke it felt like a veil was protecting them, hiding them from unfriendly eyes. It was the kind of magic that George spoke about.

Guernsey's soldiers crested a gentle ridge and a new part of France lay before them. A few hundred yards ahead nestled a wood slumbering in winter greys. Shells broke the calm, bursting among the branches or deep within the depths. A tank had stopped for no clear reason. Nobody was aboard and the platoon took a rest for a few moments in its lee. The sun chose this moment to make an appearance, casting a glint on the bayonets of the Middlesex boys way up ahead, fighting an enemy who remained invisible inside the wood.

'Neuf Bois,' said Warry. He pointed to the treeline the Middlesex were attacking. 'Nine Wood. We're going round to the left.' He jabbed his rifle and gestured heavily for the benefit of the country boys. 'À *gauche!*'

His pronunciation was off, but the men began to move.

'*Diex Aïe!*' he shouted.

'God help us,' echoed Artie.

Life shifted to a rush and a blur. The manhood of the island surged down the slope, taking cover, shooting, making short rushes. Artie saw the first Guernseyman fall spinning to the ground.

'Who was that?' Pierre called.

'Don't look. Don't ask.'

The earth was their friend and they hugged it, setting up the Lewis gun where the sergeant told them. Artie's cold finger gripped the colder trigger. He had no target but a wall of trees. He squeezed the trigger – rat-tat-tat-tat-tat. Five shots flew into the trees, then five more in quick succession.

Not too fast – mustn't overheat the barrel – mustn't cause a jam. He fired where the sergeant told him to fire. Invisible enemies in the wood or in trenches fired back. That strange swishing sound had to be bullets passing him by. Moments stretched into hours and hours became moments. When the word came the two gunners rushed into the wood with everyone else. Reaching the entrenchments abandoned by the enemy, it seemed the battle was over. A group of tanks loitered while Londoners and Guernseys mixed together as they hunted through the earthworks and the trees for any enemy that remained.

A trio of boys from Town had a bunch of Germans cornered. Cowed, frightened, ashamed, the Germans hung their heads.

'Look at this, eh!' one of the Town boys cried. 'Little Guernsey beats the Prussian Empire!'

It was hard not to feel proud.

The Guernseys spent a damp night in Nine Wood, finding shelter in the trenches of their defeated foe. By the standards of the war so far, their losses had been impossibly light, but word went around that Lieutenant Lainé had been killed in the rush on the woods.

'That young Mr Lainé was a good officer,' said Pierre. 'Liked 'im. Sergeant Brehaut was wounded too. He lives to the Castel, but I never knew him.'

'See, Dippo, we did all right. It wasn't like you said; it wasn't just target practice for the Huns. That officer, he's almost the only one killed, him.'

'Still, I wouldn't want to be the one telling his *mémaen*. And what would have happened if it had been bad, if it was the Germans with the tanks attacking us with surprise and taking us prisoner? Who would work the quarries back home and pick the tomatoes then, eh?'

Artie had to agree. Nobody had thought of that. If some horrible disaster befell the regiment it would be like a dozen steamship *Stellas* sinking all in one go. All the young men, the brave men. Now he was glad George was not here.

CHAPTER 36

Edwin Brown took an English newspaper, *The Times of London*. In the last week of November, the paper was full of news of a great victory at Cambrai and how bells had rung out across England for the first time since the war had started. Edith had avoided war news, but she was drawn to the headlines in the paper which lay beside Edwin's coffee-cup. Their paths had crossed several times and this was the fourth occasion they had shared tea or coffee.

She read the story carefully, quizzing Edwin, who knew no more than he had read in the newspaper. Artie had been posted to the front just before this huge attack. Yes it was a victory, but the whole world knew what a victory cost.

'Are our boys in this battle?' she asked.

'I don't know. For all this talk of seeing Guernsey's name on the front pages of the newspaper, there's no mention of us.'

'Surely they're doing something,' she said, frustrated and anxious.

'I guess they must be. The last I heard they were behind the lines, up in Flanders. And don't repeat that, or I'll be shot. And you too.'

She gave a very brief smile.

'If it was bad news, we'd know. So don't fret.'

'I have to get back; thanks for the coffee. Have you finished with that paper?'

'Yes, yes, take it, please, if you would like it.'

Edith found Edwin's air of authority comforting, but still

thought of nothing else than the big attack while working the tram that day. A passenger was reading another English paper – *The Daily Mail,* with a similar story making the news. Across from him, a widow was dressed in black. A man who looked too old to be in his RGLI uniform gazed out to sea from the window. Edith asked him if he had news to share, but he was 2nd Battalion, rated as unfit for the front and knew less than she did.

That evening she walked back to see George. She took *The Times* for him, to see what he thought, to see whether he and his fairy friend had any more insight. George was enraptured by the story of the tanks – battleships on land. Edith sat tense in the other chair, asking him questions every few minutes.

'You told me there was bad news coming.'

'Did I?'

'Yes. All the time, these past weeks, since Artie went back. I could see it in the way you acted, the things you did. And you are still wearing those bloney baby glasses.'

'Not while I'm reading, me.'

'You know what I mean, George Bazin, you know exactly what I mean!'

Henry came in at that moment. 'Oh, wharro, Edith, thought you'd forgotten us.'

'No, I'm just coming home for the night.'

'"Home", see, yes. It is your home, remember that.'

She felt the world slowly crowding round her. It was not a home without Artie, just this place she was expected to be for so many hours a day. At least the tram moved.

'There's a big battle,' she said, giving away the state of her nerves.

'Another one?'

'But we've won,' George said brightly.

'Now there's a turn-up,' Henry said. 'Truly won, or just newspaper-won? You know, it turns out that we lost ten thousand men and went backwards a mile.'

'Aw, Pépaen, you must believe we're going to win.'

'I just want it over, me. I want the king and the Kaiser to shake hands and call it a draw so all our boys can come home.'

'But this could be it,' George passed him *The Times*. 'Read it. We've won.'

'Put your glasses on, George,' Edith said. 'Put them on and keep them on.'

He frowned at her.

She stood up and announced she was going to bed. 'I just need... I just need to know what's happening to Artie.'

CHAPTER 37

George stared into the night. It was blustery, but there was no rain for the moment. He stood out in the yard looking vaguely south and west to where the moon was fighting to be seen through cloud. La Vallée had no view to the east, or he'd have looked that way, trying to see his brother across those hundreds of miles of sea and farmland. It would be dark in France too. Artie might need the moonlight to see his enemies, or need the cloud to shield him from their eyes.

He knew Edith was frightened. The shade of moonlight that stood behind him was frightened too. What could he say? In the past he'd been glib with his portents of doom and death, but now he saw how dangerous they could be. Edith had started to believe he had the gift of foresight. Maybe nerves drove her to do it, but she had actually suggested he probe the darkness deliberately to settle her worry. This is what Mrs Lake had warned him not to do, this is what the preacher had told him was a sin against God, yet this was exactly what he was trying to do.

The moonchild faded as the moon sought cloud. She would not be forced into prophesy, she would tell him exactly what she wanted at a time of her choosing. He gave a sigh. For Edith's sake the glasses must go away and he had to be strong. He was going to have to be strong.

The rain returned.

That same cold rain swept across Guernsey, then across the sea, then across France to chill the men dug into Nine Wood. It helped shroud them from prying and prowling Germans who nosed towards them on the second day of the battle. Artie fired away all the ammunition Pierre could pass him. When it was dark they were relieved and allowed to move into a house for warmth. The village around them had suffered in the battle and all the windows of the house were broken. An ordinary French family who once lived here had abandoned their few possessions. Troops made use of their china until it broke, piece by piece. Bed linen became towels or bandages. Artie admired a dresser, which his mother would have loved to own, and then helped his comrades break it up for firewood. In the week that followed, the village of Marcoing grew more ragged, more ruinous. Facades fell into the street, exposing the lives left behind by villagers who had fled. The bare trees of Nine Wood began to be stripped of their branches as well as leaves. Men who counted themselves lucky to have survived the first day unhurt started to feel their luck running short. Shells, snipers, aeroplanes, machine guns and mortars were nibbling at the strength of the battalion. Rain was followed by snow.

'It snowed once when George was little,' Artie said while they were shivering in a hurriedly dug trench. 'We had just enough to make snowballs. There was a big fight with the Ogier boys from Cobo.'

'Was that Tom Ogier, and his brothers?'

'Yes.'

'Saw Tom killed,' said Pierre, sadly. 'That bloney aeroplane; who'd have thought it, eh? Killed by an aeroplane. And I think one of his brothers got it yesterday.'

'Only wounded,' Artie said without emotion. 'I heard the

little 'un talking; he's really cut up about it all. Anyway at least one of them'll be going home.'

Snowflakes whirled around but melted as they settled.

'They were right little bastards, them three Ogiers,' Artie continued. 'They kept picking on George, but he wouldn't give up. He's brave in his own way.'

'We could do with him here,' said Pierre.

'No, I wouldn't want him here.' Artie held out his coat sleeve, slashed and bloodstained where some bullet or shell fragment had grazed past. 'He's a Guernsey boy, he should stay there. This is no place for him.'

CHAPTER 38

After one night at La Vallée, Edith reverted to staying at her aunt's house in Hauteville. A note was waiting for her, signed by Mr Brown. After that first chance meeting in the Markets, she had enjoyed meeting him for tea and conversation. It gave both a chance to escape their uniformed worlds for half an hour and offered a break from the demands of their families. Rich and poor suffered in their own ways.

At the hour suggested in the note, she came down the steps, slippery after the rain.

'Edith.'

'Edwin,' she breathed.

'Shall we walk?'

'It's cold – I need something to warm me up.'

'We'll walk down to the Golden Lion. It's cheery and it's close. '

Edwin held open the door of the pub for her. This was Town; she would not expect anyone to know her here. Nevertheless she preferred a table in the back corner. It was a dark November night and so many of the men were away, and the garrison withdrawn too, so the Golden Lion was a melancholy place. With coal both expensive and in erratic supply, the pub by the Markets was colder than in more cheerful times.

Edith barely let the gin touch the sides of her throat. 'My God, I needed that,' she said.

'Another?'

'Please – but don't think badly of me.'

'No, you need it. We all need it.'

Edwin brought a second gin for her and she nursed it with more decorum.

'Have you heard any more from France?' she asked.

He nodded. 'I think the lads are in the battle at Cambrai.'

'Is it bad?'

'We're winning.'

'That English paper said we'd won and it was over.'

'Wars aren't like they used to be. Battles last weeks – months even.'

'Has anyone been killed? Any of ours?'

'Lieutenant Lainé. I didn't know him, did you?'

'No.'

'There were a few others, plus a score wounded; I don't recognise any of the names. It sounds pretty light so far.'

'Light? Oh, you don't know what it's like!' Her restraint suddenly cracked. 'Waiting for Artie, not knowing what's happening to him or where he is. I try not to look at the papers. I don't let people read them to me neither, well not until this battle and now there's not enough in the bloney papers.' She paused, fiddling with her glass. 'And all the news is a week old. We call it news but it happened days and days ago. Nobody is telling us what happened today, or yesterday.'

'We'll know the truth soon,' he soothed. 'The battle will wind down, and one day before we know it, the war will be over…'

'One day. Meantimes my choice is the Hauteville convent or live on that farm with the sick old man, Jolly Jack and mad brother George.'

'I've heard he's a bit simple.'

'No, no, he's not simple. He's kind, he's too kind and he's hard to explain. No one's ever going to marry him, or give him a good job and they won't even let him go off and get killed in the war. So, you think he'd be all bitter, but he's not. He makes up for it by being really kind to everyone. He's so kind it's annoying, it unsettles me; I think, "George go away, do something else!" But of course we'll always be living with him. Even when Artie gets back it will be years and years before we can get a place that is truly our own.'

'To be truthful, I wouldn't want to still be living out in the Castel.'

'We'll move to Town,' she murmured. 'One day. When Artie is back. It's not like it's London or Paris, but it's not the bloney Castel.' Now she downed half her gin. 'I mean, there's none of the Bazin family sitting at the next table. No one's looking at us, pointing at the married lady out with a single man.'

'I'm escorting you, keeping you from harm.'

'That's as maybe, but Artie would still kill you.'

'It's all perfectly harmless; we're friends.'

'But he's a daft bastard like that. He would actually kill you, or fight you at least. He loves fighting, you never knew him at school, but the girls tell me he was always up for a fight. Now he's off fighting the Kaiser. He could have stayed at home, he could have got off. George got off. You got off.'

'No,' Edwin objected. 'I did not "get off". The Second Battalion is protecting Guernsey against invasion and German spies. We're doing our bit too. I'd be earning a lot more money if I could have stayed on at the bank. I could be building a career, especially as some of the men who were above me aren't coming back.'

She looked sharply at him.

'It's true.'

'You can't talk like the war had some kind of silver lining.'

'Every problem is just an opportunity,' he said. 'The bigger the problem, the bigger the opportunity.'

She grimaced.

'I know. There's me on the trams and George with his stone-cutting job and neither of us would be doing that without the war. And my sister too, she's gone off to work in a factory making shells and marry a man she only met because of the war. But my opportunity, Edwin, is to stay here, with George and the old men.'

She sighed, took another sip. 'He unsettles me.'

'George?'

'He sees things.'

'Like what?'

'A fairy, a ghost, an angel; I don't know. He thinks it tells him what's going to happen, like a gypsy fortune-teller. He says he saw the war coming, him.'

Edwin gave a grunt of humour. 'So he warned us all, of course?'

'No, no, no,' she shook her head vigorously. 'It doesn't work like that. He only foresees things after they have happened.' She slapped the table in emphasis. 'That tells you something, don't it?'

'So why worry?'

'Because he's had the cat between his feet for weeks, keeps looking for bad things, everywhere. Fusses like an old hen. You'd think the world was going to end the way he's going on. I just had to come away.'

Her glass was emptied.

'You're best out of there,' Edwin said.

'Yes, but for how long? I've got to go back sooner or later. I've hardly any money.'

'Artie must send back his pay?'

'Yes, but Henry has no work and neither Jack nor George work anything like the full week I do, and we have to pay a girl to clean up after them all. And somehow, Artie's expecting me to keep house until he gets back. Daft bastard. If only he'd stayed... I mean it's so selfish, leaving me here on my own! I'm lonely, Edwin, and George... scares me. And I'm so... worried.'

Edwin nodded, curling up his chin sympathetically. He was a kind man, who clearly understood women. 'If you ask me, you need another drink. Would you like something better than gin? Wine perhaps? I'll see if they have a bottle.'

He muttered a vague complaint as he brought back the bottle and two glasses. 'Not the finest vintage.'

War brought them close. Both were waiting for news, for orders, for a glimpse of the future. Neither had a friend just behind them to point the way and ease their path. Edith started talking about the books she liked, and then Edwin talked of England and the big school he attended and his university with all the pranks and parties. Through the wine she saw Edwin more and more as living a book – he was a character from another time and place. His world and her world were so different.

So soon, the wine bottle had been emptied. 'Well that was rough,' he said, scowling at the last mouthful and catching some dregs. 'Sorry, but it was the best they had. All they had, indeed. Shall we go somewhere else? It's pretty chilly in here.'

Edith's lips searched her glass for the last droplet of wine, and stood to button her coat. Her fingers fumbled, as if they were not quite under her control.

Out in the cobbled street he pointed uphill. 'This way.'

'It's my walk home,' she sighed, thinking of her route to the Castel, not to Hauteville.

'And mine.'

The Brown family owned a house on Victoria Road, five minutes' strenuous climb uphill from the Markets. Without intending to go there, Edith found herself outside.

'This is my parents' place.'

'Oh, this is just the house I want one day,' Edith declared, her words blurred by more drinks than she had count of, downed with little pause between.

'Father keeps a modest cabinet; I can offer you a Scotch or a brandy. It's either that or The Plough, which is a little rough for ladies.'

She burned with curiosity as to what was behind the door. 'Will we disturb your family?'

'No, they've gone to London for the season.'

'Oh!' She clapped a hand over her mouth. 'This is so very wicked then!'

'Not so wicked, the world is changing. The rules – the old rules, are no more!' He could have been one of those communist revolutionaries the papers had started talking about.

Edith drifted into the Brown's parlour in a dream. Her gaze took in the leather sofa, the heavy curtains, the well-made antimacassar, electric lights, fire in the grate, green wallpaper with a Chinese theme. This was a different world.

'Maid's gone,' he said, taking off the fire guard and stoking life from the coals.

Edwin had matched her drink for drink and taken half a bottle of wine with his dinner beforehand. 'Have a seat, have a seat,' he slurred.

She threw off her coat on to the back of an armchair, slumped on the sofa and gazed at the plasterwork mouldings. It felt like a palace. In an hour she would go back to the tiny rooms in the guest house, in a day or two she would return to the farm with the chickens and the male relatives. Just for an hour this could be her house.

'Napoleon brandy?' Edwin asked.

'Will Napoleon mind?' she giggled.

'I'll do large ones, saves standing up and down all the time.'

'You are very wicked,' she said.

'Gallant,' he corrected. 'Saving a damsel in distress.'

The cut-glass decanter glinted in the electric light as he poured the golden liquid.

She took the brandy in its monstrous glass. 'Gosh, it's a *bashin*!' Her first gulp was ill advised and the alcohol went straight to her head.

'Whoo,' she exclaimed, and then noticed *The Times* lying folded on the table, half proclaiming more war headlines.

'Oh God,' she said, closing her eyes.

'Edith.' Edwin sat beside her.

'This is very wrong,' she said, keeping her eyes firmly shut. 'But I don't care. The world's gone wrong; my world's always gone wrong. Just hold me for a few minutes, Edwin. I just need to be held. And tell me everything is going to be all right.'

He moved to hold her tight. 'Everything is as it should be.'

He kissed her neck gently. The tickle of his moustache made her giggle. It was familiar, comforting.

'I'm not a bad girl, Edwin.'

'Not at all.'

'But I want to be a bad girl. Good girls get nothing; they get left behind, left alone.'

He kissed her neck again.

'I could have been an actress. I could have married an advocate.'

'Or a wealthy banker.'

'Hmm, hmm, yes.'

'You are the most beautiful girl in Guernsey. You could go anywhere, have any man.'

She laughed. 'Yes, tell me that. Just keep telling me that.'

In one more gulp she finished the brandy, shaking her head. She thrust the glass at him. 'It's a big glass, but you didn't fill it even half.'

'No,' he said, taking the glass from her. 'It's expensive, very fine, something to be savoured. And you, belle of the Castel, are something very fine too.'

'Mmm, you flatterer,' she said, and let him kiss her full on the mouth, then again, and again, and again.

CHAPTER 39

The days grew darker and shorter, and minds closed to the old life once led. Nine Wood was left behind and the Guernseys occupied Marcoing, a village beside the canal whose curse was its bridges that both armies wanted to control. Some miles up ahead was the town of Cambrai, which the officers talked about in awe. Reach Cambrai and it would be over. The war? The battle? The rain? Each day more men were carried away wounded, some fell killed and some mysteriously vanished. An end had to come, while there was still a regiment left to march back through Town.

Food became scarce, and hot food scarcer. A lukewarm soup of no particular colour and tasting largely of grease and salt turned beanjar into a fondly remembered luxury. Dry, maggoty crackers made men yearn for their mothers' home-made bread. Everything about the war seemed designed to destroy the soul.

One day merged into the next, but while coming back in from manning a trench on the outskirts, Artie met some Canadian cavalry outside a half-ruined café. Their horses seemed to have no place in a world of tanks and aeroplanes and the men were frustrated, even dispirited. It was a long way to travel simply to stand around while shells from the skies butchered men and animals alike.

A group of Engineers turned out to be Americans. It was said they were coming in their tens of thousands and were going to win the war, but these were the first Artie had met.

A dozen of them stood behind the last standing gable of a building, hands in pockets or smoking. Bored, or lost, or waiting for orders, they called to Artie as he returned after running an errand for the major.

'Hey, buddy, do you know where we are?'

'Marcoing,' he said.

'Mar-co-ing,' the American recited. 'Yeah, sounds like the place. Hey, where are you from, buddy?'

'Guernsey.'

'Is that near London?'

'No – it's… near here.'

'Kinda French then?'

'Yes.' Artie went over to get a closer look at this new ally. 'Royal Guernsey Light Infantry,' he introduced his regiment.

'If you're royal, does that make you a special king's regiment?'

'Yes, must do, never thought about it. You're Americans, right?'

'I'm from New Jersey,' said the American.

'That's funny; Jersey's right close to us.'

'No, buddy, it's in America. New Jersey.'

'Well, there's an old Jersey too.'

'Never knew that,' said the American.

Guernsey bank clerk and American bricklayer talked for a few minutes about the places they had come from. About the big city of New York and the City of London, and an island too small for world maps to even show. Artie tried to explain about Guernsey and how it was neither English nor French, but realised that he was boring the American with too much detail. One of his officers was approaching with purpose in his stride, so the American quickly asked if Artie had any cigarettes. Artie said he did not.

Pierre was waiting in the shelter of a chimney that no longer had a house attached. 'Where are they to?' Pierre asked.

'America,' said Artie. 'And would you believe there's a New Jersey in America?'

'New *crapauds* then?'

'Must be.' Artie smiled. There was so little to smile about in Marcoing. 'It's funny, *mon viaer*, it takes a war to meet Americans and Canadians…'

'…and Germans, even.'

'*Cor*, when it's over, things I'll tell our George and our Edith.'

'Not everything though, eh? You can't tell them about all the bad things, like the mates we've lost and them Germans we've killed.'

'No. I'll write to George and tell him about the Americans. He'll never meet any in the Castel.'

One night, at last, the weather cleared. December was approaching and men started talking about Christmas. This war was always going to be over by Christmas and each new Christmas brought the renewed promise. Artie vaguely remembered Lieutenant Warry's suggestion that he might go home for training at Christmas. The regiment was certainly short of officers now.

Marcoing was left behind and the Royal Guernseys edged a mile or so east along the canal in the dark. Here another village straddled it, or perhaps it was two villages with the canal in between. Its bridge had given way when a tank tried to cross it and the tank still sat in the water like a dead whale.

Masnières was a dismal place, shot about and deserted by its people, and not improved by the winter weather. Catacombs ran beneath the church, so the soldiers crouched there safe from the shells and the rain. Artie could not escape the sensation that he was being buried alive. At the far side of the village was a sugar factory, a veritable fortress in this landscape of small farms. Just down from the factory lay the canal and the flat lands about it. Lieutenant Warry led his men out there in the early hours one morning, and found Artie a good place for his gun to rest. From the factory windows, he could see for miles to the east and the south.

As it grew light, a mist arose. Then, from nowhere, Germans by the thousand appeared. High in their window, Pierre and Artie watched them come out of the dawn.

'*Cor damme*,' said Pierre. 'That's enough for all the Tostevins.'

The enemy lines lay to the north, but by some cunning Hun trick they were sweeping in from the east, moving south of the canal and aiming to cut off the Guernseys and their comrades. This was war, the real war as told in the veteran's tales. It was Guernsey against the Kaiser's empire and his numbers seemed limitless. No tanks came to their aid and the skies swarmed with aeroplanes carrying black crosses on their wings. The order of the world was suddenly reversed and the easy victory of days past instantly forgotten.

Artie and Pierre had a grandstand view of the killing ground. As fast as Pierre could pass the drums of ammunition, Artie fired away rounds into the smoke and mist and waves of men in grey. Perhaps they killed hundreds, perhaps none at all – it was too far away to tell.

Around them, islanders shouted out in pain or simply fell quiet. Crossing the path of men hurrying to defend the bridges was another stream of the wounded and men helping friends who could no longer help themselves. The advocate's son fought alongside the fisherman, the grower beside the office clerk. Neighbours, workmates, relatives and brothers fell. Pierre's nightmare was come.

By the afternoon, the Germans had tired of throwing their youth to their deaths in front of the villages. Shells started to fall thick as rain. Roofs collapsed, gables fell, streets became choked with rubble, houses burst into flame. Childhood, nurture, schooling, training was all for naught as men crumpled under the shells. Dreams ended and futures were wiped away. A canal, a burning village and many thousand enemy soldiers cut the Guernseys off from their own lines.

Thank God this is not home, thought Artie. *Diex Aïe indeed.*

Another day dawned in the ruin of the twin villages called Masnières and Les Rues Vertes. The loss and exertions of the day before seemed to count for nothing as the Germans attacked again. From the sugar factory windows, Artie found his marks and fired across the canal at the swarms from the east. He and Pierre might have been the only men in the world trying to stop this horde. Its barrel red hot, its bipod shot through and useless, the Lewis gun would finally kill no more. It jammed for the tenth time, but now could not be un-jammed. Pierre and Artie could not find Lieutenant Warry, but another officer told them to take rifles off the dead and follow a sergeant who was gathering men to lead across the canal.

'We need to hold both sides of the bridge,' the sergeant said, grimacing against the noise. 'We have to stop them cutting us off.'

Masnières church was on fire, the brick houses were wrecks and the street was little more than a mess of wreckage and puddles as they picked their way down towards the bridge broken by the tank. The dead machine was called *Flying Fox* and still wallowed in the stream, helping form a bridge of sorts for them to scramble across. Artie felt a sharp pain in the back of his left leg. He paused, cursed, felt for the blood, guessed he'd live, tested his leg still flexed, and moved on. That was his third wound for the week. When things quietened down he'd have to roll up his trousers and wash the dirt out, stop it going septic.

As the day wore on the Guernseys were drawn into the confused ebb and flow of battle for the village across the canal. Dodging from ruin to ruin, the men followed the orders of officers, sergeants, corporals – then at last followed the lead of whatever man had the best idea next.

On one edge of Les Rues Vertes, that man was Arthur Bazin. A dozen men from Guernsey and Lancashire and beyond took shelter in a barn that lacked half its roof and walls. Wide-eyed boys and men too tired and shocked to do otherwise looked to this strong corporal from the Castel who seemed to be keeping his wits when everyone else's were shot away.

An explosion overhead shook the building, choking them all with dust and scattering debris across their helmets and shoulders. Pierre gave a yell. He babbled in coarse Guernsey French, gripping his right arm with his left.

'God, God, my arm is gone! Artie, my arm is gone!'

Artie was by his side, checking the nasty gash in his friend's upper arm, seeing quickly that the bone was broken and peeking through the flesh. Blood bubbled as it sought to escape. Nobody had any dressings, but strips of uniform torn off a headless German made a dirty bandage and sling while Pierre moaned.

'I'll not be picking no more tomatoes,' Pierre gasped, with his sleeve a darker red than even the ripest fruit.

'You'll be home with this one,' Artie said. 'It's your ticket home.'

'I'll pick no more tomatoes with this 'ere arm. It's gone, I tell you it's gone.'

'Shush, Dippo, you've another arm. God gave you two arms for good reason.'

Artie glanced round and saw that one of the other soldiers was wounded too – a Canadian trooper who was somehow mixed up with them. The man was pale, nursing a gash in his thigh, but still capable of standing.

'Help my friend – take him back to the hospital. Take yourself too.'

The Canadian nodded, grateful to be given permission to leave, and maybe to live.

'Take care, Dippo. Give my love to Edith and Père. Tell George…' he paused. 'Tell him to take care of them all.'

Pierre allowed the Canadian to help him to his feet. He nodded, mouth dry, shuddering with shock.

Artie touched him on the shoulder. 'À la perchoïne.'

CHAPTER 40

M en were talking within the bar of the Cobo Hotel. It was a cold December evening and three years of war had robbed the topic of novelty. Newspaper stories of offensives and counter-attacks brought the killing no closer to an end, but after so much gloom, there was suddenly talk of a victory! A real victory! The German line at Cambrai had been broken by a surprise attack with wonder weapons. English newspapers had carried the story first, but for over a week now, the left-hand side of the second page of the *Press* had been full of Cambrai stories.

'I reckon our boys are in it.'

'It would have been in the *Press*.'

'But it has – read between the lines. There must have been two score killed or wounded listed this week. There was a Lainé and a Brehaut, both Royal Guernsey. Them casualties are not happening in training.'

From one side of the tap room to the other, men condemned to sit out war on the sidelines passed fragments of information back and forth.

'I heard there's been letters delivered all over Town, and telegrams too.'

'My cousin wrote his wife from France, so I reckon they're there.'

'Hey, George, bet your brother's there, showing them what's what.'

'It's why we're winning,' he said. He joined the talk, but

knew no more than the stale news repeated by the others. A letter sat unopened on the mantelpiece at La Vallée, written in Artie's hand but addressed to Edith. Deep down, George wished his secret friend would reassure him that Artie was still fit and well.

George was surprised to see Edith through the window of the Big House, sitting in the kitchen alone, holding a cup of tea with both hands.

'Edith!' He greeted her like a happy puppy whose master had returned. He had worried each day she had been away.

'Hello, George.'

She seemed agitated, distant, not quite the confident young woman who always knew what was best. At first he thought she was ill, then maybe just tired.

'Oh don't fuss, George, I'm fine.' She waved her hand. 'You smell of pub.'

'Sorry,' he tried not to slur. 'There's a letter from Artie,' he said. 'Have you seen it?'

Her face changed just for a moment, and then she found a smile. 'Artie? Why didn't you tell me?'

'I just did.'

George fetched it from the parlour, and Edith read it aloud except for a few lines at the end which she kept for herself. The letter told of a train ride across France. It described the fields and the little villages and mentioned various friends and relatives. Artie wrote about football matches and seeing aeroplanes in the sky. He said little of the war, except that he had heard the great guns. A couple of his words had been completely blanked out in blue pencil so Edith had to guess what they were. Artie reminded George to look after Edith and Henry.

'We should write back to him, tell him all's well,' George said. 'Tell him all about what you've been up to in Town.'

'No, I'll… yes, I'll write to him,' Edith flustered. 'I'm making up a parcel for Christmas. I need to find out how to send it to him.'

'You stayin'?' he asked.

'I can't stand being up at Hauteville,' she declared, 'with that pious cow. I'd rather do the walk each day.'

She looked him in the eye then looked away, rather as he used to look away from the spirit girl when he really wanted to see her. Edith truly was the most beautiful woman he had even seen, bar one, yet he did not understand her.

On Wednesday, 5 December, Edith noticed more flags than usual as she walked through Town to the terminus. The one on the Royal Court caught her attention – this celebration was official, something big was afoot. All day as she collected fares she heard rumours, and when she got home she opened the *Press* with care. It contained a dispatch about the battle at Cambrai and how the Guernsey battalion had fought 'magnificently'. She knew what 'magnificently' meant. Bloodless victories were not magnificent. Instead of the usual short entry saying that a local man had been killed or wounded, a great list of casualties ran down the page. It was stunning. These were men she had grown up with, walked past without knowing, served with tickets on the tram. After getting over the shock, she checked each name twice, as George and Henry had already done.

'Thank God,' she said.

But God was not done with Guernsey. 'Victory' became 'Planned Withdrawal'. Later that week, another two columns of the paper were filled with the names of the wounded. More came the next day, then each day right up to Christmas Eve. Every family in the island would hear news they had dreaded.

Half the battalion had been lost. Five hundred Guernseymen were wounded, killed or simply 'missing'. Christmas was cancelled.

Edith hardly dared leave the house to go to church on Christmas Day. Curtains were drawn in houses she walked past. The wind was bitter and George and Henry walked either side of her. Henry was not much for church, but even he was affected by the loss all around him and came along for support.

Perotine was standing outside the porch. She came up and gripped Edith's hand. 'Artie?'

'No, no,' she said. 'He's not in any of the lists. And that telegram boy has stayed away. Artie will write soon, I just know.'

Perotine blurted out the name of some boy who had been wounded, and started to fuss about him, but Edith's attention faded. When she came into the nave, women in black glared her way, as if to demand to know why her husband was still alive. The organ started. She would sing especially loud.

CHAPTER 41

J anuary brought another list, a Roll of Honour, a grand total of the fallen so far. One poor woman had lost three sons, two on the same day. More lists came, of men confirmed as prisoners. Ordinary life seemed to have been suspended in the wait for news. It snowed overnight and there was a sharp frost. On the sixth all the remaining family went to church to join the Day of Prayer at the urging of the king. Oh how they prayed!

Edith stopped reading the newspaper, relying on Henry or George to nod and reassure her when they had come to the end of the casualty lists. Henry bit deep on to his pipe at some names. George would frown and ask his father whether this was the Peter that Jack had worked with, or the Arnold who lived down by the coast. With precious little work to do at the yard or the quarry, waiting for the paper was the afternoon's occupation. George wore his old glasses all the time, and Edith did not scold him. Everyone needed hope now.

One thing was certain; she would not go and see Edwin Brown. She had shocked herself, was too embarrassed to even look herself in the mirror. Artie was being brave, but she had been a coward. Her devil-may-care mood brought on by the war had turned to disgust. Even her aunt had sniffed out her guilt and sent her packing. She would not see Edwin again, not even if he walked up to her in the street and begged. The rotter, the stay-at-home shirker – he was not half the man her Artie was. More than she dreaded the telegram boy, she dreaded looking Artie in the face and giving away her bitter secret.

The telegram boy stayed away, for sure, but telegrams were for officers. Other ranks' families made do with printed forms delivered by post. Edith did not know this; she just feared the telegram that she had heard so much about. The post boy nipped down the path, but she caught him before he had time to slip the letter through the box. Edith took the envelope and the boy hurried away, not wanting to see her open it. He had a sackful to deliver.

It was a form, a plain form, with boxes filled in by hand. Artie's name and regiment were there.

She sat in her rocker for ten minutes, alone, with the clock ticking away the last minutes of her married life. A numbness grew within her.

Artie had been listed as missing on 1 December 1917.

What was 'missing'? Was it simply news that was missing, or had some clerk mislaid a piece of paper and the truth would soon out? Or was it a horrible euphemism like 'fallen' or 'lost' that hid a ghastlier truth? Since she first saw it used in the newspaper, the word had haunted her.

Henry came in, dusty, tired from actually having found a few days' work. He hunted for his pipe before even saying hello. He froze as he saw Edith sitting there.

'Not Artie? Not our Artie?'

Edith handed him the form silently, her hands shaking just as much as his.

'My Artie!'

George too must have known the instant he saw her face. She was still in the rocker, cheeks stung by trails of tears, official form fixed in her hand. Across from her sat his father staring into the fire.

'Edith?'

'Artie's gone.'

He snatched the form, reading it quickly, and then re-reading it. 'No, it says he's missing.'

'Gone!' she repeated.

'No, it means, it means…'

'Blown to pieces,' said his father. 'Just like that. And for what? King bloody George the Fifth. My Artie, my boy.'

'No, he could be a prisoner… it says here he could be separated from his regiment, which means he's lost somewhere in a fog, or a wood.'

'We'd have heard!' Edith wailed. 'It's been weeks, someone would know.'

Henry Bazin sat staring into space, gripping his cold pipe as if he would never let it go again. 'Bloody English,' he said. 'Bloody English have killed my son.'

'Pépaen, no, it was the Germans,' George said, as if it were any comfort.

'And you're the one telling me he's still alive? Lost in a fog is it? Lost on some general's desk?' Henry gave a sob. 'And they can't even be bothered to find his body and write to his wife, and his old *père*.'

Edith snapped out of her own mourning. 'Henry,' she said. 'George could be right.'

Henry looked into the distance. 'Cursed we are, bad luck from the start.' His head sagged into his lap, he sobbed without control. 'Wish your sister was here. Where's Drusille?'

'Pépaen?' asked George.

Henry sputtered, lifted his head and rolled his eyes, but they were strange, fish-like eyes. His head fell back and spittle ran from his mouth. His pipe fell to the floor.

George knelt by his side. 'Pépaen, speak to me.'

His mouth moved, but he only gurgled like a baby.

Edith shot across to help. 'Get Jack, find Jack!' she urged.

She'd never seen George move faster than he did that day. The war had come home, right into their house. His father had been struck down by that letter as surely as if it had been one of the Kaiser's shells.

February rain splashed on to those old battered glasses, reflecting her face in every drop, as if every drop were a tear. The Castel church stands exposed to the north-westerly wind and the rain cut across almost horizontally as his father's coffin was lowered into the ground to rest on top of his wife's. Heavy raindrops drummed on the coffin lid. Amid the gravestones, a spectral figure stood in sorrow. She had warned him; he had been prepared for the loss, but powerless to intervene. Perhaps that was her secret. He could not use his knowledge to change the future, only to be ready when it came.

A few days later, Artie's name was near the head of two columns of the *Press* listing missing men. All the families who had breathed a sigh after double-checking the lists of dead, wounded and prisoners knew a new fear. Letters were published appealing for information about the missing sons, brothers and husbands. Edith wrote one too. Two weeks later she received a note from Les Touillets, which had just opened up as a military hospital. Pierre Du Port was there and had news.

Edith and George walked over to the hospital that same day. A nurse brought them into a ward of metal-framed beds, where Pierre sat upright, an empty right sleeve pinned across his hospital shirt. Edith glanced at it once, then no more. Pierre produced a grin.

'Wharro, George,' Pierre said. 'Sorry to hear about your old man.'

George bunched up his chin in thanks.

'And la Missis Bazin, you come to brighten up my day? That's good of you.'

Edith sat down on the only chair and brought out a pad of notepaper and a pencil to write down any facts the wounded grower could offer.

George perched gingerly at the very end of the bed. 'And how are things with you, Dippo?'

'Reckon I'm lucky,' he replied. 'I'll get a pension and I can still work with this arm.'

He waved his left. 'Your Artie said that, him. He said, "You've got two arms for a reason, Dippo. One and a spare, eh?"' He smiled thinly. 'Half the lads are gone. Hard to think of it. Reckon they'll bring the rest home now. We've done our bit.'

'When did you last see Artie?' Edith asked earnestly. 'You said you were with Artie in the battle that was in the papers.'

Pierre frowned and was quiet for a whole minute. 'See, you've got to understand. Our battle was not the one you reads about in the papers. You wouldn't understand if you weren't there. We didn't know what was happening. Nobody told us. There would be this officer, then that sergeant and they'd get killed or we'd never see them again. It was hard to know which way was north and which way was our side and which was theirs. Just shelling and shooting.'

He told them snatches about the battle at Masnières and Les Rues Vertes and how Artie had taken charge of the group of bold men hanging on beyond the bridge.

'Then I got hit. Don't know how, can't rightly remember it happening. Must have been a shell but I don't remember it. Felt like I'd just been grabbed hard on my arm, but it was smashed. I knew straight away it was a goner. Artie sent me back – he said something. He must have been sending his best wishes to you all. Happy Christmas or something. I had this Canadian with me, we walked for miles and miles, figured we'd get killed or captured, but we both made it. He was in the bed next to me, that Canadian. He was called Rolf—'

'Who else saw Artie?' Edith interrupted.

'I was under the doctor, plenty of doctors. All keen to cut my arm off and move me on. I didn't hear anything else about what happened to Artie.'

Edith glanced at George and he nodded reassurance. 'So there's a chance, Edith, it all sounds like it was very confusing and noisy, like. Mistakes get made when things get confusing.'

'Yes,' she said.

'So, how are you now, *mon viaer*?' asked George, poking Pierre with his knuckle, trying to elicit a smile.

'I'm alive,' he said.

Edith had written down as much as she could as Pierre spoke. For weeks afterwards she asked questions of every wounded soldier she could find. There was no tale of a gallant last stand, no great poem, no song, no mention in dispatches. Artie Bazin simply faded from the story amid the confusion of a victory that turned into a retreat.

Left uncertain, perhaps a widow, perhaps not, Edith stopped eating breakfast. She was getting nowhere in her hunt for news, and eating in the morning made her feel sick. George encouraged her to eat, said she looked pale, but had she not always been pale? Was it not the curse of the redhead?

Not eating breakfast did not stop the nausea. She sat at the empty table sipping at a glass of water. She would not see a doctor, as Jack suggested. Doctors were ruinously expensive and knew nothing.

It must be the shock of the official form that caused her sickness.

It was the trauma of watching Henry die in front of her.

It was the food. Never enough of it, and not so good as in peace time.

It was the fear of being a widow.

It was the shame of that one night of foolishness.

Even her monthlies had stopped...

She gave a groan and held back her head. 'Oh no, please no,' she said.

'What?' George was kneeling by her side in an instant.

'Nothing,' she said hurriedly. 'Just, I'm sick of this war...' She burst into tears and fell on to George's shoulder.

'Oh God!'

He held her there, overwhelmed by her emotion.

'Oh George, oh George. What's going to become of us?'

CHAPTER 42

E dith had not seen Edwin since before Christmas, even by accident. The memory of one night in Victoria Road had been pushed into a dark corner of her mind and locked away, but it did not stay there. Once it was clear that Artie was in the big battle, it had crept back, daily, nightly, and her conscience bore down on her heavily. There was a saying that the guilty need no accuser.

Something inside her had snapped that November night. Some trait passed on by her mother had broken through and taken over her senses. Whenever she tried to be rational, Edith started to realise that her mistake had been inevitable. She had been drunk, but she had known what she was doing. She remembered a conscious thought that it had been wrong, but damn the consequences. War made people reckless, but she could not blame the war for everything.

Now she needed to see him, even finding Edwin Brown was hard. By enquiring at the bank, she learned he had been posted to France. She wrote a letter and hoped.

Dear Edwin

I have heard that my husband Arthur Bazin is listed Missing on December first. Pierre Du Port tells us that he was in a battle at Les Rues Vertes. This was across a bridge. Please can you find out what happened to him?

Also I am having a baby in the summer. Artie has been gone a long time and I only just knew. It is really important

you know this. I want you to write to me straight away saying
what you know and what you think I should do. I do not want
to be on my own with this baby. I have heard that the RGLI
has done its share of the fighting and is coming home so I will
see you soon.

With affectionate regards
Edith Bazin (Mrs)

It was some weeks before she received a reply, and well into
March. The war was still dragging on, the Russians had
surrendered and the papers were full of another big battle in
France. Curiously, Edwin had chosen to write to George. He
truly was the master of subterfuge.

Dear M Bazin

I do not believe we have met, although I once worked with
your brother Arthur and had occasion to meet your sister-in-
law Mme Bazin in St Peter Port some time back. I know that
you have all been wanting news of your brother. Please accept
my deep sympathies, for I have discovered that your brother
was indeed killed in the battle at Cambrai last December.
Please communicate this news to Mme Bazin in as gentle a
manner as you feel able.

I heard the story from some of the men who were there.
Your brother died defending a village when our boys were sorely
pressed. They say he fought like a hero that day. I spoke with
a man who said he was buried with some of his comrades in a
field behind the village of Les Rues Vertes. An officer said prayers
over the grave and I hope this is of some comfort. Nobody knows
what happened to his effects as the battle was very confusing.

I am sorry to be the author of such bad news, but I wished
to let you know that Arthur did not suffer overmuch and is

now at peace. Kindly let Mme Bazin know that she should feel free to write to me at any time she should choose.

All my best wishes for your family.

Yours sincerely

E. Brown (Lt.)

A corner of the Cambrai salient would be forever Guernsey. Edith folded the letter after re-reading it twice. A teardrop splashed on to the back of the letter. She passed it back to George. He had taken off his glasses to read, and was staring into the fire. He looked again at the letter, as if hoping it would say something different a second time around.

Red-eyed, she sniffed. 'I must write to Lieutenant Brown,' she said. 'Thanking him for taking the trouble.'

'I can write.'

'Your spelling is terrible! Yes, you copy beautifully, but no, George, this is something for me to do. I need something to do now. Hope is gone.'

'There's always hope,' George said.

'No, there is not.'

'One soldier looks much like another, in their brown—'

'George. The prisoner lists have come back, the wounded lists are in the paper. Artie is…' She sniffed again. 'Can you go for a walk or something? Go to the pub?'

Few men needed such licence, but George was reluctant to leave her.

'I'll look after you,' he said.

'You're so sweet. But I need to be alone.'

Now Edith would wear black. Now she would remain seated in church, with the other widows. This black flock had been growing steadily across the pews all that bitter winter.

Guernsey should start to come alive by March. Daffodils are out long before they are seen in England, and birds start to sing songs of spring. The Valpied sisters shook their heads and counted six months since Artie had marched away to war and five more until the baby was due.

''Tis a miracle,' they scoffed as she passed.

Edith was still the belle of the Castel, and until the baby began to show she still courted admiring looks from the men who rode the tram. As soon as her condition was known, she was asked to stop working – it was simply not decent. Confined to the parish, she walked the lanes wrapped in winter clothes, but when spring came, no farmer would call after her as she walked by their field. No young men would be seen with her, avoiding any suspicion of guilt, for they could count too and it was a small island. Even her friends began to shun her, not wanting to ask questions but guessing the answer. Ever the confident one, Edith began to feel scared and uncertain. Only one person remained solidly on her side.

More and more, she relied on George.

For a while Edith half expected some divine intervention, a little accident, an unfortunate illness which would terminate the life that had not yet fully come to be. As the new year progressed, she knew that the baby was determined to come. Men were dying by the drove, and the world needed babies and it needed joy.

By April, the era of trench warfare and stalemate was over. The newspapers did not seem to know where the front line was any more, and all the headlines looked ominous. General Haig had issued an order, saying it was 'Backs to the Wall' as the Kaiser's troops smashed through the exhausted British army and were once more headed for Paris and victory. With things suddenly turning so desperate, everyone in the island knew that the 1st Battalion, Royal Guernsey Light Infantry must be in the thick of it over in Flanders.

Edith read the short letter with trembling hands. How she wished she could speak to people across the miles, like with one of those telephones the posh houses had. It would be so much easier than trying to decode the meaning within written words. Edwin's second letter had none of the careful writing and well-picked prose of his last. Gone was any pretence that he was actually writing to George. The handwriting looked as if it had been written by someone completely different; indeed, it looked more like the writing of a woman.

Dear Edith

I have been hurt but am recovering well. Hope to be back to England hospital soon and then back to Guernsey. It is good news about your baby and I will see you on my return.

Yours, Edwin

He was badly wounded, that was clear, and some nurse was writing for him. Edith hunted back through the old newspapers stacked up in the dairy and found the casualty lists from three days before. *Brown, E.F.G. Lt., wounded severely on April 13.*

How severely? She pictured lost arms and legs and a disfigured face. She recalled Pierre's empty sleeve and Tom Carey's plastic mask and felt sick with horror. Then she realised she was thinking of herself, and how she would react to a man who was no longer whole. It was not the time to think of herself. Edwin had mentioned the baby, so in code had accepted it as his own. He was young, he was strong and now he would be coming home. She would be waiting, and she was determined to be a rock of strength if he needed her.

CHAPTER 43

'George!' It was Adèle Le Page who welcomed him to her father's farmhouse.

'Is your *père* in?' he asked, following her into the kitchen and laying a sack on the table. 'Or your *mémaen*?'

'Ooh, what have you got?'

'Two chancres and a flatfish. I've another fish, even, but that's for our supper. Reckon we could have a can of milk and a bit of pork in exchange?'

'We're not supposed to sell it!' Adèle said, wide-eyed.

'We're not selling, we're swapping,' he said.

Country customs ranked above States legislation, and rationing was for townies.

'One of them will be back soon,' she said. 'So, what's it going to be like, being an uncle?'

'I'm not an uncle.'

'But you will be,' she said expectantly, before her face fell. 'Oh, Edith hasn't told you?'

George started to understand.

'Edith?'

Adèle mimed a fat belly. 'Surely even you've noticed, George? Our spindly Edith isn't as spindly as she used to be?'

'She's not been well. Sick in the mornings.'

'Well there you go!'

A strange sensation came over him, a kind of relief and a kind of wonder. Amid all this death had come life.

'Artie…' he said.

'Yes, wonderful isn't it?' Adèle said. 'It… well, it makes up for her losing Artie, in a way. To know he'll have a little boy, or a little girl.'

George's hands tensed on his sack and he lifted it from the table. 'I'll come back,' he said. All this needed some thinking about.

He walked home as quickly as he could, the crabs still wriggling in his sack. Edith had offered scant explanation for why she had come back to live with the family before Christmas, nor why she had suddenly stopped working on the trams.

She came in from the yard, looking tired and pale as had become usual. 'Fish supper?' she asked.

'Yes – and two chancres. I was going to swap them with the Le Pages.'

He looked straight at her and she met him stare for stare. 'Why didn't you tell me about the baby?'

'I would have, in time.'

'Why does no one tell me things? I'm not stupid. They didn't tell me Mémaen was dying, and now you…'

'Things can happen,' Edith said. 'Babies don't always come. I wanted to be sure before I told everyone – I didn't tell Jack, either, if that makes you feel better.'

'Is it why you've stopped working the trams?'

'Yes. It's not seemly.'

'What will we do for money?'

'God knows. You'd better earn some. Sell them crabs.'

'I'll help you look after it,' he said earnestly.

'That's very kind.' Too exhausted to stand any more, Edith took a kitchen chair.

'It will be paying Artie back for the way he looked after me when I was little.'

She took a sharp intake of breath. 'George, let's not talk about this, eh? It's early days and… well, it just reminds me of all that's happened, all that's gone wrong.'

As she said this, tears began to course down her cheeks. He sat in the next chair and put a hand on her shoulder.

'Don't!' she scolded, and he drew back. 'Just don't!'

Edith took the horse bus to Town, sitting on her own, with a basket of eggs on the seat next to her. She wore a large black bonnet, borrowed from George's Aunt Irene. Its fringe came so far forward that she could only see and be seen from dead ahead. She stared out of the window and ignored the other passengers, who were all ignoring her.

Town had the usual Saturday morning bustle and it lifted her heart. Of course there were many faces she recognised, but it was not actually true that everyone in Guernsey knew everyone else. A busy market square made it all feel not so small and part of a wider world. Here were French sailors and men from their seaplane squadron. A few men in khaki or navy blue were home on leave, and women in the uniforms of nurses and auxiliary units mixed with those who stayed home to keep the island's heart beating.

Too many women were wearing black, even though it was past Easter. The Battle of the Lys was claiming what remained of Guernsey's regiment after the Battle of Cambrai. It was the same story of endless lists in the paper, which Edith never read any more. People used the phrase 'wiped out' and the cost of the stubborn retreat was carried on the faces of so many people she brushed past in the marketplace.

By Edith's reckoning the prices had doubled since the war started and the market stalls offered less to buy than in previous years. Meat was in short supply, while butter and margarine had joined the list of rationed foods. Her eggs were sold to one stallholder for a price which would have been absurd two years earlier, and in return she bought salt, flour and some corned beef. What she really needed was material to make summer clothes, as she was not certain what shape she would be after the baby was born and her wardrobe would be ruined by being taken out or modified to fit her pregnant shape. At some point she would be out of mourning and need to bring colour back into her life. She wanted to look bright and fresh when Edwin came home.

Handling the bolts of cloth, she was depressed by the price and knew she could not afford to make a single skirt. Sighing, putting down the cloth, she took up her basket. An older couple dressed in black were slowly working their way down the market. Their faces seemed grey. The man wore a top hat, and round his right arm was a black band of mourning.

Edith stared at them, but they did not even acknowledge her presence. What was one more young widow to them? Mr and Mrs Brown strode steadily past, carrying their sorrow in a cloud all around them. The cloud enveloped Edith, bringing on a state verging on panic.

'Mrs Brown?' Without intending it, she was clutching the woman's arm.

Mrs Brown pulled away, startled.

'I'm sorry,' said Edith. 'It's just...'

'Have we met, young lady?'

'I – my husband used to work with Edwin.'

The name caused the woman to sniff.

'I'm... I'm very sorry for your loss,' Edith said, backing away.

'Thank you,' said Mr Brown, and led his wife away.

Edith's world turned fuzzy and indistinct, then dark.

'Madam? Madam?'

Edith blinked open her eyes. High above her, silhouetted against the sky was a policeman. Next to her, kneeling on the cobbles was a nurse with wide, flowing cape and cap.

'Are you hurt, dear?'

Yes, she had cracked her arm as she fell. Pain stabbed through as she came back to consciousness. Her basket had taken most of the impact with the cobbles and was rather crushed. She pushed it away and sat upright.

'I'll be fine in a few moments.'

'You fainted, madam. Fainted dead away,' the policeman said.

'How is the baby?' the nurse asked urgently.

Edith touched her belly but sensed nothing unusual. That would have been a blessing, an ironic twist to the morning, a sort of silver lining. She was helped to her feet, with a crowd of people all around enquiring after her health and wishing her well. A boy picked up her basket, but its handle came away as he lifted it. Edith began to sob.

'Now, now,' the nurse said. 'This must be very hard for you.'

The nurse had added the black mourning garb to the state of Edith's pregnancy and drawn her own conclusions. Edith continued to sob, waggling the broken handle. It was one last, pathetic tragedy.

'*Madaume*! *Madaume*!' A man called from a stall further down the arcade. He came forward, clutching one of the baskets from his stall.

'The army wouldn't take me. It's me chest.' He offered the basket to her. 'It's the least I can do. I don't want no money.'

She thanked him quietly and transferred the contents of the broken basket to the new one. Then she wandered away.

Edwin Brown was dead. Now Edith was truly lost. Her bastard would be born, the war would go on forever, all the young men would be killed and any that limped back from France would have the pick of the women starved of menfolk for all those years. No one would want a faithless, penniless widow and her bastard child.

Adèle came to see her, from time to time. Tight-lipped, she asked how Edith was feeling. The way Adèle glanced at her belly made Edith sense jealousy.

'I want a baby one day,' Adèle said. 'I've got a sweetheart now, you know.' She set her chin proudly. 'He's an Engineer – from Town. He was home on leave, met him at a dance. He's called Colin—'

'Like the fairy king,' Edith observed.

'What?' Adèle scowled.

Edith was dreamy and distracted. 'It's an old story my mum used to tell. Colin the Fairy King comes to Guernsey to steal all the women, then fill the island with all of his offspring.'

'Caw, that's just old rubbish. My man's a Le Lacheur from Town. And he's ever so handsome and he's going to marry me the minute the war is over. And that has to be soon, eh?'

Edith nodded silently.

'You're so quiet, Edith, it's not like you. You should be glad, with your baby coming. We all miss Artie, but you'll have the baby.' Adèle looked searchingly at Edith, who said nothing.

'It's not his, is it?' Adèle stated.

Edith gave a shrug and a sigh. 'I wasn't a bad wife. It's like I knew he wasn't coming back. The news from France is so slow, but somehow I knew.'

'So,' asked Adèle, wide-eyed, 'the real father, does he live around here, him?'

'He doesn't live anywhere,' Edith said, and stretched her

mouth into a wide, false grin. 'God gives, then takes away, then takes away some more.'

She laid her hand on her unwanted, bloated waist. The father may as well have been Colin, the Fairy King.

In the weeks of waiting, Edith drew up plans and strategies that amounted to little more than fantasies. She could go away, perhaps to London, where nobody knew her. This dream quickly evaporated, as without a job, without a home and with not even a pension yet from the army she could see herself starving in some squalid backstreet, prey to men who did not care how wicked she was. Away from Guernsey, Edith would truly become a fallen woman.

She came to see George one day when he was working in the yard, working slowly to shape a headstone. It was still blank, one of those held back by Jack 'to be ready'.

She approached from behind, from his right. George jumped to his feet, whirling around, startled. He was not wearing glasses, but his old ones sat on a wall within reach. For a moment it was as if he were looking at a ghost, and then he realised that this was a flesh-and-blood woman before him.

Edith had never had the dark summer complexion of a true Guernsey girl, as her red hair made her prey to the sun. Today her skin looked pure porcelain white. She tossed off her black bonnet and settled on an old chair.

'I didn't mean to interrupt. Carve away. Don't mind me.'

Warily, he returned to his work.

'Will you carve me a headstone, George?'

'What?' He stopped again.

'In white marble, not that cheap stone.'

'Purbeck stone's not so cheap.'

'And I want it placed in a sunny patch, up at St Matthew's with a view out to sea, not back at the parish church with all those gloomy old tombs.'

'What are you talking about? You're not dying?'

'No, but women die in childbirth. It happens all the time. Men go off to war, but we face...'

'It will all be fine.'

'Pah. I wish I lived in your world where everything is fine,' she said. 'Did you carve the headstone for Ada Le Tocq?'

'No.'

'Died at the turn of the year, her; baby stillborn too. She was my age; we were at Vale school together.'

'I never knew her.'

'She lived over there, over by Cobo.' Edith waved her hand northwards. 'Moved down here when she married.'

'But you're a strong one, Edith. And Artie's baby will be a strong one too.'

She looked at him, hard and long. A question he dared not ask burned inside him. He stopped working again.

'Mind, your baby's a long time coming,' said George, expecting a confession.

Edith said nothing.

'I heard whispers.'

'Don't listen to them.'

'Artie went away in September last year. His baby should have come by now, but Adele says you're two months off.'

'George, you're not stupid. People think you are, but you're not. You know which way is up.'

'So Artie is not the father?'

She looked off across the Mare. 'People are saying I'm no good. Your mother never met me, but even she thought I wasn't good enough for Artie.'

'Mémaen was not right about everything,' he said. 'She and Père did their share of wrong things. We all do.'

'You're so good, George,' she sighed. 'Sometimes I think you're the only person with any heart left.'

He stopped all pretence of stone-cutting. She did care for him, after all! 'So where's the real father now?' he asked.

'Dead and gone. First Artie and then...' She wouldn't speak his name. 'I'm being punished. I lose Artie, I get this baby, I lose everyone. I'm not so evil that I deserve this!'

'You're not evil, you're beautiful.'

'But everyone knows! I see them nodding my way, talking behind my back.'

'Say it was my child.'

'No!'

'Say it.'

'It will be a lie, and what will people think of us? What I did was maybe a sin, but lying would be a double sin.'

'I don't care what they think of me, only how they think of you.'

'It's not your baby, George.'

'But it will be. I'll treat it just as if it were my own, or Artie's. Your baby is my baby, Edith.'

She gripped his hand. 'You are impossibly good. I...' She looked away, tears streaming down her cheeks. 'I'm only young, I shouldn't have to go through all this.'

Before he had chance to say what he was bursting to say, she ran from the yard in tears.

That night George walked home with purpose. An idea had been forming for some weeks. It was an idea made in heaven to quash all the conspiracies of the Devil. He switched from one pair of glasses to the other these days as the mood took him, and Edith had stopped even remarking on it. Today, for no particular reason, the old ones had come out.

George sensed that he was being followed. His original love was behind him, catching him up without effort. He was aware of a growing coldness, an all-over shiver starting at his neck and gradually freezing both body and soul. For the first time she overtook him, moved to block his path, blotting out his view. Arms folded, chin set straight, look as hard as a gravestone she glared at him.

'Get away! Get away!' he bleated.

Waving his arms to clear his way he tried to run, but the misty apparition drifted before him, dark displeasure souring her face.

'You can't keep me forever! Am I never to wed? Must I always be alone?'

George pulled off the glasses. The world fell into smudged incoherence on all sides. Trailing one hand against the hedge for guidance he blundered home. From the dresser he took his new spectacles and from a drawer he took one of his father's ties.

He inspected himself in the mirror. 'I am the man of the house now.' The way things were turning, when Jack passed on, George would be the last of the Bazins. That added weight to his shoulders, but put resolve in his breast.

Edith was working the raspberry canes to keep busy. When she saw the semblance of tidiness, the black-rimmed glasses and the look of terror on his face, she understood his mission.

'Oh George!' she said.

'I was thinking. With you, and me, and the baby, we'll be a family, a proper family again, eh?'

What else could she do? 'Yes, we will, won't we?'

'Edith, will you marry me?'

What option did she have left? She gave a laugh, possibly of relief. 'You're too good. I'm not good enough for you.'

'But you are, and you will be.'

She stood up, dusting her hands, and glanced away from him.

'I know this is not what you wanted and I know you want better things, but we're young and there's a new world coming after the war.'

Edith bit her lip, looked at the ground, considered her belly, ran through the names and faces that had deserted her or died to leave her in this strait; a woman alone, backed into the last corner of a very small island on the edge of a world at war – a war that looked like being lost after all the heartache. She forced out a smile. It was the closest she might come to salvation.

'Yes, George, I will.'

A massive relief swept over her as she let the words tumble out. She was the drowning swimmer plucked from the water by strong hands, the maiden carried from a burning building in the arms of a fireman. George had saved her.

'We can't do it until December the second,' he pulled a face. 'Artie has to be gone a year and a day, Jack said, before we know he's truly gone. But that's in time for Christmas, eh?'

He took her arm and they walked to the top of the field and she relaxed as she had not done for many months. She even found a smile. The sun was falling and sparkled off his glasses in reds and yellows.

'You are the most beautiful woman in the world,' he said.

CHAPTER 44

On Sunday the unlikely couple drove to church together in the cart, with Jack and Mrs Patterson too. George was going to have to talk to the preacher, but not with Edith around. He'd leave that until later in the week. As for those old glasses, they were firmly packed away in that cigar box.

Clopping at little more than walking pace, the cart gradually overtook the Valpied sisters also heading for the church. Edith ignored them, but George, still in fear of them, nodded a courteous greeting. He felt their eyes on his back.

'Look at him,' said the older. 'Cuckoo in the nest, brother dead and he jumps straight in.'

'Gets his house when his father died,' said the other. 'Gets his job when that young mason was killed. Now he gets the wife of his dead brother. That's the Devil's luck.'

'Là, and he works with tombstones. Death is his friend.'

In order to visit the Reverend Mosney that Tuesday, George wore his new glasses, and his suit. He was welcomed for the second time into the kitchen of the rectory, and asked to sit, but he wanted to remain standing, toying with his cap.

'You see, Rector, I wants to marry Edith. Artie's widow.'

'Your brother's widow?'

'Yes. She's with child and her family's gone. And again it doesn't seem proper for a woman and a man that isn't married to be sharing a house.'

'That's a noble thing you propose,' the rector told him. 'But you know there is an impediment?'

'A what?'

'First – do you know for sure that your brother is dead?'

'Yes, Lieutenant Brown wrote to us from France. He found the men who buried him. It was good he had a Christian burial.'

'Well, mistakes are made. Only last week we heard that Matthew Ogier was alive and a prisoner, when everyone thought him dead. Not even a year has passed. In fact I think it must be a year and a day before a missing man can be declared legally dead.'

'I know he's dead, I feel it, I know it's true. And the baby won't wait a year.'

'Ah, the baby, yes. When is the child due to be born?' the priest asked, with so little hint of suspicion in his voice that George missed it entirely.

'I don't know rightly. Summer some time. Our Edith said July or August.'

The rector nodded thoughtfully. 'Come with me.' He led through to his study and took down an English Bible. This began to feel familiar. He thumbed through to the book of Leviticus. 'You can read, George. Chapter twenty, verse twenty-one. Read it aloud.'

George frowned at the book, moved his fingers down the columns of words until he found verse 21. '"And if a man shall take his brother's wife, it is impurity…" How can that be? Artie is dead.'

'Continue.'

'"…he hath uncovered his brother's nakedness." How? What's this matter?'

'Continue.'

George huffed. 'Er, "they shall be childless".'

'Childless,' the rector said, pointedly.

The priest took the book and read the text clearly. '"And if a man shall take his brother's wife, it is impurity; he hath uncovered his brother's nakedness; they shall be childless".'

'But she's having a baby.'

'What you propose is forbidden by heaven. It is also, by the way, against the law of the land. You cannot marry your brother's widow.'

'But that's not fair!'

'It's the law, George Bazin. I'm sorry if that is what you both wish, but it would be a sin. You cannot be married on this island.'

It was if George had stepped in front of a tram. The truth hit him with a force he never imagined. His mouth went dry, he screwed his cap up into a tight ball.

'Is there anything else you wish to tell me? About the child, for instance?'

'It's Artie's baby, if that's your meaning.'

'I've heard that's not so.'

'Well, it is so. People tell lies, people round here have nothing better to do.'

He turned his back on the priest without thanking him or saying farewell. He passed the rector's wife in the kitchen without as much as a glance. George was not a man who knew anger, but now he was so angry he could choke. He rushed down Rectory Hill and then took the road leading to the Cobo Hotel, where in time he stood by the bar and ordered a pint of beer.

The bar was half-empty. Almost all the men under forty were gone to war now and those who remained tended to keep their own company out of shame. Nobody spoke to him, apart from the barman who scarcely uttered ten words.

After some hours at last he had the courage to walk home. It was a lonely walk, but at least he did not see a gloating face reflected in glass.

Edith smiled at him eagerly when he came into the kitchen, but her smile soon turned to a frown. 'George, you've been drinking! That's not like you.'

'Thought at first I might want to celebrate, but not now. The preacher says we can't be married, says so in the Bible.'

'That's rubbish.'

'Says so in the Bible.'

'Which part?'

He went to the parlour immediately and brought *La Grande Bible* that the family had shared for decades.

'The English one!' she urged. 'Oh for God's sake.' Edith went to find her own pocket bible, which was in English. She brought the good book back, starting to flick the pages. 'So where does it say it?'

'Near the beginning somewhere.'

'It's a bloney thick book, George!'

'He showed me the page, he made me read it.'

'Find it!' she snapped, passing it to him.

Of course Edith's pocket bible was smaller than the one the priest had, and the pages were not the same and nor were the words exactly. It was strange that the Word of God differed from one bible to the other, as if someone had copied it wrong over the years. It took over an hour for George to find Leviticus 20:21. Edith read it in silence. He picked up *La Grande Bible* to check whether the French version held out more hope.

Edith snapped her bible shut. 'I was never much for the church anyway,' she said. 'When I was eight I wanted to be a nun, because I wanted to look serious and dress in black, but that was it.'

'We'll live in sin,' George suddenly declared.

'What?'

'Like Uncle Jack and Mrs Patterson.'

'No we bloney well will not!' she retorted. 'My name is black enough already round here. I'll be a proper wife, not someone's mistress, your *contchubaenne*.'

'But, Edith, what about you and me?'

'Brother and sister,' she said. 'Like it has been up to now.'

'But everyone thinks—'

'Let them think. Do I care what the Valpied sisters say about me? Not one double. And neither should you.'

'But I loves you, Edith, I wants to marry you.'

'Well, God says it can't happen. And when you're dead, you can go up and argue it out with him.' Tears started to stream down her cheeks. 'We really are cursed, George, we're totally and utterly damned, the pair of us.'

He took her hand and found that he was crying too.

CHAPTER 45

George took his little boat out from Cobo and rowed a quarter mile from shore, to where his *trousse* of pots were sunk in the lee of Moulière. He kept another group over by Grandes Rocques, but they were for another day. The crabs were one of the winners of this war, as with fewer fishermen they were growing bigger and more numerous. The same went for the ormers, but George had never been sure enough of his footing to go ormering. He pulled up two healthy-looking spider crabs and a pair in the same pot that were too small to bother with, which he threw back for another year. A fat chancre and a blue lobster soon joined the spiders. Both were mean and riled by being caught and did their best to nip George as he dunked them in the keeping basket. Mrs Patterson liked lobster and would pay a good price. Yes, there were wartime rules about who should sell to whom and how much should be paid, but the joy of being thought simple was that few expected you to know the rules.

Rules, laws, God's law. The boat rocked in the swell and the sea creatures clacked in the basket.

'I am free and you are not!' He wagged a finger at the lobster, whose stalk-eyes glared back.

Free to do what? Free to marry the woman he adored? Free to serve his king? No; he was free to trap sand eels and crabs, catch sea bass, grow tomatoes, crack rock and carve the names of the dead. In the evening he could lean on the bar at the Cobo and listen to the other men moan about their wives. It was not enough, and it would never be enough. A wide blue horizon was broken only by the smoke trailing from a steamer. He was tempted to row out, and keep rowing until the island vanished and there was only sea. Then he would have it out with God.

Jack and George talked over the war news as they were repairing a wall near Rectory Hill. The Kaiser's big offensive had been defeated, and even the Red Baron was dead. Perhaps, just perhaps, the latest big battle was going as well as the newspapers claimed.

'We need to go into Town to change out our French money,' Jack said. 'Have you got any napoleons left?'

'Edith had a few, but she swapped them out last week,' George replied sullenly. 'I reckon we got a bad deal there. What's wrong with French money anyway?'

'My brother would have said it's because the English want us to be theirs, not half-French. I know the exchange rate is rigged, everyone says so, but what can you do? I've got at least fifty put by for a rainy day – I figured silver will always be worth something.'

Jack held out his hands and George passed up a block of part-shaped granite. With a few knocks of his trowel handle the stone was urged into place. 'So I'll go to Town tomorrow, get it done. Even Judas only wanted thirty pieces of silver, eh?'

'Will you go up in the morning?'

'Yes, once we're done here there's no more work this week.'

'Mr Robins from St Andrew's needs help on the vinery again,' George offered brightly.

'Tomato picking? I didn't spend the best part of my life

learning a trade to end up picking tomatoes. We've got to end this war quick, get things back the way they were.'

Jack slapped on more mortar. 'Stone – yes, the big long one.'

George hefted the stone more or less into place.

'I let Helier go,' Jack said, setting the stone with an effortlessness that takes years of practice. 'He's going to be a hospital porter.'

'He told me,' said George.

'Even then, there's barely work for the two of us. Nobody is building, hardly any repairing even. It's all just stopped, it's all like we're holding our breath.'

George sensed there was a meaning to this conversation, but it was not like Jack to be this oblique. 'Are you letting me go too, Uncle Jack?'

'No, no, it's me that's going. One man can run what's left of the business. Hire help by the day when you have to. There's a few men back just one finger down or limping no worse than you.'

'But what are you going to do?'

'Join up.'

'You're too old.'

'They're asking for men up to fifty-one from now on. All the young 'uns are used up. The Governor himself says the regiment is wrecked and there's not enough left to fill it.' Jack looked off into the distance, perhaps into the future.

'Then I'll go too,' said George. 'They have to take me now.'

Jack sighed. 'Yes, let's finish it together.'

Without telling Edith, or Mrs Patterson, uncle and nephew rode into Town the next morning. The business at the bank was quickly concluded and the French napoleons were turned into English pounds and shillings. Jack never really trusted paper and he paid half his notes straight into his account. George had actually found four napoleons in a jar and exchanged them for shillings. He had no use for notes, nor for a bank account. Business concluded, they drove the cart out to the castle, as casual as if they were tourists on a scenic drive.

The sea washed beneath them as they crossed the bridge on foot to the squat, ancient fortress. For eight hundred years it had asserted control over the harbour, assuring that even if England did not strictly rule Guernsey, it had a firm grip on its collar. Just to make the point, the arms of Queen Elizabeth were above their heads as they entered the tunnel at the end of the bridge. A sentry stopped them, questioned them, and directed them to the brick guardhouse.

Harold Torode wore a captain's pips and the care lines of a man who had been tested to his limit. He rose to greet them with the help of a stick.

'Jack!'

'Harold. Glad to see you're in one piece.'

'Most of me. The footballing days are over though.'

'Come on, *mon viaer*, they were over long before now.'

'So they were, but I enjoyed chasing my boys around.'

'Are they safe?' Jack asked cautiously.

'Both, yes.' Harold touched the tabletop for luck. 'So far, so good. A couple of scrapes, one even got himself a medal, but... we hope the worst's over.'

Harold looked from uncle to nephew. 'So, no prizes for guessing why you're here. You come to sign up?'

'Both of us.'

'For sure?'

'They're calling men my age up,' said Jack. 'At least this way I can say I volunteered. Went in with my eyes open, I wasn't dragged in.'

Harold nodded. 'But George?'

'I can walk better than you now,' said George.

'Yes, I bet you can, but you can still stay out of this. The news has been better of late, but the Russians have thrown in their cards, leaving the Germans men to spare. God knows where all those Americans have got to that were supposed to win the war for us.'

'You need more men, then,' said George. 'My brother was killed, so I figure I could take his place, get my own back.'

'Me too,' said Jack. 'I lost my brother by way of this war.'

'I heard about Henry. Great shame, very untimely at his age. So how old are you, Jack?'

He gave a Gallic shrug. 'Young enough.'

'Let's say fifty-one?' Harold scribbled on a form.

'Twenty-one,' George added, unprompted.

Another form was hastily brought out. 'Finish these, see the MO, and you're in. Both of you.'

As they came out of the castle into a sea breeze, George felt as light as air, as if he were joining his spirit. She would come with him to France, he knew. She would guide him through the smoke and the mud and she would stand and protect him like the Angel of Mons. Death held no dominion over George.

CHAPTER 46

Leviticus 20 had ended Edith's last hope. She sat in the house when the rain came, and sat in the house when the sun came out. She barely saw the summer flowers take over the hedge-banks, or the poppies spreading across the fields or the return of the swifts; she hardly ventured further than to hang out the washing or snatch eggs from under the hens. Old soldiers disbelieved the stories that the Germans were exhausted and ready to crumble, they expected the bloodshed to resume any day and braced themselves for another onslaught. For Edith, her doom was more certain. Yes, she would suffer and shed blood but after her pain and struggle would come a defeat, with all her dreams in ruins.

Her time came all too swiftly. An army recruit can desert, but not a mother-to-be. She could not delay enlistment into the ranks of motherhood, nor pick and choose her day when the time was right and her mind set. When a baby wants to arrive, it arrives.

Beatrice Bazin had an easy birth, if any birth can be called easy. Aunt Irene, Marie Bazin's older sister, played midwife. She brought George and Jack in to see the mother and child, upstairs in the main bedroom of the Big House. Edith lay exhausted in George's parents' old bed. She lay on her side, back to the child, hand covering her eyes.

'Edith?' George asked.

The mother lay still. He turned to the baby, which Jack prodded once, cautiously.

'See, she's a Bazin all right,' said the midwife.

'Hmm,' said Jack, looking George square in the eye. 'Is Edith fine?'

'She's tired. You'd be tired after all that, Jack Bazin. Just be grateful you're a man.'

Jack stepped back, allowing George to come close.

'Can I?' he asked. He leaned over the baby.

'You take care, mind,' said Aunt Irene. 'Sit down first. Here you go, hold her like so.'

George took the bundle in his arms and blue eyes looked up at him. As far as the world was concerned, he was the father of this fatherless child. By ancient custom, he claimed this role by being the first man to lift the baby. The baby gazed up at him.

'Hello, little one,' he said. 'I'm George.'

Edith remained in a state of exhaustion and torpor for several days. She had done it. Millions of women had done this before, back to the gates of time, but she was still stunned that she herself had delivered life. That nine-month nightmare of unknowing was over. It was over, she told herself, *it was over.*

'You need to feed her again,' the midwife chided.

'Again? I don't eat every two hours. I'd be big as a house if I did. Can't you…'

'No I can't. We're not posh people with wet nurses and you'll do your duty, my girl!'

Edith sat upright and pulled her hair aside. She sighed. 'Bring it.'

Aunt Irene clattered down the stair, leaving Edith to her task. Staring straight ahead, the young mother felt a tugging at her body as the little thing took its fill. The master bedroom was no more than a casualty ward and she was another victim of the war. She felt tired, she felt sick. Now what?

She glanced down at the black curly head. It wasn't a little model of red-headed self, but something completely alien.

Down in the kitchen George's aunt took a cup of tea and a slice of *gâche mêlaïe* sent round by Adèle. His first of the season.

'Edith don't seem happy with Bea,' said George. 'That's what we're going to call her, after my great-aunt.'

'Oh yes,' said Irene. 'Old Aunt Bea, she was a one. Nutty as a fruit cake, come the end. She smoked a pipe and never spoke a word of English.'

'It was my idea,' George added. 'In fact it might be Beatrice Marie, after Mémaen.'

'I'm surprised Edith didn't have a suggestion of her own.'

'She just said yes,' George said sadly. 'Like I was asking if I could have a second cup of tea. Like she didn't care what Bea was called. I said the baby needs a name and she said nothing, so I suggested Beatrice and she just said yes.'

'She's young,' said the older woman. 'But then, I was her age when I had my first. Mind, I'd seen my sisters and cousins with their babies and I knew what to do. I don't think your Edith had that kind of family.'

'We're that kind of family,' George said.

'Hmm,' said Irene, clearly thinking more than she would say. 'I'm happy to be here for you now, but there's my own to care for. Edith is going to have to take some responsibility soon.'

'I want to help,' George declared. 'Tell me what to do.'

Edith responded well to George's urge to play nurse. He soon knew all about changing nappies and burping and how to hold a child and rock it to sleep. He was a better father than most fathers.

Allowed time to herself, Edith quickly recovered her shape and her complexion. Sitting up in bed, she wrote a letter to Government House asking about her widow's pension and the special five pound grant and adding that she now had a war orphan to care for too. Money had been tight, and with three to feed it was going to become tighter.

Once she was fit and moving about, she set to working on her clothes, bringing them back down from monstrous size. What she really wanted was new ones, and fewer in black.

Two weeks after Bea was born, Edith received a letter saying that because Artie had only been missing for nine months he was not yet legally dead, and therefore Mrs Bazin was not a widow, and furthermore by extension did not have an orphan in her care.

In a fit of rage she screwed it up and threw it across the kitchen.

She stood over the cot. 'You're not an orphan. But you know what you are? Yes, yes, look at me like that, why don't you?' She wagged her finger at the helpless bundle. 'The nobs at Government House don't want to know you, and I'm not crawling to the parish. You know whose fault you are, eh?'

She had been counting the money remaining in the jar and working out the likely expenses for the next year and found they would be short. One crisis and they could be back begging the *Procureur des Pauvres* for help. Yes, there were assistance funds set up by well-meaning ladies but going to them was just another form of begging. Jack was generous and more or less kept them all alive, but his business had all but dried up. Any day, he and George could be dragged off to the war and that would be it.

The pair had finally confessed to volunteering for the RGLI. What idiots men were. Did all the Bazin men have an urge to be killed? Had it been passed down from father to son, until there were no sons left to have sons of their own? Before autumn came, she'd be on her own with a house and a cottage to choose from. At least she could rent one out.

A strong resolve came over her. Donning her widow's black for the last time, she took Bea in her arms, wrapped well against the gusty rain that came in from the west in short intermittent squalls. Travelling on the omnibus she ignored the other passengers as usual. The widow whose husband had last touched island soil eleven months earlier was carrying a two-week-old child. She alighted at the top of the Grange and walked down Victoria Road. By this time, the rain had stopped and the sun flashed out from between the clouds. This was a smart part of town, with villas in white and pastel shades build side by side down the hill. Some had basements and stairs over them to reach the front door. It reminded her of pictures she had seen of London.

She arrived in front of the Brown residence. Resolute, she stood at the bottom of its front steps, summoning all her courage. Bea was crooked in her left arm, the ultimate symbol of the wronged woman. Up she went and rang the doorbell by twisting a knob round and round.

A girl aged perhaps twelve answered the door. Possibly she was Edwin's younger sister.

'Good day. May I help you?' she asked in a polite and practised manner.

'I need to see Mr Brown.'

'Just a moment,' the girl said politely.

'Momma!' she called, running inside. 'A visitor. She wants Father.'

Edith took this as an invitation and stepped into the hallway. The floor was set with a red-framed mosaic in an Arabic style some called Guernsey Mosque. She regretted the first day she had laid eyes on it. Edith's impulses had so often ruined her plans.

Mrs Brown came from a back room, all dressed in black as she had been that day in the market.

'Yes? Can I help you? We're not buying anything today.'

'Is Mr Brown in?'

'He is at home, yes.'

'I need to speak to him – to both of you.'

'Could you make an appointment? Is this about the bank?'

'It's about Edwin, your son.'

Mrs Brown began to detect the drift of the conversation that was about to ensue.

'And who would you be?'

'Edith Bazin of La Vallée, Castel.'

'Margaret, fetch your father.'

The young girl darted away.

'You going to invite me in?'

'I think you should stay right there.' The polite tone had gone, and Mrs Brown's words carried an icy edge.

Edith took three more paces into the hall. 'It's raining out. Nasty day out the west.'

'Is it indeed?'

Mr Brown came from the back of the house. He was clutching a newspaper.

'Mr and Mrs Brown,' Edith announced. 'This is your granddaughter, Beatrice.'

For a moment there was silence. Mrs Brown's face twitched with emotion, confusion, sorrow and rage. Mr Brown's complexion lost what little colour it had.

'Get out,' the woman said coldly. 'Get out of my house now.'

'I'll not budge until you've heard me out—'

'What is the meaning of this?' Mr Brown butted in. 'How dare you! What are you insinuating?'

'Your son, Edwin, is the father of my baby.'

'Our son is dead. How dare you!'

'He wasn't dead when he had his way with me, in there.' She pointed to the parlour door.

'Harlot!' said Mrs Brown. 'You'd blacken my son's name: for what? Money?'

'Yes, money. I'm a widow, a war widow. I lost my Artie and your Edwin was going to marry me instead, and look what I've got to show for it.'

'You can prove this?' Mr Brown said.

Edith thrust Bea forward. The baby began to whimper. 'This is my proof.'

'That child could be anyone's. A French sailor's just as likely,' Mr Brown said. 'Get out of here, young lady.'

'I've got a letter too! From your Edwin.'

'Try your blackmail somewhere else.'

'But it's your granddaughter!' Edith implored. 'And we're penniless, stony-broke. I'm having to fight to get a pension from the War Office.'

Mr Brown replaced his anger with an officious tone he must use in business. 'Madam, that is all very sad and very tragic and I am sorry for your loss but we cannot take any responsibility for you or your child. And that is final.'

Edith was losing the battle. 'I'll tell people. I'll tell the people at the bank. I'll tell everyone.'

'You'll tell no one.'

'I'll write to the paper and say how it's shocking—'

'And my advocate will have you in court for libel and slander, my girl! Now off with you!' He stepped forward, threateningly.

'Off with me, eh? Off back to the country where I belong? Where I'm not fit to mix with the likes of you respectable people?'

'Which clearly you are not,' said Mrs Brown.

Her lip quivered.

'This child is not our responsibility,' Mr Brown said.

'Well it's not mine, neither.'

Swiftly, Edith laid Bea down on the entrance mat, turned and scurried down the steps. Reaching the pavement she hitched her skirt and ran down the hill as fast as she could without stumbling. Ignoring the shouts from behind she ran on as if driven by madness until reaching the Markets, where she turned aside into one of the pubs frequented by the working men.

Breathless, wide-eyed, she fetched up against the bar.

'Give me a gin!' she shouted at the barman. She banged the counter. 'Gin, now!'

CHAPTER 47

George worried when Edith did not return to La Vallée that night, staying awake until midnight when he fell asleep in the fireside chair. He did not go to the stone yard the next morning and was up early, pacing the lane until a shower came on, and then going back to the house and peering from the windows.

For the first time in history, a motor car splashed through the puddles and came to a stop outside La Vallée. A policeman got out and began to rap on the door just before George threw it open.

'Is this the home of Edith Bazin?' asked the policeman.

Behind the policeman stood a nurse from the Town Hospital with a bundle in her arms, together with one of the Castel douzainiers.

'What is it? Has something happened to Edith?'

'She's not home then?' the policeman asked.

'No, no, not since yesterday.'

Despite the jiggling of the nurse, a baby began to cry.

'Bea!'

'Is this her child?' The policeman summoned the nurse, who brought Bea over, still wrapped in the clothes she had worn the day before. 'She was abandoned on the steps of a stranger's house. Fortunately they are good, public-spirited people who arranged for her care in the Town Hospital until the mother could be located.'

'Edith's not in trouble?'

'Are you the father?' asked the policeman.

'Well, ah.'

'George has offered to marry the widow Bazin,' the douzainier intervened. 'Is that not right, George?'

'Yes, but, we can't, there's a rule. In the Bible.'

With a hard expression of disapproval on her face, the nurse offered the baby to George. He took Bea fondly. 'Thank you, thank you for bringing her back.'

'And your sister-in-law; keep her under control, Mr Bazin,' said the douzainier. 'For the child's sake if nothing else. Born out of wedlock is not her fault, but we don't want Edith Mullane a burden on the parish like her mother was.'

The policeman nodded severely. The nurse's expression was unchanged. The douzainier gave a shake of his head. 'Keep her under control – when you find her.'

Edith walked home later that day. She came in with hair unkempt and her coat wet from the rain, which had set in again. Gin and tobacco still hung about her breath when George found her at the kitchen table, chewing on a crust of bread and staring from the window.

He put his arm around her. 'Edith.'

'Don't touch me!' She batted him away. 'I'm fed up of men touching me. That's how all this happened.'

'Bea's asleep.' He motioned towards the crib.

'Wonderful.'

'So what happened?'

'Nothing happened. And don't ask again, because I'll say again that nothing happened.'

Edith took to her bed for two days. Jack and George drove Bea around to Mrs Patterson's hoping for help and advice, but it turned out that Mrs Patterson did not care for children in the slightest and knew nothing about what to do with the child. George was back to being nurse.

At least the news from France grew brighter as summer drew to a close. The Germans were in retreat and, if it was not yet another false dawn, the war might soon be over. By September, neither Jack nor George had received their call-up for the army; their fitness graded C or worse. Jack even suspected that Harold Torode had slyly hid their papers, but even if that were not the case, chances narrowed that they would ever join the Guernseymen fighting overseas.

With the U-boats all but beaten, it was safe to travel again and Mrs Patterson began taking in guests as had been her original plan. Over dinner, Jack mentioned that an American artist and his wife had suddenly arrived for the late summer and taken lodgings at Mrs Patterson's. They had planned on seeing Europe, but the war had unfairly thwarted their plans by refusing to end. Guernsey, it seemed, was as close as they were going to get.

George was by the shore the next day, attending to a crab pot that the waves had weakened. He had plenty of time for fishing now, and for crabbing when the season was right. A tall man in a straw boater strolled towards him, and behind at a short distance a woman in a pale blue dress followed, carrying a parasol. The man was well dressed in flannels, carried some form of book under his arm and was clearly a tourist.

'*Bonjour, monsieur,*' said the American, tipping the brim of his hat.

George was not often called *monsieur*.

'*Baonjour,*' he replied, drawing the word out in the island manner.

The American continued in obviously rehearsed and not terribly fluent French.

'I speaks English, sir, and I don't do the Good French that well,' George said.

'Ah. To speak the truth, neither do I.'

'We speaks the patois round here, but I don't imagine you speak a word of that?'

'No, not one word. Ah, Theodore Tulliver, of Philadelphia.' The tourist held out a hand in greeting. He was lean and tall, with a barely visible fair moustache and small, round, gold-rimmed glasses that reminded George of his old pair.

George stretched to shake the hand. 'George Bazin, of the Castel.'

'Bazin, ah. I think I have met a relative of yours – Jacques, Jack?'

'That would be my Uncle Jack – are you staying with Mrs Patterson, you?'

'Indeed we are… May I introduce my wife Marlene?'

The pale American lady nodded her head. It was clear from her manner and look that she had never done a day's work in her life and never would. Delicate as porcelain, she lacked the heartiness of the Guernsey girls and looked as if a strong westerly breeze would knock her clear over. Tulliver was some years older than his wife, who in turn was perhaps a year or two older than Edith. Artie had met an American soldier, or so Pierre had told him. George wondered why Tulliver was not in the war, now the Americans were come to win it.

'My, what are you working on?' Tulliver asked.

George explained how to repair a crab pot with string and lengths of green willow, and then where he placed them and how he outwitted the crabs. He spent some minutes on his narrative, pointing out his favourite spots.

'Spring's the best time though, especially for the spider crabs.'

Tulliver made soft noises of amazement, accompanied by a look of awe as if this were the most magical process he had ever encountered.

'And you fish just out there,' he said, shielding his eyes to peer seaward.

'And further up, that way,' George pointed to the hump of Grandes Rocques on the north side of the bay.

'I'm an artist, for my sins,' the American said. 'I paint, I sketch. I'm here to capture the majesty of the sea and the old ways of the island.'

'We've plenty of that, for sure,' said George.

The American raised a finger, as if to bring the world to a stop. 'I say, may I draw you?'

'Me?'

'I'll pay you. Ah, five dollars, what's that? A pound sterling?'

'No need to pay me,' said George. 'I'd like to be painted. Like an old general or Bailiff in his robes.'

'Ah, but I'll draw you here, with your crab pot and your boat. *The Guernsey Fisherman*. Shall we say tomorrow, if the weather is fair? If painting on a Sunday is not forbidden or anything.'

'In the afternoon?' said George. 'Once church is done and we've eaten.'

'Where will the sun be?'

'In the sky, where it usually is.'

The artist frowned, but George gave a laugh. 'Over there, behind you. Tomorrow then? I'll be here.'

So George became *The Guernsey Fisherman*, in his best Guernsey, his red neckerchief and shapeless hat. He played at mending his crab pot, seated unnaturally on the wale of his boat, while the artist sketched in his book and made little notes and painted a small version of the scene. George relaxed while the man took great pains to draw the crab pot in all its detail. He had imagined the artist would bring an easel and set up to paint in the grand manner, but instead he made a set of plans. Tulliver showed him the product of his work – a trio of pictures in his little book. For some reason he referred to his paintings as drawings.

'Back home, in my studio, I'll draw this on a grand scale. I must capture this light! It's marvellous, you know, a perfect gift to the artist.'

George looked closely at the larger of the sketches. There was the fisherman, the boat, the crab pot, Grandes Rocques and its fort in the background. Sketched indistinctly far down the shore was another figure at the very edge of the surf, possibly a woman in a long gown. George looked around him, but he and the artist were the only two on the beach.

Theodore Tulliver was seen around the parish many more times that month, sometimes with his wife, but often alone. He was full of the joys of the bucolic Castel way of life, but the wife seemed bored. Much of her time was spent at Mrs Patterson's house, reading or making little paintings of flowers.

Guernsey autumns are long and mild, and winter stays away until well into November. Mr Tulliver stayed to enjoy the turn of the season and the pounding seas of the gales after the equinox. From Jack he learned where George lived and chose a bright but blustery day to pay a call.

'Edith, Edith, come and meet the American!' George shouted from the back of the cottage.

Edith was in the yard, collecting hen's eggs. She gestured towards her dusty apron and her grubby hands.

'No, no, he likes this kind of thing. He likes Guernsey as it was.'

'There's a museum in Town if he wants Guernsey as it was.'

'Come and meet him, I've talked about you.'

She rubbed her hands on her apron and made a pass at straightening her hair, and then followed him into the hall.

'Mr Tulliver, my Edith.'

The artist took breath, possibly for effect. 'Mrs Bazin. *Enchanté, madame.*'

Edith glanced sharply at George and made an embarrassed smile for Mr Tulliver.

He kissed her hand. She drew back. 'Sorry, Mr Tulliver, but we're not fit for receiving.'

'No, no, *au contraire*. You are the image... the very image. George Bazin, you have the island's most precious secret hidden here in your little cottage. May I perhaps... with your permission, sir... may I not perhaps draw this Guernsey maid?'

'Dra...' Edith became speechless.

'Caw, that would be grand, Edith,' George said. 'Mr Tulliver is an artist, a famous American artist.'

'Well...' objected Tulliver.

'A real artist, like I told you.'

She looked at her hands. 'Not like this. I have better things to wear.'

'But I need to paint the real you,' Tulliver implored, 'the genuine Guernsey maid. George Bazin, may I paint your wife?'

'I'm not his wife!' Edith snapped.

George winced as she said this, but for an artist Mr Tulliver seemed to miss all the subtlety of their relationship.

'A maiden, how perfect!'

319

When Mr Tulliver called the next afternoon, George and Jack were away at the yard. The artist kissed Edith's hand when she greeted him at the door. She found it bizarrely charming. Then he strode around the property until he found the backdrop he preferred, and negotiated a scenario with Edith. Wary at first, she warmed to the idea.

'Beauty hidden away,' he said.

She would have worn her bonnet, but he told her to discard it and let her hair flow. She wore the better of her brown working dresses, a nearly white apron and a red paisley shawl. He wanted her to pose with her basket of eggs.

'I have no eggs today.'

'I can add the eggs. It's not as though we're doing photography – this is art.'

Edith sat on a stool just outside the door of the dairy and became *Rustic Beauty with Eggs*.

The wind had died back and the sun came out strongly, forgetting it was October.

'You're not in the war, Mr Tulliver?'

'Call me Theodore.'

'Theodore.' She made a coquette's smile and he made an 'aah' sound.

'Hold that.'

'I thought you Americans were in the war.'

'We are, my dear. I'm still waiting for the call, although I fear it will be too late. I've been trying to arrange things through my father, but wheels grind slowly. So how does a beauty such as you find herself here on the edge of the world?'

'My Artie got killed last year, being a hero by all accounts.'

'That must have been very hard.'

'It was. It is. And lots of his friends were killed too, or horribly wounded.'

The man who had all but missed the war tightened his lips and continued to work.

'So who is George?'

'Artie's brother. He took pity on me, looks after me. With his Uncle Jack – you've met Jack?' she added hurriedly. 'Until the war is over, that is, and I can move away.'

'Where are you moving to?'

'I don't rightly know yet. I hear it's a big world. I'd like to go to America – are you from New York?'

'Philadelphia. My father owns factories manufacturing boxes. At the moment he is doing well making boxes for the army. My elder brother too – he's going to be the next Box King of America. What he doesn't know about the box business isn't worth knowing and if there were a Congressional Medal for boring, he'd win two – with oak-leaf clusters.'

'So you don't like the box business?'

'Ma'am, I'm an artist. I don't knock the box business because it *allows* me to be an artist. My father thinks it terribly effete, but I have made what they call a splendid match.'

'Eh?'

'My wife Marlene. Her father is in steel, again making a great deal of money as the steel he makes goes into ships, and regular as clockwork they are sent to the bottom of the Atlantic by German submarines, so keeping up the demand for steel.'

Tulliver worked carefully as he talked, glancing up at her, then down at his art.

'I never thought of people making money out of wars,' she said.

'It has always been the case. I'm not one of those communists, but there's a good many people I know who are. They say that wars are only fought so that Marlene's father and mine and their class can make money.'

'I'm sure that's not so.'

'No, but it makes you think. Painting gives a man time to think. The more you paint the world, the more you come to understand it.'

'Have you painted your wife?' Edith asked, intrigued by her complete absence from their conversation, other than being a 'splendid match'.

'I've tried to paint Marlene several times, but she finds sitting tiresome. She's not an ideal artist's muse.'

'She's very beautiful,' Edith said.

'Yes, but a fragile beauty. It's for her health we've come here. There's a sickness stalking the cities, back in the States, and in England too. It was brought back from the war, they say, but then again I heard it started in Kansas. Fit young men and women are coughing like old-timers and dying by the dozen. They say more men at the front are dying of the flu than are being killed by the Germans.'

'That sounds horrible – are you sure it's true? It's not been in the newspapers.'

He raised an eyebrow. She found it both charming and comical.

'Do you think our governments would allow the newspapers to print the truth about the war?'

Edith suddenly felt rather stupid, as though she had been living in a box for the past four years. She loved reading and she believed what she read. Now Theodore Tulliver was hinting that the newspapers were just another form of fiction. And it made sense too – how else could the war still be raging after so many victories and gallant stands?

'Can you just turn back a little to the left, ma'am? And frown a little less?'

'Sorry.'

Tulliver began to sketch again. 'No, Marlene does not have a strong constitution – one whiff of that bad air from the trenches and I can see her falling sick with the rest. Boston was no escape, and nor it seems is London. So we're here. I had family come from Guernsey originally, long back before Independence. They sailed out to Newfoundland trading cod, then made their way down to New York State. I found this place on the map and bought the tickets in London on a whim. Perfect.'

A window opened in Edith's mind. A great, wide, French window that led out into a world richer than she had ever imagined. Theodore Tulliver moved through that world with ease, unchained from poverty, obligations and conventional thought. If she was a Guernsey donkey confined to its field, he was the bird soaring high above and away, singing any tune it pleased, migrating as the seasons turned.

Bea started to cry from within the house. Tulliver glanced that way, then back.

'Yours?' he asked.

'No – it's very complicated.' Somehow the lie just tumbled out. 'She's the child of a family friend.' So much was true. She moved on to embellish her lie to avoid it standing naked. 'I'm looking after her today – she's quite sweet really.'

'That's good of you,' he smiled. 'Do you want to go to her?'

'No, she'll wait.' Edith tried not to sound heartless. 'She usually settles down again.'

'Fine. Now, I want you to look a little sad. Life is fair and wonderful, even though you live this simple existence. And yet, there is something else you yearn for, perhaps a forbidden sweetheart, perhaps a dream you cannot quite have. Ah yes, that's it. Perfect.'

CHAPTER 48

The casualty lists had eased during the summer. What remained of Guernsey's fighting men had been pulled from the line after the Battle of the Lys and now performed gentler duties guarding headquarters and the like. Letters home became more cheerful and the survivors had even been inspected by the king. More and more the war stories were dominated by victories of the Americans, the Australians and the Canadians. The Old World was exhausted and the New came out triumphant.

While the war stubbornly rumbled on, a new fear stalked the island. Some of the soldiers who had returned wounded suddenly took sick and died. At first it was said that this was some secret weapon of the Kaiser, a poison gas that had delayed effect on the men. Then civilians began to fall ill or die in unexplained circumstances – young wives, older children and working men who had missed the war. It was a cough, an unseasonal pneumonia; even if it never came from Spain, it was soon called the Spanish flu.

Mr and Mrs Tulliver went home suddenly.

'We were just talking over breakfast,' Jack said. 'You know how he was telling us about that plague of flu they have in New York? I said it sounds like we have it here too. And that was it. His wife nearly fell off her chair and the colour went right out of him. I figure they're afraid of catching a sniffle.'

'It's not just a sniffle!' Edith burst out. 'It's killing people in America, and in France, but the papers aren't letting us know the truth! If it's come here, you'll get more headstones out of this than you got from the war.'

'Now, now, I don't want people to die just to make me richer,' Jack said.

'But you make money when people die. And other men profit from other people's misery, from this war and all.'

'Whoa – you've been talking to our Mr Tulliver. That sounds like one of his lines.'

She tossed her head. 'Maybe he just opened my eyes to what's really happening in the world. When is he going, anyway?'

'He's gone. Away, just like that. First mailboat he could catch. Guess he'll be halfway to Southampton by now, if the U-boats don't catch him.'

'Ah,' said Edith, easing back in her chair.

'They were an interesting couple, I'll grant you that,' said Jack. 'It'll be a while before we see their likes here again.'

Victims of the flu coughed blood, or bled from their ears. Most recovered but many did not and it was not clear what a patient's chances were. Nobody in authority truly knew, or would admit that they knew. The schools and concert halls closed and doctors were giving reports to the Royal Court every week on so many new cases of sickness and so many new deaths. Sales of Veno's Lightning Cough Cure and Dr William's Pink Pills surged.

Headstones were soon in demand, and once again death was George's friend.

The day Mr Tulliver came to paint his beauty with eggs, the darkness that had stalked Edith since the baby was born finally began to lift. It was as if the Americans had opened a window into her cell, but that light suddenly went out when she heard they were gone.

She gazed from the window, saying nothing, withdrawing from all the Castel could offer. George put his arm round her gently.

'Stop it!' She pushed him away roughly. 'Don't touch me – not like that! Never touch me like that!'

'Sorry.'

'We're not getting married,' she said. 'It's not happening, George, not now, not ever. So don't presume to touch me like we were sweethearts or something.'

Bea began to cry.

'The baby's crying,' she said.

George withdrew, and went to carry out his duty.

Nights drew in and for Edith it was easy to think in the way of the ancients, that the days would keep getting shorter until there was only darkness. It was hard to remember a time when there were no war clouds hanging over the island. The conflict went on and on and she did not believe the stories of heroic advances day after day and the Kaiser wanting to sue for peace. Yes, yes: she'd heard it all before.

Quite unexpectedly, it was over.

The Great War ended on a Monday in November. In the late morning, George heard church bells ringing out, and wondered what it was about. A boy rode excitedly down the lane and called over the wall of Jack's yard.

'Mr Bazin!' cried the boy on the oversized horse. 'The war is over.'

So few words carried so much meaning. George dropped his cold chisel and put on his glasses to stare at the boy, a host of thoughts crowding his mind and dozens of questions falling over each other before he could ask them. The boy did not wait, but gave a whoop and galloped on with a wave of his hat. At the turn of the lane he stopped again and shouted the news over a garden gate, before continuing his victory ride. That was one boy who would never grow to become a soldier, thought George.

As the church bells continued to ring, it was as if a great weight had lifted from him. That gnawing at his soul suddenly eased. People would stop giving him that second glance, the one that asked why he was not in uniform or why he was alive when so many bolder men were dead or maimed. Everyone would simply be glad that the killing was over and the boys would return.

At the idea of the men returning, George's elation died away. The streets would soon be full of young men, brave men with medals on their chests and tales of adventure to tell. It was easy to see the returning heroes picking up the jobs they had left behind. Work was at a standstill now, but when normal life resumed, would he have to watch all the jobs go to the fit men? And worse, what if some brave veteran marched back and swept Edith away from him? What now were his chances of finding a way to win Edith's hand? He grabbed a granite offcut and hurled it out into the field with all the anger he could muster. The rock bounced among the grass and was lost. Damn! They used to call him the Owl, but the owl has no place in the world when the sun comes up.

Edith cried after the boy told her it was over. He was whooping and staying his horse and eager to spread his message of joy. As he rode away, she burst into tears and ran indoors. She put her head down on the kitchen table and sobbed without restraint. Peace was what Artie had died for, and what Edwin had died for. Pushing their faces aside, she saw others – her cousin Jim and boys she had known at school. What a waste of lives and a waste of years!

Her years were wasted too. A widow with an illegitimate child and no money was in company with a whole generation of pretty virgins grown to womanhood during the war, all eagerly anticipating the return of the heroes. Mr Theodore Tulliver might have declared her the most beautiful woman on the island, but Guernsey's men would see the baby first, even if they bothered to look past the stories that she was sinfully married to George. Self-pity took over from gloom and she wept again.

George came home in subdued mood. Edith too was quiet. She barely looked up when he entered the cottage.

'War's over, Edith – did you hear?'

'I heard. The Ogier boy told me, then everyone else who passed.'

'It's good news.'

'You do state the bloney obvious sometimes.'

'Sorry, but it is good news and you look sad.'

'And what of you, face like death? War's over, George: cheer! Hang out the flags. The men are coming home, but not mine!'

'He was my brother!' he snapped back. 'We grew up together in this very house. I knew Artie my whole life, not just for a year or two. I'd rather it was me than him what got killed.'

'And so do I.'

'That's cruel,' he said, hurt. 'No need to be cruel, you.'

'Well, the world's cruel. The war, the flu, your leg and whatever bloody cloud of bad luck follows your family around.'

George forced a smile. 'But things balance out. I mean we've had our share of knocks, but there's good things too. Look at baby Bea, isn't she beautiful?'

'Oh, my bastard war orphan? Wonderful, thanks for raising that right now. Thanks for cheering me up like that. You're a donkey, George. Look at me, think about the fix I'm in. Tell me how it can be better, war or no war?'

'Caw, you're always thinking of yourself, you. Thousands of men are dead and you only cry for yourself. You should be happy for your baby.'

A group of men were cheering in the lane. Angry and confused, George went out and joined them, then marched in victory to the Rockmount Hotel, which was already decked out with flags. The Kaiser would be drowned in cider and brown ale.

CHAPTER 49

At one time it seemed that every man sent to France was being killed, so that all that would remain of the regiment, and the quarrying company, and the artillerymen, and the sailors and the signallers who had marched away would be photographs. It seemed a slender mercy, but as things turned out, four men out of every five survived the war. Some were shattered in mind and body, but they would return. A boy from Town, thought killed in the spring, turned out to be a prisoner. A hundred families across the island began to hope the same had happened to their missing men.

An idea crept into Edith's misery, a last hope. There was just a chance that Edwin had been wrong and Pierre had been right and that Artie was indeed a prisoner. Perhaps he had lost his memory due to shell shock, or the Germans had not bothered to send his details back to the Red Cross. It was a slender straw of hope but she grabbed on to it.

Yes, Artie could still be alive, somewhere.

Edith wrote a letter to the *Guernsey Press* and another to *The Star*. They were in the same tone as many the papers had printed during the past three years. She asked for anyone with news of Corporal Arthur Bazin, 1st Battalion RGLI to contact her urgently. In the same flurry of optimism, she also wrote to the Red Cross, the commander of the RGLI and the Lieutenant Governor.

Somebody must know.

She re-read Edwin's first letter. It was full of doubts and

guesses that could be converted to hope. Les Rues Vertes, where was that? It wasn't even on George's map of France. Even Cambrai was a tiny dot.

Artie would find his way home, somehow, but his extended absence was made worse when other men started to come back. Adèle Le Page almost skipped around Edith's kitchen while telling how Colin her sweetheart was due home in four days, and that they would be married before Christmas. Edith barely had the energy to smile at the news.

'I hope our babies are as beautiful as your Bea.'

She smiled again, thinking, *you can have her.* She did not feel the magical bond that glued other mothers to their newborns. She could not understand this baby-glee that overtook Adèle and Perotine each time Bea was shown to them. Even George displayed a girly delight in mothering the child, which seemed frankly odd.

Perhaps she was not made to be a mother. Perhaps she was just a bad person.

December had turned cold by the time Bea was taken to church for the first time and baptised. Coming out of the porch with their shared burden, the couple walked past the *Gràn'mère*, and then past the two black-shrouded Valpied sisters, almost as ancient and wicked as the stone goddess.

'Who's the father then, eh?' The senior Valpied sister gave Edith a look that was unforgiving, clearly enjoying tormenting her. At once Edith pushed the baby into George's arms.

'Not 'im, eh?' said the other sister.

Edith swore at them, but they only laughed. Once the family had passed, the two crones pointed and poked fun at their backs.

'He's bad luck, that one. A devil's foot and a fairy's child and a harlot he pretends is his wife.'

These were whispers meant to be heard. George proffered Bea.

'Edith, take your child, quickly.'

'My child?' she snapped. 'Did you hear what the hags said? It's no more my child than yours; it's a changeling, a fairy child, it's nothing to do with me!'

She put on a spurt of speed and left the cripple with the child hobbling after her. Superstitions are just rot, and fairy stories are for children, but even without the cackles of the Valpieds something gnawed at her. It was not her husband's child, and she wished it were not hers either.

La Missis Bazin was a woman of action; she would not sit by and calmly wait for fate to deal out its cards. The next Friday, she told George that her friend Violet was sick and urgently needed visiting. George happily looked after Bea and put her to bed. Edith's plan was simple and began by meeting up with Violet, who she had worked with on the trams. Violet's sickness was limited to her heart. She had spent the war pining for this young man or that, never daring to fix on one lest he be killed. At twenty-four she suddenly feared she would be left on the shelf. Edith could chaperone her while she laid out her stall and got a jump on those pretty young things of eighteen and nineteen who were new to the market.

Mrs Bazin's agenda was different. Most of the RGLI were still in France, but some were home on leave or recovering from wounds. In the smoke-filled tap rooms of St Peter Port she quizzed each man in uniform they came across, and showed the photograph of Artie. She would ask about the battle at Les Rue Vertes, and even met up with one-armed Pierre himself. He repeated the story she already knew, although blurred by the passage of a year.

Most of the men were reluctant to talk. They shrugged the

questions away, looking at their pints or glancing at each other. It was as if they were ashamed to have survived, or ashamed to have even taken part.

'No.' One corporal shook his head and leaned back, puffing on his pipe. He may have been in his late twenties, but looked ten years older. 'It's all noise, war,' he said. 'I can't recall what happened. It were just noise and smoke.'

Edith saw something in his eyes, a deep long stare that went through her and through the far wall and off to France. This quiet Guernseyman who used to be a dairyman had killed people. He had stepped over the mangled bodies of his friends and learned to become something he was not. Now he puffed at his pipe, trying to unlearn as swiftly as he could. He lifted his pint.

'Could he have been taken prisoner?' she asked. Her audience had grown to a trio of men.

'There were lots cut off and taken prisoner,' one said.

'Ah but the Jerries retreated before we were pulled from the line,' another offered. 'We held that place until the last.'

'Was he tall?' the third soldier asked.

'For a Guernseyman, if you don't mind me saying.'

'And a corporal? Tall, Artie, yes, I knows the one. Was he a Bazin? We buried him behind the village. Him and six or eight others, and a couple of Germans, even. Didn't have time to say much or bury them deep. One of the boys said the Lord's Prayer, in French as I recalls.'

'You're sure?'

'You don't want to know any more.'

'Yes I do.'

'Well he was a bit knocked about, but it was a corporal we buried, and I dug the hole meself. I gave his things to a lieutenant, but reckon he died too.'

'You have to be sure!'

'Sorry, *madaume,* I can't be any more sure than that.'

Edith went home very late, accompanied by alcohol fumes and smoke that wafted from her coat as she walked in the fresh air. She would smell like a slattern when she got in.

'Where have you been?' George demanded as she entered the kitchen.

'Finding Artie.'

'Did you find him?' George sounded surprised, as though she had good news.

'No.'

'Aw.' His excitement died away. 'Bea cried, so I put her cot in my room.'

'Oh.'

Edith had kept the master bedroom of the house for her own. Her brother in-law was relegated to the children's room and now the baby had joined him.

'I'm tired.' She slipped past him and started on up to her room.

From behind her came a whispered voice. 'Goodnight, Edith.'

Adèle's wedding was a quickly arranged affair at the parish church. Everyone knew the couple were keen to have a family, and few would be surprised if the returning soldier had not already made a start. Wedding celebrations and La Laongue Veille were rolled into one. By this time, Edith held two letters offering snippets of information she already knew and a longer one from a survivor of Artie's platoon who more or less repeated Pierre's story. On Christmas Day, she sat in the rocker, close to the fire and re-read them. That year and a day had passed.

'Edith,' George said. 'I don't like to say this, but our Artie is not coming back. And if he did there would be a story to tell about how Bea came to be, and it would break his heart. So in some ways things are best left as they are.'

Break his heart? Yes she had. Edith bit her lip, wondering what a wicked girl like her should do next. But 1919 was a new year and she would need a new plan.

CHAPTER 50

The New Year came with a great storm from the south-east. It took six panes off the vinery and knocked a chimney pot off the Big House, carrying three slates down with it. At least this gave George and Jack a challenge to turn their hands to. While they were up the ladders, they decided to replace the guttering at the back of the cottage too, as it leaked more water than it channelled.

Edith folded away her three letters, plus two more that arrived after Christmas, plus the two she had from Edwin. These went into a box with Artie's four letters home and she tied it up with an old pink ribbon. *Old year out*, as the saying went. She put the box in the bottom of her hanging press where some of her mother's things still rested in a pile.

She spent time on her appearance and went round to visit Adèle and find out if she was truly pregnant already. Adèle offered to cut her hair in what she said was the latest style – Edith had let her hair grow after Mr Tulliver had raved about her flowing locks or some romantic twaddle like that. Now the women picked a new style from a catalogue. Edith's hair was soon no longer than the nape of her neck, keeping its natural wave at the sides.

Mirror in hand, she admired her new self. Goodbye *Rustic Beauty with Eggs*.

Whenever there was an excuse to get out of the parish, Edith took it. She visited distant relations or women she used to work the trams with. She went to the better shops in Town, if only to browse, and always called at the library. Men of learning came here, or at least had done before they learned to kill. She even went up to the Guille-Allès Museum, despite having no interest in stone axes, stuffed monkeys or masks from the South Seas. Her hidden hope was that someone would notice her, and knew that George's hope was that they would not. Her mother had said that marriage was like trade. Yes she had a baby, but she was a war widow and proud of it. Yes there were hundreds of young, fresh girls who had never known a sweetheart, but Edith was the beauty of the parish.

Wasn't she?

Edith looked hard into the dressing-table mirror.

Was she still?

A flush in her cheeks would just not go away. She patted her waistline, convinced it was firmly back into shape after the birth of Bea, if not quite as slim as before. Wearing just her bodice and knickers, she gave a half-twirl in one direction, then the other, criticising her look. No, she did not feel slim, but thin.

Bea could rest with Adèle while George and Jack went to the pub, it being Friday. Adèle just couldn't get enough baby practice. Edith would go to Town and meet Violet in a café off the Pollet. There was a dance at St George's Hall and some of the smarter young men would surely drop by. If not she'd have a drink with Violet and the tram girls. Somehow the war had made it acceptable – if not entirely respectable – for women to drink in pubs.

The conductorettes were always a laugh, and they spoke English too. One or two still had brothers, even. For a moment, Edith was reminded of her mother and the French sailor. Ruth Mullane had written to say Marcel had married her, in the end. She now had a French name once more and was living in Toulon. Quite possibly, she was happy.

Edith opened her purse and counted the doubles and English sixpences. If she walked, she would be able to afford the café. Her feet were tired and her muscles ached and those two miles to Town seemed like an awfully long way.

Down at the Cobo Hotel, the jokes began to bite. George did not have a wife, just a woman whom he shared a house with. One who was far too good for him. Nobody believed his stories that they were going to be married one day. Even if that was so, he'd be a cuckold. His 'wife' went drinking in Town on Friday nights. Always seen with this soldier, or that sailor, close in talk. Some days she was in the cafés, rubbing up against the bright young things who had survived the war. Was she charging by the hour?

What self-esteem George had built up during the war years ebbed away. He started drinking at the new Rockmount Hotel instead. At least people there knew him less, but they knew Edith just the same. The Rockmount was trying to be a select establishment. It was perched at the very top of the beach at Cobo and when the sun went down over a pint of beer, there was not a millionaire on any yacht in the world who enjoyed a finer view. That February night, the sun was gone well before the men made their way to the coast. It was dark and almost cloudless, without a moon.

Jack and George talked with the men, hearing again the war stories of a neighbour who had joined the navy and sailed the whole way around the world chasing German cruisers. Other neighbours fresh back from the army said little. Their war stories were their own and only those who had been through the Somme, Passchendaele, Cambrai or the last stand of the

RGLI at Doulieu-Hazebrouck had earned the right to hear them. They drank to the memory of a lad from Richmond Corner, who had survived the whole war without a wound, only to die of the flu while waiting for his discharge.

George had worn his new glasses every day since he had proposed to Edith, although they were not strictly new any more and were almost as chipped and worn as his childhood pair. He gave them a wipe with his sleeve and was pleased to put them back on without any form of revelation. He had no wish to see beyond the end of the bar or deeper than the bottom of his pint pot.

Normally, George had a rule of three. More than three pints and he lost count and on an uncounted number of pints he could not trust his legs on the uneven walk home, with only the stars to guide him back. Jack had always drunk in moderation and had given up his pipe when he met Mrs Patterson. She had a very civilising influence on him. That Friday, Jack stopped after his second pint.

'I, erm, I ought to check that Victoria is all right,' he said. 'Mrs Patterson, I means. She was having trouble with that back door of hers again. Needs easing I reckon.' Friday night in the dead of winter was not the right time for carpentry and both men knew it. 'And I can get me a cocoa or a malted milk for my walk home.'

His uncle patted him on the shoulder, and left George to drink his third pint alone. February is a dreary month without the hues of November, the sparkling frosts of the deepest winter or the storms of March. In daytime, an English incomer such as Mrs Patterson might think spring was on the way. She would find the air almost warm at night if there was cloud and not too much wind, but on this night a near constant breeze came cold from the sea as George walked home alone and in the dark.

The lamp burned in the kitchen of the Big House. He came in to find Edith with her head down on the table, arms around her head muffling a sobbing, panting noise.

'Edith?'

He had drunk enough to be elated, but not yet enough to feel depressed. Beer gave him confidence.

'Edith!' he said sternly. 'Are you drunk? Are you drunk again!'

She gave one moan. He stepped around to oppose her, braced for an outburst, even an assault. 'Edith, where's Bea?'

Every man has limits and George's had come. He grabbed her arm in anger, then immediately let go. It was hot and wet. Edith lolled her head and looked up at him. She usually looked pale in lamplight, but now she was flushed and sweating.

'George?' she said feebly.

He touched her burning forehead. 'You're not drunk again? How much have you drunk?'

'One sherry, I swear. I'm just so tired, George.'

'Where's Bea?'

'Adèle... Adèle has it. I want to sleep, I just want to sleep. Walked back from Town, but I can't walk.'

'I'll get you to the green bed.'

He hurried to the parlour and cleared the green bed in a moment. The fire was unlit and the room cold. Was that good, when she was so hot? George found the balance to help Edith stand and totter across the hallway and on to the bed. He brought blankets downstairs, and poured her a glass of water. Edith was panting, burning up.

'What can I do?' he asked. 'What's wrong?'

As he said it, he knew. The whole island was talking about it. All had thought it had gone away in the autumn, but it was back for a second round. This was the Spanish flu and his chisel wrote the story of those it took away.

Bea remained at Adèle's in fear she would catch the infection. Jack and George carried Edith upstairs and laid her in her marriage bed, not knowing how much of her walking out clothes to take off. Coat, shoes and shawl were easy but the rest must remain until she was well enough to climb into her nightdress of her own accord. Mrs Patterson came around next morning, frowned a little, donned a mask she had bought in Town and then saw to it that Edith was dressed in her nightgown and her soiled clothes put to wash. She wore fine gloves all the time, but nevertheless washed her own hands three times afterwards with carbolic soap and nipped out into the fresh air as soon as she could.

Jack explained that Mrs Patterson could not be expected to be nurse to Edith. George understood. Every second family who had been spared in the autumn was going down with this illness. Young men just back from the war, or the sweethearts who had waited four years were sickening and dying. It was a challenge to the courage even to stay in the Big House now.

'I'll go for the doctor if you'll stay with her,' Jack said.

'I can't afford no doctor…'

'But I can, George.'

'I can't take your money.'

'Aw, I've got no children, me. So one day,' Jack spread his hands, 'all this will be yours. And the business, what's left of it. So I'm spending your money, in truth.'

Jack fetched the doctor, and then said he would keep out of the way as best he could. La Vallée became a plague house and only one person would enter it other than the doctor. The women of the parish told George that onions were good for the flu, as was salt placed up the nose. Edith could eat little, but

George ate onions every day and snorted salt as if it were finest snuff. He heard that cinnamon in milk was an effective remedy and fed Edith by the spoonful whenever she was taking food.

More and more, George's thoughts were drawn to the box beneath his bed. After months of drawing close, weeks of taking the box out before sliding it back and days when he opened the cigar box before closing it once more, George sacrificed what remained of his free will. Just to feel the pinch on his nose was to wear armour against reality.

Hope for the future was fading, so he turned hope back in a familiar direction. He winced at the world as he had not seen it for many months, but it was an empty world. He was afraid she might not return. The spirit would be angry. His angel would not forgive him for being unfaithful. How angry she had been when he proposed marriage to Edith! Pure fairy jealousy was not to be dismissed lightly.

A day passed and Edith grew sicker. George began to doubt his own childhood as his old friend failed to appear. Edith grew delirious and vomited the food he brought her, and George's faith faded. He stopped looking for help from beyond, and sat on his own, staring into the fire.

Gazing into the flames, he remembered how the firelight used to bring out the dancer from the shadows of the room. In that moment he saw her, and his heart jumped. When she came, her face carried neither anger nor jealousy, only pity. He ad misjudged her. Her anger at the proposal had been aimed aving him the pain now being endured. It had been another ing misunderstood. She was indeed his one true friend.

're doing a grand job, George. Artie'd be proud of you.'
d well back in the yard, hands in pockets. 'You're a
ı than me.'

'They wouldn't let me join the army. If they had I might be dead now, or be short one arm like Pierre. So I reckon this is my war now. Saving Edith. And if that flu takes me, well, it could have been a bullet last year. End's all the same.'

George felt his throat tighten as he spoke. He touched his brow and knew what was happening.

'Are you well, George?'

'No, not as well as I was. Have you got money for another doctor, Jack? I can carry on for a day at best.'

'Aye. I'll get him directly.'

'And if it does take me – get Elias Hamon to carve my tombstone. He's not so bad, on a good day.'

'You'll need no tombstone yet. They make us Bazins tough.'

'Purbeck stone,' George added grimly.

Edith had lived through a nightmare where she was running up a hill trying to escape someone. Edwin, no – Artie. No – some German. No – it was George! The hill grew steeper until she had to claw her way up inch by inch. It was so steep that she would fall to her death unless she clung on. She fell and she woke. Drifting back to sleep she tried once more to grip that slope of greasy grass. This dream had gone on for days.

In between, George was there, spooning her food, mopping her brow, passing her the chamber pot and leaving the room while she swayed unhappily. She did not bleed as that poor pregnant grower's wife from up Le Préel had done before she died. Edith clung on and after four days became stronger once more. The temperature started to fall, the dreams eased and she ate some bread.

'Thank you, George.'

He smiled, a puffy-faced smile.

'You're wearing your baby glasses.'

'Couldn't find the others.'

She gripped his hand and he gripped hers.

'Bea is fine,' he said.

'Bea?'

'Your baby.'

Oh yes, not all the nightmares were caused by the flu.

'Adèle has her. She's having a baby of her own, even. Look, Edith, now you're awake, mind if I go lie down? I'm very tired, me.'

The shade-woman came to him that night, lay down beside him and laid a hand on his breast. George slept deeply, allowing himself to fall away in her arms. Wherever she led he would follow. The places she took him were strange, unearthly places beneath the dolmens, the *pouquelai* where the fairies feasted and demons danced. Only his knowledge that she was with him kept him from terror.

'Good morning, George, how are you feeling?'

She was holding a cold cloth to his forehead. Opening his eyes he saw it was not the crow-haired phantom but a gentle elf-faced redhead with short curls.

'Edith?'

'My turn to be nurse, yours to be patient.'

'Oh, Edith, let me up.'

'Stay there, George Bazin. Stay in that bed two more days.'

Edith stood wearily. Her own strength had not returned and her muscles ached, but Artie's brother needed her just as she had needed him.

'How's Bea?'

'Jack says she's well.'

Edith came back to health within the week, and Bea was

brought down to La Vallée once more, but the baby was more of a stranger than ever. Edith would ignore the crying until she could bear it no more, and as she could no longer feed the child herself it was easy to send George for the bottle. At times she would stare into the crib, shaking her head as if this were not her child at all. More and more, she was convinced that this was so.

CHAPTER 51

Even the birds knew the war was over, that spring of 1919. The spring brought an idea into George's head. Edith dreamed of moving to England. He wanted her to be happy and he wanted so much to marry her that he reasoned it must be legal over there. Everyone said how backwards Guernsey was, that things were done in certain ways because they had been done that way since Norman times and nobody had seen fit to change them for fancy modern ideas. Out in the big world, things moved faster and the old ways were left behind.

George had never been to England. He had never truly left Guernsey, as the one trip to Crevichon he had made with Artie and Uncle Jack barely counted. Leaving the White Rock on the steamer he wondered if this was how Artie had felt, sailing away, and watching the spires and rooftops of St Peter Port fade. Herm and Jethou became lumps on the horizon and Guernsey fell away against the southern sky. The sea was the colour of broken slate and rough, but George was used to smaller boats and choppier water, so he just watched the horizon and the gulls weaving above the wake of the steamer. A few travellers were sick over the side, or ran for the restrooms and did not emerge for hours. France slipped by, and Alderney too. A stubby lighthouse marked the Casquets reef where Gràn'père Bazin had become a hero in his final moments. Next came the English Channel. A flotilla of destroyers chased across their stern, with little to do except wait to see whether the Armistice turned into lasting peace. A day of grey sea and grey sky passed.

England appeared as a smudged line along the horizon, much like France looked from Guernsey on a clear day. Details became clearer, and colours grew to reveal green fields and dark woods. Chimney smoke and glittering windows marked the towns and villages. *This is a big world*, thought George, with room for everyone and a solution to everyone's problem somewhere.

The Isle of Wight came up finally on the starboard side, with its chalk cliffs and red lighthouse at the end of the Needles. A pair of four-funnelled cruisers steamed sedately towards Portsmouth, their work surely done. George gazed in wonder at the huge harbour and bustling town of Southampton that unfolded out of the sea before him. Many of the ships in the harbour still bore their warpaint of grey, white and black zigzags designed to dazzle and confuse submarines. George thought them strangely beautiful, almost the work of an artist. That would have been good war work for Mr Tulliver if he never got to join the American army.

Friends had warned him to take only English money and not try to pay his way in francs and doubles. He might even get arrested for passing fake money. Just beyond the harbour George found a public house advertising cheap rooms for sailors and figured that he counted, having just made the longest voyage of his life. The room he was offered was tall and narrow and stank of stale smoke, but gave a long view down a side street towards mast-heads and he could hear the sound of gulls, so felt at home.

Fish and chips made a great supper and he enjoyed the English beer. A pretty woman, older than him and wearing too much make-up wanted to know what ship he was from and where he was bound.

'I'm going to find a church that will marry me and my Edith.'

'Your Edith? Is she your sweetheart?'

'Yes.'

'Are you marrying her soon?'

'Soon as I can.'

'I see. You have a nice time, dearie.' The woman went away and for a moment George felt lonely and wanted to call her back and talk some more. Then he saw how she pounced on two more sailors, resting her arm on the shoulder of one and sweet-talking him in the identical way she had just sweet-talked George. This was her trade and she knew it well. He finished his beer and went upstairs alone.

Drizzle greeted George the following morning as he set off to explore Southampton. He found churches for Baptists and Catholics, a Methodist chapel plus a synagogue for the Jews, by which time he was lost in a maze of backstreets. At last he saw a policeman and asked the way to a church – 'a proper church'. The one he was sent to was a grim, soot-stained brick building, not at all like the island churches. He went inside and found a lay person cleaning the altar brass. The vicar would not be in until noon, so George waited, studying the tombs and memorials one by one. Lots of people lived here and lots of people died here. If he moved to England, there would be no shortage of work.

Noon came and the vicar appeared soon after. George introduced himself and was shown to the vestry where he stumbled through an explanation of his heart's ambition and Guernsey's backward attitude to such things. The vicar nodded, barely allowing George to finish his preamble before bluntly quashing the dream without a shred of Christian sympathy. It was illegal to marry your brother's widow, even in England. George received the verdict in silence.

Out on the pavement, out in the drizzle, he determined not to give up. The policeman he first spoke to had said there was a registry office in Southampton, which sounded a bit like the Greffe in Guernsey, and people got married there too. By the time he found the right building it had closed for the day, but the next morning George managed to make it inside and speak to a man in a suit who seemed to know all about marriage.

'It is actually illegal,' the man said. 'Against the law. It would be like marrying your sister.'

'I don't have no sister, she died when she was a baby. And my brother got killed in the war, being a hero.'

'Well, I'm sorry, but there you have it.' After a moment, the man offered another thought. 'Mind you, I've heard there's talk of changing the law.'

George's mood brightened.

'With so many men being killed in the war, and so many widows at home, it only seems natural. I'd hang on a few years if I were you.'

'A few years?'

'Laws take time to change.'

A few years? Yet, there was hope.

'George, you're mad!' Edith said. She chided him for spending all that money on travel, and now for nothing.

'No, no, listen. The man told me that they are going to change to law in England. So we can wait here until they do, then move to England and be wed and start our lives afresh.'

There was an odd look in her eye. Pity maybe, terror perhaps, certainly indecision.

'George. I'm not marrying you.'

'But we can, in England.'

'Not here, not in England, not in Timbuktu.'

'But you said yes. You said you'd marry me!'

'I did, and I dearly wish I hadn't. That was before we knew about this law and before the war ended. And I've said since, more than once, that I'm not marrying you.'

George drew back. 'We'll just wait then.'

CHAPTER 52

With peace came work. The quarries never again became as busy as they had been, but the market for tomatoes picked up swiftly. People started to rebuild their walls, repair barns and extend their houses once more, and even without meeting bullets, gas, shells or the flu they continued to die at the rate God ordained. George was moving finished granite cobs in Jack's yard when a black-clad woman came slowly round the corner of the barn. He first caught her reflection on the inside of his glasses – his new glasses. He spun round, expecting to see nothing, but in front of him stood the elder of the Valpied sisters, her cheeks thin and drawn.

Neither sister spoke a word of English, and had never spoken a good word to George.

'Our Annie is dead,' she said stiffly. 'That flu took her yesterday.'

He had not known the younger Valpied sister had been called Annie.

'I want you to do her a gravestone,' she said. 'Nice, like.' She brought a folded piece of paper out of her pocket and gave it to him. 'This is what I want it to say.'

George took the paper and nodded. The dedication was in Good French, but her spelling was awry.

'Your letters are good – seen 'em I have,' she continued. 'Seen every one you've done. All the old people. Everyone we knew.'

George nodded. 'I can do this. Do your sister proud, I can.'

'Leave space underneath, as I expect I'll be following her soon enough.'

'Do you want Guernsey granite? Polishes nice. If not, we've got some nice Purbeck stone that carves better. I can't do much with granite except plain lettering, but it lasts longer. You'd not be wanting marble?'

'That white stone,' she said, pointing at a broken slab.

'Purbeck stone, then.'

'We've been saving,' she said. 'How much will it be?'

'Hard to say exact.' Then he guessed at a price.

'That much?' The elder Valpied nodded. '*Cor là*, so be it. We're burying her at St Matthew's, Tuesday if you'd come along.'

'I will,' he said.

The elder Valpied sister left without another word. She seemed tiny now, less than half a whole, a ghost of a woman. As a child George had feared the sisters and as an adult he had loathed them, but he felt the loss of the survivor, whose forename he still did not know. Death settles all accounts, as Uncle Jack once said.

George went to Annie Valpied's funeral and Uncle Jack came too, seeing as how she was now a customer. Mrs Patterson accompanied them, looking very smart and proper in black. She rarely said much, and had a quiet smile as if her thoughts were many miles away.

'Buried at sea' was the gravediggers' jest about St Matthew's Cobo. It was high up – just inland from the Guet and the spur fell away sharply to Cobo on the north and Vazon to the south – yet the water table was high here. Annie Valpied's coffin splashed into six inches of water, and then was covered with the clammy orange soil.

After the funeral the men walked Mrs Patterson down to Cobo, and came back to La Vallée as a pair.

'I was going to ask you about Mrs Patterson,' George said.

'She's very well, thank you for asking.'

'No, I mean: will you be marrying her?'

Jack took off his cap at the suggestion, looking away for a moment. 'Oh I don't know. She's been married once and in no rush to go there again. And I'm not so much the marrying kind, me. At that last wedding we went to, the preacher said marriage is all about getting children and I reckon we're both past that now.'

'So you won't get married?'

Jack re-set his hat. 'Secret of life, George, is to be happy with what you've got and with who you are.'

So that was the secret. Perhaps life could not get better than it was and he should not dream of what could not be. If Edith spent as little time with him as possible, George poured his affection into little Bea. She had bright blue eyes and tight dark locks – paying no resemblance to the fair Edith at all. Her first words were Pa-pa-pa, but not even the love of a child could blank out all the cares in his world.

His determination to marry Edith had finally worn away. War, death, love and tragedy had passed him by and left him standing as the rocks at Cobo stand unharmed when a storm churns the water, re-shapes the beach and smashes boats to pieces. It takes courage to face the future not knowing what it will hold, and George had run out of courage. On any given day he would wear whichever pair of glasses he chose, and damn whatever Edith might say.

The wife who was not a wife, the sister who was not a sister, was out late again that Friday. It had become her night to court scandal, to be seen out drinking, to be seen in company with other men. George believed less than half what he heard, but tonight she was late. Bea began to cry. George was on his feet quickly and moved to the corner of the kitchen.

'Hush.' He leaned over the cradle.

Another leaned close too.

'Isn't she precious?' George asked.

The figure stayed, leaning as close as he. For moments they enjoyed a stillness together, then the door opened. Edith came in without a word.

'Bea is awake.'

'So?'

George noticed that his companion stayed with him. She did not flee in the face of Edith, nor shy away. At last he had an ally.

'You should care more for your baby!' he said, firmness in his voice.

'My baby? Whose baby? You've heard the stories, you heard what the Valpieds used to say. The Wise Women of the Parish.' Her voice sounded shrill – she had been drinking alcohol again, he was sure.

'One old witch is dead,' Edith continued, 'but her sister still sneers at me. They were right you know, right all along. About this baby, this… this… bantling.'

'Look, I know being a mother doesn't come natural to you, but we must still care for her—'

'Care? What do I care? Its father runs away and gets killed. My husband leaves me with his idiot cripple brother. Leaves me with… this thing crying and mewing all the time!'

Edith swept past the three of them: man, baby and spirit of the air.

'You know the old story,' she said. 'Ask the last of the Valpieds – she knows, she'll tell you. A *pouque* comes into a farmhouse, steals a baby from its crib and puts its own in its place.'

She pulled Bea's blanket back just far enough to reveal her face. 'And its mother knows it's not her child, but nobody will believe her. So,' she took in breath, and adopted a baby voice as if to entertain Bea. 'One day when the furze fire is roaring, Mémaen takes up the baby to throw it into the flames. At the last moment, the *pouque* appears to save its child. Then everyone knows she is speaking the truth.'

George looked at her aghast. Edith nodded. 'And that's a true story.'

For a moment he saw his own mother, despairing at the crippled, helpless Drusille. His father, out of work, unable to offer an alternative.

Bea started to cry again and broke the spell.

'Hush,' George took up the child and held her close. 'No one's going to hurt you, Bea. Mémaen's tired.'

Her cot was back in his room.

CHAPTER 53

In time, a name would be carved on a memorial in Smith Street and on a great monument at Louverval, but after all Edith's enquiries, it was clear that Artie Bazin was not coming home. Over fourteen hundred of the twenty thousand men who once lived on the island had been killed in the service of the king. Of the rest, a good quarter had seen action and many bore the scars. The brutal statistics of war left a thousand women doomed to spend the rest of their lives as widows or spinsters, and Edith knew she was firmly in these ranks.

May arrived, but for Edith it remained winter. She let George keep Bea in his room and was relieved of the weight of the baby's constant demands. It was hard to hate George. He did not have a bad bone in his body, but his attention had become obsessive. She would not marry him; she could not stay here forever. His jaunt to England had been the last straw, and she could cheerfully kill Jack for lending him the money.

It was Saturday and George was always happy to play *pépaen*, so Edith could escape the house and the little pink intruder who dragged her down and reminded her of everything that was wrong with her life. She had the first volume of Emily Brontë's *Wuthering Heights* on the table in front of her, and would dearly like a quiet hour just to read past Chapter Five and lose herself in somebody else's misery.

As she sat at the kitchen table she could hear George baby-talking in the yard. He was showing Bea the chickens, telling her some silly farmyard rhyme as if a baby that age would understand.

...In patois. He was teaching her patois and Beatrice Bazin would grow up to be a country girl and chase chickens the rest of her life. A tear ran down both Edith's cheeks and one fell straight into her tea.

Without any particular reason or destination she grabbed the book, grabbed her bonnet off the peg and left the house, turning left for the coast. Coming up the lane the other way was Mr Theodore Tulliver of Philadelphia. She came to a dead halt. What business had he back here again?

He was startled to see her, almost like a robber disturbed red-handed.

'Madame Bazin,' he said quickly, then recovered his composure and tipped his straw hat. 'Beautiful day.'

She had not noticed.

'Why, my dear, you have been crying.'

Had she? She hugged the book close to her chest as if to protect herself.

'May I?' He advanced a finger and wiped a tear away. 'You're looking so well,' he said. 'I heard you'd contracted the flu and worried for you, but here you are, picture of health.'

Edith gave a sniff, tried to smile.

'I see you are planning on reading. You're headed for a quiet place, no doubt, seeking solitude.'

'Ah,' she said, as she was not quite sure what she was seeking.

'If so, I shall not detain you.'

'I'm just... I'm just walking. This is just...' she waved the book uselessly.

'Which way are you walking?'

She pointed away from La Vallée, back the way he had come.

'An excellent choice. May I accompany you?'

Edith put on her bonnet properly and tied it in a neat bow, then artist and lost soul walked together down the lane, down the valley towards the sea. That arc of blue soon came into view, the west coast spread wide below spring sunshine. Green fields, carpets of flowers, birds alive in every hedgerow. Edith stayed silent.

'It is good to be back,' Mr Tulliver said. 'I feel alive again.'

'Good for you – I feel dead.'

'But here? With all this?'

'It's the edge of the world, Mr Tulliver; you said it yourself.'

'Theodore please, Theodore. Or Theo if you prefer.'

'Theo.'

'And it's not the edge of the world – three thousand miles that way, as the albatross flies, is New York.'

She sighed and glanced up at him; straw hat, little blonde moustache, tiny spectacles and all. All the men she knew were rough men, tough men, hard men. Strivers like Jack, fighters like Artie and stickers like George. Theodore Tulliver was none of these.

'Are you staying at Mrs Patterson's again?'

'Yes, for a week or two.'

'How is your wife?'

He caught a little breath before he replied. 'Marlene died at the turn of the year. We did not escape the Spanish flu after all. No matter where we travelled, it stalked us – it finally caught up with us in Florida. I was devilishly feverish, but recovered. Marlene simply wilted like a delicate flower in too much sun. She was taken away before I even recovered.'

'I'm very sorry.'

'So I have run away again.' He gave a thin smile. 'To here, to the last place I was able to paint. To the last place… I felt inspired. Sometimes I think I might settle here, buy a little cottage like yours. Don an old fisherman's vest like your brother's. Give my life to the waves and the dunes.'

'Don't!' she said. 'You can paint pictures and write poems, but you never want to live like this. Why do rich people think it's so jolly being poor and never going anywhere and never meeting anyone who isn't a cousin or a cousin's cousin?'

'I'm so sorry, I suppose we must do that. It's wrong, I admit, romanticising the rustic life.'

'There we go. What's a rustic life? Is that me? Here? In my one dress that isn't black or brown?'

A blackbird was startled by their approach and took flight straight from the hedge, chattering alarm. Tulliver glanced at it briefly, then back to Edith.

'Forgive me, I'm an artist. I look for beauty and inspiration even where there is none.'

'You're running away, Mr Tulliver, like you said. That's what you're doing. You ran away from America, from being rich, from the flu…'

'I ran away from the war,' he added. 'Is that shameful? I didn't believe in it and I ain't one of those men who felt he had to prove himself in valour. And also, I think, I know, I ran away from my wife.'

'What?' She was staggered at such a confession from a near stranger.

'You cannot hold something so fragile. You cannot cherish something so well bred, so well connected, so fine and…'

'You didn't love her?' Edith was incredulous. 'But you still married her?'

'We do what we have to do, what feels right at the time.'

'You can tell me! Story of my life, but you're rich; you can do what you like.'

'If only that were true.'

'But it is! Being poor is a trap. This rustic thing all around me is a trap. Paint the pretty *flleur*, paint the pretty *mêle*, but I walk past them every day. I've seen as many pretty flowers and blackbirds as any woman could ever want. I can't get away, ever. You can leave here tomorrow, go anywhere you like, be an artist if you want.'

He gave a little laugh. 'Money does not make you free.'

'Oh but it does, Mr Tulliver. I don't have ten pounds to get me to London, let alone enough to stop me starving when I get there. Then what do I do? Go into service? Work as a barmaid? Now the men are back, they don't even want us women working on the trams no more.'

'A beauty such as you should never have to work.'

It was late in the afternoon, and George had looked after Bea all day. Jack had worked around the greenhouse for a while, but since then had taken the cart over to Cobo where Mrs Patterson needed some small job doing. George made a bottle of milk for Bea, wondering where Edith and their supper were.

Jack returned. 'No Edith?'

'No.'

'I'll scrub up a bit, then. Been down to Mrs Patterson's. I thought she might offer me a bite of supper, but that Mr Tulliver is back.'

'The American?' George asked.

'Yes.'

'And his wife?'

'No.'

George had the oddest sensation, like that of a man in the condemned cell who has just heard the distant chink of the gaoler's keys and the footsteps of the chaplain.

'Where's she to?'

'She died of that Spanish flu,' Jack said. 'In America, even. Seems the whole world had it. Shame, nice lady she was. Very refined.'

George went out into the gathering dusk. Edith had still not returned, and waiting for Edith was becoming the theme of his life. He chose to go towards the sea and had not walked far before he saw her silhouette, and that of a man. It was the tall gangly American, and his alien voice carried far in the stillness of the summer evening.

The Owl flitted over a field gate and shrank into the hedge. He stood motionless and unseen, a shadow among deeper shadows. Through a gap in the branches he watched the couple talking. Mr Tulliver waved his arms and something he said made her laugh.

Once the pair parted, George made his escape down the back of the hedge, head full of conflicting thoughts. Suspicion, jealousy, uncertainty and indecision crowded in on him. What to do? What to say to Edith? Or was this warning all just his imagination and Mr Tulliver would vanish as quickly as he had the year before?

He'd confront her – or maybe she'd confess and blurt out what she'd done. Instead Edith mumbled some apology and set about supper in haste – fried sausages and boiled potatoes. Jack mentioned Mr Tulliver once over supper, but Edith merely paused between mouthfuls and said nothing. George tried to catch her eye but she avoided his stare. Bea started to cry, and for once Edith was the one to go to her.

Sunday morning saw the ritual ride to church in the cart. Mrs Patterson joined the family, but Mr Tulliver was nowhere to be seen. Perhaps he was Chapel or Baptist, Jack surmised.

George was extremely quiet and Edith noticed. After the service she nudged him.

'George?'

'Come with me,' he said.

She carried Bea and followed him round the back of the church and partly down the slope. He stopped in front of the tombstone to his mother, father and sister.

'You brought no flowers.'

'No,' he said.

She sensed an odd mood about him. 'You did a perfect job on the tombstone,' she said brightly. 'It's quite the best in the row. They would be so proud.'

'Once, you said we were cursed. The Bazins.'

'Did I?'

'Bad luck, was it? Well here's where it comes from. And here's why I won't take your nonsense about changelings and wanting to lose Bea. I had a sister named Drusille. She was like me, crippled, sickly, slow. Too much for a poor family to bear, it was. So—'

'Stop it.'

'So, my mother, or my father, or both of them—'

'Stop it, I don't want to know!'

'– let her drown.'

Edith sucked in air, closed her eyes and breathed deeply.

'They took her picnicking down the Mare, when it was still winter. They let her run off, or crawl off. Or they just led her to the pool.'

'Oh God, George.'

He stared at the gravestone, not at her.

'So you see, you shouldn't wish your child away. It dogged Mémaen and Pépaen their whole lives. Took it into this grave. They hated me after I worked out the truth.'

She gave a little laugh, of embarrassment or shame. 'This is just another one of your stories, like the fairy woman.'

'No – Jack knows. Or he worked it out for himself – you can ask him. Why do you think he never wanted children? He didn't want another Drusille, or another me, and he didn't want that temptation.'

'George, this is just mad!' She began to walk away from the grave.

He caught her up. 'So, we've been given a last chance, the Bazins. Bea is a gift, we've got to love her and care for her.'

'Because of your dead, drowned sister?' she said coldly. 'Because I've married into a family of heroes and mad people and murderers? Why? Why me?'

She pushed Bea into his arms. 'Here's your gift – she's getting heavy. She's not even a Bazin, lucky girl.'

On Monday morning, Edith waited until George and Jack had left for the yard before changing out of her working clothes and into her cornflower-blue dress. The cotton was thin and the colour was heavily faded. Taking up the silver-plated comb Artie had bought her, she worked at her hair until it fell just right, wetting it in places. In the mirror and the poor light she saw that pale face stare back. In due course, squinting at the bright sky would give her crow's feet around her eyes. The west wind would beat roughness into her cheeks and the sun would spoil her skin. She would not turn a jolly honey-brown like Guernsey girls of the old families; her face would simply burn and shrivel.

She gathered up Bea and walked her over to see Adèle, who had moved with her husband to a vacant cottage a few dozen yards from her parents' house just beyond the Castel school. She was well into her own pregnancy, tiring but still game for baby practice. Perotine Guille was there already, and brimming with excitement. Quite out of the blue she had agreed to marry the grower from Le Préel whose pregnant wife had fallen to the flu. Both Edith's old friends were full of their news and the new lives that were opening up to them. Such happiness almost felt obscene after all the world had been through. Edith stayed for a single cup of tea, and then walked down to the coast.

Mr Tulliver had asked to meet her again and she'd agreed before he'd even finished his sentence. Although he said he'd sketch her, this pretext was forgotten and they merely walked and talked. Meeting near the old round tower at Vazon, they walked round to Hommet headland almost as far as the big fort. The sea lapped on both sides, long lines of surf running on to Vazon's wide beach, while calmer, darker water filled the narrow bay at Albecq. Glancing at Albecq's pink rocks towering over the deep blue sea, rimmed by white surf and thrown against a cloudless sky, Edith could see why an artist would be pulled to the island.

'I never complimented you on your new hairstyle,' he said. 'Very modern. Very up to the minute.'

She had deliberately avoided wearing a bonnet today. 'Thank you. I thought you'd miss my long, flowing tresses.'

'Oh, but that was a different Edith, was it not? Once you were oppressed by war, but now you are free. This Edith is ready to spread her wings.'

He asked about Bea. 'It's George's child, ain't it?'

She said nothing.

'I saw you two together in the road, last time I was here. It was clear, from the way he holds the child and you stand a little way apart. He loves the child but you do not.'

Saying nothing is a form of lying, but Edith gave a shrug.

'George is devoted to Bea. It's a small island, Mr Tulliver, and people talk, so you mustn't believe everything you hear. Not half of it, even. Strange things happen in wars and we don't get a lot of choice what happens.'

'And the mother?'

Edith shook her head. 'It's a sad story... now George wants to marry me. I said yes, foolishly, last year. I was mourning for my Artie and George was the nearest to family I had left. He wants us to be a real family – me, him and that baby.'

'Gee.'

They had reached the rabbit warren at the neck of the headland. From here it narrowed towards the gaunt Fort Hommet which blocked further progress, but a path bore northwards along the edge of a low, crumbling cliff. Edith nodded that way and he followed her lead. The mound of the warren and thick furze breaks and outcrops of pink rocks made them invisible to the shore, and no one else was walking the headland. It was a small island, but you could still get away from everyone else.

'So you're marrying George?' he said, with a strain in his voice.

'No, I most certainly am not! And, as it turns out it's not allowed under the law, marrying your brother's widow, but George keeps hoping the law will change and some fool has told him it will. And even then, I won't marry him, I can't. I don't love him, he can never offer me what I want, and I can never give him what he wants. I'd be a bad mother to Bea and a terrible wife to George. I'd end up like my own mother, looking for refuge in gin and French sailors.'

'Life can be terrible.'

'Can it be anything else?'

'Yes. There's beauty, art, tranquillity.'

'Love and excitement?'

'That too, in proper measure.'

In his hawkish face, Edith saw true sincerity. There was no obsessive gleam that afflicted George, nor the predatory look that Edwin had adopted when seducing her and stealing her from Artie. Tulliver was no jaunty boy like Artie had been, full of plans and dreams of one day and might be. Theodore Tulliver was a man who had seen the world, lived his dream and carried out his plans.

'So I don't want to be rich, and you don't want to be poor,' he said.

'We could swap,' she suggested brightly. 'I'll have your money and travel the world on ocean liners and steam trains. You can stay here and live with George. I'll be fine. I'll take plenty of books, and learn to paint. Meantime, you can learn the patois and buy a Guernsey. You'd love feeding chickens and cleaning out *bashins* – it's really… rustic.'

Theo had this curious twisting smile he used when both amused and surprised. She loved it.

'Oh I would love to have you as company at some of the dinners I have to attend, surrounded by pompous people who think that a crisis is when the wine is the wrong temperature, or they cannot find a word to rhyme with "orange", which means their insipid poem is *simply ruined*. You would really pop their balloons.'

'Me?' she laughed.

He bowed his head slightly and removed his boater, leaned over and pecked her gently on the cheek. She did not shy away, nor did he move to take further advantage of her. Tulliver replaced his hat.

'I came back for you, my dear,' he said. 'I came away from this island with so many images of beauty, but one shone out above all else. All through my illness, I kept my thoughts fixed on your face. In my mourning for Marlene, it was as if you were at my side. My painting of you, your basket of eggs, is on the wall of my New York apartment.'

'It takes more than beauty, Mr Tulliver. Beauty fades, it's only skin and hair.'

'No, your beauty is deep down.' He ran his hands in front of her like a magician, miming her shape from waist to breasts. 'All this is just its earthly projection.'

He wafted his hand over her cheap cornflower dress. 'And this – the army would call it camouflage.'

'But I don't have... what is it, breeding?'

'You're a woman, not one of your prize Guernsey cattle. And if you're talking class, rank or privilege, I care nothing for them and the war has wiped all that away.'

'And education, and learning?'

'I'll wager you read as many books as I do. There are women of my acquaintance who pretend to be ignorant, so as not to overshadow their dim-witted husbands, but I can't see you doing that. Nobody learns spirit from a book; the finest finishing school in the world doesn't give you a soul.'

'But I've done some horrid things.'

'A caged animal will bite because it wants to run free. My dear, the world has just spent five years doing the most monstrous things for what it thinks were the noblest of reasons. If you have sins, weigh them against all that has happened.'

Every word he spoke lifted her heart and her spirits. He offered so much and was demanding nothing.

'We need to have a good talk,' she said.

CHAPTER 54

War's legacy, and the flu, and the broken hearts that followed gave the masons plenty to catch up on that spring. Annie Valpied's stone was cut and ready for George's attention. George had put on his old glasses that day, squinting as Jack and Phillip the new boy moved the stone to where he could work on it.

'Can't you find your proper glasses, George?' Jack asked.

'Ah, I'm wearing these for Mr Tulliver,' he said. In truth he felt more secure in his old glasses, now things had suddenly turned uncertain. 'I'm thinking that Mr Tulliver might come by and ask to paint me again, him. These old glasses make me look all country, just how he likes.'

'I saw him to the Guet,' Jack said. 'Looked like he was waiting for something. Just standing there, him. Not painting, like you'd expect, but just standing like he was waiting for the bus.'

Except there was no bus which made its way up to the Guet.

'Did you see Edith?' George asked.

'Yes – heading off to Adèle's, I reckon. It's nice to see her out with Bea. It's a fine afternoon.'

A cold hand gripped his heart. Until she had her own baby, Adèle would always take Bea to nurse and play with. From Adèle's it was only a short walk along the spine of the hill to the lookout point at the Guet.

'Jack, can you spare me for an hour?'

'Of course. The old witch'll still be dead tomorrow.'

He nodded thanks, dusted his hands and set off uphill with purpose. The narrow lanes were overhung on both sides with furze and bramble, long grasses and ferns, so for the first few minutes he saw little beyond the path in front of him. Sunlight glinted off his glasses, then shadow, and then shafts of light again. Anyone would have imagined shapes following on either side.

From the high ground the world was spread wide. It started to open up as he passed St Matthew's church. By the time he reached the bare rock of the Guet the whole west coast was laid before him – from the *hougue* at Les Vardes in the north to Lihou Island in the south. Rows of glasshouses hugged the lower slopes of the hill before the Mare was reached. Two steamers were on the horizon and a fishing boat worked closer in. Down by Fort Hommet, across from the pink rocks of Albecq, were two figures. One was in pale clothes and hat, carrying what could be an easel or sketch pad. The other was dressed in cornflower blue but wore no bonnet, her red-golden hair flashing in the morning sun.

George ripped off his glasses, tired of the things they showed him. A strange taste came into his mouth and a muzzy feeling in his head. He remembered the moment his father had suffered that stroke, falling away from reality. He thought briefly of those who would welcome him into the netherworld, and pushed those thoughts away. In a moment the glasses were back on his nose and he set out down the hill.

The boulder-choked bay at Albecq lay between him and the couple. Edith and Mr Tulliver were out on the Hommet headland, walking up the rabbit warren towards the old fort. Completely engrossed in their own private world, they did not see him approach. He circled around the bay, losing sight of them behind a deep bank of furze. The gorse was in bloom, but then it was always in bloom.

Using stealth worthy of the Light Infantry with whom he never served, he moved behind the bushes, and then hurried from one furze break to the next. He was soon at the warren and by working his way to the top should be able to see anyone further to seaward.

Footsteps were approaching. He dodged into the best cover he could find. Edith came past not ten feet away, singing some song very quietly to herself. George had not seen her so happy since the early days of her marriage. He did not challenge her, but watched as she skipped as lightly over the grass as if she were a *pouque*. It took five minutes for the figure in blue to disappear completely behind some greenhouses inland. In that five minutes, George's spirits declined steadily until all around was blackness other than that receding blue smudge.

She came from behind. Her hair may have been no more than the reflection of the dark gorse, her eyes no more than a distant glimpse of the sea, but she was here. The look on her face was stern and determined, angry even. There was a glint in her eye he had not seen before, and it frightened him.

George stood up and moved swiftly away, taking the path through the gorse out along the headland to where the land ended abruptly and where the sea had carved a cave, the fairy cave which was the gate to the underworld. Mr Tulliver sat close to the edge, staring out to sea, not even holding pencil or pad. George halted, brain full of hot blood that drowned his thoughts.

On the ground, half-hidden by the gorse, lay an object curved and brown. Distracted, George picked it up. It was a sickle-like tool known as a *faucille*, used for cutting furze. To George it felt like a weapon. Rusted and forgotten, it could have been carried by an eager Militiaman six hundred years before when Guernsey's men had rushed down here to repel the French invaders, then dropped when its owner fell in the massacre that ensued.

Repel the invaders! Protect hearth and home! Mr Tulliver had still not seen him and there was nobody about. The *faucille* would cut a throat as easily as it would cut gorse. And wasn't he from a family of murderers? It would be a simple matter to drag the corpse a little way along the low cliff and drop it into the fairy cave. George might even scramble down to make sure it was well hidden under rocks and boulders and seaweed. Let the *pouques* take Mr Tulliver! He smiled, thinking the deed already done and Edith secure as his wife.

His grip on the handle grew tight.

CHAPTER 55

As his hand clenched around the handle of the *faucille,* George sensed something beneath his thumb. Letters, three of them, carved into the wood. He felt their shapes, glanced down at them.

PLP.

The notion that this was a mediaeval weapon was ridiculous, of course. It was a furze-cutting tool dropped and forgotten last autumn or the autumn before by one of the men of the parish.

Pierre Le Pelley?

Peter Le Prevost?

Paul Le Page?

One of his neighbours or distant relatives, no doubt. They would miss this, it felt like a good tool. George's anger ebbed away. No matter how cleverly he could conceal his crime, the American would quickly be missed. Even if he was not found immediately, in time the sea would disgorge its secret. The spectre of murder would follow George for the rest of his life, as surely as the spirit woman had. Its face would be foul and he would never be free of it and never at peace: this was Drusille's lesson to her brother. Mr Tulliver had still not noticed him and things would stay that way.

With mind so fogged he was almost blind, George made his way slowly back to La Vallée, relaxing his grip on the tool before grasping it hard once more. He let it slap against his trouser leg, he toyed with it and re-read the carving. He fingered the rusted blade. He ignored whatever was following him. On reaching home, he took the tool round to the back of the dairy and left it there, promising that he'd ask all the PLPs he knew, one by one, until he could return it.

As George came into the Big House by the back door, Edith came through the front at almost the same instant. She was carrying Bea and the child was gurgling quietly.

Edith glanced at him only quickly. 'I need to get the food ready,' she said. 'Take Bea.'

He took the baby without a word and she turned away to the cupboards.

Edith too was in a fog, or at the bottom of a deep well. In her mind was a wall, and each way she turned was another. She would drown, she would suffocate. Everyone conspired to smother her; George, the baby, the relatives, the neighbours, even the stupidly happy Adèle and Perotine. And there was Theodore Tulliver at the top of the well, free as a bird. If she called to him, he would throw down a rope. Why was what she ought to do in constant opposition to what she wanted to do?

She put together what food she could find, which was bread and cheese, plus an onion for George. He sat down without a word, concentrating on his food and not looking her in the eye. He hacked bread from the loaf as if it were toughest oak, or the neck of a hated enemy.

'I'm not hungry,' she said after taking a few bites, and went upstairs.

In her room she stared from the window out at the spring garden. God had never devised such a beautiful prison. She noticed she was breathing heavily, as if at the end of a long run. George was good; too good. She despised him and he did not deserve it. Now she began to fear him. He could indeed be completely insane and all that goodness simply a mask.

And Bea? Edith gave a little laugh, smiling to herself. Nostalgia and affection often produced tears, but you could be wicked with a laugh on your lips. In her hand was the photograph of her mother and her father, the only one she possessed.

'I am what you made me,' she said.

CHAPTER 56

I t was the front door that awoke George in the morning. He was usually the first to rise, so he was confused. Perhaps he had overslept. Bea was still in the cot at his side, sound asleep. He reached for his glasses and in his haste he could only find the old ones. From the window he could see nothing but a bright morning, the flowers, the lane and the trees on the far side.

Quietly he stepped on to the landing and went downstairs in his nightshirt. All was silent apart from Gràn'père's clock. The photograph of Edith's mother and father in its frame was gone from the sideboard. When had she moved that?

Her winter coat was gone from its peg beside the door, but her summer coat remained. The field boots she wore to work in the garden were still there, but not her better shoes. Perplexed he went back up the stair as fast as he could. He tapped on Edith's door, whispering her name. He put his ear against it but could hear no breathing. He spoke her name louder, and again heard nothing beyond Bea stirring at the noise. Pulse rising, fearing a scolding or fearing worse, he turned the handle and pushed at it gently.

Edith's bed was empty and unmade.

'Edith!'

It was not only his would-be-wife that was gone, but the best of her things. The mirror remained, but not her silver comb or her purse or her pocket bible. He checked the hanging press and found only her winter and working clothes.

Her drawers contained only one worn-out summer skirt and some old stockings and night-things. He hurried downstairs, calling her name. He checked the parlour and the kitchen and went out to check the dairy.

He went round to the cottage, but it was silent.

Quite pathetic, he tapped on the door of *la p'tite maisaon*.

'Edith, are you in there?'

Of course she would not be there – he was putting off the conclusion that had dawned on him five minutes before: Edith was gone.

Still in his nightshirt, he went out into the lane. Birds called, chickens clucked, seagulls wheeled, but there was no human life in sight. A panic seized him, a mental cramp that prevented action. Breaking out of it, George went back inside, upstairs, removed his glasses once more and dressed. He lifted Bea from her cradle and put a shawl around her.

'Pa-pa,' she said.

After his Guernsey went over his head, he put back his glasses. The old friends pinched him, but the view they offered had a familiarity that broke his indecision. Something drew him to turn left out of his gate. That Mr Tulliver had to be behind this, and he was down at Mrs Patterson's at Cobo. Edith might have ten minutes' start but she would hardly be there yet. With Bea wrapped in his arms he went into the lane and up towards the road. Here were fresh horse droppings, and a little way ahead Albert Thoumine the carter was watering his horse at the *abeurvaeure*.

'Albert! Have you seen Edith?'

'Lost her, have you, George? That's careless.'

'No, she ran this way.'

'Well I saw a woman, a mite overdressed for the time of year if you asks me. She had all baskets and bundles hanging from both arms, her. She was headed towards the Route Cobo and seemed in a desperate hurry. That's not going to be your Edith, is it?'

'Yes, yes.'

'Because I saw one of them private motor cabs go to Town not ten minutes back, even. But Edith's not one to take a cab, is she? It's not like you can just whistle for them.'

Town, yes. And Tulliver was the kind of man to arrange a cab – and pay for one. Town was the obvious way for them to flee. With his cursed foot and a heavy child to carry, George would make heavy work of the two miles or so to St Peter Port. 'Albert, you'd not be going to Town, you?'

'Sometime,' he said, but sounded as if he had all the time in the world to get there.

'Edith has fled – she's running away with an American tourist.'

'What? Well I never…'

George shook his head, almost feeling drunk with despair and indecision. 'It's true, I know it's true, I've seen them together even.'

Bea gurgled and Albert frowned. 'Well, the mailboat's due to sail.'

'When?'

The carter looked skyward as if to tell the time. 'About now.'

'Take me to Town.'

'George, I've me work to do.'

'I'll give you a pound. Two pounds.'

'George…'

'Five pounds – look at the baby, she needs her mother!'

Bea turned her head and snuggled up to George.

'I don't want your money, you. Pass the baby up, and climb on.'

So George passed Bea to the carter, and then sat behind him and took her back. No cart would beat the motor cab to

Town, but Albert hurried his old grey mare as best he could, past the big house at Haye des Puits, past Rectory Hill with the church on the skyline. Up the slope above him spread the churchyard, with George's clients stacked in rows and his family looking down on him.

George expected to be followed, but he saw no glint reflected in his glasses. Of course, when he looked for her, when he needed support most, she was not there. She only came unbidden.

Albert's mare trotted along at fair pace, as the road was near level at the foot of the Castel hill and the ground to the north was swampy, even. Once upon a time, Artie had taught George to catch freshwater eels in the *douits* by Foot's Lane. By the big house called Vimiera, shrouded by huge pines, the road began to rise towards Town. Now the grey mare slowed to an agonising pace. A motor car passed them. That was the way to travel to Town! George wished he had a motor car, or a friend with a motor car. The houses on the edge of St Peter Port stretched down the hill to meet them.

Over the rooftops from the very top of the Grange they could see the black smoke of a steamer firing up its boilers.

'I'll take the Avenue down,' Albert said. He'd tried to make conversation all the ride, but George's mind was full of anxiety, and hopes, and regrets.

As they passed between Elizabeth College and the towering St James Church, a horse bus came up past them, trotting out of Town step by step. The cart eased down the tree-lined Avenue, past Candie Grounds, scene of concerts and parades, past the Boer War monument that Uncle Jack helped build. Little pieces of George's life passed him by as valuable minutes slipped away.

St Peter Port harbour was swollen with a high tide. A

mail steamer rode high at the White Rock pier, black smoke streaming skywards. Was it twenty years since Gràn'père went down on such a steamer? And two years since Artie had left, maybe on this very same boat? Now his Edith was being carried away. The horse was urged into a trot, but sailors threw down the ropes and pushed the vessel away from the quay. If only he had not stopped to dress, if only the horse had trotted faster, if only he had awoken earlier, if only he had seen through Edith's silence and guessed her plans!

And what would he have done to stop her? He felt the ghost of the sickle in his hand. What would he have done? Fate can be cruel, but it can make decisions easy.

Three blasts came from the steamship's horn.

Albert pulled the cart to a halt to allow a large dray to pass. Once the path was clear, George could see the mailboat reversing out into the harbour basin towards the castle. Albert drove his horse forward on to the harbour arm, momentarily gaining on the lumbering ship. It was no longer moving backwards, and was making that awkward turn to bring its bow to point seaward. Once at the White Rock, George struggled down from the cart to the quayside.

Bea gave a cry and Albert held her out for George to take. With the child in his arms, he began to hobble towards the retreating ship. It finished manoeuvring as he approached the end of the quay.

'Edith!' he yelled.

He could not see her figure on the deck.

'You can still come back!'

With one hoot of its horn, the ship began to move forward with purpose. George started to walk sidewise, crab-like, keeping pace with the ship. He held up the child for the passenger to see.

'Edith! Think of Bea!'

He brought Bea back down to his breast, a tear forming in his eye. In his glasses, the face was smiling. That face! He glanced down at Bea and for a moment…

No, it was his imagination!

Bea was growing heavy. He lowered her to the ground, setting her among some coiled ropes. As he released her, he overbalanced, stumbled, threw out a hand and grazed it on the quayside as he fell. The glasses continued to fall, exploding in a shower of fragments as they bounced from one cobble to the next.

'No!' He picked up the wire frames, shards dropping into his hands.

Desperate, wild with emotion, he flung the empty frames towards the vanishing ship. Hitting the water with only the slightest splash, they sank into the depth of the harbour and were lost forever. Before the ripples had ceased, the ship had passed the harbour light and was gone behind the sea wall and into the Russell. Only a swirling black cloud remained. George was left at the end of the quayside, almost blind, hardly able to tell sea from sky. The last wisps of smoke were caught by the breeze and dissolved.

'Edith!'

As he shouted the name he knew he cared nothing for it and never spoke it again.

'Bea,' he said gently.

The child was unhurt, lying on her back amid the rope coils as if they formed one huge basket. Picking up the child, he drew her close, so close that he could focus on her face – a face so familiar, a face he had known since childhood. Eyes as blue as the sea at dusk, hair black as the crow.

Bea smiled, and for the first time he noticed the glint in her eye.

In an instant he knew that his story was all about her. George's life so far had been as the lesser part of the brothers Bazin, the little brother, the one people thought a fool, the one left behind. He had hidden in the shadow of his brother, relied on his uncle for work and let the ill luck of others steer his life. He had been obsessed by a woman who was never there and another he could never have. Now he and Bea were the last of the family Bazin, and yet he was strangely content.

Jiggling her gently, George carried Bea back towards the waiting carter.

'Can you take us back to the Castel?' he asked. 'I can't see a thing, me.'

But he could see – his future was clear. This was the way things were always going to turn; his life could never have taken a different path. His destiny was here. All his love would be for Beatrice Bazin.

AUTHOR'S NOTE

The quote from Chekhov which gave this book a title came to me at a time when I was racking my brains to find one – messaging friends, phoning my mother, beta-testing ideas on social media. My working title was *Glint* so when I came across the quote it suddenly felt like destiny. Except Chekhov never actually said this verbatim – the 'quote' is a contraction of his advice to writers on how to write. What we think is true turns out to be apocryphal; we live in a world of folklore, superstition, myth, part-truths, half-lies and selectively filtered 'news'. Like George, we build our own reality.

Literally hundreds of books, pamphlets and papers have been written about Guernsey's history, biography and folklore. All these would form a grand bibliography for this book, running to a dozen pages if this was a factual work. Any research on the Great War has to start with Eddie Parks' *Diex Aïe*, supplemented in the digital age by the website *The Channel Islands and the Great War*. The *Transactions of La Sociéte Guernèsiaise*, which has been published annually since Victorian times, contains a wealth of detailed articles. Books which were essential for me to consult included Sir Edgar MacCulloch's *Guernsey Folklore* and Marie De Garis' later *Folklore of Guernsey* as well as her *Dictiounnaire Angllais-Guernésiais*. P Barbé's paper *The Decline of Guernsey English* was invaluable, as were many conversations about Guernesiais with Yan Marquis, who kindly read through two drafts and made valuable suggestions. Liz Walton and Gillian Lenfesty also kindly read early drafts and helped sharpen up some of the period detail. I'd like to assert that all remaining historical errors are deliberate! Dea Parkin of Fiction Feedback helped polish the final draft, encouraging me across the final hurdles to publication.

I have spent two decades living in the Castel, sat on the sand with a cider in hand and watched the sun sink towards America. Artie and George strolled past my gate on their way to sign up with the Militia at Les Beaucamps. I have visited the memorial to the fallen at Louverval and walked over the new bridge that links Masnières with Les Rues Vertes, but this is fiction, not a history book. Novels come from the heart – or maybe from something we thought we saw in the corner of an eye.

Jason Monaghan, Guernsey 2016
www.monaghanfoss.com